Somebody's Someone

Somebody's Someone

Annie Mick

Copyright

Cover design by Josh with Pro-design-X

Dedication

Hey, Jude
You waited, anxious, encouraging me to get moving and finish this book. Told me you couldn't wait to read it. I missed the mark by about six weeks. You left this world a better place because of you. You left empty spaces in hearts because we will miss you. The one thing we will never do is forget you. Your laughter, your jokes, your honesty, your encouragement, but most of all, the "I love you" at the end of conversations. This one is for you. I hope you can read it from heaven.
We will forever hear your "Whispers in the Mist".
See you on the other side.

Table of contents

Chapter 1

Deacon

"People, if I may have everyone's attention." Captain Garner's booming voice calls from the entryway of the squad room. *"If I may."*

That's hilarious, Cap. *"If"* would indicate it's a question. We all know you're not asking. The corner of my mouth tips in a smirk as I wait for the ever-familiar smell of fear to invade my nostrils.

The rookies in the room spin so fast that their shoes nearly exchange right foot to left as they trip over their own feet. File drawers are slammed shut quickly as the overbearing authority of the man standing in the doorway takes precedence over the case files about to be set in their proper place. Phones are set in the cradles after a swiftly muttered, "I'll call you back." Chairs squeak as their occupants sit up straight, eyes fixed on the man in the doorway. Papers are shuffled as they're abandoned on the desktops. Donuts are either gagged down in one swallow or set back in the box – absent a bite or two. Hence the reason I don't indulge.

Next to me, Rodriguez spins in his chair and nearly chokes on the chips he was obnoxiously munching – spewing the remnants a good three feet in the air – before he murmurs, "Hot damn. Come to papa."

I raise my head slowly from the monotonous paperwork I'm filling out for another perp – one more in the long line of assholes this city seems to dole out on a daily basis – and I suddenly understand the silence that has befallen the room, as well as Rodriguez's inappropriate comment. It has nothing to do with Captain Garner. Though I appreciate their shock and awe, mine is for totally different reasons. The stunning beauty before them would stop traffic on the Autobahn. Kings would bow down to her. Big Ben would stop ticking if she visited London. It's a timeless beauty one never forgets. I'd only seen her at her worst and yet never have I been so permanently altered as I was by . . .

"Everlee Remington." Her name is but a soft whisper from my lips. My heart bursts into the same flames I had to tamp down so long ago while my stomach knots so tightly it's painful. I've only whispered that name to myself on occasion over the years; in my sleep, in my dreams. Worse yet, in my nightmares. I would know those eyes and that face anywhere. Even more beautiful than I remember. You would think after all these years, after all the cases I have solved, I could look her in the eyes. But I can't.

Rodriguez nearly salivates as he stares. "All the things I could do with that body."

"Show some respect, asshole," I mutter low through gritted teeth.

His slimy snicker makes my skin crawl. "I'd be respectful, Gray. Break her in slowly. Hell, I'd even wine her and dine her before I take her home."

I shoot him a side-eye. My lips barely move as I grind through a clenched jaw, "Shut the fuck up before I knock your teeth to the back of your throat."

"Don't worry," he chuckles softly. "I could share with you, Deacon. I'm a generous guy. But only for one night. She looks to be a keeper."

"One more word," I threaten so only he can hear. "And I will cut your dick off and feed it to you."

He bobs his eyebrows like the sleazeball he is, relentless in his daily pursuit to piss me off. "Can you wait until after I feed it to her? Making her my last trip around the world could be worth it."

Standing from my desk to make a fast exit down the hall by way of the only other door out of here before I put his nose out of joint, I grab a pen and discreetly jab it into Rodriguez's side as I pass. He yelps loudly and swears under his breath.

"I said shut the fuck up," I warn him again quietly as I pass, letting him know one more word will land my fist in his face. It wouldn't be the first time. He's not a bad cop – not my favorite by a longshot – but his cocky attitude and his dick need adjustment. I really don't care about either one, as long as he keeps them out of the department and away from the job.

"Gray!" Cap calls before I can get out the door. "Where are you headed?"

"Need to make a call," I shoot back, my eyes fixed on the escape path ahead. I don't want to see her. Whatever he needs to say, he can say it to the room. Right now, I need to slow the pounding in my chest and breathe. I can't do that with Everlee Remington this close.

"It can wait," he orders. "I want you all to meet our new forensic scientist. People, this is Everlee Remington. File on up here and introduce yourselves. I ain't got time to babysit you. Rodriguez, if your handshake lasts any longer than two seconds, I will have your ass on a silver platter, got it?"

My insides freeze as the ice water crawls through my veins inch by painful inch. Our new forensic scientist? I'll be seeing her day in and day out. The lab is in our building. It's been six years and I still can't give her any answers.

Parnell makes his way to me before he takes his place in line behind the others, keeping his voice low against the chatter in the room. "Did I hear him right? Is that . . .?"

"Don't say anything, Vic," I warn him.

"Who the hell would I say anything to, Deac? You and I are the only ones in this division familiar with that case."

I turn to face the crowd, watching as they shake her hand, welcoming her into the fold. She smiles, though it's forced. The pain in her eyes is well masked, unless you know what you're looking for. Forensic scientist. That's a helluva lot of schooling. She hasn't given up. Well, Everlee Remington, neither have I. The case has been shelved for years; dormant. I still study the file now and then; peruse witness statements, rewatch the video collected from the single street cam working that night. I made copies of everything – including the deleted portion of footage my buddies had no choice but to erase – and keep them in my home, convincing myself that one day I will see something we all missed.

"Let's keep it that way," I say as we edge our way toward the depleting line of detectives and officers.

"Hey." He nudges my arm before we reach the others. "Spencer had no business being on the streets. Compassion is part of being a cop. He was so far out of line, you couldn't find a line. You did the right thing, Deac. *We* did the right thing."

I stop, dropping my chin to my chest, my hands tucked safely into my pockets so no one sees my knuckles turning white with my clenched fists. "I know that. My only regret is I didn't grind his face into the glass the way he did her knees."

He nods toward her, a puckish grin that only I understand, and whispers, "Looks like she healed pretty well. Spencer doesn't have any kneecaps to speak of."

"Vic, we still haven't solved . . ."

He slaps my back and eases me forward. "You can't solve them all, Deacon."

Vic goes first, taking her hand in his for only a moment in a professional handshake, and smiles. "Ms. Remington, welcome aboard. Detective Victor Parnell. I look forward to working with you."

My turn is next . . . and last. Damnit! I should have moved faster. I could have rushed through this little meet-and-greet on the pretense of someone waiting behind me. Her hand feels like silk, heat, and poison at the same time. The temptation to pull her into a comforting hug is as overwhelming as the urge to run, but I muddle through.

"Ms. Remington," I utter, avoiding eye contact yet yearning to look into those eyes I've never forgotten. "Detective Gray. Welcome to the 83rd."

Her grip is firm for such a dainty thing and feels like hot coals against my palm. I don't squeeze hard – Everlee was only meant to caress, hear whispers of comfort and reassurance. Feel safe. She grips harder as I try to release my gentle hold, causing me to lift my gaze and make contact with soulful gray eyes surrounded by thick dark lashes that have haunted my dreams for years. Still mesmerizing, bordering hypnotic. Porcelain skin, narrow nose with unique teardrop shaped nostrils above a cupid's bow surrounded by full lips. I only ever saw her lying down, but I had plenty of time to study her face, note every feature; bone structure, jawline, every last little freckle, the tiny scar above her left eyebrow.

She studies my face as if recalling – or searching for – a memory; her eyes narrowing the slightest bit as her head tilts a fraction.

Don't do it, Everlee. Please don't do it.

"Just Detective Gray?" she asks, her voice as melodic and haunting as those eyes.

I release her hand – the cruel reality that mine now feels empty gripping my chest like a vise – and nod once and look away. "Yup."

What the hell is wrong with me? All she has to do is ask. How many Deacons are there? Outside of churches anyway. And I haven't been to one of those since I can't remember when.

Turning quickly to find that infamous backway out, I weave through the desks toward the door, and nearly run to exit the building. Once outside, I stand against the brick wall, catching slow deep breaths and wait for my lungs to fill and my heart rate to decrease. Six years I haven't seen her, other than in my dreams. If I thought young, beautiful Everlee Remington haunted my dreams, the grownup version is about to cause some pretty severe insomnia.

Six years ago

"Jonah!!!" The piercing screams and cries of the young woman bent over the body of the man lying on the ground filled the night air around us. Her hands and clothes soon smeared with blood as she dropped to her knees and captured his upper body in a tight grasp and held him close to her, sobbing as she rocked him in her arms.

"No! Please, God, no!" she wailed at the sky above, squeezing him closer as if she could transfer life into the limp, motionless body in her arms.

I was a rookie, working crowd control and rolling out the yellow tape to cordon off the area. We had arrived shortly after the call had come in; the report of a man down outside a club in the downtown district. Anonymous call – of course. Suspected stabbing. The victim was a musician from the band playing at the club, who at the time had been on break. By the looks of the scene though, the victim hadn't been stabbed with a knife. He'd been attacked with a broken bottle – or several of them. There was glass shattered all around him. And this young woman, in her shock and agony, was apparently immune to it.

"Hey!" Lieutenant Spencer ordered harshly, reaching for her shoulders to pull her away. "Get outta here. This is a crime scene."

"This is my brother!" the woman shrieked as she fought his grip and ignored the orders of the lieutenant, clinging to the young man in her lap. "My baby brother," she whimpered.

"Let go!" Spencer yelled, grabbing under her arms and yanking her up. She fought hard – a worthy opponent to a man twice her size.

She sobbed harder, pulling the body of her brother with her as Spencer yanked her upwards. "I can't leave him! He's bleeding!"

"He's dead!" Spencer barked, yanking harshly, the weight of both bodies in his grip as she held steadfast to her brother. "It doesn't make any difference now."

"No! He can't be! Jonah, wake up. Please, wake up." The horrified sobs of the woman were enough to make a grown man cry.

"I said let go!" he hollered with another brutal pull of her shoulders.

Spencer should have been handling her with care; showing compassion, gentility. Using words like, "Let us help him. We need to get to him to help him. You're hurting yourself on the glass. Let me check him so I can try to stop the bleeding."

Mind you, it was pretty easy to see the young man was gone, but this was her brother. The tape was already on the concrete around the body. The street cam would give us the info we needed. She'd busted through the line to get to him – a force to be reckoned with. Who knows how one of us would react if that was our loved one on the ground?

My gut churned as I took in the scene before me. There was no reason for his cruel treatment. Spencer was causing more damage to the crime scene by mishandling things the way he was than she possibly could. But what happened next was inexcusable, and unforgivable.

He dropped her hard and pushed on her shoulders, pressing a knee to her lower her back, twisting her body forcefully and in the process, grinding her bare knees into the broken glass on the concrete beneath them.

"There!" he grunted as he held onto her shoulders one last time and twisted her upper body. He seemed to take a sick satisfaction with her sudden groan and shriek as the glass ground into her skin. "You want to stay with him, bleed with him, you dumb bitch."

Something within me snapped. Higher ranking officer or not, this was inhumane. I was twenty feet away, but I don't think it took more than five seconds to be diving at Spencer. He never saw me coming. I knocked him to the ground and was on top of him, pummeling him as if he were a punching bag.

"You sonofabitch! What are you doing?! She's just a girl!" My fists found his face to be an easy anger outlet, over and over – every punch feeling like an ounce of justice for an innocent victim.

I felt hands grab my shoulders and pull me off the still body on the ground. Spencer was out . . . cold. They pulled me away quickly, but not quite far enough to prevent me from landing one hard kick to his ribs for good measure. Low life asshole. He'd already been on suspension once for a domestic abuse investigation. Why was he even on the force? He had a wife and two kids. Emphasis on "had". Smart woman dumped his ass and left him far behind, taking the kids and leaving the state.

"Your shift is up in an hour," Vic said sternly as he walked me away from the damage I had left behind, his strong and firm hand on my shoulder. "You're going to escort the girl to the hospital in the back of the ambulance. Nobody here saw a thing. As far as Spencer will know, somebody from the crowd jumped him. I'll see to it myself."

"Did you see what he . . ."

"We all saw it," he interrupted. "You're damn lucky we have who we have on duty tonight. They like you, rookie. They hate Spencer. Get your hands checked while you're there. We'll report it as an incident with crowd control."

"They're fine," I barked, clenching and unclenching my fists to check for flexibility and broken bones. "Where's the girl?"

He tipped his head toward one of the two ambulances parked at the curb. "They're loading her up. She's a mess, Deac. That was her little brother. We'll take care of the witness statements. The farther away we can get you from Spencer, the better off you'll be. As far as he'll know, you were nowhere near when he got jumped, got it?"

"Thanks, Vic." My utterance came with a shitload of gratitude and a half ton of worry that I had just lost my job. Eight years in the service, two years as a firefighter before changing my career route, and another half year to get through the academy before being hired on with the force. My jaw was aching due to clenching my teeth, my heart racing due to the adrenaline pumping through my veins, and my lungs burned with every breath I tried to suck in. I didn't fly off the handle like that. Hell, I was one of the most self-controlled and patient guys you could meet . . . up to a certain point and circumstances.

"You're scheduled off the next three days, aren't you?" Vic asked.

"Yeah."

"Good. I'll clock you out at the station." He slapped me on the back before we reached the ambulance for me to accompany the young woman to the hospital. "Lay low. If you need anything, call me. I'll keep you posted if there's anything to report."

"Just find the guy that did this. After what Spencer did to her, I feel like we owe her justice as much as we do her little brother."

He snorted and shook his head. "If she sues the city, she may be getting a whole lot more than justice. Spencer just opened a whole can of worms." He slapped my shoulder once more and gently pushed me forward. "Go on, get outta here. We got a little street cam footage to clean up before that asshole sees who attacked him."

"It was worth it," I sneered before climbing into the back of the ambulance where the girl laid on a gurney; the EMTs working hard to calm her down, blood seeping onto the mattress beneath her.

He smirked. "Pretty sure his ex-wife would send you a thank you card and a box of chocolates."

I glanced back over my shoulder to see a slowly waking Spencer being helped to his feet. "Send him to a different hospital, will ya?"

He eyed the same scene I was and laughed. "Think I'll razz him first and tell him to go home and take some ibuprofen. Make him feel it for a while. See ya later, rookie." He closed the doors to the ambulance and tapped them twice for clearance.

Once inside the ambulance, the EMT asked me to sit at the head of the gurney – virtually out of their way – and simply talk to her, try to calm her, and see if I could soothe her while they worked on the bloody mess Spencer had caused.

That's when I got my first true glimpse of her. This wasn't a girl at all. She was young, yes, but she was no girl. Tear-filled, gray eyes flecked with green that bore into mine. Thick black lashes, porcelain skin, and full lips that weakly pleaded through her pain, "My brother. You have to help my brother."

"What's your name?" I asked in an effort to distract her.

"Everlee Remington," she whimpered. "Please help Jonah."

"Everlee," I said through the calmest voice I owned then told a lie I'd probably never forgive myself for, but the truth wasn't mine to tell. "They're helping your brother in the other ambulance.

There wasn't room for both of you in this one."

She reached for my hand, desperately seeking comfort in whatever form she could find it. "Stay with me?"

I answered her with another lie as I held her small and delicate, blood-coated hand in mine – because I had no other choice, "I'm right here, Everlee. I'm not going anywhere."

And for nearly two days I didn't. I stayed outside the curtain in the ER, listened intently as she cried and whimpered while they examined her, answering their questions the best she could, all the while asking where I was – "the man in the ambulance".

"Deacon Gray rode in with her, didn't he?" one of the ER techs asked. "I thought I saw him hopping out of the ambulance."

"It's no wonder she's asking," Shar, the nurse who offered an open invitation anytime I was willing and available, said with a giggle. Her tone changed to condescending when she obviously addressed Everlee, "Sweetie, Deacon is taken. He has that effect on lots of women."

Taken? What the hell?

"Shar!" Dr. Hayes snapped. "Call for ortho stat. We need some repair here."

She whipped the curtain open and I stepped back quickly in order to remain hidden from Everlee. Shar's face lit with her usual salacious grin that I found extremely unattractive – I didn't play where I worked – but the look on mine left no doubt I had overheard her comment and her grin fell as her face turned ashen.

My glare spoke for itself as I ground through a clenched jaw, "Call for the ortho."

I waited for Parnell to show up and supervise the investigative portion of the incident. Then I contacted my sister to bring me a change of clothes and a duffel bag in order to keep my uniform and gun with me. I held vigil in the surgical waiting area while they repaired the tendons in her legs. I waited outside recovery until they got her situated in a room. I sat in a chair outside her room to ensure she was recuperating properly.

Obtaining her emergency contact information from Parnell, I volunteered my services. Her mother was the listee and on vacation out of state at the time. So, I waited until she arrived – two days later. A dead son and an injured daughter, and it still took her two days. I even offered a plane ticket to get her back sooner; an offer she refused.

Was it against department policy? Absolutely.

Did she know where the offer came from? Absolutely not.

I tried.

They kept Everlee heavily sedated and partially restrained due to her persistent attempts to get out of the bed and find her brother, struggling to rescue a young man who couldn't be saved.

For two days, I sneaked into her room while she slept; checked on her. A virtual ghost. A ghost in sweats and sneakers. A ghost who whispered words of encouragement to her while she slept. A ghost who brushed her hair away from her face, traced his finger along her cheek and jaw, held her hand, kissed her knuckles. Eventually her mother showed up and Everlee was finally . . . no longer alone.

After it was over, I went home and slept for a day before I had to go back to work, where I spent nearly a month waiting to be called into the captain's office. Anticipated being released from my duties, fired for insubordination, brought up on assault charges for beating the piss out of Spencer – itching to do it again.

I'm still on the force – now a detective in the 83rd precinct – not too far from the original scene of the crime. The city settled out of court; Everlee's mother raging for justice. According to all accounts, I was simply one of the cops cordoning off the area, oblivious to what had happened.

Spencer? I scratched my itch. More on him later.

I never saw Everlee Remington again . . . except in my dreams.

Going forward, she was – and would be – forever to me, sweet Everlee.

Chapter 2

Everlee

Six years, a change in majors, and what seems like a lifetime of agony to get where I am. Four years to earn my bachelor's – all done in Louisiana prior to the incident – two years in forensics and another two to earn my master's degree in Chicago as well as one more in fellowship. You lose a lot of time when you're trying to heal.

How many phone calls had I made to hear "Nothing yet, ma'am" or "We're still working on it"? The crushing blow came when they told me all avenues had been studied and no answers had been found. Technically it wasn't closed. If anything came up, they would let me know.

But I knew what that meant: Jonah's death was filed as unsolved. AKA: put the evidence in a box in a room in the basement, never to see the light of day again. The paperwork would be scanned into a computer system, any items they had confiscated would be collecting dust or lost, and Jonah would be a number – one of many. A statistic in the next crime risk assessment of the south side of Hasselback, Louisiana.

I stayed for a year before I left for Chicago; hoping for answers, a resolution, maybe a little peace of mind knowing Jonah's killer was behind bars. But Chicago had an excellent forensics program and getting as far away from here was the best thing for me at the time. I always knew I'd come back. If the Hasselback PD wasn't going to solve the case, I sure was. I also still had a bone to pick with one Lieutenant Dylan Spencer. However, in order to do any of those things, I needed an in. A master's degree and an education in Chicago would pretty much guarantee that for me. Can't say my name didn't carry a bit of weight as well. They wouldn't dare turn me down. The last thing Hasselback would want is another . . . hassle, so to speak.

The settlement with the city more than paid for my schooling outside of my scholarships. In all honesty, it would have paid for my schooling without the scholarships, had my mother not taken a good portion for herself. As it was, I had enough for housing, food, clothing, and any other necessities that came up. The settlement also paid for all of my medical care and the physical therapy that followed the tendon repair in both legs. I don't limp anymore – I even run for exercise – and it's not like I wear miniskirts, so there's always that.

My mother, on the other hand, had enough for travel, wine, fancy clothes, and a new car. Pretty sure she pocketed a few boyfriends in that time span as well. The last time I saw her was right before I walked out the door after hearing her say, "What's done is done, Everlee. Let it go. It's time to move on." Letting her go was easy. I did move, but I refused to move on until justice was served.

I was only minutes late that night. If I hadn't gotten delayed in traffic maybe Jonah wouldn't have stepped outside on his break. Maybe we would have all stepped out together instead. Maybe we would have stayed inside and sat at a table and had a drink. Maybe he would have picked out a couple songs for me to sing with the band. It was kind of our thing.

I still tolerate my mother's occasional phone calls; generally with gritted teeth followed by a massive headache, but she is my mother. And now that I'm back – thank you, Gram for leaking that little tidbit of info – I'm afraid phone calls aren't going to be enough for her. We're all we have left, besides my grandmother, who constantly reminds me we can't choose our family. Which truly is unfortunate. But then Mary Poppins wasn't real, was she?

My phone barks no more than two minutes after I've set it and my keys on the counter after a grueling first day. I loathe orientation. It's my lab now and organization apparently wasn't the last forensic scientist's forte. Five weeks minimum is what it's going to take to straighten out the godforsaken mess left for me. Not to mention filling out requisition forms to order the supplies I'll need. How in the hell things got done properly is beyond me.

"Yes, mother." My voice is clipped as I answer. Nothing really out of the ordinary and today is no exception.

She releases an exasperated sigh, and I easily imagine her rolling her eyes. "Haven't we had this conversation a thousand times already, Everlee? I prefer you call me Beverly."

Of course she does. She's 46 yet styles her hair like a teenager, wears sky-high heels, orders manis that resemble talons, and swears that God only invented wind and rain to ruin her hair and makeup. My plan is to show up for her 50th birthday party with a fully lit cake, announcing flame retardant frosting, with the explanation that due to her reduced lung capacity brought on by smoking and advanced age, I would never expect her to blow out the bonfire.

"No worries here, folks. Let me just grab the fire extinguisher."

"Afraid your new boyfriend might overhear and get the impression you may be a little older than you told him you are?" I snort laugh. "We're not sisters. You birthed babies. We weren't ordered and grown in a Petrie dish. Unless of course there's something you're not telling me."

She lets go another long sigh that breezes through the phone line. More a hiss really – like a cornered cat when you piss them off – and I pull the phone away from my ear. "I called to see how your first day went."

"It went fine," I reply curtly, wondering how long it will take for her to inquire what my salary is. "It was only the first day. It was more orientation than anything. I'm not even hands-on yet."

"So, you didn't cut up any bodies today?"

Annie Mick

"Mother!" I yell in frustration. "I'm a forensic scientist, not pathologist. I don't cut up bodies! What is wrong with you?!"

"What's the difference? I thought you saw bodies and did things with them," she replies, indignant.

Took less time for the headache to hit with this call than I thought it would. I generally name them Beverly or mother. Today, it's simply "PITA". No, not the yummy bread on the gyro sandwiches I can devour in two minutes flat. It's short for "pain in the ass".

"I gotta go, *mother*." I emphasize the name, knowing will piss her off the most. "Should you decide you want to know the *difference*, Google it."

I end the call without giving her the opportunity to respond. She thought I did things with bodies? No, mother, that's your job. Not sure what his name is this week but it shouldn't be a problem for you. There will be a new one before long.

Opening the fridge, I scan the contents inside. What'll it be tonight, Everlee? Leftover blech? Frozen and thrown into the microwave blech? Or chop 'til you drop salad blech? Ooh look! Wine for the win! Well, that and the take out menu on the counter.

Thanks, mother. Or is that Beverly? Can't wait for the day she decides her name is too old fashioned and changes it. Will it be Muffy, Buffy, or Tiffy? Possibly Princess. No problem. She can study a book of names until the cows come home if she wants. The one she'll never get from me is "mom". She didn't want it when we were young; she's sure not getting it now that I'm older. Had she known that Jonah and I called her *Beverage* when she couldn't hear us, she may not have been so averse to being called mom.

Having finished the Thai food and sipping the last of the half bottle of Pinot, I stack the requisition forms I studied while I ate. My only hope is the city is willing to cough up a few more bucks to fill that lab with the latest technology. If not the city, I'll hit up the state for funds. They plan on using me in different parts of the state; why not ante up for the lab I'll be working in full time? Favor for a favor. You scratch my back – I'll scratch yours. Besides, my first and foremost interest is searching the basement for the box with the case number they've filed my brother's death under. I'll solve their cases, I'll do my job, but in the midst of it all, I'll be doing the job they never finished years ago. I'm good at puzzles.

"*Cut up bodies.*" Good God! I roll my eyes, recalling my mother's words. I deal with evidence. I shoot photos, analyze, collect evidence from crime scenes. Then, I bring it back to my lab and piece it together.

Do I see bodies? Of course, I do.

Do I have to touch them? Sometimes, in order to obtain fingerprints, maybe skin or hair samples, blood or skin from under the nails.

Do I wear rubber gloves? Is that even a question? You'd be amazed.

Do I sleep at night? Did you miss my mention of half a bottle of pinot?

My phone lights with the face I'm going to miss most from up north. His goofy grin is one made of magic; lighting up a room as he enters and leaving his mark wherever he goes.

Theo Masters pushed his way into my life the day we met and saw to it I never walked home alone or rode the train by myself from that day forward. We shared a condo just outside Chicago in Rogers Park on the shore of Lake Michigan for five years. Two bed, two bath. No sex. Just friends. Good reason for that. I believe his future husband may have objected. Theo wanted a clean, easy-to-get-along-with roommate who shared the same interests. The fact we were attending the same school for the same thing, well – can you say perfection?

I was on the train my second day in Chicago, on my way to check out a rental, when two shady looking characters were making their way toward me, and Theo stepped in. He wrapped his arm around my shoulder and said, "There you are, sweet cheeks!" He leaned close and whispered, "Play along. I swear to God, I'm safe. They're not." He glared at the two men and they turned around and left. Guess it's not too hard to ward them off when you stand six foot-three and weigh close to two fifty. Did I mention it's solid muscle?

"Hey, you," I answer cheerily.

"Hello gorgeous," he returns with a voice so velvety and smooth it feels like a blanket on your skin. "Did you dazzle them with your brilliance today?"

"I sparkled like tarnished silver."

He lets go a throaty laugh. "Evs, I could paint you with charcoal and you would still sparkle. Now tell me, love, how did it go?"

I sigh heavily. "I've got a lot of asks. The lab leaves a bit to be desired."

"Everlee Remington," he chides. "Did I teach you nothing? You don't ask, you demand. If they want your best work, they give you the best to work with."

"If they gave me the best to work with . . ." I chuckle lightly. "They'd give me you."

"You miss me already, don't ya?"

"I really do," I reply with all sincerity.

"I need my four seasons, sweetie," he tells me. "Rain, sun, snow, and a shitload of wind. A city named Hasselback? Sounds like a preemptor to raucous. Besides, them gators would love me for breakfast."

"Probably lunch and dinner, too," I groan. "You'd be a smorgasbord."

"Oh baby," he hums sexily. "I'm a delicacy. You forgot dessert."

I giggle without measure. "You're crazy is what you are."

"And my goal has been achieved," he says softly. "I made you laugh."

"You always do, Theo. I miss you."

"You know I miss you, baby girl. Keith and I will come see you in a few months. How's that?" he proffers, then adds a twang to his voice. "You can treat me to some Cajun food and maybe I'll buy me some gator boots."

I belly laugh. "You will not."

He continues with his silly twang. "We could slide on into

Nah'lins and have some o' them there beenays and earn ourselves some beads."

"They're beignets and you don't have boobs," I correct him.

"We'll let you flash yours and give us the beads to take home. Can you imagine the tales we could tell?"

"Theo?" I say softly as my eyes start to well with tears.

"Yeah?"

"I love you."

"I love you too, sweetheart," he whispers. "You're going to do just fine. Don't let one goal be your only goal. Be happy, Evs. It's all I want for you. Now, go get 'em, tiger."

We end our call and I stare at my phone. Theo knows the whole story. I'll be happy; once my one goal is accomplished. Until then, I can fly by the seat of my pants.

* * *

I wake with a start at quarter after three. It's dark outside and the breeze through my sheer covered window is humid with the night air. My breath is caught in my throat and my neck is wet with sweat. My body feels weak and tremulous; like I've just run a 5K.

"I'm right here, Everlee. I'm not going anywhere."

Those eyes. Green like moss on a stone. And that voice. So deep you don't just hear it; you feel it. At least I did, all the way to my bones. Gentle and compassionate. I haven't dreamed about him in so long. The man in the ambulance. The only thing I remember about that night outside of holding my little brother's bloody body and begging God not to take him. Well, other than the agonizing physical pain that went with being shoved to the ground and feeling like my skin was being torn from my knees and shins. The displacement of two vertebrae in my back didn't help much either. But I had a year of treatments and physical therapy to remind me of all that, day in and day out.

"It's being back here, Everlee," I mutter to myself. "Time, you just need time."

Annie Mick

Throwing the sheets off, I climb out of bed, too shaken to lie back down again so soon. Two weeks I've been here, moving in, getting settled. Taking my time to acclimate before stepping into a new world, a new life.

My condo is perfect. I had searched for two months before finding one that fit me. Convinced I wanted a two-story – you know, in case I didn't feel like making the bed – but Theo talked me out of it.

"So, you're going to try to finagle stairs blind every morning, Evs?"

"What are you talking about?"

"You do realize it's best if you're awake before you attempt stairs, don't you?"

"I'm not a sleepwalker!"

"Everlee, you need two cups of coffee before you even open your eyes." He shrugged and grinned. *"Just sayin'. My girl's not a morning person."*

He was right, as always. My condo here is a little bigger than the one we shared in Chicago, a lot newer, and in a quiet neighborhood. Theo demanded I not take the first floor and lease the one available on the third. Said "gators" don't climb walls and to let them feast on the first floor tenants instead. It didn't matter how many times I tried to explain I was nowhere near the swamps; he simply wanted me above the first floor.

I'm not stupid. He didn't want anyone to have easy access to the windows and a way to bypass the doorman. Yes, he worries. And, he's like the big brother I never had. Not that Jonah didn't act like one. Age was no factor when it came to protectiveness. We'd grown up having virtually only each other, other than our Gram.

My feet slap heavily across the wood floor as I make my way to the kitchen for a glass of water. Yeah, I'm not a middle of the night kind of person either. That dream though. I can't remember the last time I'd had it. Still as vivid as the first time. Maybe even more so tonight; as if it had been given a fresh coat of paint.

Somebody's Someone

Opening the fridge door, I eye the bottle of wine lying on the second shelf versus the Brita pitcher sitting on the top shelf. My eyes shift to the clock on the wall. Half past three.

"Don't even think it," I scold myself out loud.

Reaching for the water pitcher instead, I pour myself a glass, holding it up before I chug it. "Nectar of the gods. Might not be as tasty, but it is the smarter option." Setting the empty glass on the counter, I roll my eyes and head back to the bedroom, mumbling, "Besides, Captain Garner would probably be hard pressed to believe you use Pinot flavored toothpaste."

Annie Mick

Chapter 3

Deacon

Two hours of frustration, tepid Chinese take-out by the time I got around to eating it, scattered papers all over my coffee table, and the video having been played over and over on the big screen TV before I gave up once again; packing the evidence neatly into the folder I keep tucked away in the bookcase.

How many times can you read the same statements, watch the same video, study the same evidence and still come up empty? Damnit! Did we lose something in the cuts they had to make in the street cam video because of me jumping Spencer? It was only seconds, but seconds can mean the difference between solved and unsolved. Something, or someone, in the background? But how much more damage would that asshole have done if I hadn't stepped in?

The same things I'd seen over the years of studying the video. The same motions and reactions as people came and went. The camera captured the victim leaving the bar and walking out toward the street, waving to someone, only to return a few minutes later, bent and stumbling while holding his stomach. The broken glass found on the ground all around him was there before he fell. The broken beer bottle found implanted in his belly was new. It had cut right through the abdominal aorta. It was either a well-aimed hit or a lucky strike. Either way, he bled out before they could help him. He really didn't stand a chance.

Why had I pulled the evidence out and viewed it all over again last night? Everlee Remington. Seeing her yesterday put me in the back of that ambulance once again. *"Stay with me"*. I did stay with you, Everlee. But I let you down as well, and I've been trying to make it right ever since. I've dreamed of the day I could call you and tell you we found justice for Jonah. Apologize for lying to you that night; for telling you your brother was getting help in the other ambulance. But only because I didn't want you to hurt any more than you already were. Apologize for telling you I wasn't going anywhere, then left you in the hands of your mother. I heard her lie to you; tell you she had been there the whole time. Shatter your heart when she told you she had your brother cremated. Never gave you the opportunity for a final goodbye. All the times I've wanted to call you just to see how you were. To tell you I've never forgotten you. To say you were the most beautiful thing I'd ever seen in my life.

And now? Now you're even more beautiful than I remember. There was no ring on your finger yesterday. No tan lines to indicate residence of one recently either. I'm observant like that.

Oh sweet Everlee. Why couldn't you have been married with children by now?

As soon as the light blinks off on the Keurig, I pull the cup off the tray and put it to my mouth. Strong, black, hot. Just the way I like it. By cup number four, I might be feeling human again. I laid awake and stared at the ceiling for hours last night. How am I going to work side-by-side with her? How am I going to be within close proximity and not touch her? We're the perfect moth to a flame analogy.

I steeled myself yesterday before approaching where she stood, I had prepared. However, I now realize the problem. I can steel myself all I want, but Everlee Remington is a magnet and if I get close, I may never be able to detach.

It took every ounce of willpower I had to not pull her into a hug, to tell her to run. Warn her away from this seedy side of life that's loaded with drug runners, murderers, wife beaters, and the dregs that we deal with on a daily basis. Ask her to give me a little more time to solve her brother's murder. She's too young, too vulnerable, too innocent.

Which rounds out the other reason she shouldn't be here. I am not that young, and I'm anything but innocent. I may not play where I work – never really been tempted – but I'm a damn good athlete outside the precinct. Remember the report cards we received as children that commended us: 'plays well with others'? I'm a straight A student as an adult as well. And never has a coworker looked so tempting.

Rinsing the cup and setting it in the dishwasher, I take a long, deep breath and release it slowly. "She's not a playground, Gray," I mutter to myself, heading to the bathroom for a shower to get ready for work. "But damn, taking her for a spin sure would be fun."

Under the hot water, steam fills the room, and my mind floats to memories over the last six years. I've punished myself in peculiar ways; setting the thermostat on my heart to ice cold, never allowing women to get close, always placing boundaries of physical pleasure with no attachment, no reruns if the movie was over. AKA: "The End" a literal closing statement. That one is for the clingers. "Hey, it's been fun" or "Take care of yourself" the typical send off . . . or take off. Waking up alone is my MO and my preferred method of avoiding awkward morning-after situations.

I thought my time in the military had tainted my view of the world . . . of people. Turns out being a cop can do a whole lot more damage to your faith in mankind than witnessing the damage in a war-torn country. It can make you cold and emotionless sometimes. Because if you're not, it will break you.

Trips to the hospital to interview victims or perps have always been a trigger of that night and the two days that followed. Those eyes and that face I studied so closely. The hand I held, the words of comfort I whispered, the promise I spoke. That was the last time I let myself get emotionally involved. There was no reward in the end; just a sensation of loss like I had never felt before, and promised myself I would never feel again.

Annie Mick

Everlee Remington all grown up. She must be about 28 now. She wasn't really a girl when I first met her; she was a victim. A helpless, injured, broken, young woman. But now? She's a powerhouse, and she's on a mission. *Damned if I'm not proud of her.* I'd have to be a fool not to see it. Returning so close to the scene of the crime and in a position to have full access to all of the evidence. The same force to be reckoned with that she was before Spencer ground her knees into the broken glass. Oh, sweet Everlee, what rain from hell do you plan on dousing the city of Hasselback with? And what are your plans for the perp once you find them . . . *if* you find them?

Do I try to stop you? Do I help you? Are you here to solve what we couldn't or do you have another purpose? Possibly retribution? Believe me, love, Spencer paid. Do you know something I don't? Would you share it if I asked?

The longer I perseverate all the possibilities of Everlee – that face, that body – the more my blood heats. Unfortunately, all the blood drains south and I find myself hard and needy. I slam the faucet off – my moral compass consuming my need – then chastise myself as I wrap a towel around my waist and stomp to the bedroom to get dressed.

"Good God, Deacon." I reach for my jerseys and pull them on. "One fucking day and she's under your skin. Either pull your head outta your ass or resign."

Opening my cell phone to the contacts list, I send a quick text.

Me: "Your place. Seven o'clock. No dinner, no frills."
It takes two minutes.

Her: "You're such a romantic, Duncan. No clothes either?"

I smirk as I read the text. *Duncan.* Best idea I ever had. Incognito and inaccessible.

Me: "You know the drill."

Somebody's Someone

I finish dressing and ignore the successive pings of my phone as I tuck it into my pocket. Never been one much for conversation or texting. Keep it simple, in and out, go home . . . alone. They enjoy themselves – I'm not that selfish – I relieve some pressure and tension. Seems I may be needing relief a little more often if my thoughts go places they shouldn't.

* * *

"Gray!" Captain Garner calls out from the doorway. "My office, now."

"Ooohh," Rodriguez singsongs. "Somebody's in trouble. Steal a donut, did ya?"

I feign a deep yawn and look bored. "Nope. He just wants the names of your regular hookers. Seems they've all come down with a nasty rash. The work doc will be up soon to get you for an exam."

"I ain't been with no hookers!" he grinds through a clenched jaw as he scouts the room for any witnesses to our conversation.

Lifting a brow, I scoot my chair back and stand. "No? Hmmm," I hum and nod contemplatively. "Did you know masturbating will turn your palms purple?"

As if by reflex, he immediately turns his palms up for inspection and checks them. His chin lifts as a scowl joins a nasty shade of red on his face. "You're real funny, asshole."

Lifting one shoulder in a shrug and smiling cockily, I reply, "I thought so. See you later, Handy."

"Gray!" he growls low.

"Purple," I mimic his growl.

"Fuck you!"

"Nah, I'm good."

Crossing the hall to the captain's office, I hear chatter coming from the room. *Her chatter. Day two, Cap? Are you kidding me?*

"Gray, come on in," he says when he sees me in his doorway. Everlee sits in one of two chairs in front of his desk. Cap waves to

37

the empty one. "Take a seat."

"I'm good," I nod from inside the doorway where I've stepped, keeping my eyes fixed on his. "What's up?" I know I'm pushing my luck. Garner has a thing about eye level when he speaks, or preferably looking down upon his subject.

He arches his brows then glances at the chair and back to me, waiting for me to follow his order. I reluctantly take a seat on the edge of the chair next to Everlee, elbows on my knees. The soft scent of jasmine infiltrates my nostrils and a sudden flashback of that night hits like a lightning bolt. Sweet Jesus, she hasn't changed her perfume in all this time. My mind wanders helplessly as I breathe a little deeper, capturing the scent I've never forgotten, *not to mention the stupid fucking shrubs I planted in my backyard as a reminder of her.*

" . . . so, I'm pairing you two up as a team for a couple of weeks so Everlee can get a feel for things and familiarize herself with the area." The Cap's voice is echoing in my head before the words register, but once they do my gut bottoms out.

And since when did she become Everlee? I think the only people he's ever called by their first names are his wife and kids. Maybe the dog. And that's only speculation.

"So, she can what?!" My voice is harsher than I intend and to make matters worse, I don't stop there. "Doesn't she already . . ." I manage to stop myself before I slide both feet in my mouth and clear my throat instead. There has been no explanation of Everlee's history and therefore, no way I should know she would be more than familiar with the city.

"The 81st is already on site," Cap starts. "It's the abandoned lot where the old Kmart used to be on Mackinaw and Lotus. Construction crew was about to start work on tearing out the old concrete. The body was found in the bottom of a storm drain in the parking lot. They're waiting for you."

"If the 81st is on site, what do you need me for?" I wave a hand in her general direction. "And why in hell does Ms. Remington need an escort?"

Captain Garner squares me with his well-known and ever

famous *because I said so* look. "You're not *escorting* her, you're driving and assisting her."

"Does she not know how to drive?"

Everlee looks up at the ceiling and chuckles sarcastically before speaking to herself. "Don't worry, Everlee. Eventually they'll remember you're in the room." In my periphery I see her turn toward me. "Not only do I know how to drive, Detective Gray, but I'm quite capable of doing my job without any assistance." She then turns back to face our supervisor. "Captain Garner, I'm not sure why you thought this was a good idea, but I can handle myself quite well. I'll find my way."

"Everlee," Cap says with a calm and gentility I've never heard from him before. You'd think he was talking to his daughter, a victim, someone fragile. "The forensics assistance team had already taken off with the van before checking in to see who was leading. They've been reprimanded. Nobody has touched anything. Hawkins used to drive himself from here." He rolls his eyes. "Or from home half the time because he hadn't shown up for work yet."

He's right. Hawkins was the former head forensic scientist for Howard county and was not known for reliability, nor was he the epitome of competence. Hence, the reason Everlee has replaced him. Apparently, she has not been introduced to the entire district yet.

"Why not just let me go from here?" she asks. "I can drive myself."

Cap heaves a heavy, drawn out sigh. "It's your first time out in the field. It doesn't sound like a very pleasant case to start with. We're a team around here." He smirks as he looks at me. "Deacon needs a little work on his team skills anyway, and there is no time like the present."

Everlee stiffens next to me before slowly turning my way. I feel her eyes study the side of my face, her gaze nearly burning a hole in my skin. Her voice is but a whisper as she inquires, "Your name is Deacon?"

Rising from the chair, I turn toward the door. "Let's go, Ms.

Remington."

Chapter 4

Everlee

My ID, credentials, and phone are always with me. I usually carry some cash or my debit card for emergencies as well, but I need to stop in the lab to grab it before we leave. "I need to stop by the lab. I'll be right back."

"You don't need to carry a purse, Ms. Remington." Detective Gray slides his sunglasses on as we walk toward the exit. Correction: He walks, I nearly run. Long legs and lest we forget, not a team player. *Apparently, he's a jackass as well. A gentleman lets the lady walk ahead or by his side.* "It's just one more thing for someone to steal from the car."

"Good thing I'm not going for my purse," I snap back. "I'll only be a minute."

He mutters behind me as I turn down the hall that leads to my lab, but I hear him clearly. "Probably a fanny pack to stash the tampons."

I stop dead in my tracks and turn. "That was last week but if you need some, I keep a few extras in the lab. Want me to grab a couple for you? I understand they can come in handy in case you lose the stick up your ass."

His cheeks flush the tiniest hint of pink below his aviator shades before his jaw sets tight. "I'll be outside. Don't be long." *Yup, definitely a jackass.*

Theo would be proud of me. He may have had a better retort but he would be high-fiving me right now. I stand a little taller, my jaw squared as I walk toward my lab. *Deacon.* Why does that name ring bells? Not church bells, mind you. No, that man is anything but angelic.

* * *

The ride to the crime scene is silent until Detective Gray sets the radio to classic rock at a volume that doesn't allow for easy conversation. If he knew it was my favorite, I truly doubt he would have chosen it. He grips the steering wheel so tightly his knuckles protrude and turn white against his otherwise tanned skin. He has large hands with long fingers, well-trimmed nails. The muscles in his thighs bulge beneath his dress slacks. He's a runner; has to be. Probably does leg-lifts too. Everything I see is viewed from side-eyed glances; thick, dark blonde wavy hair that's a little mussy, well-trimmed short facial hair, a sharp angled nose, defined jawline.

"We're here," he announces, pulling the car to stop near the vehicles in the parking lot full of a variety of construction cranes and diggers, police cars, the coroner's truck, and the forensics van. A mass of navy blue shirts and khaki pants on the forensics team as well as blue jeans and chambrays on the construction crews discern who's who. A few uniforms as well as shirts and ties with sport coats are in the mix as well.

I resist rolling my eyes at his announcement. I'm well aware we're here, Detective Gray. I could have found it with my eyes closed and without a GPS. My childhood home is two miles to the north, the high school I attended is five blocks to the west, and the bowling alley is still standing about a mile to the east. It may be a large metropolis, but when you're unsupervised as a teenager, you find your own entertainment.

"Gray," a good looking, smiling face greets him as we make our way toward the group. "Whoa! Who do we have here?" he asks with a flirty grin and a slow perusal before extending his hand to take mine. "Please tell me you're single."

"Knock it off, Marty," Deacon sneers. "She's here to do a job."

I'm not sure if I laugh at Marty's flirting or Deacon's gruffness, but as I do I extend my hand to Marty's, playing along, and answering most of his questions, "Everlee Remington. Senior forensic scientist."

Marty takes my hand in his, then tucks it inside his elbow and walks me forward toward the cordoned off area. "Well, Everlee Remington, beautiful name by the way, I'm Detective Marty Striegel with the 81st. We'll talk about the details when I take you to dinner on Friday. In the meantime, we have a body in the bottom of the storm drain over here. You ready to show us what you got?"

"Ready and able," I reply. "Where's my hazmat gear?"

He waves a hand toward the forensics van. "Right over here."

"No one has been down there, have they?"

"No ma'am," he reassures me, his southern drawl strong. "They've been waiting for you. We have been shining the lights and checking for snakes and such." He eyes me curiously. "You sure you're ready for this?"

My steely glare must speak for itself because he flinches before I ask, "Are you questioning my skills or my backbone?"

He smiles impishly. "I wouldn't dare, Everlee Remington."

Nor should he. He'll learn. And if he's got half a lick of sense, he'll be a quick study.

"Good." I nod curtly, pulling my hand away from his bent elbow and head for the van, leaving him in my dust. "Let's do this."

Behind me is an unmistakable growl followed by Deacon's unwavering threat, "Touch her again and I will break your arm."

I don't wait to hear any more of their exchange. My stomach is already roiling. I have no idea what awaits me in that storm drain. I've seen it all, I've smelled it all. I've felt deeper and stronger than I've ever wanted to. But this is my job, and if it helps bring justice for those who have been wronged, then I've served a purpose.

Suited up in hazmat gear and heavy boots that reach my

knees, I start to descend the ladder that leads into the pit below.

"Everlee, wait!" Deacon yells from just feet away. He's in the same gear I am, suited from his head to his toes. Which, quite frankly, is not his job and quite unexpected. Ignoring his order, I continue my descent step by step.

Soon after I reach the bottom, Deacon hops off the last rung of the ladder and steps to the ground. "I told you to wait! Damnit, Everlee, is this the way you always operate?" The mask over his nose and mouth underneath the full gear face shield muffles his voice slightly but doesn't hide the anger in his voice.

"As a matter of fact, it is, Detective Gray. I have a job to do."

"So apparently you don't follow orders?" he hollers.

"You don't get to give me orders!" I exclaim indignantly. "You're along for the ride."

"I gave you the ride!"

"I've had friendlier rides on the subways in Chicago!" We stand toe-to-toe in a heated glare, our face gear nearly touching. The space we're in is barely enough for one, much less two. The little I can see of his eyes is full of fire, the face gear fogging with his heavy breaths and reflecting the bright light from the lamp he holds in his hand. "I don't want your ride, Detective Gray."

"You sure about that, Ms. Remington?" His voice is low and laced with what I would swear is sexual overtones. And why it turns me on is far beyond me, especially given the circumstances. Geez, wine and dine me first, pal. Try a little tenderness. How about somewhere other than a storm drain with a dead body in the vicinity.

Oh yeah, there's a body in here.

"I just wanted to make sure it was safe down here," he mutters softly.

"Now that that has been established, mind if I do my job?"

The "body" is a virtual skeleton with skin, rotted clothing draped in various places over it. Still hair and fingernails, but no identifiable visual remains. DNA is all we will have to go by. This isn't a fresh death. The poor thing has been here for some time.

And due to the fact it's rained countless times in the interim, it's going to inhibit the investigation a thousand fold. I snap dozens of pictures first, then collect hair samples, scrape the underside of the fingernails for evidence before clipping samples of the nails. We strip some bits of clothing from the corpse and package and label it to check for probable, but not impossible, nonexistent blood samples. Deacon stays throughout the process and actually is quite helpful. The forensics team lowers the equipment I need and hoists it back up when I'm done. They will collect the remains, now that I'm done collecting what I need, and move them to the morgue. It appears to be a female; the pelvic bones and chest cavity are evident of that – you can never assume by clothing. But the clothing we did remove may be indicative of a particular nighttime job – sequins and such – fishnet stockings, garters, sky high heels. You get my drift.

Stripping the hazmat clothing off after ascending from the drain, I strain for a few deep breaths. The air is humid and thick in the Louisiana daytime; the heat a degree or two short of hell. One of the forensic team members hands me a cold bottle of water.

"Thank you," I tell him before chugging half the bottle in one go.

"Truckers used to use this lot as a bit of a rest area," Deacon says between long pulls of his water. "Hookers found it a good place to earn their keep during the week when downtown business was slow."

My head turns slowly and I let out a bitter huff. "Earn their keep?"

He lifts one shoulder in a slow shrug. "Just an expression. She probably picked up with the wrong guy and he dumped her when she demanded to be paid."

"Dumped her?"

"Killed her, Ms. Remington," he deadpans. "If you're going to live that way, there's every chance you're going to die that way. A hooker is a hooker."

How dare he!

"Everyone is somebody's someone!" I shriek angrily. "She

was somebody's daughter! Maybe somebody's sister! Who knows? Maybe even somebody's mother!"

His brows lift in casual indifference over the top of his aviators before he finishes his water and throws the bottle in the container by the van. "Then maybe she should have been home with her kids. I doubt you'll find anyone crying at a funeral for her. Like I said, a hooker is a hooker."

I stare at him in disbelief and shock at his cruel statement. "Tell you what, Detective Gray, should you suffer your demise when I'm still around, I'll be sure to show up for your funeral. I'll even do your eulogy. Let them know their tears are in vain." I toss my water bottle toward the bin and score. "Because a dick is a dick."

Pulling my phone from my pocket, I pull up the Lyft app and head toward the edge of the lot. I'll walk before I get back in a car with him. It's not like I have a purse with a stash of tampons in it. He certainly doesn't need them either; that stick is wedged so tight up his ass it's a wonder he can walk. The team has all the evidence I collected loaded into the van. Besides, I haven't known them long enough to convince them to hide evidence from a fresh murder; namely Detective Gray's.

Behind me is the voice I heard the moment we stepped out of the car. "Damn, Gray. That one's got lady balls. You can break both my arms, but I'm goin' after that. Think I'll come visit at the 83rd."

Chapter 5

Deacon

"Damn, Gray. That one's got lady balls. You can break both my arms, but I'm going after that. Think I'll come visit you at the 83rd." Marty laughs as he stands beside me.

"Go anywhere near her, Striegel, and they will not find your body," I warn him. "Stay on your own turf."

"There is no turf. She works with all of us, Gray," he reminds me with a tilt of his head and a cocky grin. "You lucky bastards simply house the lab in your building. Think I might find the need to check on a case that Hawkins was in the middle of when he left. Maybe the lovely Everlee and I can work on it together. We are having dinner on Friday after all."

"In your dreams. She never agreed to it, asshole." I warn him once more for good measure, "Stay away from her, Marty. She's too young and innocent for a prick like you."

He smirks as he studies her retreating backside. "She looks teachable."

Grabbing the front of his shirt, tie included, I twist hard. "And you look breakable. She's not one of your whores. Hunt for pussy in your own neighborhood."

Setting a fast pace – not quite a dead run but damn close – I head toward the departing Everlee. "The car is over here, Ms. Remington. Let's go." I reach for her elbow and as we connect,

I fight pulling her to me. Shaking her hand yesterday was hard enough – the memory of kissing those knuckles, caressing that skin.

"Feel free to use it, Detective Gray," she says as she snatches her arm away. "I have a car on its way. I don't feel like riding with a dick."

The low growl that leaves my throat catches me by surprise. Hearing her say riding and dick in the same sentence sounds like a good idea to me. Oh wait! She said *don't*, didn't she? Damnit, I need a drink . . . and a cold shower.

"I'm sorry," I relent with a heavy sigh. "I shouldn't have said what I did."

She turns and studies me with an arched brow, though she can't see much. My shades thankfully cover my eyes. Otherwise, she just might see they're fixed on her mouth.

"Are you apologizing to me or what was once a human being?" Her voice cracks the tiniest bit. "With a heart, and a soul, and feelings?"

"To both of you." I shove my hands in my pockets because if I don't, I'm afraid I may place them on her hips. "This job. It can change you. You see the worst of . . ."

"I came here from Chicago, Detective Gray," she interrupts, her voice strong and once again confident. "I assure you I've seen my share of the worst." She narrows her eyes. "More than you'll ever know."

No, Everlee, I do know. I watched you. I was there.

A blue Toyota pulls up to the curb and the driver calls out from the open window, "Everlee?" She moves to open the back door to get in.

Reaching for her once again but stopping short of touching her, I nearly plead, "Ride with me. I apologized, didn't I?"

She pulls on the handle of the car door and opens it. "Apologies aren't a free pass, detective. Follow-up is the determining factor for sincerity. I'll see you back at the precinct." She slides into the backseat with ease and closes the door. The driver takes off and I'm left to eat crow.

Somebody's Someone

My deflated ago takes a blow until a smirk slowly tips the corner of my mouth which then grows into a full blown smile. Everlee Remington – the force to be reckoned with. The first woman I've ever known to piss me off and make me proud at the same time. Yeah, Garner's going to have my ass when I get back to the station. Vic may have a few questions of his own as well if word gets around. Oh hell, what am I thinking? That place is worse than a church bingo hall. You know how it is. By the end of the evening, once they've called O-69, there's not a poor bastard in town gotten his balls waxed or a woman received a Brazilian without the whole parish knowing. Worse yet? It's not the esthetician who let the cat out of the bag.

Let that sink in for a minute, folks.

Pulling my phone out of my pocket, I send a quick text:

Me: *"Not going to make it. Something came up."*

Is it my conscience? My moral compass? Or is it my sudden hope that after six years of only memories, there is a reason she's come back into my life? Or . . . it could be the simple fact I have never in my life been drawn to anything or anyone like I am to Everlee Remington.

The phone in my hand buzzes.

Her: *"I'll stay up late. Doesn't matter the time. I'm sure you'll make it worth my while. I promise I'll make it worth yours."*

Sliding my phone into my pocket without responding, I make my way back to the car. It's tempting; I could use the release. So easy. In and out. But the thought suddenly strikes me as repulsive. I've got a shower, and soap, and a hand.

* * *

Garner yells as I pass his office on my way to the squad room. "Gray!"

49

Oh yeah, suddenly a good shot of whiskey and my couch sound good right about now. I suppose I really should have given this consideration on my way back from the scene. A lame excuse, a reason, a bit of smoke to blow up his ass as to why Everlee and I didn't return in the same car. I stop at the threshold of his office — makes for a faster escape if I need one.

"You called?"

"You wanna explain?" He stands from his desk, hands fisted as he leans forward on it. His stern glare speaks volumes, but he says nothing more. I mean really, his inquiry could be related to anything from the coffee spill in the box of donuts this morning (sorry, not sorry), the price of eggs in China, the political upheaval in Venezuela. Or . . . maybe the dead crawdad in Rodriguez's desk drawer.

"Explain what?"

"Close the door," he orders.

I start to step out and pull the door behind me.

"With you on the inside, smartass!"

It was worth a try.

"Why did Ms. Remington come back in a Lyft?" he asks, crossing his arms over his chest. "What did you do to piss her off?"

I shrug then lift my hands. "What makes you think I pissed her off?"

"It's what you do, Gray." He scowls. "I swear to God, you took online classes to learn how. You've probably earned your PhD by now. Hell, for all I know, you're moonlighting as the professor teaching the classes."

"What did she say?"

"Not a damn word." He smirks. "Other than you could use a good shower before you come to work in the mornings. Said the storm drain smelled better than you. Couldn't take the close quarters in the car."

My jaw drops. That little shit! My personal hygiene is stellar. My cologne costs a fucking fortune. I manscape! And no, the church bingo ladies don't have a damn clue. Discretion is the better part of *my* valor. My hookups are in the next county over, as a construction worker by the name of *Duncan Greene.*

"Yes, Gray. We all know you have perfect teeth," Garner says with a wry look. "Close your mouth. I don't need to see them." He arches his brows and narrows his eyes in unison. "Seems you may have met your match in our little Everlee. I don't know what happened out there, but what I do know is it had better not happen again. When I send you out together, you'd better return together . . . with smiles on your faces. Do I make myself clear?"

It's not a question. I know it and he knows I know it.

"Yup."

"Deacon." He turns toward his window as if searching for an explanation and sighs. "She's a little green. Fresh out of school and off the assembly line, but she was top in her class. Don't make her job any harder than it's already going to be."

"Why me?" I ask him.

"Why not you?" He lifts one shoulder and lets it drop, then tips his chin in question. "How did she do out there today?"

I shake my head and chuckle softly. "She was a pro. You'd think she's been doing it forever."

He nods. "She's probably had a bit of practice. She is from Chicago."

No she's not – she only studied in Chicago – but I don't tell him that. I noted she didn't share that little tidbit in the discussion before we left either. I was pretty sure she could have found her way to the scene without any problems. I'm aware the city settlement was hushed. It wasn't in this precinct. Word gets around, but it was a long time ago and swept under the rug faster than politicians caught with prostitutes.

"Yeah, that's what I hear." I twist the knob and open the door. "I'll do my best."

"Counting on it," he says, an unmistakable warning in his tone. Before I can get the door closed, he calls out, "One more thing." I wait with bated breath, my back to him, jaw clamped. "You're accompanying Ms. Remington on calls until further notice."

I whirl back, eyes wide, nostrils flared. "I'm what?!"

Annie Mick

His face is stoic, hands folded in front of him on the desk. "Play nice, Deacon." He smirks. "Be sure to shower."

I don't slam the door, but it takes every ounce of restraint I have not to. If he only knew what he was asking. Correction: demanding.

* * *

The rest of the day goes by in a blur. One robbery, a domestic call, two arrests and a shit ton of paperwork. All in all, typical. Same shit, different day. Unless of course, you consider my morning with Ms. Remington and the shitshow with Garner.

Which brings me to where I'm standing at the present time; right outside her lab. I saw her car in the parking lot and came back in to check on her. It was a shit day and I only made it worse. She was right, too. My hostility should have been aimed at the criminal instead of the victim.

It's six o'clock and the lights shine through the small window in the door to the lab. Why is she still here? I thought she clocked out at five. I study her for a moment, feeling that ever familiar skip of my heart, before tapping lightly on the door and pushing down on the handle, then poke my head in.

"You got a minute?"

She doesn't look up from the slides she's carefully placing in individual slots in a tray. "I suppose I could spare you one. I'm just about to head out. What can I help you with, detective?"

I step farther into the room, letting the door close behind me. "You doing okay?"

She moves across the room and places the labeled tray onto the shelf in the glass temperature controlled cooler then closes the door. "Is there a reason I wouldn't be?"

"Have you had dinner?" I ask, stupidly because I came down unprepared. I could take her to dinner, couldn't I? I'd give anything to learn more about her. What she's been doing. How her time in Chicago was – aside from subway rides being more pleasant than mine. If she has anyone special in her life.

"Dinner?" She chuckles. "It's five o'clock. A little early for dinner."

"It's six o'clock, Ms. Remington. You're working late."

"Huh, guess I wasn't watching the time." She gathers a few tools and places them in the steamer, locks the chamber, and sets the timer for cleaning. "Not sure why I'm working so hard on this one. It's not like she has a funeral to get ready for. Probably no one waiting to bury her remains. No one to cry for her. Maybe they don't even miss her. Isn't that right, detective?"

I run a fast and frustrated hand through my hair. "I said I was sorry."

"I heard you the first time." She has yet to spare me a glance as she opens the drawer of a file cabinet and pulls out her purse — the one containing those spare tampons I'm sure — and slings it over her shoulder. *I am such an asshole.*

"Do you have someone to get home to?" *Yes, I know. But it's a good segue for asking if she has someone special in her life.*

She stands in front of the computer and taps a few keys, studying the screen. "Are you asking if I have a dog or a cat, detective?"

"That would be a *thing* to get home to, Ms. Remington."

"Dogs are people too!" she exclaims. *Damnit! She's eluding the question and she knows it!*

"Do you have a dog?"

"No, I have a Roscoe. And he gets hangry about seven o'clock so I'd best be going. Anything else I can help you with?"

"You have dinner to fix for *Roscoe*?" My brow furrows, my hopes dashed. "By seven? Does he ever cook for you?"

"No," she says. "I'm the cook at our house. I'm a fan of sushi and he isn't." The screen goes dark and she turns toward me. "Well that, and he has trouble with utensils."

"Trouble with utensils?"

She holds her index finger and thumb about half an inch apart. "Those little fins can't quite get a grip."

I stare at her, that mouth so close to tipping a grin. "Roscoe is a fish."

"Don't tell him that," she warns with a pointed finger. "He is the king of his water castle."

I snatch her finger up with two of mine and curl them around it. "You told the captain I stink."

"I could have told him you were an ass."

"He already knows that."

Her eyes meet mine and she freezes, drawing in a quick breath. The impish grin she wore only moments before vanishes. Her brow furrows as she gazes into my eyes then she looks away with a fast shake of her head as if to clear it. She yanks her finger out of my grip and rakes a hand through her hair. "I'm sure you have somewhere to go. Goodnight, Detective Gray."

She pulls keys from the pocket in her lab coat before hanging it on a hook, then scurries toward the door before yanking it open. "You first. I need to lock up."

A slow silent breath leaves my lungs as I walk slowly to the door. "And you need to get home to Roscoe."

"Yup," she replies with a nod that easily averts her gaze.

I stop in front of her, mere inches between us. "You can call me Deacon."

Her chin lifts, those stormy gray eyes filled with emotions I can't read. "No," she whispers, "I don't think I can."

Does she remember? From the looks of it, if she does, I will forever be the reminder of the worst night of her life.

God, I want to say her name, feel it roll off my tongue. But instead, I nod and murmur, "Goodnight, Ms. Remington."

Chapter 6

Everlee

"Hey Roscoe," I greet my Siamese betta fish as I drop a few flakes into his bowl. He swims to the top and nibbles at the flakes as if to say *thank you* as well as *what took you so long?* His magnificent flowing red and blue fins sway in the water as he dives for the few pieces sinking to the bottom before they reach the floor of the tank. "You didn't forget me, did you?"

Tears stung my eyes all the way home as reality sunk in. It's him, and he doesn't remember me. I had no idea he was a cop. An EMT maybe, but not a cop. Those unique moss-green eyes. Scolding with a hint of mischief today, but they're the same ones that were so filled with compassion years ago. His voice is gruffer; a cold edge that wasn't present before. The man in the ambulance that I've dreamed of off and on for six years is a cocky, bossy, bitter cop. Oh God, he's beautiful. More handsome than I remember. He's older than me – not sure by how much – but that only works to his advantage, given the morons I dated throughout my early college years. I could have drawn bullseyes on my target points and they'd still miss.

Newsflash college boys: An E-zone is not the endzone. It's not a race to the finish line; it's a pathway!

Spoiler alert: If you have to repeatedly ask a woman if it feels good, you're doing it all wrong! Use some intuition, for God's sake!

Does he know about Jonah? He must. He was there. *Not that he stuck around. Contrary to what he told me he would do.*

If he finds out who I am, will he try to prevent me from solving Jonah's case?

Is he one of those cops who protects their own, no matter what they do, and thinks Lieutenant Spencer's behavior was warranted?

Theo answers on the second ring. "Hey, sweet cheeks, miss me?"

His warm welcome makes me smile. "I found my ambulance guy."

The silence is deafening before he finally breaks it. "Tell me he's a hot, single EMT that's been searching for you for years and fell on his knees and proposed the moment he saw you."

"Well," I drawl. "You've got the hot and single part right, I think. Hardly a marriage proposal. He doesn't remember me, Theo."

"What?!" he shouts unexpectedly. "No way. You're – you're you, Evs. Unforgettable. Get the poor bastard some glasses."

"No, Theo." I chuckle softly. "I think he's a player. And, he's a cop."

"Holy shit," he breathes on a drawn out shocked whisper. I picture his wide eyes and raised brows. "A cop?"

"A detective actually," I admit. "In the same building. His captain has assigned him to work with me on site calls for the next couple weeks."

He groans. "Oh, baby girl. Want me to come down there and kick his ass?"

The laugh I needed has been delivered – as always. Keith pipes up in the background – apparently I'm on speaker phone. "Theo, she can kick your ass and mine in a dark alley without blinking twice. When we go down there, it's gonna be for fun. Show them what you're made of, Everlee. You've got this in the bag. I'll bet you anything he knows exactly who you are and he's been sweating bullets since he saw you."

"There's not even a hint of recognition," I tell them.

"He's a cop," Keith says. "They're trained to wear poker faces. Give me his name, I'll check him out for you."

Keith is former military and works in security; though I'm not sure in what capacity. But he can track, trace, and relocate. It's all I know, all I've ever wanted to know. One of those *If I told you, I'd have to kill you* jobs. He's the straight man of the duo. Well, in a sense. You get my gist.

"I don't know as if that's necessa…"

"Everlee," he draws out slowly.

"Deacon Gray," I concede. "Detective with the 83rd precinct in Hasselback."

There's a long uncomfortable silence before Theo breaks it with the exaggerated southern drawl he loves to tease me with. "Deacon Gray, from the lovely metropolis of Hasselback, Louisiana. Does he speak Cajun or is he refined like the rest of us?"

"Refined," I groan. "Diction-wise anyway. His mannerisms are more like a bull in a China shop."

They both laugh at the description I give. "Good thing our little teacup isn't fragile, love," Keith reminds me.

"Bull riding is a sport, you know," Theo adds with a wicked cackle. "Don't they have rodeos in Wheeziania? Yippee-ky-I-A and all that? Could be fun."

"Theo!" I gasp.

"I'm rolling my eyes on your behalf, Everlee." Keith chuckles. "I'll get back to you with what I find. Keep your chin up."

"Love you, Gorgeous," Theo says.

"Love you guys, too."

It's nearing eight o'clock by the time I've finished the phone call and my shower. Chop-'til-I-drop salad and wine for dinner is the choice tonight, unless I want to order takeout again. Takeout is the easier choice, but not the healthier one. And I do prefer my given name of Everlee over Bubble Butt.

Papers remain strewn across my table and are beckoning me once more. So many requisitions, so little time. Let's just hope the one thing I don't hear from the city council is . . . so little money.

Three hours later my head finally hits the pillow. Eventually, Roscoe and I will be able to sit and watch TV in the evenings – crime shows of course – and simply enjoy each other's company. I've considered getting a dog. Maybe a Belgian or a German Shepherd. With the proper certification, I could take him on jobs with me. But then there's the lab. Nah, too much hair. I guess a girl can dream, can't she? So long as I don't end up a cat lady. In my eighties, shawl on my shoulders, a rocking chair on the front porch, feral cats seeking food under the floorboards. Too mean to pet, but too cute to exterminate. You think I'm joking? Come down to the south sometime. They're here. The ladies . . . and the cats.

* * *

"I'm right here, Everlee. I'm not going anywhere."
My pillow is once again soaked with sweat when I wake up gasping. Damnit! It was so long ago. Reaching for my knees, I run my fingers over the last two ridges of scars that remain; one on the right kneecap, one below the kneecap on the left. The lengthier scars that decorated my shins for years are minimal now; the plastic surgeon's talented hands having performed their honed craft to the best of their ability. Winters in Chicago were rough sometimes, but the icy cold weather is no friend to bone or tendon injuries.

Theo was the best. He attended PT sessions with me, learned the techniques used in order to study my movements while I did my home exercises. He would ensure the ice packs were always at the ready, keep a heating pad at my bedside and one by the sofa so there would be one available at all times. He'd rub some kind of Japanese ointment on my back to soothe the pain, pour a hot bath for me to soak in. Keith even bought us a hot tub for the closed-in patio so we could use the jets for massage. Truth be told, I think Theo may have enjoyed it more than I did but a glass of wine and a tub of bubbles felt pretty good after a long day of work and/or school.

Somebody's Someone

"Deacon Gray rode in with her, didn't he?" someone had said after I had pleaded with them for the man in the ambulance. *"I thought I saw him hopping out of the ambulance."*

"It's no wonder she's asking," a giggling female voice contributed. *"Sweetie, Deacon is taken. He has that effect on lots of women."*

All these years, I'd never had this dream. When Captain Garner referred to him as Deacon, it stirred something within my brain. A quick flash of déjà vu that made zero sense at the time. But, I was on my way out to my first crime scene . . . to a dead body . . . in a storm drain . . . in an abandoned parking lot. Priorities, ya know? Not to mention it took the man all of two minutes to reveal his ability to piss me off. Tampons in a fanny pack! Ha! Joke's on you detective. I get the Depo shot. An average of six periods a year. Take that, jackass!

But this evening in the lab. *"You can call me Deacon."*

Wait a minute! Taken? Deacon Gray is taken? I flip my pillow over so the dry side is up and lie back down on it. Staring at the ceiling, I let those words float around in my head again. *Taken.* I roll over onto my side and punch the pillow a few times in an attempt to fluff it.

"Good luck, Mrs. Gray," I grumble as I settle in once more. "Let's hope he keeps his word better these days than he did six years ago. Wouldn't want him going anywhere."

* * *

Back in the lab the next morning, I watch the computer screen as the system pieces together the information I fed it. I know better; it could be days. Hell, it could be weeks. DNA searches are oftentimes fruitless, especially in unidentified victim cases. However, if what I scraped from under her fingernails is identifiable and in the database, it could lead to something – anything. Yes, I'm trying to identify the victim. That might actually be easier via dental records which have been fed into a different system and are being analyzed at this very moment. It's a puzzle. I wish it were as easy as a jigsaw, but it's not. My goal is to not let Jane Doe be a Jane Didn't, because Jane Did…exist. The same would apply to John. But today I'm working with other remains from the storm drain. I want to catch a killer as well.

Leaving the computer to work its magic, I look at the stacks of files left behind by Hawkins, the former forensics scientist. There must be thirty cases here. His departure was abrupt; therefore, his backlog a shitshow. Notes should be done on the computer – not by hand. His handwriting is all but indecipherable. No dictation to back up anything. I've yet to inquire about the circumstances behind his departure, but I anticipate it.

The two taps on my door is quickly followed by it opening and a cheery greeting.

"Good morning, Sunshine." Ah, Detective Striegel. "How is the lovely Miss Everlee today?"

"I'm fine, thank you." I open the first file on the top of the stack and frown at the contents. "What can I do for you Detective Striegel?"

He moves to where I stand at the counter, too close for my comfort, and places his hand on my lower back. "I came to see what time I should pick you up for dinner on Friday."

"I didn't agree to dinner with you on Friday."

He laughs as he moves his hand a little lower, placing pressure on a vulnerable spot that took a long time to heal. "Oh, Everlee. You didn't have to agree, it's a foregone conclusion. You, me, dinner, drinks." He leans in and whispers, "Magic."

"How much do you value that hand you have on my back, detective?" I ask him.

He snickers. "Why would you ask that?"

"Because if you don't remove it right now, it's going to be out of commission for about six weeks." I turn my head to meet his eyes straight on. "Because that's what will happen after I break it."

"She's not joking, Striegel." Deacon's low growl rings from the open door that neither of us heard. "And whatever she doesn't break, I'll add to it myself."

"Ah, Detective Gray," Striegel pitches a little high after

removing his hand immediately. "Good to see you too. Thought I might make an appearance and check on a case Hawkins hadn't completed for me."

Deacon holds the door open as if waiting for our guest to use it. "Next time use the phone. Ms. Remington has her hands full cleaning up the mess Hawkins left behind. You're not top priority. Clear it through Captain Garner before you set foot in the building again."

Detective Striegel smiles at me, a glint in his eye that makes my skin crawl. "We'll talk later, Everlee." He heads for the door and exits with Deacon on his heels. The conversation on the other side doesn't escape my ears though.

"I warned you once," Deacon threatens. "Stay the hell away from her."

"A little territorial, aren't we, Gray?" Striegel chuckles.

"Try me one more time, Striegel, and you'll find out just what I can be. Get the hell out of here."

The sound of one set of footsteps echoing in the hall fills my ears as I stare at the files in front of me. My hands shake, though I don't know why. I'm a fourth degree black belt. It took me years to get where I am, but I'm here and I'm not about to leave before I finish what I came to accomplish. I can handle my own. *Not all cops are bad,* I remind myself as the sickly tingle in my spine makes me shiver. The door opens once more, but there is no need to turn to see who it is. I can feel his presence. I rearrange a few files on the counter in front of me simply to have something to do.

"You okay?" he asks, stepping into my lab, yet keeping a safe distance.

"I don't need your protection, Detective Gray," I snap. "I could have handled him without your assistance. I'm quite capable of taking care of myself."

He moves closer, a scolding tone as he says, "You don't know Marty Striegel."

I whirl around, my sense of self-preservation and dignity in high gear, and take a few steps of my own toward him. Years I've thought about this man. He knew my name for God's sake!

Somewhere in my deepest fantasy filled daydreams, I had hoped he might one day see me again and wonder what he'd missed. Regret not staying to watch – or help – me battle through the biggest fight of my life. Maybe just tell me how proud he was of me for winning the battle. Am I that forgettable?

"And you apparently don't know me, Detective Gray." I shouldn't have said it. Damnit, Everlee! He's *taken!*

A shadow passes through those magnificent green eyes as they crinkle at the corners. His voice is softer, the edge now gone. "We could fix that."

"I think that ship has sailed." I shove my way past and throw open the lab door, rushing down the hall toward the restroom. I was young, vulnerable, and so needy that night. I'm not her anymore and the man in the ambulance is dead to me. Nobody murdered him though, and I have real killers to catch.

Tonight, I'll start my search in the bowels of the records room where they've stashed the evidence of Jonah's case. I'm coming, baby brother. I'll figure it out, eventually. One way or another, I will find justice for you. From the looks of the mess Hawkins left behind, it's no wonder he never solved your case. Or was he covering for someone?

Chapter 7

Deacon

"And apparently you don't know me, Detective Gray." Was it pain or anger I saw in those eyes? So hard to read. I thought she had recognized me the night before. Maybe it was wishful thinking. Do I fess up? Do I want her to come to me first? Do I want a chance to explain or do I simply want a chance . . . with her?

That entire incident nearly broke me six years ago – the first *and last* time I've ever let emotions get in the way of my job or my life. Her mother would have found a way to draw me into the shitshow and my career as a cop would have been over. She waltzed into the hospital as the star of the show and kept the spotlight on herself throughout the entire production. I watched from the audience at a distance and took my leave as if my ass were on fire. Parnell had worked hard to cover for me. I learned the hard way through Everlee and never looked back. That's not to say I ever forgot her. I simply let her go.

Emotions are dangerous. Sex is a tool, mechanical, a release of tension and pent up energy. I've never had to vie for a woman's attention. Am I trying too hard? Do I even know how? I know what to do with them – pretty damn good at it too – but it's a whole lot easier to put your dick in than it is the effort.

That was over two weeks ago. Everlee has found a way to avoid me at all costs; buried in her lab, in meetings seeking funds for equipment upgrades, on the phone with state officials collecting information regarding cases Hawkins fucked up, and finally, three days working as a Locum for Summit county – *my stomping grounds as Duncan Greene.*

Which is where I just so happened to make a typical trip over the weekend. In the door, down the hall to the bedroom, clothes off, the woman on her knees, when it all came to a grinding halt. I was hard as stone, could have delivered for hours, but it was the wrong recipient and my dick suddenly lost all his zest for life and lust. She wasn't a brunette with stormy gray eyes and a voice I could listen to for hours. She wouldn't have been whispering '*Deacon*'; she would have been screaming '*Duncan*'. I was a gentleman, though. I gently pulled her to her feet, tapped her on the nose, and said, "I think we'd better call it The End."

I was sure to demand her phone and erase my number. My departure was not a quiet one. The shoe being thrown against the door as it closed was a strong indicator the lady was not happy. It might have had something to do with my pointing out her generous collection of vibrators in the nightstand and my recommendation she use one . . . or two. I am nothing if not considerate.

"Thought you could get away without me, Ms. Remington?" I hasten my steps to catch up with her before she can get out the door. The forensics van sits in the parking lot ready to leave – Everlee at a near dead run to join them.

"You weren't here when the call came in, Detective Gray," she tosses over her shoulder as if I'm an afterthought. "If you can't get to work on time, then you will be left behind."

I snatch her elbow before she can climb in the van and spin her around. "It is five minutes before seven, Ms. Remington," I grit through a clenched jaw. "The call came in at six. I'm hardly late. You pull this shit again and I'll make damn sure you're riding a bike to get to the site. Now get in the fucking car. We ride together, like it or not."

"I don't like it and I don't need an escort." She pulls her elbow out of my grasp with a huff. "I can ride in the van."

"You can." I arch a brow and grin smugly. "But I'm not your escort and I showered today. Even put on deodorant, just for you. Now get in the car. We're a team, Captain's orders."

"I thought you weren't a team player," she says, throwing the captain's words at me.

I take her elbow once again, gentler this time, feeling the charge it pulses through my fingertips – remembering how it felt to brush my knuckles across her cheeks, whisper words in her ear – and lead her toward the car. "I'm counting on you to teach me."

"What if I'm not a team player?"

Halting my footsteps, in turn stopping hers as well. My fingers hold their gentle grip on her elbow while my thumb moves lightly over her silky skin. I don't want to fight with her anymore. I love her sass, her strength, the determination she's shown. But I have yet to see a genuine smile or hear her laugh.

Art and music; I'd bet my life on it.

"I think we could be really good together," I say with a boyish grin. "What do you say, Everlee?" Her name. A mix of teeth on my lip and roll of tongue in my mouth feels like candy.

She arches a brow. "You don't think your wife would object?"

I nearly choke on my own spit as I sputter, "My what?!"

"Your wife, Detective Gray," she snarls venomously as she pulls her arm away. "You remember her, don't you?"

"Unless I'm suffering amnesia, no." I dip my chin and narrow my eyes. "I am many things, Ms. Remington. Married is not one of them. Never have been."

She eyes me skeptically before heading for the car. "Fine. I suppose we can ride together, but I'm still going to keep my window cracked. Maybe next time you shower, you'll remember to use soap."

Patience, Gray. You've never had to work for it.

The crime site is on the south side in an alley where dumpsters are located behind restaurants in the area. One of the staff from a restaurant happened upon a body part lying beside a dumpster while taking out a bag of trash this morning. Not the preferred wakeup call most of us look forward to, but definitely an eye opener if the coffee doesn't work.

Gotta admit, the guy has good eyesight. The body part he found is a finger. The remaining parts seem to be packaged in wrappers of newspapers, brown paper bags, and boxes placed in various dumpsters. We've so far collected two arms and two legs – minus the fingers and toes, but we're still counting those – the torso, and . . .

A low sickly groan sounds from our left. "Is this what I think it is?" One of the officers helping with the search holds up a small brown paper bag held between his fingertips and thumbs as if it might bite him. His skin has turned pale with a fine mix of green – a definite indicator the man is about to lose his breakfast. He bends a little, his knees nearly locked together.

Everlee leans in to take a peek as he holds it out to her. Her voice is calm and cool as she answers, "Why yes, officer, that is indeed a penis."

"Holy shit!" another exclaims as he grimaces. "Can you imagine the pain when they cut through that bone?" *Idiot.* We have no idea if the guy was alive when they dismembered him. Though I will admit, the thought does have a tendency to cause the boys to do a little tuck upwards.

Everlee rolls her eyes and advises, "You might want to brush up on your anatomy lessons. There is no bone in a penis."

"Really?" He scrunches his nose, then gives his best shot at flirting with Everlee as he winks and asks, "Then why do we call them boners?"

She shakes her head and proceeds to bag the godawful wrinkled appendage. "Probably for the same reason you idiots use what should be an acronym for yourselves when referencing a woman's vagina." She shoots him a wry look and emphasizes, "Because you **Can't Understand Normal Thinking**."

It only takes a moment for most of us to laugh while the confused moron chortles uncomfortably so as not to be left out of the rather clever response. As soon as Everlee's back is to him, he looks to his partner and whispers, "What's an acronym?"

Everlee mumbles as she writes another tag for the bagged dick, "Too early in my day to start drinking and too late to call in sick. Theo is going to love this one."

I lean into her from behind, dropping my face mask so I can capture the scent of her hair, and whisper so close she can feel my breath on her skin, "I thought his name was Roscoe."

She shivers and huffs, "Detective Gray, do not sneak up on me."

"I wasn't sneaking up on you," I say softly, the effort to keep my distance a challenge. "Roscoe was a conversation between the two of us. Thought I'd keep it that way."

"There's no head." She frowns as she tallies the contents removed from the dumpsters and in the process, changing the subject. "We've emptied three dumpsters and there is no head."

"It's probably been mailed to the family," I tell her. "Typical gang war behavior. It's their way of guaranteeing silence and a warning at the same time."

She turns slowly, her face so close it would take mere inches to swallow her mouth in a kiss. "Typical?" she asks on a shaky breath.

I want to take her in my arms, shield her from this cesspool of crime and inhumane acts of violence. She had to have seen this type of shit in Chicago. Not that it's easy to see it anywhere, but the storm drain incident and today's dumpster diving has really seemed to hit her hard. It pisses me off the pathologist couldn't be called in this morning, but the state is so backed up and short on forensic specialists, the jobs are being divided the best they can be at the present time.

And who the hell is Theo?

"I think that's it, doc," Morris hollers from his position next to the last dumpster that's been emptied.

"I'm not a doctor," Everlee calls back to him, snapping off her gloves and removing her mask. "Everlee is fine. I'm just a scientist, not a pathologist. Let's finish loading up the van."

"Hey," I nearly scold as I take her arm. "Don't diminish your accomplishments. Don't ever let me hear you say *just* again."

She pins me with a questioning gaze. "You are not *just* anything. You've worked hard to get where you are."

Her mouth tips in a small, appreciative smile. "Thanks, detective."

Someday, Everlee Remington, you will call me Deacon. And someday, maybe you'll smile without forcing it.

Why would she think I was married? Did Striegel tell her that? Could it have been the hospital? Does she remember? After all these years? Taken?

Shar, if it was you, I hope you've gained a hundred pounds, been divorced twice, and have five kids that drive you nuts.

We're in the car on our way back to the station from the dumpster diving expedition. "Did you have breakfast this morning?"

Everlee sits quietly, hands in her lap, staring out the window. Her stomach growls as if on cue. "Not hungry, thanks."

"Well," I say, turning into a diner I frequent on weekends. "One of you is lying and since your belly spoke first and loudest . . ." I put the car in park and shut it off ". . . it wins. Let's go."

Exiting the car, I close the door behind me and head for the door of the diner. I look back to see her sitting in her seat, arms folded over her chest, a hard stare fixed on me. I curl a finger to beckon her. She lifts her middle one to flip me off. I wave my hand to beckon her again. She lifts both middle fingers. I hit the alarm button on the fob and set off the ear piercing screech, turn to open the door and step inside.

She'll learn.

The door of the diner swings open after I've been seated at the front window and enjoyed approximately two minutes of watching Everlee stew. I hit the button on the fob and silence the alarm.

She points her finger hard and glares. "You are an ass!" The fiery glow in her eyes is literally the sexiest thing I've ever seen. The slight southern twang when she loses her temper is delicious. I'd bet my left nut she's worked hard to lose that. The flush of her skin is the rosy tint I want to put there with heated moments as she screams my name. She may be my undoing, but as I study the enigma before me, I realize she'll be the one to put me back together, because she's been holding my heart for years. Everlee Remington has finally come home.

I shrug and smirk. "I don't stink. Care to join me? They make awesome pancakes and a pecan roll that will melt in your mouth."

Her brows lift and a small gleam lights her eyes as she whispers, "Pecan rolls?"

My mouth twitches at one corner and I wink. "And pancakes."

She folds her arms over her chest, boosting her already tantalizing breasts even higher. But I'm a better man and hold eye contact versus staring at those delicious tits, leaving a coppery taste of blood in my mouth while I bite the inside of my cheek.

Patience, Gray. She's the first, and only, woman you've ever wanted to wake up next to.

"What if I want both?" she challenges.

"If you sit your ass down at the table . . ." I proffer as my resolve grows weaker. "I'll buy you anything you want, Ms. Remington."

"Chocolate chip pancakes."

"Sit down, Everlee." My voice is so low it sounds like a growl, but apparently it works because she finally slides her ass into the booth and my suffering – or was it torture – ends. Somewhat. Her tits are still visible but they're not three feet from my mouth and begging for me to take a nipple in it.

Chapter 8

Everlee

Yes, I've avoided him for the last two weeks, but I've been extremely busy as well. No onsite calls – gratefully – but dealing with bureaucracy is enough to make a Mormon school teacher drink. Funny the city has plenty for new office furniture, repainting the mayor's offices, a budget for luncheons that would make a poor man cry, and a new fleet of cars.

My solutions? Grease the wheels on the chairs, learn to love the current beige, eat a damn sandwich like the rest of us, and employ a mechanic! Aesthetics and appetites be damned! Probably didn't make them too happy that I had obtained the list of their planned and current projects, presented them to the council, and compared them with the necessary items for the lab. Not to mention the outstanding and unsolved cases the medical examiner's office is dealing with at the present time. Being short-staffed is one thing. Being denied the best and sufficient equipment is another. There are families waiting for reasons. Loved ones waiting for closure. Budget cuts are not rocket science. Households do it on a daily basis.

My closing line? "If you want my best work, you need to give me the best to work with." *Thank you, Theo Masters.* Now, we wait. My hopes aren't high, but that meeting was only city level. I can still deal with the state. Hasselback vs. Louisiana. A little like

Rushmore vs. Everest. Tornado vs. hurricane. But mostly? Everlee Remington vs. Bureaucracy.

I was able to manage two nights in the basement poring over Jonah's files, the evidence collected; once I got through the tears and the roiling in my stomach. It's hard to be objective when you look at pictures of your little brother's body on the ground, his shirt soaked with blood, his favorite navy blue beanie lying next to his head instead of on it. I borrowed (stole) the street cam footage collected from the scene and am waiting for the high resolution software Keith is sending me – shouldn't take too long. He's a little worried, as is Theo, that the emotional distress caused by watching it may be a bit too much for me – a setback. It's been six years though. I may have snapped pictures of a few other items as well. I simply want closure . . . justice.

"Good?" Deacon asks, a knowing grin smattering his face as I moan over my first bite of a pecan roll. Warm yeasty bread, cinnamon, caramel, pecans. Oh yeah, I'm in heaven. He had me at pecan rolls; my weakness. I was ready to chew my own arm off after having raced out this morning without food, but keeping a safe distance from him is my best shot at staying focused on the tasks at hand. Maybe after I finish my goal here, I can go back to Chicago and be amongst friends, the people I miss most. Away from my mother and all that haunts me.

My mouth is full, so the best I can manage is an eye roll, a nod and a long moan of pleasure. "Mmhmm."

He shifts in his seat as he studies me, then clears his throat. "I take it you like it."

"Oh, this is so good," I nearly hum after swallowing. "I'm glad you didn't recommend sausage and eggs. After handling a squishy, wrinkled penis this morning the sausages may not have . . ." My statement dies as the server sets down a plate of chocolate chip pancakes in front of me and her eyebrows shoot skyward.

"It's okay, Alva." Deacon holds up a hand and reassures her. "The wrinkled penis was unusual circumstances. Although, first thing in the morning I think she would have preferred a hard one." He looks to me and smirks. "Am I right?"

I glare at him before turning to the waitress. "It was a work thing."

"Oh, honey," the middle-aged, now grinning server placates me with a gentle pat on my shoulder. "You don't need to explain. We don't discriminate here. What you do for a living is your own business."

My jaw hangs slack as I search for an explanation then sputter, "No, no! I – I'm not a…"

"Ms. Remington," Deacon taunts with a chuckle. "The more you protest, the worse your case looks."

Apparently he's a regular here and knows the staff. Wait a minute! My case? Is he giving her the impression I'm his perp? Not so fast, asshole.

Turning back to Alva, I release a long, exaggerated sigh. "He's right. Disclosing Detective Gray's shortcomings wasn't very ladylike. Maybe next time he'll have more stamina."

She snort-laughs as she looks to a wide-eyed glaring Deacon while I slice into a large stack of chocolate chip pancakes and smile cockily before I stuff a bite in my mouth. She smacks my breakfast companion's shoulder with the back of her hand and cackles. "Think you may have met your match, Deacon. I like her more than Parnell. Be sure to bring her back."

His glare is strong but not as harsh as Alva walks away. I arch a brow and tip my chin. "Don't spar with me unless you're prepared, Detective Gray. I told you before, I'm quite capable of handling my own."

The corners of his mouth tip before a soft smile lights his face. There's a glint in his eyes that only makes them more haunting, taking me back to a time I wish had never happened. He nods slowly then whispers, "Yeah, you are. I am so damn proud of you, Everlee."

Proud? Why would he be proud of me? He doesn't even know me. Yet, why does it cause a flutter in my chest to hear him say it? I turn away from his moss green gaze and clear my throat. "I think our food is getting cold. We should hurry up and get back to the station."

Annie Mick

* * *

Back in my lab after our late breakfast, the call I've been waiting for finally comes through.

"Everlee Remington," I answer in anticipation, though nervous at the same time.

"Ms. Remington." The sharp, high-pitched, southern-accented voice of Mayor Peters rings through the receiver and strikes cranial nerve 8, causing an ever familiar lightning bolt to shoot from my ear through my brain. Thanks a lot, pal. Someone needs to grip your throat and drop your decibel level and pitch a notch or two. *Need a bingo caller for the hearing impaired? He's gotcha covered.* "Mayor Peters here. You know, I'm not sure how you pulled the strings you did, and rest assured I will find out, but you got your money. We gotta meet with the forensic pathologist now that he found out you got what you did. Young lady, you opened a whole can o' worms."

"Mayor Peters," I start. "I assure you . . ."

"Stop right there!" he snaps harshly. "You listen to me. We had our budget set for the next two years and you came bargin' in demanding all sorts of fancy new equipment . . ."

"Have you ever lost a loved one, Mayor Peters?" My own voice is just short of yelling as I take my opportunity to interrupt. I hadn't demanded anything. I pleaded my case for the sake of accuracy and efficiency – not to mention grieving families. "Have you ever had to wait *months* to find out how they died? Have you had to bury your spouse, maybe your child or a sibling, without having any idea what, or who, killed them? Our backlog is astronomical."

I wait and wait . . . then wait a little longer.

"I can hear you breathing, Mayor Peters," I say lightly, then grant him one more breath before offering a morsel of food for thought, "I guess you're luckier than the victims' families, huh?"

"Are you finished, Ms. Remington?"

"Is the decision final?" I ask. "The papers are signed, the check is in the mail so to speak?"

74

"You know it is," he barks. "I wouldn't have called you if it wasn't."

Ah, what's the matter, mayor? Beige not your color? Did your wife slip one night and whisper her true sentiments in your ear when you were on top pumping into her? "Beige, I think I'll paint the ceiling beige."

"Wonderful," I nearly sing as I fist pump the air.

"Ms. Remington," he growls slowly, his threat unmistakable. "I will find out who your friends are on the city council. I've only been in office for two years, I have plenty of time. This won't be happening again."

Oh shit! I hardly have friends on that committee, but with his resources and enough research, he just may find out who I am. The city may have settled out of court to avoid publicity, but whereas the public doesn't have access to sealed records, he does. It's not impossible for him to find. Go ahead, mayor, open that can of worms. I'll personally feed them to you. Best you leave it alone though. Learn to love beige, grease the wheels on your office chair, and eat a damn sandwich for lunch. Wouldn't hurt to pass on the scotch as well.

Thoughts of food take me back to this morning's breakfast with Deacon. Why would he be proud of me? And Everlee? He didn't just say my name. No, he tasted it. Slow, sweet, as if savoring . . .

The red alert light on the computer comes to life at the same time the soft chime rings. I've got a hit! I enter my passcode, then enter the second set of numbers to bring it to life. My heart races as the identity and picture of a young woman appear on the screen. Two weeks after we collected her remains from the storm drain and we have a name. Her family had offered DNA samples months ago in the hopes – and dread – of at least finding her and an answer. It accelerates the process in the unfortunate circumstances of finding a corpse versus a live person. But it delivers closure. Tears fill my eyes as I hit print, collect the papers, and rush to the squad room.

"Detective Gray!" I shout from the doorway, holding the papers up. My tears mix with joy as a bubble of laughter escapes.

Every head in the room turns my way, except for his. He's not here. In all my excitement, I failed to notice his empty desk. My bubble bursts and my shoulders deflate. Of all the people I wanted to tell, he was the first. He was there with me – even though he was an ass. This is proof of my worthiness, my capabilities. And the one person I ran to . . .

"Ms. Remington?"

I turn at the sound of his voice, the papers in my hand held high as I run to him and jump into his arms, giddy with excitement. "We did it! We found her."

"Whoa." He chuckles. "Okay, slow down." He gently peels my arms away from his neck and glances around us. An audience has gathered in various places throughout the hallway, eyebrows lifted, grins on their faces. My face flushes a deep heated red with embarrassment. "Let's go in here," he says, leading me to an empty interrogation room, closing the door behind us.

"I – I'm sorry," I stammer. "I kinda got lost in the moment."

"Feel free to get lost anytime." He shakes his head and grins. "What's up?"

"We found her! The woman from the storm drain." I hold out the papers and point to the picture. The same long red hair as the body we removed. "Her family reported her missing six months ago. She's from Houma."

He studies the picture in my hand, brow furrowed, mouth twisted, then looks at me. I see the guilt wash over him, I hear it in his voice as he humanizes the rotted corpse from the storm drain. "They can give her a funeral," he whispers. He takes a deep breath and blows it out slowly as he closes his eyes. "And they can cry."

Tears find their way from my eyes to my chin. "We did it."

He takes my cheeks in his palms and studies my face, wiping the tears away with his thumbs. "No, you did it." His gaze falls to my mouth but he closes his eyes before dropping a kiss to my forehead. "I am so damn proud of you, Everlee."

"I haven't found her killer yet," I murmur beneath his chin and shrug. "Not sure I ever will. But we need to tell her family we found her." The victim's hyoid bone and thyroid cartilage were fractured – as well as her neck – there's no doubt she was murdered by strangulation. The pathology report was completed three days ago. "Will you contact them and let them know?"

He tips my chin with two gentle fingers. "It was the 81st district, Everlee. It's not in my jurisdiction to do so. There's protocol to follow."

PROTOCOL – I hated that word

Six years ago in a hospital room: restrained, machines beeping, drugged, my legs in bandages and braces from the ankles to the knees, in traction. Fractured vertebrae as well. So much pain. My mother telling me Jonah was dead. She had already had him cremated. I couldn't say goodbye. I would never see my little brother again; even if his eyes were closed. They were waiting for her to give me the news.

It was protocol.

"You what!?!"

"Everlee, the price of caskets and funerals is outrageous. I can't afford that."

"I needed to see him! You didn't let me say goodbye!" Pulling at the restraints, the machines started to beep louder, the rate increasing. The pain in my body nothing compared to the pain in my heart.

"If he had been working a regular job like he should have instead of trying to become a rock star, it wouldn't have happened," she scolded. "Now settle down before . . ."

"Get out!!!" I screamed, pulling harder at the restraints until the IV snapped and blood spurted in every direction – my mother bitching that I'd soiled her outfit.

Nurses and assistants appeared out of nowhere; more drugs, more needles, lights out. The beginning of the silence and solitude I took solace in for the following six months. Once I was able, I took Jonah's ashes down to the Gulf and cast them out into the water. His best friends and bandmates accompanied me. We held each other and cried, said our goodbyes, and came home.

Jonah was all I had. He got our tears, but he never got a proper funeral.

"Hey." Deacon gently grasps my shoulders and bends at the knees slightly, dipping his head to capture my gaze. "Where did you go?"

My eyes meet his and another flashback occurs as if it were yesterday. *"They're helping your brother in the other ambulance. There wasn't enough room in this one."*

Ignoring his question, I repeat that loathsome word with nod, "Protocol. Would you handle it for me?" Turning quickly, I exit the interrogation room and stumble toward my lab, locking the door behind me.

Where did I go? Better question is where did you go? Was he already dead, Deacon? Were you following protocol back then? Did you lie to me that night?

Bits and pieces. It's all coming back.

Chapter 9

Deacon

I shouldn't have kissed her on the forehead. But it was that or her mouth. Have you ever been in a candy store and the mere sight and scent of your favorite makes your mouth water? Your tongue starts to roll a little and the next thing you know, you're either licking your lips, salivating so hard you drool, or diving for the treat that has set your taste buds in motion. I'm not a kisser – never have been – just ask the women I bed on a regular basis. *Correction: Used to bed.* I haven't had my dick anywhere but in my hand in well over a month. But Everlee Remington? Never have my lips, tongue, and teeth been so desperate to taste and touch every inch.

Damnit! I am proud of her. But we're coworkers as far as she's concerned. We should be slapping each other on the back and saying *good job, nice work*. She has come so far. She doesn't know I've seen her at her worst, weakest, her most vulnerable. She doesn't know I sat in that hospital room and whispered how proud I was of her for being so strong, for fighting to heal so she could . . . *take care of Jonah.* Yeah, I'm an asshole. But Jonah was all I had to give her. I wanted her to fight, give her a reason. I'd been on the battlefield. If you have nothing to look forward to, to fight for, you have no reason. After her mother's refusal of a plane ticket to get home faster, her less than panicked voice, I had a gut feeling her brother was all she had.

My mother would have flown a fucking broomstick to get to me faster, my little sister on the one behind her. My dad would have hijacked and piloted the damn plane.

Telling me "We did it". No Everlee Remington, you did it. You saw that rotting body dressed in hooker's clothing as a human being. A person. Somebody's daughter. Me? I saw it as another statistic, a number for the books.

How long will it take before this job turns you cold? Numb, just like me.

Staring at the picture and information in my hands, I shake my head. 23 years old, five feet-four inches, 120 pounds. Life summed up in numbers on paper. Yet, Everlee made her a priority. She made her a somebody.

"Got a minute?" I step in as I tap on Captain Garner's door. It was open, what the hell.

"What's up, Gray?"

"Ms. Remington ID'd the body from the storm drain." I set the papers in front of him on the desk. "Wants to make sure it's handled diplomatically. Victim is from Houma. Reported missing six months ago."

He scrunches his forehead in question. "Diplomatically? Wasn't that a presumed hooker in the 81st district?"

I nod to the papers I set on his desk. "Don't you have daughters about that age?"

He glances at the report before he crosses his arms over his chest and scowls. "I do, but they would never…"

I hold up a hand to stop him. "If they were to commit the ultimate sin, fuck up big time, lose their way . . ." I shrug. "You'd cry at their funeral, wouldn't you?"

He stares, waiting for an explanation.

"Ms. Remington believes everyone is deserving of tears being shed at their funeral." I grin wryly and roll my eyes. "Unless it's me of course. Because a dick is a dick."

He pinches the bridge of his nose and groans. "I ain't even gonna ask."

"Probably best if you don't."

"So, what do you propose?"

"You make the call to Houma PD," I explain. "You have contacts there. Victim's neck was broken; strangulation. Ms. Remington is still working hard to catch a killer. Try to find a female to deliver the news and soften the blow. Give the family half the closure they need. Let them know we're working hard on the other half."

He studies me with narrowed eyes before his mouth twitches. "She making you human, Gray? Sounds like you might actually care."

"Just doing my job."

"Mmhmm." He ponders for a moment. "Houma's only 80 miles away. Think Everlee would want to do it? She worked hard on this. You could make the trip with her. Leave tomorrow morning, be back by lunch."

"No," I state in no uncertain terms. Not after watching her a little while ago. Something set her back. I had to take her shoulders in my hands before I could even get her attention. "Ms. Remington has enough on her plate. It's going to take her months to clear up the disaster Hawkins left behind. Besides, I think she got too emotionally involved in this case to begin with."

He smirks and leans back in his chair. "Is that why she was clinging to you like Glad Wrap in the hallway a while ago?"

Great. I was hoping he was not witness to that.

Tugging at the shirt collar that at the current time feels like a noose around my neck, I clear my throat. "She was excited about IDing the victim. It was her first case." I point to the papers on his desk. "You'll take care of Houma?"

"Yup." He lifts a brow and steels me with his ever famous *don't cross me* glare. "Gray, we all know you're a lady magnet. I made you two a team. I want you to watch *out* for her. But you also watch your step with her. She's young."

Our stare down lasts for a good ten seconds, maybe more. I've never crossed the line at work. He doesn't know our history. But then, apparently neither does Everlee. Do I want her to know?

Maybe. I'm only seven years older than she is. Would it stop me? Hell no. She's not that damn young. Do I want her? More than my next meal.

But first, I need to know who Theo is.

I heave a sigh and nod. "Keep Marty Striegel away from her, would you? He's been circling like she's fresh meat."

A vein pops in his forehead as he scowls. "Dickhead Striegel from the 81st? How does he know Everlee?"

"The storm drain incident. He was on the scene when we got there."

His brow furrows as he tips his chin. "Did he get out of line?"

"Just a bit."

He nods sharply. "I'll leave orders at the front desk that he doesn't get in without a pass." He grins slyly. "And after he gets the pass, he'll have a chaperone."

"Appreciate it. I'm off to court." I tip my chin, lightly tap on the frame of the door, and attempt my escape; just not fast enough.

"Deacon." Keeping my back to him I wait. I hate that tone. He's not my father, though he could be age-wise, bits of wisdom here and there. "She'd be good for you, you know. Just not so sure you'd be good for her. Don't fuck this up."

He's right. I was a different man six years ago though, not that he knew me. I had a few hard edges; two tours of duty will do that. But something changed that night, and in the months after. I became harder, colder, numb. The more scenes we encountered, the more my emotions shut down. The more faces I saw, the less defined they became, unless they were still alive. It became more about facts and evidence than it was about the people, with the exception of one. One *Jonah Remington.* I could never let it go; rather never let her go.

* * *

Six months after that night outside the Blue Velvet Lounge, I made my way to the evidence room seeking the box labeled

0097465 containing all the physical evidence pertaining to the death of Jonah Remington. I was there to read the notes again, see if the statements taken would shine any new light on the case.

Vic had delivered a copy of the uncut version of the street cam footage a couple months ago as a bit of a 'welcome to the club' gift. The note attached read: "This is the uncut version. Never lose perspective on who we serve. You did good, rookie. Throw a damn good punch too. Three broken ribs, broken nose, and two busted teeth. I hate dirty cops. City settled out of court. The girl will receive compensation to cover all medical costs and a nice chunk of change to go with it. Thought you would want to know. You can burn this or keep it as a reminder: you were somebody's hero that night."

None of the information was on microfilm yet; records was behind – aka short staffed. If the city's budget committee were to find better things to do with the tax proceeds than painting government buildings and buy new office furniture, they could afford salaries for a few new staff. Probably wouldn't hurt to cut back on comped meals and fancy dinners either. Eat at Burger King or McDonald's like the rest of us once in a while for God's sake!

I was pissed to hear that they had listed Jonah's case as unsolved after only six months. As I was nearing the aisle for R-U, I heard the sounds of heavy breathing and grunting followed by tearing of clothes. I was about to back up and leave what I thought was a risky, heated rendezvous (shit happens) when I heard the woman attempt to scream before I heard the loud slap followed by a choked gag.

"On your knees is where all you bitches belong." Spencer's familiar sickening growl came from the other side of the aisle. "Take it all. Suck it clean."

It was hardly a heated rendezvous. Spencer was shoving his dick in the woman's mouth while she gagged and fought furiously, her hands shoving at his thighs. He had one hand gripping her hair tightly, the other clamped on her jaw to hold it open to prevent her from biting down hard.

"Get off her!" I flew down the aisle, shoving him off and

knocking him against the rack behind him. His head hit hard on the metal rack and he fell to the ground; his pants around his ankles.

Spencer was stunned momentarily; flat on the floor, dick at full salute. He reached for the back of his head with one hand and threw a hard finger at me with his other. "Don't you fuck with me, rookie. Get outta here. She wanted it."

I looked back at Tess, our records room assistant; shirt torn, no bra, sobbing and swiping her mouth with her forearm. "Did you want this?"

Her whole body shook as she stared, her face filled with mortification before she choked, "N-no", then proceeded to puke all over herself.

Every muscle in my body went rigid and geared up for what I knew would feel so good as I glared at Spencer. He'd beat his wife. He'd ground poor Everlee's legs into glass so hard, it took multiple surgeries to fix them. I had no idea where or how she was. He had scarred the most beautiful thing I'd ever seen in my life . . . and she was gone. He took from me. And now he had taken from Tess. The city had paid for his damages before. He'd been charged with domestic abuse and gotten away with it. And yet, he was still here. Still employed. Still a public servant. I just didn't care anymore. Job be damned. I apparently hadn't beaten him hard enough that night.

"On her knees, huh? How are your knees, Spencer?" I sneered, eyeing the crucial joints between his thighs and shins before collecting his gun from the holster and tossing it out of his reach. "Maybe you can learn to crawl on your belly." My boot landed hard on his right kneecap, and he let out a howl so loud it could probably be heard on the third floor. Mind you, pants around his ankles, because the dumbass didn't move fast enough to pull them up, didn't leave him at a great advantage.

"You sonofabitch! I'm gonna . . ."

"No you're not," I told him as I shoved his upper body back down to the floor with my foot. His left kneecap was next, the crunch mixed with his shriek of pain a delightful sound to my ears. Watching him writhe in pain, knowing I had just blown out

both of his kneecaps, may have bordered on sadistic, but it felt like retribution. Not for Tess, not for his ex-wife, but for Everlee Remington. "You seem to have a problem with your knees, Spencer. Might want to find yourself a desk job."

I turned to the sobbing Tess, stripped my own shirt off, leaving me in a T-shirt, and held it out to her. "Use this to cover up."

The room filled with fellow officers shortly thereafter; having heard the bloodcurdling screams. Spencer immediately started spewing lies, accusations of assault, and was carted off by EMTs in an ambulance. I collected his gun from down the aisle and handed it to a fellow officer. "He was going to shoot me with it. Didn't leave me with much choice."

The entire investigation took three days, four long, tedious internal affairs meetings, five paid days off for me, and sexual assault charges against Spencer with immediate dismissal. Word had it he needed to have his knees replaced but still carried a chip on his shoulder.

As always, it was kept internal. A bit like what happens in Vegas stays in Vegas.

I continued with the 79th division for another year, achieving rank of lieutenant within that year. Then Parnell transferred to the 83rd and asked me to follow. Now, I'm a detective. Best decision I ever made.

Annie Mick

Chapter 10

Everlee

Three taps on the door and the futile wiggle of the handle reminds me it's locked. I've been granted one hour of solitude. I really could have used a couple more. But it's Friday and I'm not on call this weekend, so Roscoe and I will have plenty of solitude. There's laundry and groceries to do and let's not forget Netflix. I won't be poring over proposals and filling out requisition forms for the budget committee for a while. Mayor Peters made it pretty clear the pocketbook is zipped tight.

Pizza and a bottle of wine can't come too soon.

Crossing the room, I turn the lock and open the door to a grinning Captain Garner.

"I wanted to let you know Houma has been handled by me personally, and to congratulate you myself." His face beams with what I assume is a fatherly smile. I've only ever seen one on Theo's dad – mine left when I was four. "That was good work, Everlee."

"Battle's only half over, Captain." I shrug and wince. "Still haven't caught the bad guy."

"Sometimes we never do," he says, tilting his head and crossing his arms over his chest. "This is a job, Everlee. Don't make it your life."

I huff a pitiful sigh. "I just want the answers."

"You can't catch 'em all." He spots me with a knowing look

and a soft smile. "What helps me sleep at night is knowing there's still a nice hot spot in hell for those we don't." He turns back toward the hall and finishes as he walks away, "That, and a couple shots of good bourbon. Have a good weekend, Ms. Remington."

Two hours later I've managed to finalize specific equipment orders for the lab, send them for approval, and even rearranged an entire file in alphabetical order. Apparently, Hawkins was either severely dyslexic or extremely sloppy. My day is over, my head is full, my body is weak. I wish Roscoe needed walks; it might give me incentive to get out more. As it is, my run will take place on the treadmill at home or I'll visit the gym once again. Maybe tomorrow.

On my way past the squad room, Lieutenant Rodriguez calls out as if we're old friends, "Everlee! We're going out for a few drinks at the Blue Velvet Lounge. Would you care to join us?"

My footsteps falter and I stop in the hallway, staring at Rodriguez. He couldn't have knocked the wind out of me faster if he'd thrown a punch. That's ten miles from here . . . and on a street I've avoided like the plague since I've returned. Though I am waiting to view it via street cam footage once Keith provides me the proper equipment.

The Blue Velvet Lounge. Is Rodriguez taunting me? Did the city not keep it under wraps as per the agreement? The mayor might have access – if he dug deep enough – but he'd need a pretty big shovel and an IQ higher than 95. The records are sealed.

Deacon isn't in the squad room, but Victor Parnell rises from his chair quickly, throws some papers at Rodriguez and mumbles an incoherent order. He then makes his way toward me and stands in the doorway, blocking my view of the squad room. "I heard the good news, Ms. Remington."

"Wh-what?"

"The funding for your new lab supplies." He smiles easily. "Deac also told me you ID'd the woman from the storm drain. Good work. I'm not sure Hawkins would have ever put the effort in."

"Uh," I falter, my breath still caught in my lungs, glancing toward the exit. "Thanks. I'm headed home now. Goodnight, detective."

"Can I walk you out to your car?"

Walk me to my car? Where is all this attention coming from? He's about mid-forties, *married*, and has partnered with Deacon for years – information obtained during breakfast this morning. I let him talk, I listened. Not exactly gossip with a book club, but more general information to help with acclimation.

I blink fast, once – twice. "No!" I snap harsher than I intended. I'm on edge. The mayor's threat, Rodriguez's invitation. *Protocol.* I run a fast hand through hair that I've forgotten is tossed up in a messy bun, in the process getting my fingers caught under the hairband and dislodging a pen I'd stuck in the bun earlier.

Victor bends to retrieve the pen and holds it up, grinning. "My wife does the same thing. I'm trying to convince her to switch to pencils, though. They'd be handier for the crossword puzzles we do and a lot easier for me to wash out of her hair."

He was just being nice, a gentlemanly offer of seeing you to your car. He mentioned his wife. Chill out, Everlee.

"I'm sorry I snapped at you." I take the pen he holds out to me and tuck it into my bag. "It's been a day. I can get myself out, but thanks for the offer, detective." As I turn to leave, I look back over my shoulder. "Isopropyl alcohol works well for removing the ink."

"Nah," he says with a laugh. "I like takin' my time. The little touch of blue makes her eyes sparkle, too."

A happily married man.

Not another mention of drinks with the squad room, no secondary invitation. Almost as if he wanted me out the door as fast as I wanted to leave. Odd.

All the way home the images of the Blue Velvet Lounge dance through my mind. Caleb with his signature tattoo of a hula dancer on his forearm playing keyboards and Jonah on guitar wearing his treasured navy blue beanie, carrying the night through music consisting of soulful blues, rock, and even a touch of jazz when requested. Their three mates: Trent, Cody, and Micah were rowdy but lovable. All of them dedicated musicians with a dream of a recording contract. I wonder where they are now.

When I left for Chicago, I didn't look back for the five years I was gone. I had one goal and until it was finished, I had no intention of returning. I worked hard, my goal was to be the best. I cut all ties with a time that once was, with the exception of my Gram who did visit three times in total; but never my mother. If she did, I wasn't aware. I held my promise to Gram that I would begrudgingly accept my mother's phone calls once every two months, and she kept mine to never disclose my address. Gram loves Theo and he is quite fond of her as well. Truly, I think the heavy southern accent might play a part, but Gram does have her charm as well. Kinda wish some of it had rubbed off on my mother.

And speak of the devil.

The barking dog ringtone starts from inside my purse before I can get it set on the counter. Am I ready for this yet? Nope. Roscoe first. Priorities. I plop my purse on the counter along with my keys and round my neck over my shoulders, stretching the muscles begging for a massage. One more thing on my to-do list.

"Hey, buddy," I sing, making my way to his tank where he edges to the glass, awaiting his meal. "Miss me?" I sprinkle his usual dinner over the top of the water and watch his magnificent blue and red fins wave through the water. It's relaxing. Small wonder they put fish tanks in nursing homes. Patients sit in front of them for hours, finding the serenity of nature in a tank.

My phone barks again and I take a deep breath as if by reflex to calm myself before taking the few steps necessary, pulling it from my purse. I study the screen for a moment. Nope. Wine first. At least one swallow to take the edge off. Maybe two. If it were an emergency, she would have sent a text to indicate such to ensure I answered. She also knows better than to send a spurious one to render immediate attention. The last time cost her six months of unanswered phone calls.

I open the fridge door, remove the bottle, pop the cork and pour. Four swallows later it rings once more.

"Yes, mother."

"Beverly," she drawls in correction.

"Sorry, wrong number," I deadpan. "No Beverly here."

She huffs in frustration, "I wasn't asking . . ."

"You never do," I interrupt her before releasing a resigned sigh. No, she doesn't ask, unless of course she wants something. "What's on your agenda tonight?"

"What makes you think I have an agenda, Everlee?"

Wait for it . . . wait for it.

"Fine." She sighs dramatically. "I'm a little strapped."

Told ya.

"Well, if you were able to call me, you must have access to your phone. Call the fire department." I swirl the liquid gold in my glass and smile to myself. "I know these situations are embarrassing but I'm sure they can cut you loose. Might want to tell your latest to ease up on the bondage."

"Everlee Remington!" she shrieks indignantly. "That is not what I meant and you know it."

"What did you mean, mother?" I know exactly what she meant, but it would be interesting to see how far under she's gotten herself. The woman is a couple decades away from retirement – or should be – and my bet is she doesn't have one dime to her name outside of what's in her purse. Worse yet? She's pissed away every penny she got from my settlement. *My caregiver, my ass.*

"I-I'm short on funds," she stammers. "I-I need a loan."

"A loan," I say lightly. "You do realize a loan is with the intent to repay it. How do you plan to do that? Am I to assume you've gotten a job?"

"Not yet," she snaps defensively. "I haven't been able to find anything."

I roll my eyes and swallow another delightful taste of pinot. My mother hasn't held a job in over ten years. Back then the boss's wife felt her bent over her husband's desk was not a part of the job description and therefore let her go. "Really? I see help wanted signs everywhere all over the city."

She huffs an irritated sigh. "They're not within my field of expertise."

Bite your tongue, Everlee. Don't say it. Draw blood if you have to.

"How much are we talking, mother?"

"Ten thousand?" she asks sheepishly.

"Ten thousand," I repeat slowly. "That doesn't sound like gas, grocery, or rent money. You have a nice car. What's it for?"

"A cruise with Drake," she whispers so low I almost miss it.

"A what!?" I sputter. Damnit! There went that mouthful of wine that's now splashed onto the counter and kitchen floor.

"Everlee," she whines. "It's been so hard without Jonah here. I don't have a gravesite to visit. He moved out before he died and I don't have any of his things to hold or look at." She hesitates, as if searching for the trail to my Achilles heel. "I thought maybe the sound of the ocean, the feel of the waves, and the wind in my hair could make me feel closer to him. That is where you put him, ya know."

She really did say that, didn't she?

My blood boils as my temples start to pound while my fingers flex on my one free hand so as not to grip my wine glass and shatter it in my hand.

No gravesite to visit? She's the one who had him cremated.

No things to hold or look at? Where are the childhood pictures? Oh wait! She didn't take any!

He moved out the day after he graduated high school; two months before he turned eighteen. Because he couldn't stand being around her anymore.

Had she ever gotten her grubby paws on it, she would have sold his guitar to the nearest pawn shop to cover a liquor store run, a new hairdo, and a mani-pedi. His guitar alone would pay for this cruise and mark my words, she wouldn't hesitate to spend it. One item she will never have access to is Jonah's Gibson. He scraped and saved for it for years. It's in storage, preserved and reserved for a little boy or girl I hope to one day have. Jonah would have been so proud. The only reason I have it is because Caleb kept it safe and out of Beverly's claws until I recovered and was able to decide what to do with it.

Somebody's Someone

I released Jonah's ashes into the Gulf – his memories are in my heart and in my head. How dare she use him as a ploy for a vacation with her latest boy toy.

Taking a few deep breaths, I blow them out slowly. I could simply press end, throw my phone across the room. I could scream, call her names, read her the riot act. I could release years of pent up anger in words I can never take back. Or . . .

"Here's an idea for you, mother," I say calmly. "Since you're so set on the sound of the ocean and feel of the waves and the wind in your hair, I recommend you get a sound machine and a box fan and rent a room with a waterbed at the No-Tell Motel on highway 61 to shack up in with your latest quest. I hear they rent by the hour if you can't afford weekend rates. The bank of Everlee is closed. You are now on my do-not-answer list for two months. Try this again, I'll make it six."

I end the call and shut down my phone before she has a chance to protest. Theo and I chatted last night. I talked to Gram last night as well. I'm not on call. Just Roscoe and me . . . and a nice chilled bottle of Pinot. I've lost my appetite – pizza can wait.

Chapter 11

Deacon

Judge Eli Walker almost never lets court run over, much less on a Friday. But lo and behold here we are. And here I sit, having been called to testify in the case of another of our city's finest, surreptitiously checking my watch every two minutes. Worse yet? I've been in this fucking courtroom for three hours for nothing.

He's let defense counsel run their typical bullshit – new evidence, added witnesses, bonus DNA collected at the scene – until four o'clock and now he's droned on for another half hour, I swear, just to hear himself speak.

On any given day, I could set my watch to 3:55 and count on that gavel hitting the bench followed by, "Court is in recess until 9am tomorrow" . . . or Monday in this case.

It's nearing five o'clock before I'm on my way down the hall to leave the courthouse as the voice I dread every fucking time I'm beckoned here calls out behind me.

"Deacon!" The jaw grinding, ear piercing, ball shrinking bellow of prosecuting attorney Della Marlow ricochets off the wall and lands against my hypersensitive eardrum. Good God, sharing space in the same room with this woman is bad enough. In the same bed? Not a chance. One would think *no means no* should apply to the fairer sex as well, but . . . here we go again.

"Deacon," she purrs as she latches onto my arm with cat-like, blood red, manicured nails. "I was hoping to catch you before you got out." *Yup, gotta improve my running skills.* "Dinner and drinks? I know a good place for dessert."

"Already got plans, Ms. Marlow," I decline without one hint of disappointment. Why bother? I'm not disappointed. She is delectable – not gonna deny it – but a few too many have feasted at that banquet table and, quite frankly, there just ain't enough penicillin east side of the Mississippi. I also will never be beholden to anyone who can pull strings or cut them. Or in her case, take you on the magic carpet ride then pull the rug out from under you. To put it bluntly, *I don't shit where I eat.* I don't do favor for favor. I do honor for honor.

She squeezes tighter and digs her nails into the suit jacket I'll be stripping off as soon as I step out into the sweltering heat. "It's been a long week, Deacon. We could probably both use . . ." She squeezes tighter and purrs, ". . . some release."

The only release I'm looking forward to right now is my arm from her hand because it feels more like a vise on my balls, making them shrivel inside my taint. Her perfume doesn't smell like jasmine, her hair is bleached blonde, her eyes are muddy brown, her makeup caked on and pasty. Her tit is stiff against arm AKA *au implants and plastic surgeon.*

My phone buzzes in my pocket and I pull it out, seeing a text from Vic.

"Need a call ASAP"

My brow furrows as I study the message. If it were an invitation, I'd be looking at a time and place. If it were a simple question, he'd ask and expect a simple answer. This implies a problem.

"Duty calls," I say, snatching my arm out of her unwelcome grasp.

"Next time?" she asks, nearly falling forward as she reaches out in one last attempt to hold me back.

"Have a good weekend, Ms. Marlow." Taking the stairwell in lieu of the elevator, because I'm a helluva lot faster and ready to snap, I rush to my car, start it, and blast the air conditioning at the same time I tap Vic's number on the screen.

"Court run over?" Vic answers with a question.

"Apparently Walker wasn't in a hurry to start his weekend," I reply, skipping the details that despite spending nearly four long-ass hours in the courtroom, I never made it to the stand; that I will be back here Monday, pissing away however much time they determine it takes to hopefully put away another fine example of wasted air space. I think of Everlee and how happy she was identifying the woman in the storm drain and how elated she would be if she could find the party responsible for putting her there. To feel the way she would hug me again, the warmth of her body against mine, the smile on her face, the light in her eyes. I'll help her find him if she wants. Oh hell, what am I thinking? I haven't even found her brother's killer yet.

"Deac, you still there?"

"Yeah," I mumble as I switch to Bluetooth and turn out of the parking lot. "What's up?"

"You've been working with Ms. Remington lately," he starts. "Whether you want to admit it or not, I know you've got a personal stake in her wellbeing. Thought I would let you know, Rodriguez invited her to join the gang for drinks tonight."

Gripping the steering wheel tighter as I grind my teeth, I keep my reaction in check, as all good detectives do. "Thought Garner made his stance clear with Rodriguez."

"His invitation was innocent enough."

"But?"

He hesitates then sighs. "At the *Blue Velvet Lounge*."

"Fuck," I groan low and slow. "What happened?"

"Truth? I've never seen that shade of pale before," he says. "I'm worried about her, Deacon. I distracted Rodriguez by throwing some paperwork at him and got Ms. Remington out of there as fast as possible. Wouldn't hurt to check on her if you can."

"I gotta drop out at the station before I go home." I press on the gas pedal a little harder to expedite my trip as I enter the ramp onto the interstate.

"You need her address?" he asks with a hint of playfulness

in his voice I don't find amusing.

"I'm good," I reply.

He laughs heartily . . . and a bit too long. "Didn't think so. I'm headed for home. Takin' the wife out for dinner." True Victor Parnell brotherly compassion rings through as his tone changes. "Deacon, I saw your reaction the day she showed up. I've also seen the way you look at her every day since. Although we've never spoken of it, I know where you were for two days after that night. I always figured eventually you'd get past it, but you've never gotten that woman out of your system." He sighs in disappointment. "No matter how many you've tried to replace her with. Put as much effort into winning her as you do your thoughts of wanting her, you might stand a shot. At least I know Duncan Greene won't be in Summit County tonight. Have a good weekend, buddy."

He disconnects before I can respond, before I can remind him I haven't solved Jonah Remington's case. Wait a minute. The eyes bugging out of my head stay focused on the road, though with difficulty, as his words sink in. How in the hell does he know about Duncan Greene? Well, that's one conversation I don't want to have with him but you can bet your ass I'm going to.

Once done at the station, I stop at home to shower, change, and prepare for the unknown. Throwing on some worn jeans, a green ARMY T-shirt and a spritz of *fucking fortune* cologne, I collect my badge and strap on my ankle-carry weapon I never leave home without when off duty. *One never knows.*

On the way to the car, I stop short and mutter to myself, "Damnit, do it now or you'll forget. It's been hotter than hell." Stepping into the backyard, I grab the hose from the storage bin and turn it on, taking aim at the jasmine bushes that line the edges. The one solid investment I've ever made is this house. This house, with the hope that someday it would become a home. A true Louisiana treasure. Three bedrooms, two baths, large yard for kids to play, a front porch with a swing that only my mother and sister use, a back porch with two Adirondack chairs for my dad and me, and a picnic table for friends. It even has a damn parlor. Not that I ever use it.

As I work my way around the yard with the hose and note

the shrubs I've put the most effort into to keep them strong, keep them alive and thriving; the delicate blossoms and scent that take me to a place I never wanted to leave, I laugh to myself. "He was right. You never did get her out of your system. She's been here all along, because you didn't want to let her go." I wind the hose up and put it back in the bin and look up at the house. "Time to start working on making you a home."

I know the different squads sometimes mix and meet at various places – the Blue Velvet Lounge being one of them on rare occasions. Some of us have worked together throughout the years. Hence the reason I know Marty Striegel, as well as his proclivities. I'm not an angel, never claimed to be. But where my dick has been and what it likes is not, nor will it ever be, public knowledge. Hence the reason the bingo ladies are oblivious. I'm a lover, not a talker – unless you consider the filthy things I might let slip in the middle of chasing an orgasm and upon release. It's amazing what true thoughts you can masque with swear words.

One flash of my badge is all it takes for the doorman to let me enter the building. One warning to not give her a heads-up that I'm on my way to her door is all it takes for him to set the desk phone back in its cradle.

"You're not going to shoot her, are you?" the initially shocked and wide-eyed, now somewhat chary doorman asks. "She's a really nice lady. I'll personally vouch for her." He's about 45, graying around the temples, fatherly type, with a wedding a ring on his finger.

"You will, huh?"

He tips his chin slightly. "Yes, I will. She's the only one in this building who even knows my name."

"And what would that be?"

"Garvis Harrington," he answers proudly. "Been the doorman since the building went up two years ago and Ms. Remington is the first tenant who's ever asked. Got 65 residents in this place and not a one of them knows me from Adam, but that young lady asked. Says hello and goodbye. Always adds on a have a good day, too."

"Well, Garvis Harrington," I say with a smirk. "I'll know who not to shoot, provided you don't let her know I'm on my way up." His jaw hangs agape as he stares. I shake my head and roll my eyes. "I'm not going to shoot her. We work together. She had a shit day and I'm checking on her."

A slow puckish grin spreads before he chuckles and waggles his finger. "You like her."

Good God, I'm back on the playground in fifth grade. Am I that transparent? I walk toward the elevator and push the button, looking back once more. "Do not call her." He reluctantly nods in agreement. The doors open and I heave a sigh, looking back once more. "Have a good day, Garvis." The doors close with the added echo of a chuckling doorman.

Maybe she is making me human.

Chapter 12

Deacon

Three taps, ten breaths, and a shitload of patience later, the door opens only enough for Everlee to narrow some pretty glassy eyes and tip her chin. "Detective Gray. How did you get up here?"

"I have a badge, Ms. Remington." I arch a brow. "It gets me in many places. May I come in?"

If I had a dime for every expression she runs through as she studies my face, it would total a dollar. Crinkled nose, furrowed brow, squinted eyes, puckered mouth, etc. If I didn't recognize the inebriated state that accompanies them, it might be humorous.

"Why?"

"Open the door, Everlee."

She holds her finger up and weakly points it at me. "I have a black belt, you know."

"Good to know." I carefully push the door open as I reach for her to assure she doesn't stumble, then slam the door behind me. "Let me know where you keep it so I can use it to whip your ass the next time you wallow in alcohol."

She pulls from the hand I have grasped around her arm and stumbles backwards, but I catch her by the waist. "I was celebrating, Detective Gray. I declined the invitation from your friends in the squad room and decided to have a drink at home. Speaking of which . . ." She holds up her free hand and points but looks over my shoulder as she asks, "Why aren't you there with them?"

The same reason I never am, but I don't tell her that. "Have you had any dinner?"

"I will when it gets here," she replies with a slow blink.

"When is it due?"

She closes one eye, opens it, then closes the other and opens it as she eyes the ceiling and considers her answer. *Definitely inebriated.* "I gotta call it in first."

Hiding my disgruntlement, I lift her by the waist and walk her to the sofa, setting her down gently on the center cushion. "Sit. I'll figure out dinner."

"You forgot my wine," she pouts, pointing to the kitchen counter where her glass and the last of the contents of a bottle of red remain. Stepping to the counter, I pick up the glass and the bottle and proceed to empty both into the sink. "Hey!" she shrieks. "That was mine!"

I smirk in satisfaction. At least I didn't have to wrestle it out of her fingers. "It belongs to the city's sewer system now."

Her stormy gray eyes flare with a true anger I've only ever dreamed of. It's bold yet spunky, sassy and strong with . . . no pain. I knew it was in there. Her slack jaw stirs fantasies of all the things I could do with that mouth. *Rein it in, Gray. She's a lifetime of fantasies. You don't want "The End" with this woman, you want "Forever".*

"You ass!"

I shrug casually, keeping with our usual banter. "At least I don't stink."

She folds her arms over her chest and tips her chin. "Did you use soap this time?"

Opening the fridge, I see a choice of Brita filtered or bottled water. I take the easy route, grab two bottles, walk to the sofa and plop down beside her. Handing her one, I grin. "Even used cologne. Wanna sniff me?"

She scowls before setting the bottle on the coffee table and attempting to stand on wobbly legs. "Already did when you came in. I need to pee." I stand to catch her before she falls, but there's not much I can do about her tripping over her own tongue. A frustrated growl leaves her throat before she huffs, "I didn't mean I *sniffed* you. I could smell you when you came in. You must have bathed in it."

"Got it." I wink. "You didn't sniff me."

We stand with my hands on her biceps steadying her stance – despite the reason, it feels good to touch her – before she looks up and narrows her gaze. "Why are you here, detective?"

"I wanted to make sure you knew Houma was handled the way you wanted and to congratulate you on the funding for the lab equipment," I explain, grateful I had thought this through on my way over. "You do have a way to get things done, Everlee."

She eyes me skeptically. "Captain Garner already did. You could have just called or waited until Monday. Don't you have a hot date?"

"Nope."

"Why didn't you go out with the others tonight?"

Lifting one shoulder in a slight shrug so as not to lose our connection – she hasn't pulled away; I'm sure as hell not going to let go, I answer easily, "Missed the invite, I guess. I got back late from the courthouse."

"Do you go there a lot?"

"The courthouse?" I grin wryly. "Only when called upon to assist in rehousing the city's finest."

Every effort afforded me to avoid the true reason that brought me to her door tonight flies out the window as the storm passes through her eyes. She's back there, holding her brother's dead body, her knees being ground into the broken glass. Her searching gaze nearly burns a hole in my conscience, and my soul, as she whispers, "The Blue Velvet Lounge."

"Not one much for the after-work gatherings." It's not a total lie. I participate on a semi-regular basis – enough to keep my friends close and my enemies closer – but I really am not a fan. I also don't go to the Blue Velvet *a lot* but I have been. Not to drink or cavort, but to investigate.

"Doesn't sound like a good place." She turns away from

my hold and heads for the hall, somber but seemingly steady until she sways slightly.

I rush forward and reach for her elbow. "You need some help?"

She pulls her arm out of my grasp. "Once upon a time I did." She shoulders the wall as she looks back. "Thought I had a hero, too. But I found someone else to rescue me. He keeps his promises. Lock up on your way out."

What the hell is she talking about?

The door to the bathroom opens minutes later and she appears in the entrance to the hallway as the toast pops up, warm and crispy.

"Why are you still here?" she asks, then hiccups.

I plate the toast, sans butter, and take it to the coffee table. "Sit down. Eat this and drink the water. Tell me what you want on your pizza."

She eyes the toast then looks to me and wrinkles her nose. "God, I hope you cook better at home. That's toast. Without butter, it's bird food. Unless you lived with my mother. With peanut butter, she called it dinner."

There's a bitterness in her tone that tugs at my heart. I knew I didn't like that woman. She added to all the reasons I didn't want to leave the hospital; abandon Everlee. Had she been a child, I would have called CPS to investigate.

Guiding her to the sofa, I gently force her to take a seat. "Dry toast. It'll soak up the acid in your stomach from too much liquor." I pull my phone out of my pocket and pull up the app for the best pizza place that delivers on this side of the city and take a seat next to her. "Now tell me what you want on your pizza."

"Onions, onions, and onions," she answers with a healthy helping of snark.

Tapping the correct buttons to order half pineapple and shrimp (gag) the other half pepperoni and sausage, I close out the app and pocket my phone. I know what she likes. She's ordered it twice in the last month from her lab. I'm a detective . . . and nosy. I also ordered pecan roll twists with caramel sauce to dip them in.

I'm nice that way, I think. I've never done it before. Real kicker? I added on a mini all-meat for Garvis downstairs. "Done. Now eat the toast."

If I were an artist, I would paint the expression on her face on a huge canvas and hang it on my wall, but as is, I'll store it in my memory bank for the ages. Her expressions are genuine and unguarded tonight. Adorable. "Did you really order me triple onions?"

"It's what you asked for." I lean forward and snatch a piece of toast off the plate and hold it up to her mouth. "Now eat the toast."

She gasps. "I wasn't seriou..." Taking the perfect opportunity to shove a corner of the toasted bread into her mouth, I wait for her to bite down. She glares instead, the fire in her eyes stirring a helluva lot more than my emotions.

"Bite down and chew," I growl slowly.

Her entire demeanor changes as her eyes light up and she bats her lashes, hollows her cheeks, and garbles around her mouthful, "Do you want me to spit or swallow?"

My well practiced composure ends up somewhere in no man's land. Do grown men whimper? She warned me not to spar with her. "Jesus Christ, Everlee." I let go of the toast and bolt off the couch, running both hands through my hair. "Save the euphemisms for the proper place and time."

She pulls the toast from her mouth, arches a brow and dramatically tips her chin. "Then learn not to stuff things in a woman's mouth without her consent, Detective Gray." She folds the piece of bread in half, licks from one end of the crust to the other, chomps down hard, chews dramatically, then sips the water to wash it down. She grins smugly. "Proof that my bite is worse than my bark. Kinda bland, I've had better things in my mouth."

"Like what?" I have no right to ask, no room to talk, but the thought of her with other men, any man, makes my skin crawl.

"Wine," she replies with a smirk. "And if you'd leave, I can get back to it."

"Do you drink like this often?"

She smiles cockily. "Only when I'm alone or with someone."

The intercom buzzes and before she can rise from the sofa, I'm by the door to answer. "Garvis, I want you to bring the order up."

"Uh, Detective Gray, was it?" he asks. "I'm not supposed to leave my post. I was calling to let Ms. Remington know the order was being delivered."

"I'm flashin' that badge again, Garvis," I warn. "You've got two minutes. Bring the order up yourself."

"On my way."

Waiting by the door for the delivery, I open it as soon as I hear his footsteps. Yanking a twenty from my wallet for his tip, I pull the large pizza box from the bottom of the stack, check to see which of the smaller two is the pecan twists, and hand back the mini all-meat along with the money.

"Thanks."

His eyebrows shoot skyward as he stares at the box in his hands. I think the pizza is more important than the cash in his hand. "You bought me a pizza?"

I shrug. "What can I say? She's rubbing off on me."

The corners of his mouth tip. "She has a tendency to do that. Thank you, sir."

"Best get back to your post. Have a good night, Garvis."

The door closes behind me with a quick thud as I make my way to the sofa and set the pizza on the coffee table. By the time I'm back with plates, napkins, and silverware from the kitchen, Everlee has the box open and is staring at the contents.

She frowns before she stiffens her chin and turns to me. "How did you know I like sausage and pepperoni?"

Damn, she's good. So stubborn. If I have to choke down pineapple and shrimp to appease her, so be it. If she needs to squeeze my balls to keep the upper hand, I'll pass them to her. Anything to keep her from drinking more to try and forget, to use alcohol as an elixir for pain. It doesn't help, sweetheart. Believe me, I've tried.

"Lucky guess," I tell her as I pass her a plate. "Dig in."

She doesn't take the plate from my hand, but instead just stares until tears rim her eyes, then whispers so softly it's almost inaudible, "My own mother doesn't know what kind of pizza I like." A single tear rolls down her cheek and she sniffles. "Why are you being nice to me, Deacon?"

Deacon.

This is a fresh pain I see in her eyes. The mention of peanut butter on toast for dinner and now this. "Did you and your mother have a falling out tonight, Everlee?"

"Sh-she's so c-cruel," she hiccups through her first sob. "Always aiming for m-my weak sp-spot."

On instinct, I pull her into my arms and she sobs against my chest. She doesn't try to pull away, doesn't tense; simply cries. And I let her, for as long as it takes. And it takes until she falls asleep, against my chest, limp as a noodle and passed out cold.

The buzzer sounds once again and I lie her back on the sofa, on her side, as gently as possible, and place a pillow under her head.

Turning the receiver volume knob to low before answering, I clip, "Yeah, Garvis, what is it?"

"Detective Gray," he replies cautiously. "There's a woman in the lobby demanding to see Ms. Remington. Says she's her mother." His voice drops to a whisper, "Not a very pleasant person, I must say."

"I'll be down in a minute. Do not let her up."

Spotting Everlee's keys on the counter, I collect them before checking on her once more. Her breathing is even and deep. Her brows furrow-free. Pressing my lips to her temple, I leave a whisper soft kiss. "Don't puke before I get back."

Taking the stairs down to the lobby, I find a platinum blonde arguing with Garvis. Face caked with makeup, leopard print mini skirt, high heels. Beyond middle age but trying hard to relive her youth. She'd fit well under a streetlight, twenty bucks a pop. Oh yes, I remember her.

Beverly Remington: what nightmares are made of.

"Evenin', Garvis," I greet him casually then glance up

toward the two electronic devices recording the activity in the lobby. "Security working?"

He nods, then reaches into his pocket and discreetly pulls out his own phone and whispers, "Back up video?"

I nod once. "Good idea. Do we have a problem?"

"I want to see my daughter! Give me her apartment number!" Beverly shouts before Garvis has an opportunity to reply. "What the hell is the problem and who the hell are you?"

"First of all," I start. "No, you won't be seeing Everlee. Second, not a chance in hell are you getting her apartment number. Third, the problem is you. Fourth? I will be your worst nightmare if you don't walk out that door, find the rock you just crawled out from under and slither back under it."

"How dare you!" She charges at me, teeth bared, hand raised high ready to strike.

Grabbing her wrist to halt her strike, ready to grab the other should she decide to use it, though it is holding her purse, I warn her, "Do you know what the charges are for assaulting an officer?"

She pulls from my grasp, eyes wide in shock mixed with a healthy side of rage. "You don't even know who I am!"

"Did you get all that, Garvis?" I ask him, never taking my eyes off the vile, narcissistic bitch in front of me.

"I most certainly did, detective," he answers proudly.

"Perfect. Now switch to the camera on your phone and take a pretty picture of *Beverly Remington*." She does exactly as I expect and flashes her glare at Garvis. Garvis does exactly as I expect and takes more than one, as in plenty. "Be sure to connect that phone to your printer. Print some good 8x10s and tape them up behind the desk. Make damn sure she doesn't get in the building again."

"You can't do this!" she shrieks, and just like water from a faucet that can be turned on as easily as it can be shut off, the tears start to flow. "I just wanted to see my daughter."

Looking to Garvis, I grin wryly. "What do you think, crocodile?"

He rolls his eyes and nods vigorously. "Definitely crocodile."

"My tears are real!" she bellows. And just like that, the

tears are gone, replaced by rage once again. "Who keeps a mother away from her child?"

"People who care about her," I reply, holding back the contempt I've felt for this woman for the last six years. "And she's not a child. Go home, Beverly. For once in your sorry ass life, put Everlee first. Just let her be."

I turn for the stairs, knowing deep down this is far from over, but I can help stave off some pain for at least a while longer; give myself one less thing to worry about. I look back over my shoulder before opening the door. "The no-contact orders will be in place by next week. I'll see to it myself."

Now to find her brother's killer.

I find Everlee exactly where I left her; asleep on the sofa. The pizza box still open on the coffee table, water bottles beside it. Visiting her bedroom first, I turn down the blankets and fluff the pillow. I retrieve two Tylenol, a bottle of water, and leave them on the nightstand. Returning to the living room, I gently slide one arm under her shoulders, the other under her knees, and lift. She feels so tiny, so fucking perfect in my arms. She leans her head on my shoulder and wraps her hand around my neck and sleepily mumbles, "Don't leave me."

The weight of her words nearly crushes me. Does she remember? Is it me she remembers or is it the stress of tonight that has conjured up otherwise long forgotten events of that horrendous night? I hold her to me a little tighter, relishing the feel of her body next to mine before I steal a kiss to her temple and whisper, "I'm right here, Everlee. I'm not going anywhere. Not this time, I swear."

She's in leggings and a loose T-shirt so she should be comfortable enough for sleeping. It wouldn't be right to strip her down to anything less anyway. That time will come, *with her consent.* She barely stirs as I lay her head on the pillow and tuck a pillow behind her so she doesn't roll over onto her back. Pulling the sheet and a lightweight blanket over her, I leave the comforter at the end of the bed. She's at peace, for now. Her porcelain skin free of worry lines. High cheekbones, unique teardrop shaped nostrils over slightly parted lips. Even more beautiful than I remember.

Sliding a light knuckle across her cheek, I smile and drop a kiss to her temple. "Sleep, angel. I'll be here in the morning."

Leaving the door partially open so I'll hear her if she wakes in the night, I make my way back out to the living room to pack up the leftovers, aka the whole pizza, and prepare for a restless night on the sofa. She'll either be cranky or grateful in the morning. I can live with either, as long as I know she's okay.

Chapter 13

Everlee

"Someday, you little rat bastard," I mutter as I try to peel my dry eyes open. "I will find you and stuff that sand back up your ass." Rising slowly, I press the heels of my palms to my temples. Someone left their bowling ball inside my head and . . . "Ooh, they're still playing. That was a spare," I murmur and wince as I move to get up. Mere eye movement hurts.

There are two Tylenol and a bottle of water on the nightstand staring at me, whispering words of wisdom, *"Take me, take me now."* My mouth feels like it's been stuffed with cotton and my tongue sticks to the roof. Sip first, swallow after. Now, I'm generally prepared for almost anything, but leaving Tylenol and water on my nightstand are not usually in my wheelhouse. I generally pay my penance for being an idiot through the self-inflicted pain of rolling my butt out of bed and finding my way to the bottle of pain relief.

Deacon. He's my Tylenol fairy.

Taking the time to brush my teeth and relieve my bladder first, I pad down the hall and out to the kitchen where I find Deacon Gray in an army green T-shirt and blue jeans and . . . barefoot. Tattoos peek out from under the sleeves on the upper portion of his biceps, making me all the more curious just how far they reach under those sleeves. Like an idiot, I dip my chin and tilt my head as if I can get a better view from a different angle. It's the equivalent of leaning forward in your chair while watching TV to see if you can spot the villain hiding around the edge of the screen before they attack. *Newsflash: you can't.* Were they there last night?

"I can take the shirt off if you prefer, Everlee," he teases, stirring something in a skillet at the stove. My apartment smells like a touch of heaven at the current time; a mix of bacon, eggs, and toast. "There's more where these come from. Coffee?"

"Why are you still here, Detective Gray?"

Ignoring my question, he proceeds to pour a cup of coffee, adding one sweetener and topping it off with the perfect amount of creamer. Even worse? He tosses in the tiny dash of salt I have a tendency to add to remove the bitterness. It's soon joined by a plate of bacon, eggs, and toast.

"Come on," he prods. "There's no arsenic in it. I'll save that for later if you're obstinate. You missed dinner. Sit down and eat, Everlee."

"I have to feed Roscoe," I retort, aiming my footsteps toward his tank.

"Already did." He sets his own plate on the bar. "We've had quite the enlightening conversation while waiting for you to rise. Now sit down and eat."

My brows pinch – a sore reminder that facial expressions are not my friend until the Tylenol kicks in. "Roscoe doesn't talk."

His eyes widen in shock, then he turns his gaze to Roscoe's tank. "Roscoe, have you been holding out on her?" Roscoe waves his silky fins through the water and releases a single bubble from his mouth that seems akin to sticking his tongue out – if he had one.

I look back at the man standing at my kitchen counter, wondering why he's back in my life. Why he can't remember me when I remember him so clearly. "You're an idiot."

"Better than an ass, isn't it?"

"Barely," I grumble, making my way to the kitchen bar where he pulls out my chair and I take a seat.

"How's the hangover?"

"I don't have a hangover!" I protest loudly, though the moment I do, I regret it.

Hands are on my shoulders in the perfect grip before I can speak. Thumbs at the base of my skull apply the perfect amount of pressure as two index fingers massage my temples. In unison they work so well together I forget where I am, forget who's applying the majestic touch. A whimper and a moan leave my throat at the same time my head falls forward and I nearly faceplant into the plate of breakfast in front of me before those two large hands gently keep me upright. As God as my witness, this is the closest I've been to an orgasm in, well – a very long time.

"Okay," I say breathlessly, barely hiding the shivers that massage induced as I pull away. "Thank you."

His breath on my ear only produces more shivers as he whispers, "Better?"

I nod shakily, only able to muster, "Mmhmm."

"Good," he whispers against my ear again. "Do you want me to warm up your breakfast?"

"No. No, no," I nearly whimper. "C-cold is probably best right now."

He chuckles low before taking his seat next to me and forking a bite of eggs. "Eat, Everlee, or I'll feed you myself."

His phone buzzes on the counter next to him. He picks it up and as he reads the screen, his brow furrows. "Aw shit," he murmurs, rising from his seat. "Please eat. I've gotta go."

"What is it?" I've got no right to ask, but the worry – and the fury – in his eyes is concerning.

"Work," he replies sharply, then releases a deep sigh. "Everlee, please eat your breakfast."

"What are you doing here if you're working?" He only sighs again. I'm not stupid. He wouldn't be here if he were on duty. I dive for my own phone that lies on the counter. I had turned it off last night and haven't checked it for hours. If it's work, he's being called in for something major, and he's not exclusive. He tries to get to my phone before I do, but I masterfully snatch it up before he can and power it on.

ALL AVAILABLE OFF-DUTY LAW ENFORCEMENT, RESCUE AND RECOVERY, EMERGENCY PERSONNEL,

Annie Mick

AND FORENSICS OFFICIALS PLEASE REPORT. MASS SHOOTING AT SUMMIT COUNTY FAIR. MULTIPLE FATALITIES AND INJURIES.

I look up from my phone. "Summit County isn't your district."

"We work in six different counties as off-duty if we're needed in emergencies." He nods toward my phone. "Summit is one of them."

"I'm a locum as well. I work all over the state if needed. This message came in for me, too." I rise from my seat, but he gently takes my shoulders and forces me back down into my chair.

"Please eat first. You were drinking heavily and you didn't eat last night. You'll be running on fumes. It's hot as hell today." He scowls. "You've got to eat something or you're going to end up one of the victims."

"I'll eat on the way." I slip off the chair and rush toward the bedroom to change.

"Then I'll drive the both of us!" he shouts after me.

"You didn't eat either!" I shout back.

"Then I'll order from the diner and you can feed me!" He finishes on a low growl, "You stubborn little shit!"

When you live alone, closing doors for privacy isn't something you make a habit of. It's not like Roscoe watches me pee or change clothes. And this morning is no different, because there's an emergency, and I'm not thinking. I whip off my T-shirt and leggings and open the dresser drawer in search of underwear. The next trip is to the closet for my field clothes. My boots and supplies bag are in the closet by the front door. I dash across the hall to the second bathroom and grab the cap I washed after the last outing by the dumpsters. The last thing I need is my hair hanging in my face, and the cap was dirty so I hung it on the hook in the shower to dry and never took it down.

Cotton undies go on first. Sports bra next. It's too damn hot for lace – it's nonabsorbent and gets itchy. I'd love to take a shower, but what's the point? I doubt my armpits will be the spotlight today.

"Deacon?" I call out as I'm slipping on my pants.

He clears his throat loudly and his voice sounds strained. "Uh, yeah?"

"Do you need to go home and change?"

"Nope, I'm good."

"I won't be long," I reassure him. "I'm coming."

"I doubt that," he mumbles. "But *I'm* damn close."

"What?"

"Let's go, Everlee."

When I walk out into the living room, he's standing at the door, keys in one hand, the other in his pocket. "You ready?"

I snatch my keys, phone, and the lanyard with my credentials off the kitchen counter and see that he's cleaned up the mess from the breakfast we didn't get to enjoy. "I need to grab my boots and bag from the closet."

He smirks. "The fanny pack?"

"Why?" I smile cockily. "You need a tampon?"

"I need to tamp somethin'," he mutters as he pulls the door open. "Put your boots on in the truck."

Once in the truck, I tie my hair back in a ponytail that I pull through the hole in the cap, then twist into a messy bun at the back, and lean down to lace up my boots. All in all, it took approximately ten minutes to get out the door. "Would two more minutes have killed you?"

"Yup," he says. "They just might have."

Chapter 14

Deacon

Perfect tits. And on her way back out of the hall bath and into her bedroom? *Perfect ass.* I've seen my share, more than my share. But never have I seen a more perfect pair than Everlee's. And that ass? More please.

She was on a mission; tunnel vision. Carefully calculating and collecting everything she would need to get through the day – apparently forgetting she was not alone. Being an afterthought might annoy me on any other given day. Today? Not so much. I nearly choked on my own spit. Not sure if it was the shock or the sight though. I was putting fresh socks on (yes, I keep a bag in my truck for *various* reasons) while sitting on the sofa when the fast moving peep show darted across the hall. I did a double take, certain I had been mistaken, but when she dashed back out and that tight little ass bounced with each step back into the bedroom, I nearly put holes in the toes of my socks from yanking them on so hard. The vertical scar on her back was a painful reminder of her past, making my fists clench with a strong desire to find Spencer and put him six feet under this time. A decent man would have looked away. And I did . . . eventually. As soon as she disappeared into her bedroom.

I spent the remaining few minutes cleaning up after breakfast i.e. food in the trash, dishes in the dishwasher, and skillet in the sink. That, and talking down the semi in my jeans. *'Not now, buddy. All in due time, junior. Win her, Gray.'*

Oh, for God's sake! She can't even make field clothes look drab. Army green T-shirt, same color cargo pants, lace up boots with thick soles. Hands and body of a woman, mind of a soldier, and heart of . . . glass. Very thin, cracked glass ready to shatter if last night was any indication.

"How's the head?" I ask her as we pull out of her parking lot.

Her phone rings before she has a chance to respond and she pulls it out of her pocket, grinning when she sees whoever is calling. "I know why you're calling," she answers guardedly and turns toward the window.

"It's all over the news!" the voice rings through the phone. A *man's* voice. "Baby girl, tell me you haven't been called in. You haven't had a weekend off since you started."

"Volume," she warns softly. "We've all been called in from near and far."

"Volume?" he asks, still loud enough to be heard. "I don't care about someone hearing me. I care about you, sweet cheeks. Have they apprehended the shooter? Are they sending police protection with you or is dementia dick meeting you at the Tilt-O-Whirl?"

Everlee tucks the phone tight to her chest and turns to me, cheeks flushed. "Do you know if they've apprehended the shooter yet?"

I keep my eyes straight ahead, my jaw clenched somewhere between cracking a molar and snapping a root. "Dead."

"Shooter's taken care of," she tells him. "It's a matter of investigation and recovery now, I guess."

I don't catch his next question as his volume has decreased significantly but she eventually stammers, "Oh, um, Detective Gray and I are on our way to the scene now," then grumbles, "and you may as well be on speaker phone."

Ah, I'm back to being Detective Gray.

A long pause of uncomfortable silence ensues before a

burst of laughter rings through the phone and into the cab of the truck as I pull into the lot of the diner. What the hell, it's on the way, and I'd already called ahead. I hop out of the truck and slam the door behind me. *Dementia dick? Is that how she refers to me? Is it the age difference? There's not a damn thing wrong with my dick! I could make those college boys look like preschoolers! There's a lot to be said for experience. And what's with sweet cheeks? Not that he's wrong. I saw them this morning. More please.*

Alva has everything ready to go and bagged by the time I get to the counter. She frowns, her eyes watering as she hands me the bag and two coffees, fixed the way I ordered. "On the house today, Deacon. I put regular silverware in there, too. You'll bring it back. I see Everlee out there in the truck. Tell her hello for me. I wouldn't want to be in your shoes for nothin'." She knows where we're heading. Half the fucking state is heading where we are; those who aren't working a regular shift. You don't remove your own workforce to care for someone else's territory. The crime rate would skyrocket and it would be the equivalent of leaving your citizens behind to be eaten by the wolves.

As I open the door of the truck, Everlee is tucking her phone back in her pocket. I hand over the coffees then climb up and hand her the bags, start the truck and back out of the parking space. Slapping the magnetic flashing light on the top of the truck, I pull out onto the street and head for the highway. She opens one of the bags and pulls out a Styrofoam tray filled with biscuits and gravy. Any other day the scent would have my mouth watering. She forks a bite of biscuit and scoops some extra gravy onto it, leans over the console, and holds it up to my mouth.

"Eat, Deacon."

God, I love the way she says my name. 'Eat me, Deacon' would sound even better, but . . .

"Don't you mean dementia dick?"

"What!?" she snaps. "I didn't say that!"

My eyes flash to her in challenge. "Your boyfriend did."

She rolls her lips between her teeth in an effort to hide a grin but doesn't deny it. "Eat your biscuits and gravy or I'm going to tell Alva."

"You first."

She takes in the whole bite without hesitation and moans as if it's the best thing she's had in the last year. Knowing Alva's penchant for a special touch on a shitty day, it probably is. "Oh my God, this is heaven in a tray." She takes another bite and moans just as loud before chewing lightly and swallowing. She goes in for a third and my balls clench at the thought of hearing her moan one more time.

"Are you going to share?"

"This fork has my cooties," she teases.

I could take the fork, dip it in the tray myself, and eat on the go. I've done it so many times, I could do it blindfolded. But the thought of Everlee doing it for me, the fact she's willing, turns that simple tray of food into a buffet.

"Put it in my mouth, Everlee," I warn slowly. "Especially the cooties."

After sharing the first tray of biscuits and gravy – from the same fork – she pulls out a hash brown patty and holds it up for me to take a bite. As we get to the final portion, she holds it up, "You want it?"

"I do." She just doesn't know why. She holds it close to my mouth, waiting for me to open. Instead, I snatch her wrist first and hold it steady as I accept the offering, chew and swallow first, then suck each of her fingers clean of any remaining oil.

"Well," she says breathlessly as she rubs her fingers together. "So much for needing a wet wipe."

Take that boyfriend. I've waited six years for her. Maybe I didn't know it, maybe deep down I always knew it. She said "Don't leave me" last night while I was holding her. I stirred something inside of her. She hasn't forgotten . . . everything. I'll explain why I had to leave, let her go, but that I stayed as long as I could . . . someday.

* * *

Somebody's Someone

Pandemonium is a weak description of the scene when we arrive. One mile up the road from the entrance starts the fiasco of flashing our credentials every 500 feet – my badge and driver's license, Everlee's state license. Shades off so they can match the face to our IDs. It's understandable, but frustrating. There are days I wish I weren't so anal about keeping my truck clean. The sun glaring off the fresh wax shine doesn't help. Our caps will be beneficial once under the sun – a good barrier from heat stroke – but shades are a must to fight reflections.

As we get closer to the grounds, the screams become clearer, louder, ear piercing. The closest I can park my truck is approximately a quarter mile from the entrance so we leave the truck behind and run toward the arch logoed with SUMMIT COUNTY FAIRGROUNDS.

I grasp Everlee's elbow before she can veer off in another direction. "We stay together. This is pure chaos. I don't need to worry about where you are in the midst of this fucking disaster. Got it?" She only stiffens beneath my touch and glares as she drops those shades to the tip of her nose. I know that look and I don't like it, one little bit. "Everlee," I say slowly.

She pulls her elbow from my grip and squares her shoulders. "Out here, it's Ms. Remington. Time to go to work, Detective Gray."

Law enforcement has done their best to corral non-injured survivors to one end of the grounds to await word on loved ones and friends, which is where most of the screaming is coming from. Minor injuries are being tended to by field workers and EMS personnel are busy tending to the most severely injured and loading them into waiting ambulances. There are bodies already covered in white tarps in various places on the ground and some still, unfortunately, exposed. Crowd control is, even more unfortunately, becoming less and less controlled.

"Oh my God!" Everlee's eyes are glued to the Ferris wheel before she drops her bag at my feet and takes off at a dead run that a champion sprinter would struggle to keep up with. The Ferris wheel is at the far end of the midway, but I now see what caught her eye.

The majority of the emergency workers and police on the scene are so distracted by crowd control and tending to the injured, they haven't seen the disaster unfolding about four cars off the ground.

"Everlee!" I scream at the top of my lungs as I try to keep up. She winds her way around the heavy cables on the grass, bodies lying on the ground as well as the officials standing on their feet, pushing and shoving the ones that get in her way. One cop grabs her arm and as God as my witness, I've never seen a woman dropkick a man as fast as she does and continue on her way. He reaches for his gun while still lying on his back.

"You pull that firearm," I warn him, stepping on his chest, "and it will be the last thing you do. She's personnel, you stupid fuck." I flash my badge and take off in another lung-burning run behind her.

By the time I arrive at the Ferris wheel, she's already climbing the outer frame like a fucking spider monkey, out of my reach, on a mission to get to the little boy. He's standing on the bench of the car screaming in absolute terror, his mother grasping his arm doing her best to calm him. His *very pregnant* mother. Everlee is halfway to him, about twenty feet in the air, and already calling up to him as she continues her ascent; crotch against the frame, arms pulling her up while her feet boost her climb.

"It's okay, buddy," she shouts to him. "I'm on my way. You take care of mommy and I will buy you the biggest ice cream cone you've ever had."

She's gathered the attention now of not only the cop she counter-assaulted, but of a few other rescue workers.

"Get a fucking ladder over here!" I scream at any and all. "Get a bucket! Whatever you've got!" And then I start my own climb behind her. The bar is thick, hot from the sun, and how in the hell she's climbing this damn thing at the speed she is I'll never know. The only thing to grip with your boots is the bolts that hold it together.

She reaches the car as a siren from a firetruck blares below us. I'm too squeamish to look down. My goal is above me and one wrong move is all it will take to turn this ride into a bungee jump with no cords. I wonder if Everlee will still do my eulogy. I finally make it to the four-seater car and edge my way in. It's shaky, sways with my weight, but one foot is on the solid bottom of the car and all I have to do is get the other in.

"This nice officer is going to hold you for a minute while I check your mommy, okay?" Everlee sits on the edge of one seat, holding fast to the little boy around his bottom as she presses him tight to her chest. "Then you'll get to take a ride in a firetruck. I bet they'll let you ride up front and blow the horn. Would you like that?"

Uh, Everlee, think you might want to let me get my other foot inside the car before you hand me a kid?

"I think he needs help," she turns the little boy in her lap and holds him tight around his belly, his back to her chest. "Can you take his hand and help him in? You'll have to pull really hard. Are you strong?" The little boy nods at the same time mom hollers in pain. Everlee shoots me a look of impatience and grinds through a clenched jaw, "Got a bit of a *laborious* job here, Gray. Step right in anytime. Watch out, the floor is slippery."

The little boy reaches out for my hand, which I virtually ignore, and let go of the pole and dive for the car at the same time – realizing Everlee is using me as his distraction – landing in the middle and plopping on my ass on the other side. Thank God for four-seaters. The slippery floor? Yeah, that's amniotic fluid. She hands the little boy over with a tight smile. "Good job. You sit and I'm going to check your mom."

She turns back to the woman at her side and tells her, "I need you to lie back and let me check you, okay?" The woman nods shakily and whimpers. As soon as she's reclined, Everlee lifts her dress and pulls down her panties. "Ooh, boy. Looks like somebody's ready to say hello. Hang on, mom. Gray, undo one of your shoelaces and keep it handy. We're crowning."

We're crowning? No Everlee, I'm ready to shit my pants!

"Can't they move this thing to get us down to the ground first?"

"Might want to gander above you, Gray."

I look up to see the top half a body hanging over the edge of the car above us. *A shooting victim.* Nope, they can't move us to the ground at the present time.

She strips off her T-shirt and lays it out on the bench at the edge of the woman's fanny, leaving herself in only a sports bra. On any other woman, it would be running gear. On Everlee, it's . . .

"I could use another T-shirt if you're willing to hand it over, Gray. Need something to wrap the baby in." Everlee snaps her fingers impatiently. "Shirt, Gray. Get ready to push, mom."

Multiple pained hollers and three pushes later from mom, we have a new set of lungs announcing her arrival to the world. The little boy in my lap had simply watched with fascination mixed with worry as I tried to explain that he was on his way to being a big brother.

Not gonna lie, trying to calm a child while Everlee does all the work has a tendency to make one feel a bit emasculated. Trying to hold back from strangling her in the process is even more of a challenge.

I will find the cop that damn near shot her.

I will point out the stupidity of impulsivity on her part.

I will make her see just how damn close she came to being a victim today.

Strongminded is one thing; bullheaded is another. She's a beautiful mix of both, but each has their place.

The fire company manages to maneuver a bucket on an arm in the air to transport mom and her two children down and into the ambulance first. Everlee and I follow in the return – both shirtless, adrenaline still pumping at a fast rate through our veins, I'm sure. For different reasons as well, I'm sure.

On the way down, because I can't help myself and I'm shaking so hard with anger, I lean close so only she can hear. "You should have called for rescue units. That was the most reckless thing I've ever seen. What the fuck were you thinking? There is protocol. Damnit, Everlee! Do you really have no regard for your own safety?"

The rescue workers all take their turn appreciating a half-dressed Everlee, one of them asking for a date – the promise of champagne and lobster – as our feet barely touch the ground. The low growl I release accompanied by the *accidental* shoulder clock as I pass him provides little satisfaction.

The little boy screeches from the back of the ambulance as he holds his arms out, "Eberwee, stay wit me!"

Her breath catches in her throat before she looks at me. Her chin trembles and her voice cracks. "The least I can do for him is explain why I can't."

She walks to the ambulance where the little boy waits then virtually jumps into her arms when she's close enough. She embraces him as if they're long lost friends, tells him how brave he was, and promises to come see him once they're back home and settled in. I've no doubt she'll follow through – probably with ice cream and a trip to the fire station so he can blow the horn on the truck.

Those assholes will probably all have her phone number before she leaves the fire station, too.

Annie Mick

Chapter 15

Everlee

The forensics team for Summit county is more than accommodating once I make it back to the front of the fairgrounds. A tank of water for cleaning up as well as medical grade soap to accompany it. Delivering a baby without gloves wasn't exactly what I had in mind today, but I doubt the little girl planned on being born on the Ferris wheel either – a month early, but seemingly healthy. Bottles of electrolyte water to rehydrate, a T-shirt to replace the one I lost. Wrong logo – right purpose. They also had the bag I dropped when I ran toward the Ferris wheel. I also received one marriage proposal and two invites for a night out. I think Deacon received the equivalent so I didn't really feel extra special. But then, watching him approach the van shirtless drew the attention of many – men and women. They even gave him one of their own shoelaces to replace the one I demanded to tie off the umbilical cord.

And yes, his tattoos extend far beyond the biceps. Not that I care. He's lucky I don't dunk his head in the muddy water on the ground left from washing up. If I'd wanted to be scolded like a child, I could have called my mother. He can follow protocol all he wants. No one on the grounds had even noticed the child that was ready to leap off that Ferris wheel. He was traumatized, sunburned, and scared to death.

"Duncan!" A woman from the cordoned off area shouts

out and waves. Deacon bristles with the sound but ignores it as he slides his shades back on quickly and pulls his cap lower on his forehead. "Duncan Greene!" she calls out again. "Where have you been? You haven't been answering my calls or texts."

I turn to see a rather buxom blonde in short shorts and an off the shoulder skin tight top staring at Deacon. "I think you have a fan," I tell him. "She's staring at you. Wrong first name and a little off on the color, but she seems pretty homed in on her target."

"No clue," he says.

"You haven't even looked in her direction."

"Don't need to," he says tersely. "She's not calling my name. Let's get back to work. By the way, you got aloe vera at home?"

"I don't think so."

"We'll stop on the way back," he informs me. "Your shoulders are pink. You got sunburned up on the rollercoaster."

"Duncan, you asshole!" the woman screams.

"I don't need a daddy, Detective Gray." I glance back over my shoulder at the woman who looks like she's ready to carve a hole in Deacon's backside. "Maybe she needs some tending to. Her shoulders are exposed. You never know, aloe may be her rub of choice."

"What I know . . ." he says gruffly, grasping my bicep and moving me away from the area as fast as he can, ". . . is that you are rubbing me the wrong way. We have bodies to tag and evidence to collect. We will discuss your behavior when we're done, Everlee."

"Ms. Remington," I correct him.

"Everlee," he growls.

"Ms. Remington," I say again then enunciate, "Detective Gray."

"Deacon." He pulls harder, dragging me alongside him at a pace that he knows is difficult for me to keep up with. "Are we really going to start this shit again?"

"You're the one who insists on *protocol,* detective," I snark. "Just following your orders."

He veers off to the right toward a set of trailers belonging to the traveling carnies, pulling me behind him, until he has us tucked between two of them, away from the crowd, out of sight. He backs me against the side of one of them and stands so close I feel his shuddered breaths as his whole body shakes. He's angry.

"Protocol! Really?" he yells so loud it hurts my ears. "Do you have any idea how fucking close you came today?!" He slams the side of his first into the trailer near my head. "You damn near got shot by a cop you had just assaulted! You climbed the frame of a carnie ride like you had a death wish! No safeguards in place, no net, no safety straps, no request for help. You wouldn't know protocol if it bit you on the ass!"

His words hit hard. There are rules to be followed, steps to be taken, *protocol*. But sometimes mere seconds make all the difference in the world. What would it have taken for Jonah? The little boy looked like he was going to jump.

"He needed help," I protest weakly.

"And I need you," he says, his voice less harsh as he pulls his shades from his face, then reaches for mine and gently removes them. I see the eyes I remember so well and recall the night I needed him. "Don't ever do anything like that again. Promise me."

"Promises are . . ."

He doesn't give me the opportunity to finish as he grabs the nape of my neck and crushes my mouth with his, the whole of his body pinning mine to the wall of the trailer behind me. It's harsh, claiming; feels like punishment really. But honestly? I'll take this over being scolded any day. The bill of his cap goes one way while mine goes another.

As our lips part, he finishes my comment with a guilt-ridden whisper, matched with the crinkles at the corners of his eyes, "Sometimes unavoidably broken." He kisses me again, softer this time, tilting my head so his mouth fits mine perfectly. My lips are drier than I prefer for a kiss – thank you Louisiana heat – but somehow he makes it flawless; his tongue seeking to soothe the sore spots he had just caused. It's the kiss I've dreamed of for years, filled with passion and heat – the heavy bulge against my stomach a surprising, but welcome addition. The *man in the ambulance* wants me, but he doesn't even know who I really am. He was the light to my dark, a juxtaposition of sorts, but only for a short time. I'm still in the dark, and the light at the end of my tunnel lies in solving Jonah's case. Would he help me or hinder my efforts?

He straightens the cap on my head, hands me my sunglasses, and gingerly bends – probably so as not to crush the hard-on behind his zipper – to pick up his cap that's fallen onto the ground, slapping it against his thigh before putting it back on his head. "We should probably get back out there. Still got a long day ahead of us."

"Yeah." I chuckle sarcastically. "Priorities and protocol."

"Everlee," he starts on a sigh.

"Work, Deacon." I stumble past him on shaky legs. "Tag 'em and bag 'em."

"At least you got the name right," he mumbles behind me.

Turning one last time before we're back out in the thick of things, I smirk. "Are you sure about that, *Duncan*?"

His scowl isn't hidden well behind his shades as he grunts, "She wasn't calling my name."

"There she is!" a voice calls from a group of workers as we step out from behind the trailers. One rushes over with phone in hand. "I got some excellent video of your climb up the Ferris wheel. Can I get your name before I turn it in to the news so they have all the info for the full story?"

Deacon grabs the phone from his hand before the man can stop him. "You recorded her? Without her permission?"

"Well, uh yeah," the man says. "We're on public grounds. It's public information."

"It's a crime scene, fucknuts," Deacon grinds through a clenched jaw before he throws the phone on the ground and stomps on it with his boot, shattering the screen.

"Hey!" the man shrieks. "That's a thousand-dollar phone!"

Deacon smirks. "Looks pretty worthless to me."

The man tips his chin and grins smugly. "I have the video stored in the cloud."

Deacon grabs him by his T-shirt collar. "And I have your face stored in my brain. I guaran-damn-tee you it will not look the same when I get done with it if you release that video. Got it?" He twists his collar in his fist, then throws him to the ground where he lands on his ass. "Liability, lawsuit. Think long and hard. You can't be that fucking stupid."

As we walk to join the group from our own county, I glance at a fuming Deacon. "You're pretty good with that F-word, aren't you?"

He takes a deep breath and blows it out slowly, gathering composure before he arches his brow over his aviators and smirks. "It's not the *word* I'm best at, Everlee."

"Hmm," I hum. "Is that what she said?"

He sighs, then throws his arm over my shoulder. "I was trying to protect you. I lost my temper back there."

"Was that before or after you kissed me?"

He pulls slightly on my shoulder to halt our footsteps. "What I lost when I kissed you was my mind."

"Oh," I say, disappointed. "So, you didn't mean to."

He pulls at the back of his neck in frustration. "Did it feel like I didn't mean to?" I shrug under the arm he has over my shoulder. "Everlee," he says slowly, taking my both of my shoulders in his hands, bending at the knees due to his height and dipping his chin to ensure my attention. "Did it feel like I didn't mean to?"

When I don't respond, he simply leads me toward the group, who is now staring at us, and says, "We'll discuss this later."

"Yeah," I snort lightly, yet in the back of my mind thinking *if you don't go anywhere.*

Chapter 16

Deacon

"Deacon, Ms. Remington," Victor Parnell greets us as we approach the small group gathered near one of the strategy points at the edge of the grounds. "Been looking for you. They said you were at the forensics van getting new, uh," he grins, "clothes."

"Yup," I reply flatly, stepping forward. "What do ya got?"

"We've got men posted in the south quadrant." Vic points to a sketch on the table in front of him. "A few more throughout the grounds and searching vehicles in the parking areas. The shooter came in from under an opening in the fence at the east end. No witnesses to his entrance so far."

"Got an ID yet?" I ask.

Vic shakes his head. "Not yet. Didn't have any on him. Came in guns blazin'. Two fully loaded machine guns. Went through both belts of ammo, then turned a handgun on himself."

My head whirls toward Vic. "Machine guns? Where the fuck did he get those?"

Everlee tsks beside me. "Those who can, do. Those who can't, swear."

My head turns slowly. "That's not the quote."

She lifts one shoulder and smiles cockily. "Potato, potahta." She looks to an extremely amused Vic. "Do we have a body count yet?"

He grimaces. "We have a ground count of 24 so far, but we won't have a total until we have a survivor count from the hospitals. I understand you took a rather unorthodox approach to saving three a little while ago, Ms. Remington."

"Call me Everlee, please. Did you get the body down from the Ferris wheel yet?"

"They just brought him down," he tells her. "There were five other people up there lying down on the seats too scared to move."

"Can't say as I blame them." Her brow crinkles under her cap and then she scouts the area around us. "Are we sure there was only one shooter?"

"As sure as we can be," Vic replies. "We've got sharpshooters all over the place. The entire perimeter as well as strategically placed within the grounds."

She slides her cap up off her forehead as if wiping sweat from her brow as she slowly and discreetly scans the trees, which here in Louisiana are plentiful and full this time of year, be it in backyards or fairgrounds. "Are they all in uniform? Special colors?"

"Black or navy blue," I answer before Vic can. "Why?"

"Victor," she says. "Step closer, please." He does as she asks and she speaks softly as she informs him, "Don't look now, but there's a guy in camo at my two o'clock in the magnolia tree behind the funnel cake stand, about twenty feet in the air. He's either scared to death to come down after witnessing a blood bath or he's an accomplice biding his time. Since he's hugging the branch like a lifeline, I'm betting on the former. I can't tell if he has a weapon. Remind your sharpshooters he is most likely a bystander who is too petrified to move. Tell them not to get trigger happy."

Vic picks up his walkie talkie and starts the communication that will put him through to the proper channel. As he does, I move closer to Everlee's side in order to scope out the point of interest and mimic her movements. How in the hell she sees what nobody else does, I'll never know.

"See him?" she asks.

"Mmhmm. Good eyes, Everlee."

"His blood is on their hands if they *fuck* this up." She turns to walk toward the line of bodies covered in white tarps and tosses back over her shoulder. "Yes, Deacon, I said it. You must be rubbing off on me."

If she only had any idea how much I want to.

* * *

It's nearly ten o'clock when we pull into the parking lot of her complex. The day turned into night, floodlights shining all around us, helping to guide us through the massacre that had taken place this morning. I stopped at the grocery store to grab some aloe vera on the way back. Her neck was more than pink; can't imagine how red her shoulders are from the time spent up on that damn Ferris Wheel. I truly anticipated her falling asleep in the seat beside me. Fourteen hours from start to finish, one breakfast shared on the way, cold sandwiches and chips lunch catered by three different diners, which she barely ate after much pleading from yours truly, and two iced coffees as well as a shit ton of bottled waters and Gatorade. She is exhausted. We both are. But the adrenaline hasn't worn off yet. Once it does, she's either going to crash and burn or she's going to have a meltdown. After tending to a scene like today, it's policy, and mandatory, for every participating employee to undergo a psychiatric evaluation. I would imagine after the Ferris wheel incident, Everlee's evaluation will be accompanied by a stern reprimand for not following protocol. The end results don't always justify the means, but I will do everything within my power to back up her decision. I was mad as hell at her, yes, but I was scared to death of losing her too. Who knows if the little boy wouldn't have jumped? Who knows if they would have gotten to the pregnant woman on time? It's going to be hard to be impartial after watching that scene unfold.

The young man in the magnolia tree was exactly what Everlee had suspected; a panicked and terrorized witness. He'd already wet his pants, thrown up all over himself. He could barely breathe, much less talk. His two friends that he'd arrived with this morning were victims of the merciless killer. They were there to celebrate one last week of freedom before leaving for bootcamp . . . together. Fresh out of high school, 18 years old, and only one of them would see another year. He will either make one helluva stone-cold soldier, or he will never make it to bootcamp. Everlee's intuition is uncanny. She followed protocol, but it came with a warning. I've never been more grateful for precautions being taken. She called it as if she knew exactly what was happening in that tree. For all the lives that were lost today, she saved one – four, if you count the Ferris wheel incident. She's not a force to be reckoned with; she's a force you get out of the way of, because she will knock you on your ass before you ever know what hit you.

"I'll see you up," I tell her, opening my door to round the truck and get to hers. She sits in the seat, motionless, her eyes devoid of emotion as if she's taught herself how to turn it off and on. She is *Little Girl Lost.*

"I'm okay, Deacon," she says quietly, though not moving from her position. Her seatbelt remains buckled, her gaze fixed on the dark shadowless night out the windshield. She is anything but *okay.*

I reach over her to undo the seatbelt, the closeness my own undoing. I'm so tempted to slide my arm under her legs, gather her in my arms and carry her upstairs. She worked hard today; a concentrated façade for every body she examined and identified – a tear shed for each that no one but me saw. A whisper shared with every cadaver, a compassionate word of apology she didn't owe, yet felt compelled to give.

I should have never left her side.

"Come on," I gently urge. "Let's get you upstairs. I'll feed Roscoe. You get a hot bath and I'll get you something to eat."

"Do I get a glass of wine?" she asks sardonically. "Or am I still on probation?"

I hold up a single digit. "One."

She takes in a long breath and lets it out slowly, leaning her head back on the seat. "I have big glasses on the top shelf. If you can't reach them, I have a stepstool I use."

Somebody's Someone

I should have followed her to Chicago. I should have solved her brother's case. I should have never let her go.

"Come on, tiger, let's go." Grabbing her backpack off the floor of the truck, I set it on her lap and slide one arm under her legs and the other behind her back, lifting her into my arms. I spin toward the building and slam the door shut with my foot, then tap the lock button on the fob. The lights flash and the locks click.

"Deacon!" she squeals though it's weak. "I can walk."

"Yup," I deadpan. "I hear you can climb too."

She gasps and kicks her feet, then slaps at my chest as if she's gotten a second wind. "You're not going to let that go, are you?"

"Nope," I say as I boost her higher in my arms and squeeze. "Now quitch'yer bitchin'. I gotcha."

She lays her head on my shoulder as if too exhausted to argue then slides her hand up to my neck and murmurs, "You don't even know me."

"I know you better than you think I do, Everlee Remington," I whisper into her temple. If it stirs anything inside her, she doesn't let on. It's not time yet. I'll spend a lifetime apologizing for leaving her behind if I have to.

Garvis opens the front door for us, his brow furrowed in sympathy, his head shaking slightly in disbelief. The entire country knows by now what took place today. The fair will be shut down. There will be flowers lain at the entry, memorials and funerals to attend for the next few weeks, dignitaries visiting to make speeches over the next few days.

Will it change anything? No.

Will it calm the nightmares of the witnesses? No.

Will it heal broken hearts? No.

Will it bring loved ones back? No.

Will it wipe out evil or cure mental illness? No.

The Summit County Fair will go down in history as *"the place where it happened"*. The body count rose by three before we left.

Garvis quietly walks to the elevator and pushes the button

for the third floor. "You'll call if you need anything?" he whispers.

I nod and step in when the doors open. "Thanks."

Once inside her apartment, I carry her through the bedroom and into the bath before setting her on the counter. Turning to the tub, I start the water, reach for the bubble bath that sits on the shelf and pour some in. I have no clue what I'm doing – not much of a bath person myself – but a good couple splashes seems reasonable to me. The scent of jasmine fills the air and I pause to breathe in one deep lungful.

Everlee sits on the counter, watching me. I begin by releasing the messy twist of hair at the back of her head and removing her cap, tossing it on the counter. Kneeling in front her, I unlace the boots and gingerly tug each one off and set them to the side. The water and bubbles have reached the proper depth so I turn to shut off the faucet.

"Hop in the tub," I tell her. "I'll get you some dinner."

Stormy grey eyes meet mine as she tilts her head. "You're not going to stay and wash my back?"

Pinning her with a glare that only seems to entertain her and add heat to an already steamy room. "Don't tempt me."

She yanks the T-shirt up and off her head, leaving her in the sports bra. "If you change your mind, you know where to find me."

The bathroom door slams me behind me as I pull it shut and call out, "Dinner will be waiting."

Chapter 17

Everlee

As I lay back in the tub of bubbles, I bask in the feel of the warm water soaking muscles I didn't realize ached so much, the scent of jasmine versus the smell of death. I try to rid my head of the vision of bodies on the ground, some on the rides not taken; the smiles taken away, the laughter replaced with a scream, or worse yet ended by silence. I've seen murder scenes – plenty of them – but none like today's. From children to grandparents and every age in between. Never have I been closer to calling for a prescription for sleep aids. Wine shouldn't be my best friend; especially given my mother's history. I've always promised myself I'd be better than that. Wits over wine. Tenacity over tequila. Brains over brandy. Cognition over cognac.

My fingers are prunes and the water is cooling before I push the drain button and rise to my feet to start the showerhead in order to wash my hair.

Three taps on the door are followed by, "Everlee, you okay?"

"Just washing my hair," I tell him. "I'll be done in a few minutes."

"Perfect timing," he returns. "Dinner will be ready in five."

"What are we having?"

"Food. Make it snappy."

Good grief. The man can go from zero to sixty in a millisecond and from soft to grumpy in even less. Admittedly, through it all he never loses that sexy edge that makes you want to run your fingers through his hair or slap him. Something tells me that either one would cause the same reaction though. Eyes that flare before he takes what he wants, but a passion in them that makes me believe he gives as good as he gets. I certainly got a dose of it today.

Oh, that kiss. "I know you better than you think I do, Everlee Remington."

How, Deacon? From watching me work? Knowing how I take my coffee? What kind of pizza I like? Ha! So, you've observed me at work. Kudos to you. The real me was a desperate young woman who needed you by her side so many years ago. She believed you. She believed *in* you.

I shut the faucet off and wring my hair out. Snatching the fluffy towel Deacon laid over the rack, I dry off quickly and throw on a dark tank top and lounge pants. It feels good to be clean. If soap and water worked as well on our brains as it does on our bodies, the world would be a better place.

Padding down the hall back out to the kitchen, I see Deacon at the counter unpacking fish and chips from a restaurant five streets over from my complex. He's poured two tall glasses of ice water, one glass of white wine at my place, and set out the plates and silverware already. He sets the containers of fish and chips at each place and nods. "Sit, eat."

Taking my place on a bar stool, I open one of the containers and plate a piece of fried cod and a few fries as well as three pieces of shrimp. Must admit, it is done to perfection, smells good, and makes my stomach growl.

"Why fish and chips?" I ask.

He proceeds to plate his own without looking over. "What does it look like?"

"What?"

"What does your dinner look like, Everlee?" he asks again.

"Uh," I crinkle my brow, "food?"

"Exactly," he says, stuffing a bite in his mouth.

"Deacon, what am I missing?"

"Any reminders of today. Hope you don't mind dipping your shrimp and fries in tartar sauce. No ketchup or cocktail sauce allowed. I think we've seen enough red to last us a while, don't you?"

Tears well in my eyes before I can stop them. He's either done this a time or two or he put a lot of thought into it. White wine instead of red. Italian could have been a disaster. Thai could have been questionable at best. Chinese could be a reminder of any number of things. A burger any less than well done and rubbery could be a real stomach churner. Many a night I've set down my fork due to a trigger. He chose a colorless yet tasty dinner. He was being considerate and protective.

I slide off my stool and wrap my arms around his neck. "Thank you," I whisper then sniffle against his neck.

He wraps a single arm around my waist and whispers back, "There's a slice of lemon cake in the fridge for you as well. Now sit down and eat before it gets cold."

The glass of wine sits untouched. My stomach has roiled in on itself so many times today, wine doesn't even sound appetizing. We eat in quiet comfort, a few words here and there, but the day has taken its toll. What is there to talk about?

The mother on top of the little girl shielding her body?

The man who died on top of his fiancé so she didn't get shot, but she laid underneath him until we found her?

The carnies who carried no ID, so now we wait until the news spreads and families hopefully come to claim them?

The granddad who shoved his three grandkids in a porta-potty to stay safe? His dead body on the ground in front of it blocking the door. The kids were pretty dehydrated before we found them, but they were alive. Grandpa's mission accomplished.

No, not very good dinner conversation.

"Would you stay with me?" My voice is shaky and weak as I stare at my half empty plate. When he doesn't answer, I find the courage to look up at him and see him biting his bottom lip. That war within finding him once again.

"I . . . uh, Everlee," he says then grimaces. "I'm not sure that's a good idea. I haven't showered. I've gone through my change of clothes and . . ."

"I have a shower! I have a washing machine," I interject quickly. "And you don't have to sleep on the sofa. I have a spare bedroom. I wasn't propositioning you, Deacon. I just don't want to be alone tonight. I've never had a day like this and . . ."

"Everlee . . ."

My shoulders deflate when I realize how desperate I sound and I lift one in resignation. "Unless you have a late date. Maybe that woman on the fairgrounds. Sorry, I didn't think about that. Maybe she needs you tonight."

"Everlee . . ."

"You shouldn't have to babysit me, Deacon," I continue in an effort to hide my embarrassment, my cheeks flushing, my skin growing hot. "I can handle my own. Been doing it for years and . . ."

He places a gentle hand on my shoulder. "Everlee, you need to shut up now. I don't have a date. I'll stay, provided I stay in the spare room. I do need to toss some clothes in the washer and get a shower. Okay?" He rises from his seat and takes the containers to the trash. "And you need to call Theo. He's been lightin' up your phone like a damn Christmas tree."

Finding my phone on the counter half hidden under a dishtowel, I flip it over to see 14 missed calls and numerous missed texts. "Oh God, Theo. I promised to call him. I didn't see the screen light up. I thought my phone was shut off."

He grumbles as he passes to the foyer to grab his duffle bag, "You only silenced it. I flipped it over so we could eat in peace. I'm going to start the laundry and then get my shower. I'll give you some privacy."

I watch him saunter toward the short passageway to the utility room. "Deacon?" He hesitates but doesn't turn around. "Are we going to talk about that kiss this afternoon?"

His chin dips toward his chest and he shakes his head. "No,

we're not. It was a mistake, Everlee. Call Theo, he's waiting."

A mistake? But, he said he meant it and . . .

"Are you going to stay with me?"

"I told you I would."

"And you're always good for your word, aren't you, Deacon?" I snap harshly without thinking, the pain of being forgotten and left behind consuming me, before I snatch my phone off the counter and head for my bedroom. It wouldn't be the first time he left. I survived then, I'll survive it again. Don't let the door hit you in the ass on your way out.

"Hey!" he calls out after me. "What the hell is that supposed to mean?"

"I'm right here, Everlee. I'm not going anywhere". The words play like a reel in my head as if he's whispering them in my ear. A voice so deep I could swim in it, so comforting it felt like a hug. The hand that held mine giving me strength instead of pushing me away. I swear to God he was with me, even when I was unconscious. I woke to the horror that was my mother and the truth – Jonah was dead. The man in the ambulance had simply done his job.

I take a couple minutes to step into my bathroom to splash my face with cold water and gather my composure before calling my best friend. The woman staring back at me in the mirror is tired, worn out, and a bit heartbroken. "Your life is not a fairytale, Everlee," I whisper to her. "And he's not your Prince Charming. Do what you came here for and move on."

"Tell me you're okay." Theo's shaky voice rings in my ears as he answers my call.

"I'm okay, Theo," I reassure him. "Just a shitty day in paradise."

"Alright, sweet cheeks," he says on a deep sigh. "First things first. You know I love you to the moon and back. And now that we've gotten that out of the way," he hesitates, then shrieks, "What in the name of all that is holy were you thinking?!?"

"Theo!" Keith scolds in the background. "Ease up."

I burst into tears. It's been the day from hell – one I don't want to ever relive. I can't even remember the climb up the Ferris wheel. I do remember delivering a baby. I remember holding that little boy and comforting him. I remember the ride down in the firemen's bucket. I remember Deacon telling me how reckless I was.

I remember the kiss. *The mistake.*

"He didn't mean it, Teacup," Keith says lovingly. "We were worried sick."

"A bit pissed dementia dick didn't keep you from doing something so dangerous, too," Theo grumbles.

"Yeah, well," I sniffle. "He's pissed enough at me for all of you."

"He's just doing his job, Evs," Keith defends. "You gave him the slip, didn't you? I would imagine he's pissed at himself as much as anything."

"Speaking of the detective," I say in an effort to change the subject. "What did you find on him?"

"Not a damn thing," Keith replies. "The guy is so clean, he squeaks. Former military with honors who got on with the force when he got out."

"That's it?"

He chuckles. "How much more do you want?"

"Nothing," I grouse. "He'd be a whole lot easier to dislike if I had some ammunition, you know?"

"Baby Girl," Theo scoffs. "Your arsenal is full. You just need to remember which weapon to use. It's not what they're lackin', it's what you're packin'. Have you forgotten everything we taught you?"

"Only a little," I admit. "Keith, how are you coming with the special software I need to go over the footage?"

"Shouldn't be too much longer," he replies confidently. "Sorry about the holdup. I'm hoping it will give you a whole new view and some sharper images, and maybe some answers nobody else has been able to get."

"What is taking so long?" I ask. "It amazes me we have satellites that can scope a license plate number, but getting software to sharpen the view on street cam footage? Like pulling teeth."

"Everlee," he drawls. "We're not talking about tuning a TV screen here. It's government property that I have to sign my life away for. And yes, it's legal, sort of. You're licensed in three states; that proved government enough for them. I just hate the idea of you doing it by yourself."

"You can walk me through it."

He sighs heavily. "That's not what I meant and you know it. We'll figure something out, okay?"

Theo laughs. "Maybe we could get Dudley Do-Right to sit with her."

Inhaling a deep breath with a yawn, I say, "Guys, I'm all out of Everlee. She's checking out for the rest of the night. I haven't even called Gram and I see she's called me half a dozen times."

"How about I call her for you?" Theo offers. "Get her calmed down and you can talk to her tomorrow."

"That would be perfect, Theo," I groan in gratitude. "Better hurry. She's probably asleep in her chair."

"What about Beverage?" he sneers. "Has she given you any grief or cough, cough, indication of concern?"

I roll my eyes, not that he can see it. "She called last night, asking for ten grand for a cruise with her latest shack up."

"What!?!" they holler in unison.

"Yeah," I reply, my voice cracking. "It gets worse though. Said she didn't have any of Jonah's things in her house and since I tossed his ashes in the Gulf, that being out on the water would make her feel closer to him."

"Are you fucking kidding me!" Theo growls.

"Nope, no joke."

"Aw Evs," Keith says sympathetically. "You have got to cut her out of your life, regardless of what Gram says. The woman is poison. We can talk to Gram if you'd like."

"No," I plead. "Don't do that. I'll tell her myself."

"Everlee," Keith whispers. "We love you."

"I know," I whisper back. "I love you too. I'm gonna get some sleep now. We'll talk soon."

"Hey, Evs," Keith adds. "If you want to go climbing again, call me first. I hear the sherpas on Everest are looking for work."

"Not funny, big guy."

"Yes, it was," he laughs. "And you needed it."

"Love you, sweet cheeks." Theo says softly. "Get some sleep."

Chapter 18

Deacon

I wasn't eavesdropping – initially. Fine, I'm lying. I'm a detective, what can I say? Damn glad her floors don't squeak? Two voices coming through loud and clear from the speaker phone in her room made it too hard to resist. Two male voices, and the mention of government property perked my ears. Theo must have a friend over. Where the hell is he anyway? If he were worried about her, he should have been here waiting for her.

So close to walking out the door due to anger, I changed my mind at the last minute. My laundry was in the washer, I'd already showered, standing in the one pair of gym shorts I had that was clean. I could have driven home wearing those, no problem. But I told her I would stay.

Not good for my word? When have I not been good for my word . . . that she knows of? And a date? I don't date, I fuck. At least I used to before she showed up, but I wasn't about to explain that to her. Lydia Cromwell. Best mouth in Summit county. Sucks like a Dyson and swallows like a champ. And there is no mistaking my tattoos. She was so damn easy to ignore with Everlee by my side. Made me wish it had never happened. My replacement T-shirt read SCFT. Summit County Forensics Team. Still untraceable.

Aw shit! The news! Everlee's stunt on the Ferris wheel today has already been plastered on every social media account available and will be national news by morning. Unfortunately, that stunt included me following her climb right behind her. Neither of us did interviews, no matter how many inquiring minds wanted to know, and the media was not allowed on the grounds. They were all kept at the entry and the only videos released were the ones recorded by the assholes on the grounds. But city officials will be releasing our names due to pressure by the media.

The real teeth grinder of my entire evening? The text I got from shithead Striegel with an attached picture of our climb about halfway up. *"Nice vantage point for a view of that ass. Yeah, I might have risked my life too, Gray. Lucky you."*

Lydia Cromwell eventually discovering my true identity means *Duncan Greene* has met his demise and Deacon Gray has lost his location for easy ins and outs. I'll find a new one. Maybe the next county over in the other direction once the story dies down. Possibly *Damien* this time. He was the devil's spawn, wasn't he?

Concession is not my strong point, but I will not chase another man's woman. What was I thinking? Everlee Remington is not mine to have. Hearing her tell Theo she loves him – the sweetness in her voice, the sincerity in his when he returns the sentiment – takes me back to the day I walked out of that hospital. *I should have never left her.*

I also shouldn't have kissed her, because now that I have it's all I can think about. Six fucking years and I never forgot her. I would have killed for her; nearly did. Spencer is lucky to be alive. I should have given Tess my gun and let her do the honors. No one would have held it against her.

When her phone call comes to an obvious close, I step away from the door and walk back to the kitchen to finish cleaning up from dinner – the one short time shared together this evening without interruption. Yes, I had silenced her phone and inadvertently (total lie) covered it with a dishtowel.

I now know what her mother did to her last night. Ten grand for a cruise. Using her brother's death as a weapon. What else has she done to her over the years? And what government property is this guy getting for her? If I had to hear Theo call her sweet cheeks one more time, I was going to go out of my damn mind.

Dudley Do-Right. *Fuck you, Theo.* About as funny as Dementia Dick.

Sherpas on Everest. *Glad you can laugh. I'm still shaking.*

Who the hell is Gram? *If she has a grandmother here, why wasn't she called when Everlee was in the hospital?*

"I can get those," she says, stepping up behind me to collect the silverware from the counter. "I had to call him before he started calling the state police. He's kinda like that."

"Saw the video, did he?" I ask, sharper than I mean to but jealousy is something I've never dealt with and apparently I suck at hiding it. I snatch the silverware up before she can. "I got this."

She reaches for the untouched glass of wine and before she can tip it back, I drop the silverware and place two fingers on the underside of the glass to keep it from spilling and my other hand on hers. Our eyes lock, neither of us edging the glass forward or back. I'm not challenging her; rather pleading. You can't wash away the dirt and grime with anything more than soap. You cannot flush away the pain with alcohol. You can, however, replace the pain with pleasure, counteract the sad with happy. Still trying to figure it out myself, but I will not watch her go down that rabbit hole. I've seen too many others lose themselves in artificial means of trying to numb their senses in order to deal. I'm the one who put her drunken ass to bed last night. She's stronger than that. I'll take her to a 24-hour gym if she needs to release some pent-up energy – since apparently I won't be taking her to bed.

She slowly releases her grip on the glass and I take it to the sink, emptying it into the drain. "So much for that," she grunts and rolls her eyes. "I'm going to bed. Do you want to tuck me in?"

I grind my teeth a little harder, the pain in my jaw a good reminder how many times I've done it already today. "Where's Theo, Everlee?"

She scrunches her nose the tiniest bit. "Theo's in Chicago."

"Ah, long distance relationship," I state out loud as if solving the puzzle. No wonder he wasn't here waiting for her.

Her mouth quirks and her eyes light with mischief. "In a

sense."

"And this gives you open license to . . .?" I narrow my eyes in question. When she doesn't respond, I ask, "Does he know that I'm staying here?"

"I might have neglected to mention that." She lifts one shoulder and grins. "Do you want me to call and get his permission?"

This is not my Everlee Remington. She's tired, exhausted. She wouldn't be a cheater. I scrub my hand over my face and heave a sigh of frustration. *I told her I would stay. It's past midnight. Six hours and I'll be gone; having kept my word. I'm good for my word . . . or will be this time. I owe her.*

"Go to bed, Everlee. I'm going to put my clothes in the dryer. I have a lot to do tomorrow and court again on Monday. I'll be out of your hair early in the morning."

Her brow pinches as she protests, "You're not in my hair, Deacon. I asked you to stay. If you don't want to, just say so."

"Everlee, please," I whisper, a few breaths short of begging. If she doesn't walk away, I may end up doing what I want now but will regret later. She isn't mine to have. "Please go to bed. I'll be here through the night. Okay?"

She looks dejected but nods slowly before she walks down the hall and closes the bedroom door behind her; the barrier feeling like a concrete wall.

Swear to God this is going to be the longest fucking six hours of my life.

* * *

"Deacon?" Her breathy, soft whisper comes from the doorway where she stands and waits, a soft light behind her from the hallway that makes her look ethereal.

I shoot up in bed, startled to find myself in a strange room. Normally, I'm more aware of my surroundings, but after so little sleep last night and the day of horrors, my mind is somewhere between half dead and uncomfortably numb. My muscles feel like they've gone three rounds with a sumo wrestler, and suddenly

Allman Brothers' "Whipping Post" is echoing through my head. Yes, it's my go-to. Therapy.

"Everlee?" My voice is raspy from the dust and dirt breathed in today and my eyeballs feel like they're being rubbed with sandpaper every time I blink.

"Can I come in?"

"Sure," I reply, throwing back the sheet and sitting up. "You okay?"

Her voice is weak and she sniffles as she makes her way to the bed. "Can I stay in here with you?"

O-kay, I'm awake now. "In here, with me?"

Her attempt at humor is admirable, but it comes out more a half sob. "Roscoe's waterbed is too small and he hogs all the blankets."

I can't help but chuckle as I slide back into the bed as far away as I can get and lift the sheet. "Come on. Don't know about being a blanket hog and I can't guarantee I don't snore, but I'll do my best."

She lays down on the middle of her half of the queen size bed, facing away from me, and tucks the pillow under her head. "Thank you," she whispers.

I lie down on my back, stiff as a board, as far away as I possibly can. "Did you have a bad dream?"

"No. Just couldn't sleep."

"Can I do anything for you?"

"You already did, Deacon." She hunkers down into her pillow deeper and murmurs softly, "You stayed." A few seconds later I swear I hear "This time."

It could have been a puff of air, a small whistle between her teeth, a tiny hum. Most likely penance though, because the slice of guilt it shoots through my chest is unyielding.

I had told her I wasn't going anywhere – but I did.

Tonight, I told her I would stay – so I will. One last time.

Tomorrow will be a new day and I can start over. Everlee Remington is not mine to have. Never was and never will be. She's in love with Theo what's-his-name from Chicago. Duncan Greene, construction worker, will rise again – literally and figuratively – in *Harbor* county. Or was that Damien?

* * *

My dream has me so lost in ecstasy, I don't want to open my eyes. Soft, luscious curves, the scent of jasmine filling my nose as I drop my chin to caress the silky skin of her shoulder with my mouth. My dick is so hard it aches as my hips tilt forward against . . . Oh shit!

I slide away from Everlee as quickly and cautiously as I can, trying hard not to wake her. At some point in the night I had not only moved close but had wrapped around her like a second skin; spooning her from behind. She's a magnet and unfortunately, I've got an aching piece of steel seeking a home this morning.

"I already felt it, Deacon," she says with amusement in her raspy voice as she looks over her shoulder at me. "Good morning to you too."

Rolling over to sit up with my back to her, I grumble, "Pretty sure you studied biology. Morning wood. Normal reaction, Everlee."

"The same normal reaction as your mistake, Deacon?" she quips. "Like the kiss you refuse to discuss?"

Running a fast hand through my hair and marching toward the door, I glance back for one last look at the woman lying in the same bed I was in. "Just like that."

Stepping into the bathroom, I lock the door, take a quick piss – which is not easy when you're hard as stone – wash my hands, and run my fingers through my extreme bedhead. I take an extra minute to splash some cold water on my face and plan a strategy for a fast exit: grab a T-shirt, stuff my clothes in the duffel, slip on my boots, and run like hell. Maybe I can transfer districts. The captain and Vic will keep Striegel away from her. I may have to see her once in a while, but I wouldn't be in the same building every day. I stare at the face in the mirror and whisper my resolve, "Make her hate you as much as you hate yourself."

Somebody's Someone

Finding Everlee in the kitchen preparing coffee, I walk past her and head for the utility room. Popping open the dryer door, I grab my laundry and stuff it inside the duffel, sans one T-shirt that I slip over my head. The wrinkles smooth out immediately with the tight fit over my chest – as if I care. My six o'clock plan went right out the window once I realized we'd slept until eight this morning. Don't know if it was the exhaustion or the total bliss of holding my sweet Everlee for the first – and last – time. And now it's time to get back on the Deacon train – aka be an ass, keep my distance, pretend she doesn't exist.

"Do you want some coffee?" Everlee asks as I make my way toward the door.

"Can't," I reply, slipping a foot into my boot. "Got a lot to do today. Court in the morning and probably a lot of answers to give for yesterday. Be ready. I doubt the bosses are going to be too happy about your little climbing stunt and the press is probably going to be on a headhunt." I shoot her a stern glare. "It's what happens when you don't follow protocol."

She scowls, and I see the same fire in her eyes from our first journey out on a call – the woman in the storm drain. I see a sliver of the strong and inimitable Everlee Remington returning. Her mother won't be back to bother her – I'll get the no contact order done this week. Forged signatures aren't that hard to come by. She'll become focused on her brother's case again. I know she collected (stole) information from his casefile in the records room. I'll focus harder on her brother's case as well so hopefully she can get the hell out of here and go back to Chicago and she and Theo don't have to be long distance anymore.

"How do you do that?" she whispers as if fascinated.

"Do what?"

"Go from being a decent human being to an absolute ass in two seconds flat?"

"Because I'm a dick, Ms. Remington," I say flatly and open the door. "And we all know a dick is a dick." I turn my head slowly and narrow my eyes. "But I don't dip mine where it doesn't belong and I'm not a cheater. Go call Theo. I hear phone sex can work during times of absence.”

Her eyes nearly bulge from their sockets before she shrieks, “You pompous ass! Theo and I aren’t . . .” Her words are lost to me as I don’t let her finish, slamming the door before she can. The last thing I do hear is the sound of her coffee cup shattering against it behind me. It’s over. I can go back to fucking without conscience . . . or commitment.

Damn, I hope she remembers to feed Roscoe.

Chapter 19

Everlee

Stalling for time and the energy it will take to talk to Gram, I clean up the mess I created by pitching my coffee cup at the door. It was my favorite cup too!

Sticks and stones may break their bones, but gloves will always protect me.

A customized cup Theo had made for me upon the end of fellowship and before my departure from Chicago. Handwashed every time I used it, carefully placed on the countertop waiting for the next pour. My temper got away from me and as I gather the broken pieces and place them in the trashcan through blurred vision, I've never felt more akin to an inanimate object than I do right now. *Broken.*

"Go stick your dick wherever you want, Deacon," I mumble to myself as I scrub down the remaining spots of coffee from the wall. "Call the blonde from the fair. You probably don't know her either. And FYI, you jackass, your bosses aren't my bosses and can't touch me. I work for the state of Louisiana." I stand from the last of my task and walk toward the kitchen sink to rinse the cloth. "If the state decides to do away with me, so be it. I've got the footage I need and Keith has the software. You assholes haven't solved anything in six years. I'll solve Jonah's case on my own and go back to Chicago where I have real friends, real people. Screw you all."

"Hey Gram," I say sheepishly when she answers. I've never questioned the true reception I'll receive when I call her. She loves me, always has. She's been the one solid throughout my entire life. The rock when my mother would roll. It wasn't Jonah's and my fault we hoped that roll would be off a cliff.

Her deep sigh accompanied by a hum of relief indicates forgiveness in its highest form. Not sure if it's for putting the fear of God in her or my negligence in her calling her yet, but . . .

"I don't know if lettin' you climb that big ol' oak tree like a monkey was a good or bad thing, child. But seein' as you birthed a baby and saved a little boy and his mama, all I'm gonna say is I'm glad you're safe." She hesitates. "Nope, changed my mind, that's not all. Everlee Remington, you ever do anythin' like that again and I'm gonna tan your hide."

Apparently, Theo and Keith have talked her down. I expected an earful.

I sniffle and chuckle at the same time, wiping a tear away. "I love you, Gram."

She sucks in a short indignant sniff, though I know there's a handkerchief at her nose, and says, "Yeah, well love me better and let me meet our maker first. Not that you didn't give my ticker a good run for its money. Now, when are you comin' to have tea with me?"

We chat for a good half hour before we're done and she asks for details – of the rescue, not the climb – and we bid each other goodbye, the promise of tea together in the near future, and a heartfelt "I love you".

My rock when my mother rolled – in the sheets with her flavor of the weekend.

There's an army green T-shirt in the back of the dryer when I open it to toss in a load from the washer. Deacon must have missed it due to his rush to get out of here this morning. I remove it and hold it to my nose. It smells like my laundry. Not a trace of him left behind. I hold it up to my shoulders and see it falls to mid-thigh. It's soft, big, loose. I'm tempted to burn it, but I think I just found a new sleep shirt.

I'm mad, but I'm hurt more than anything. He could have just asked me who Theo was rather than assumed. He kissed me, damnit! And what a kiss it was. It felt real, as if he didn't just want it but needed it. However, deep down I needed him to remember me. But he doesn't, and maybe that will make it easier to stay on task and remember why I came back here.

Now, to work up the courage for a trip to the Blue Velvet Lounge where Jonah's bandmates are playing next weekend. I don't have their phone numbers anymore or I would give them a heads-up. My last communication was with them when we placed Jonah's ashes in the Gulf. I've read their statements over and over, as well as all the others taken at the scene. It's a wonder the Hasselback PD kept them. There's a glitch in the street cam footage that still has me baffled. It cuts out in the midst of that asshole Dylan Spencer shoving me to the ground and resumes a short time later with him on the ground after a bystander attacked him. The background of the footage is fuzzy, but my hope is Keith's software can help.

* * *

Monday morning brings a wash of anxiety I did not see coming. I knew my actions over the weekend were going to bring repercussions in some form; Deacon had warned me of that, but I did not see this coming. I'm walking out the door of my building toward my car in the parking lot when . . .

"Everlee Remington!" A man bolts toward me from across the street with a cameraman running beside him. Behind them is a group of approximately ten other people rushing toward me, all shouting my name and bombarding me with questions so fast I don't understand any of them.

The next sound that greets all of us is a shotgun being cocked and the growl of James, our daytime doorman. He's an enormous black man with a heavy southern accent and a friendly smile with a laugh so deep it rattles your bones. But today . . .

"You take one more step into this *private* parkin' lot and

you boys are gonna be givin' me reason to shoot ya'll. Go on, git!"

When they push forward, ignoring his warning, he fires one shot in the air. The reporters freeze in their tracks. "You got a hearin' problem?" James asks, smirking, then points his gun in their direction. "Next one's gonna land in somebody's ass if ya'll don't git outta here." He looks to me and tilts his head toward the building. "Inside, Miss Everlee."

Once back in the lobby, James holds his hand out. "You gimme your car keys in case my wife calls with an emergency. Otherwise, it ain't goin' nowhere." He hands me a set of keys of his own. "You take my truck. It's out back. The red Ford F150. You have one o' your policemen escort you back home. My wife'll pick me up after work and drive me back in the mornin'. Just leave my keys here at the desk. We gotta git this problem taken care of."

"Y-you're n-not going to get in t-trouble, are you?" I stammer.

"Nope," he answers confidently. "Got a license for the gun and they was trespassin'. Endangerin' one o' my residents."

I nod vigorously. "I'll vouch for you."

His deep booming laugh returns. "I'll let ya know if I need ya. Have a good day, Miss Everlee. You best be gittin' to work."

"Thanks, James," I tell him as I rush for the back door.

"Miss Everlee," he calls out after me. I turn back to see him arching a brow. "Should you run over any reporters if they git in your way, I'll vouch for you too."

Maybe I do have some people here.

* * *

Cora greets me at the front desk as I enter the building and holds out a piece of paper. "'Mornin' Everlee. Captain Garner left this for you."

The pit in my stomach opens a little more. "For me?" I step forward and take the tiny folded scrap into my hand, forgo opening it and make a request instead. "Can I get a lot pass while I'm here? I have a different vehicle for the day and I need to put a tag on it."

"Sure thing." She pulls a tag from the drawer. "Whatcha got?"

I hand her the paper with the info for James' truck, i.e. make, model, plate number. She fills out the tag, holding it in the air, but not handing it over. "Secret for a secret," she says conspiratorially.

"Huh?"

She leans forward and whispers, "Are his abs and tattoos as hot up close and personal as they are on TV?"

Ah, Deacon. They most definitely are. They're even better pressed against your back in bed while there's an impressive erection poking your ass cheeks. They'd be best if he were . . . My cheeks flush hot with embarrassment.

"I'll take that as a yes," she says with a giggle as she fans her face.

"I – uh . . ." I hold up the tag she's finally handed me. "I'd better go put this in the truck before they tow it."

As I'm exiting the building to the parking lot to tag James' truck, Deacon is entering. The courthouse doesn't open until nine, so pretty sure he's checking in first. "Ms. Remington," he mumbles on his way past me.

"Fuck you, Detective Gray," I mutter back. I meant it for his ears only, but as luck would have it, Rodriguez appears out of nowhere.

"Mornin' Miss Everlee," he singsongs with a tip of his chin and an impish smile. Before the door closes behind me, he laughs loudly. "Wifey troubles, Deacon?"

Once back inside and in my lab, I unfold the message from Captain Garner.

Meeting at one o'clock in the conference room. Meet me in my office ten minutes ahead of time. We'll go together.

Lovely.

Annie Mick

Chapter 20

Deacon

When I left Everlee's Sunday morning I had one mission in mind: clear my head, my space, my memories, and everything that had haunted me for the past six years. First on the agenda: Jasmine . . . until I remembered the irreparable damage one person could do to her. *Beverly Remington.* The jasmine could wait.

Finding Beverly was no problem, waking her was a bit of a challenge. To say Beverly Remington is not a morning person is the understatement of the century. Judging by her lackluster and hungover appearance, not only is she a loyal customer of cosmetic companies everywhere, she's a pretty damn good contributor to liquor stores and local establishments as well. She lives in an apartment complex on the south side of the city that has seen its better days. From the looks of her that morning, she has seen hers too.

Answering the door in her half open robe and a scowl on her face, she didn't look too happy to see mine. "What do you want?" she sneered.

"Wanted to make sure I made myself clear, Ms. Remington," I warned her. "You get any ideas about selling a story to the papers or trying to grandstand your daughter after her heroics yesterday, you won't make it to the bank to cash the check." My glare was harsh, but left no room for doubt as I finished, "I will *toss* your body into the Gulf myself and watch as you feed the fishes."

"How nice for my little girl." She laughed bitterly. "Bodyguards wherever she goes. Guess she did learn how to use those assets after all. Sorry, detective but you're a little late. Theo already called and threatened me." She tilted her head and batted mascara crusted lashes. "But if you ever get bored with her . . ."

It took everything in me not to shudder . . . or vomit. One cold, hard stare later and I closed the conversation, "I'd rather roll in pig shit."

I went home after, still feeling the need for a shower. The woman is poison.

Discovering Theo had gotten to her first didn't help my disposition at all either. But did confirm my place in Everlee's life. And hers in mine; *The one that got away.*

* * *

"Deacon, what the hell are you doing? Those are in full bloom!" Dory shrieked from behind me after entering the yard unannounced. Dory is my little sister; six years younger, pain in my ass but lovable, too smart for her own good, and a self-appointed guardian by proxy until I get married. Little does she know, she'll be burying me first. She's as nosy as one of the church bingo ladies, but the difference between Dory and them is she's all ears and no mouth. Good reception, no microphone. Unless, of course, it's me.

I continued another slice into the dirt at the edge of the roots with the spade and forced it deeper with the sole of my boot. I'd already removed three of the shrubs at the back of the yard; only sixteen to go. I could get the whole thing done before day's end; I was sure of it. With each dig of the shovel, I had thought of Theo, his friend on the phone, Dylan Spencer, Striegel, the fireman's proposal, Duncan Greene. The list was endless. My life had been so fucking easy before she showed up.

"Deacon, stop!" Dory grasped my sweaty bicep and yanked hard, making me drop the shovel. "I supplied those, you idiot! Those are primo jasmine shrubs. The crop this year was shit! I couldn't get a new supply if I begged, borrowed, or stole!"

Dory owns one of the most popular floral and landscaping stores in midtown Hasselback. And yes, she's right. She did go out of her way to find me the best, and she did handpick every one of these shrubs. She also taught me how to trim, fertilize, and keep them healthy over the first year they were in so they wouldn't die.

She eyed the gaping holes left from the three I'd already removed and gasped in horror. "Get your ass over there and put my babies back in the ground. You want to throw a temper tantrum, go throw axes or get drunk like normal men do. What the hell is wrong with you!?"

"I don't want them anymore," I grumbled as I reached for the shovel.

She reached for the shovel at the same time and held it back. "Then I will have my crew come out and dig them up properly. I've got buyers that will be more than happy to take them off your hands."

I didn't really want them gone. I wanted her. I'd always wanted her. I never woke up with women. Sunday morning was a first and not only did I not reap any reward, I found out doing the honorable thing hurts like a sonofabitch.

I looked to Dory and grimaced, a plea that only she would understand, "Would you help me put those three back in?"

She rolled her eyes and slapped my arm. "For dinner, a six-pack, and a ride home. Shower first though, you stink."

After we got the last shrub reset and in the ground, she looked at me as if in thought and studied my face. "You ever gonna tell me who she is?"

"Was, Dory," I corrected her. "She's the one that got away. Because your brother's an idiot."

"Got away?" She arched a brow. "Or you let her go?"

Changing the subject in one fell swoop, I asked her, "How does fried chicken sound?"

She gave me one of her typical *you dumbass* looks and shook her head. "Fitting. Go shower. I'll peel the taters."

Annie Mick

* * *

"Gray!" Captain Garner calls out to me as I pass his office Monday morning. My fists are already clenched tight with extra effort being put into keeping them at my sides in lieu of putting one into Rodriguez's jaw. *"Wifey troubles, Deacon?"* But then hearing Everlee utter, *"Fuck you, Detective Gray"* wasn't exactly the icing on a donut either. However, seems my goal was achieved – she hates me.

A few wolf whistles at the front desk might have been funny on any other given day. Not so much today. *Note to self: keep your shirt on.*

I stop at the threshold and lean on the doorframe. "You beckoned?"

"Conference room, one o'clock," he states as if there's no choice.

"I have court at nine."

"Be back by one and we won't have a problem." He tips his chin and smirks.

"I'll let you call Judge Walker and inform him of his time limits this morning. I'm sure he won't mind setting his watch to accommodate." I shrug and grin wryly. "It's not like putting away the criminals should take precedence over a meeting."

He heaves a sigh and rolls his shoulders. "Make it back as soon as you can. Mayor Peters called for it."

"Why?" He simply sits back, arms folded over his chest, and stares at me. I snort laugh. "It was Summit county. Peters has no jurisdiction."

"Roll with it, Gray," he placates. "Let him stomp his feet and get out of our way."

"What about Ms. Remington?"

He shoots me a puzzled look, probably due to my use of her proper name, before saying, "Everlee will be there. I left her a message."

The knot in my stomach twists; the scent of jasmine already filling my nostrils. Thoughts of putting her to bed on Friday after

164

she cried in my arms. Her naked body crossing the hall Saturday morning. That kiss. Waking up wrapped around her on Sunday. I fed her fucking fish! I don't want her to hate me. I want more. I'm not resolved – I'm dissolved . . . into a big fat puddle of Everlee goo.

"Gray?" Garner's brow is furrowed as he stares up at me.

I straighten off the doorframe and nod. "I'll be there, provided I'm out of court on time."

"Check in with me ten minutes before," he orders with all the confidence in the world that I will be back in time. "We'll walk down together."

* * *

My stint in the courtroom this morning is minimal, limited to sworn testimony, and zero direct contact with the lovely Della Marlow, leaving me plenty of time to make it back for the meeting. I would have loved to stick around for the verdict but that is a luxury saved for the prosecutor and those who don't earn a living arresting the assholes in orange who occupy the defendant chairs.

I even find time for my two pieces of leftover fried chicken from the fridge in the breakroom. The dark container wrapped in a hazardous materials bag and labeled "*Stool Sample*" usually guarantees no takers.

The door to Garner's office is closed and while the conversation from inside is muffled, it's pretty clear Everlee is not happy. I rap on the door three times and wait.

"Come on in," Cap hollers.

My intuition rarely lets me down and today is no exception as Everlee turns in her chair and sees me in the doorway, then turns back to Garner and sneers, "What is *he* doing here?"

"Close the door and take a seat, Gray," Garner bypasses her question and orders me. He arches a brow as his eyes flit back and forth between the two of us as soon as we're seated side-by-side, then smirks. "So," he says with a hint of amusement, "I take it the honeymoon is over. What did you do, Deacon?"

Everlee shoots to her feet, nearly tripping over me to get to the door. "I don't need Detective Gray to defend my actions to the mayor. Not that he would." She scowls at me. "He doesn't *dip* into things he doesn't belong in. I can make a phone call if I need help."

She slams the door behind her before Garner glares at me and shouts, "What the hell did you do, Gray!?"

I breathe a pitiful huff before standing and turning for the door. Keeping my back to him, I hesitate before turning the knob and go with the truth. "Walked away when I should have stayed."

Chapter 21

Everlee

"Come on, come on. Pick up," I whisper into the phone as I stand in the ladies room. Mayor Peters threatened me the last time we spoke. I anticipated a phone call, maybe a scolding email, but a meeting? I can barely stand watching the jackass in a press conference on TV.

"Everlee," Keith answers, his voice laced with concern. "Everything okay?"

"Not really," I whisper back. "In need of a 9-1-1 favor. Rupert Peters, mayor of Hasselback." Keys start clicking in the background immediately. "He's been out for blood since I got my funding for lab equipment. I've got a meeting with him in seven minutes because of Saturday. He threatened me when I got the funding, Keith. Said he was going to find out who my friends were on city council. I'm afraid he may have found a lot more than that. These people don't know who I am. All those records were sealed, but if he dug deep enough, I'll never have access to what I need to solve Jonah's case."

"Settle down, Teacup. You're an employee of the state," he reminds me. "It's not like he can fire you."

"N-no," I stammer, "b-but he c-can tell everyone who I really am. Th-they think I-I'm from Chicago."

"Everlee Remington," he says sternly. "Four in, five out

right now. Do it with me. Ready? One, two, three . . .”

We breathe together, four counts in, five counts out, slowly. It’s a military tactic he taught me a long time ago.

“Do it again,” he instructs gently. So, we do. “Better?”

“Yeah.”

“Keep your phone handy. Go to the meeting with your head held high. You are Everlee Remington, warrior.” He chuckles. “If you want, we can add carnie ride climber to your resume.”

“You’re not funny,” I sniffle.

“I’m kinda funny.” His deep soto voice is comforting as he finishes, “I love you. Now, go knock ‘em on their asses.”

The door to the conference room is open and everyone sits at the rectangular table; Peters on one side, facing Garner and Deacon on the other, waiting for me. Mayor Peters rolls his eyes and heaves a deep exaggerated sigh as if he’s been inconvenienced by my two-minute tardiness. “Nice of you to finally join us, Ms. Remington. For someone who showed the extreme flexibility skills and speed as you did on Saturday, I would think the least you could do was show up on time today.”

“Ah, well,” I say unapologetically as I take a seat next to Captain Garner. “I’m here now. What can I do for you?”

“We’re here to discuss your behavior on Saturday.” He places his elbows on the table and folds his hands together as he leans forward. “I think you’re a liability to the city.”

“Now wait a minute,” Captain Garner fumes beside me.

“It’s okay, Captain. I’ve got this,” I reassure him. “Mayor Peters, I don’t work for the city, I work for the state of Louisiana. I also locum for two others due to a severe shortage of professionals in my field of work. Why we’re having this meeting is beyond me as what happened on Saturday was in Summit county. The only thing I’ve heard from the mayor of Turnstile was a phone call yesterday to thank me for helping. How about you tell me why you’re even here.”

“Because you live in my city,” he sneers, then lifts his eyebrows in a *gotcha* glare. “The city you’ve found an abundant amount of funds in.”

Still unsure if he's referring to his beige office and squeaky chair or my history, I take my chances. "Your city?" I lean forward and narrow my eyes. "I would think as mayor, your best interests would be to protect your citizens. Why didn't you protect me from the reporters staked out by my home this morning?"

Deacon acknowledges me for the first time since I stepped in the room. "There were reporters at your place this morning?"

My smirk feels oh so good as I answer, "The threat of buckshot in their asses did a pretty good job of holding them off."

"You threatened someone with a gun, Ms. Remington?" Mayor Peters inquires as a sinister, smug look crosses his face, and the moment his eyes meet mine, I know he's found what he was looking for. Sealed records or not, it won't matter how the information is released, only that it is. He arches a wicked brow in challenge. "Sounds like you gave those reporters a reason to dig into your *past*."

My phone buzzes in my lab coat pocket and my heart pounds in my chest as Deacon jumps to his feet and he and Captain Garner yell in unison, each one expressing their disdain, "Did you just threaten her?" and "What the hell are you playing at?"

"Louisiana is an open carry state, Mayor Peters," I add. "It's not like I shot them."

Phone in hand, I smile to myself as I open Keith's message. *"This ought to do it, Angel."* Two links – each one holding a goldmine of information, or rather, guarantee of anonymity. Blackmail at its finest and a jail cell for him once I find what I came for.

Keith Sommers, you are my hero!

"Are you done playing with your phone, Ms. Remington?" Mayor Peters huffs, outraged my attention is not on him.

"Gentlemen," I say nonchalantly, addressing the captain and Deacon. "Could you give me a minute with the mayor? Alone."

"No," Deacon snaps harshly from above, still on his feet. "I don't trust him."

"Neither do I," I reply smugly, my eyes fixed on the mayor. "Stand outside the door. I'll call if I need you."

Annie Mick

After another protest and much hesitation as well as a soft reassuring grip on my shoulder from the captain, they leave. I hold up my phone, screen facing the repulsive asshole across the table from me, the first picture prominently on display. The gray pallor his skin has turned in a nanosecond is delightful. Turning the phone back to myself, I flick to the next disgusting display of true debauchery. Huh. Who would have thought our own Mayor Peters was into BDSM? Full costume, no less. Not kidding.

"I could have them blown up if you'd like. Give you a better view. A good 8x10 should do it." I smirk. "Pretty sure it would do for the general public."

"Where did you get those?" he grinds through a clenched, ticking jaw.

"What? These?" I nearly singsong, clicking out of that link and into the next one showing receipts of deposits. "That was just a warmup. Your sexual proclivities would only provide short term shock value. "However," I hold up the phone once more so he can see the screen, "I believe interest in your offshore bank accounts might be significantly piqued. Tell me, Mayor, how would you explain deposits of fifty thousand dollars a month for the last year on your yearly salary of just over a hundred thousand?"

Have you ever seen gray pallor turn green? Kinda cool, really. Nothing I'd paint on my walls at home, mind you, but it's a good look on a crooked politician who realizes he's just been handed his ass on a silver platter.

I stand from my chair and hover over the table, leaning toward him, my eyes flaring with hatred. "As far as my *flexibility and speed* on Saturday? I earned it, mayor. Took years and a lot of work to heal. The money I got from the lawsuit? It paid for the repairs from the damage one of your officers inflicted. The rest of it? My education. Lose the information you've obtained. Go back to your plushy office and learn to love beige. Maybe use a bed in a cheap hotel instead of the backseat of a fancy car for your depraved antics."

He only narrows his eyes and stiffens his shoulders. *Stubborn bastard.*

Somebody's Someone

Standing upright and straightening my cuffs after I pocket my phone, I grin. "I could use one more steamer in the lab as well as two more microscopes. I'll send the requisition form soon. I expect immediate approval and delivery even sooner."

His eyes are nearly black as he stares at me. "You think you've won?"

"Yeah, I do." I tilt my head, praying my casual indifference is convincing. "Should anything happen to me, Mayor Peters, not only will all of this information get out but be rest assured your wife be spared any of those pesky expenses of an autopsy, because there will be no body left behind." I grin devilishly. "My kind of friends aren't on the city council. I brought back more than just an education from Chicago."

Ever hear of a Kodak moment? I don't need a picture though; the look on his face is imprinted on my brain. Pure terror. *Mission accomplished.*

Getting one last dig in before I leave, I scratch my upper lip. "You've got a little white stuff under your nose. You don't strike me as a powdered donut kind o' guy. Your aim should be more precise. That shit gets expensive. Don't they do drug testing at city hall?"

Sure enough, the back of his hand flies to his face and he swipes under his nose and sniffs.

I roll my eyes.

Such a tool.

Captain Garner and Deacon may as well have had their ears pressed against the door they're so close as I exit the room. It's a wonder they didn't fall back inside.

"You okay?" Garner asks with a brow furrowed so deeply, the hair meets in the middle.

"All good," I answer cheerily, ignoring the hand Deacon extends, and head back to my lab on wobbly legs I can only hope they don't notice.

Just another day in paradise.

How I wish I had someone to hug, maybe a high-five to slap, someone to share this victory with me. But what is my victory? My past here won't be revealed? My secret is safe? Would anyone care? Would Deacon even remember that night? Really, what difference would it make?

Jonah. Jonah would be the difference. Solve the case, Everlee!

I'd never woken up in a man's arms before Sunday morning. I'm not a poster child for purity, but the very few one-night stands I'd had during my early college years were more like half-night stands because I always left before sunrise. I had a dozen or so dates while in Chicago but I was so engrossed in school, nothing else mattered. Not to mention the physical therapy, the plastic surgery, and the scars. And they were simply dates; nothing more. I honestly can't remember the last time I was romantically kissed before Saturday.

But he blew it. He didn't ask about Theo; he assumed I'm a cheater. No, Deacon, that would be my mother. The reason Jonah and I didn't have a father. I was six years old when he left, Jonah was only four. I remembered everything, Jonah remembered nothing. It was for the best.

Pulling my phone from my pocket, I send a text to Keith.

"Don't think the mayor will be bothering me again. Thank you. I am so lucky to have you in my life."

It takes only a few minutes but my phone buzzes with what I need.

"I'm the lucky one, Everlee. One phone call away. Love you."

Three solids in my life; Theo, Keith, and my Gram. How many people even have one? Sheer luck sent me two of them. Maybe I can get my Gram to move up north with me. I'm here on a mission and need to remember my goals. I'm not sure my intent was ever to stay. Hasselback let me down six years ago. I'm using them as a means to meet my goal. There's a killer out there with my brother's name on his back, and I won't rest until I find him. The man in the ambulance was a silly little approach to wile away the hours when I was bored. The fantasy of a dumb, young girl who believed yet another lie. And now that I've met him, I once again

Somebody's Someone

am reminded how forgettable I am.

Maybe that's why it's so important to me that even the dead know they were, at some point in time, *somebody's someone.*

Chapter 22

Deacon

The door slams against the wall as I push it hard, reentering the room we'd been banned from as the mayor and Everlee had their private chat. "What the hell is your problem with Everlee Remington?!"

"Deacon," Garner mutters a warning next to me.

Peters smirks. "Detective Gray. Perhaps you've forgotten who you're talkin' to."

"Haven't forgotten a thing," I spit through the clenched jaw that hasn't eased up since we got kicked out of here ten minutes ago. "Again, what is your problem with Everlee? What happened on Saturday has nothing to do with you."

His eyebrows lift and his smug expression is so damn tempting to punch. "Seems you're a bit of a ride climber yourself, detective." He holds up one finger and smirks. "And you are a city employee which makes you my business."

"Don't you even start." Garner's low growl comes from my side before he steps forward and leans over the table, sliding it forward into the mayor's midsection, hands fisted on the top, making Peters slide his chair back and gasp. "You want the rain of hell down on you, Peters? Try goin' after two employees who saved three people on Saturday. The public ain't gonna give a damn how it was done. The reporters will eat you alive. I'll see to it myself. You will be out of office before your secretary can get off her knees. I got one of the highest ranking police districts in the state." He lifts a hand and points a hard finger, mere inches from Peters' face. His voice is low, the depth of which leaves the mayor's eyes wide. "You're gonna find dealin' with the devil is easier than dealin' with me. Stay the hell away from my people. Best stay the hell away from Ms. Remington too, because she is one of my people. Get outta my building. We're done here."

Annie Mick

Less than a minute later the room is clear, the mayor gone; having shoved paperwork loosely into his briefcase and storming out the door. Captain Garner and the police commissioner work closely together; they're tight-knit, good friends. I do believe the mayor has met his match.

Garner and I stand in the hall watching Peters' retreat before he looks to me and releases a deep sigh and shakes his head. "Let's get back to work."

"Thanks for that," I tell him.

He pats my shoulder. "No thanks needed. That guy's an asshole."

"By the way, it was actually four, Cap."

"What?"

"She saved four."

He scrunches his brow, puzzled. "People?"

I nod and chuckle. "Yeah, people. She spotted a young man wearing camouflage hiding in a tree. All the kids are wearing that shit these days like street clothes. Who knows what might have happened to him if he'd been spotted by a sharpshooter. He climbed that tree to get away from the shooter. He was terrified. She saw him when nobody else did."

His brow furrows deeper. "The kid okay?"

"I don't think anybody's gonna be okay after that. He was there with his buddies celebrating before they were supposed to leave for bootcamp next week together." I feel an old, unwanted, familiar burn behind my eyes. It's been years. Some came home, some didn't. But I've never seen a situation where they never got to go.

"Where did the others hide?" he asks.

"Can't hide when you're dead, Cap." I slap him on the shoulder and head back to the squad room.

"Wait!" he calls out after me. "Why am I only hearing about this now?"

I turn back slowly and shoot him a wry look. "Because it was Everlee. She hates attention. And if she doesn't find another occupation, she's going to be ruined." I pocket my hands and stare at the floor for a moment before I meet his gaze once more. "Nothing that pure belongs in our world."

The moment the words leave my mouth, I know I've made a mistake. Those are my thoughts, my feelings. I know her weaknesses, her strengths, how she takes her coffee, what she likes on her pizza, how she feels in my arms.

I fed her fucking fish!

He didn't see her in that warzone on Saturday. He didn't watch her shed tears over people she'd never met, mourn for lost souls because they wouldn't see the light of the next day, whisper words of apologies she didn't owe them as if they could hear her, wish them well on their new journey as she tagged their bodies and covered their faces.

Hell, maybe she could find a new job as a professional eulogizer. Is there such a thing? She'd be perfect at it. She's a stranger to no one. Most of those carnies don't even have homes, much less families. Don't tell Everlee that though – she'd be back there collecting their remains and offering her services for memorials because *"Everyone is somebody's someone"*. Little does she know.

"Gray." Cap snaps me out of my thoughts and eyes me suspiciously. "Something happen between you and her that I should know about?"

I nod slowly and let out a pitiful huff. "Yeah, I fed her fish."

His nose scrunches so tightly it looks painful. "What did you do, kill it?"

Turning to walk away, I mutter more to myself than him, "Nope, just told him the truth."

I'm in love with her.

"I'm gettin' too old for puzzles, Gray," he calls out after me.

"Try shuffleboard," I toss back over my shoulder. "I hear the senior crowd loves it."

"Smartass!"

* * *

Annie Mick

Three hours later, Garner calls my name from the doorway of the squad room. "Bring your jacket. Let's go."

It's one hour from quitting time. I'm tired, pissed off, have just finalized the paperwork for another of the city's finest, and wearing a nice bruise on my rib cage from a cheap shot the asshole took with his elbow during a struggle in a takedown an hour ago. A raging woman charging toward you with a baseball bat can distract you from the task at hand. The flying bat that landed on my back didn't feel too good either. Hurts like a sonofabitch, actually. It wasn't me that shot her, but it was a fellow officer. Therefore, the paperwork was a bit extraneous compared to the usual simple arrest.

"What?" I ask impatiently once in the hall, expecting to be sent for another inquiry over a cop simply doing her job.

He dips his chin and eyes my midsection. "Ribs okay?"

I roll my eyes and grind through a clenched jaw, more pissed at myself for being distracted than the pain itself, "They're fine."

"Really ought to get that checked."

"I'm fine," I reiterate. Omitting assault charges on a dead woman only seemed reasonable. The bat flew out of her hands when she got shot. Besides, it also saves me more nagging from Garner to seek medical attention for some bruises.

"Have it your way. Until your stubborn ass follows strict protocol, you'll be doin' it my way." He holds out a slip of paper. "Not quite desk duty, but it'll keep you off the streets. Forensics van just took off. 85th has a body out in the sticks. Everlee's with the team in the van so I want you to go meet her at the scene."

"What the hell!? Off the streets!? My ribs are fine!" I snap harshly, too worn out and pissed off to hold back the frustration I've been battling over Everlee since Sunday morning. "And what the hell does this have to do with Everlee? If she's already on her way and the 85th is there, she's got what she needs."

He stuffs the paper into the pocket of my shirt before he taps over it as if to ensure its placement. "You work as a team until I say otherwise. Let me know when you're ready to see the doc. Play nice, Deacon. Hope you showered today. She is to ride back here with you." He smirks as he jams his thumb toward the exit. "Move it, before I poke you a few times myself to see if you flinch."

I could argue, but it would be pointless. "The sticks" isn't exactly the seedy part of Hasselback – we have much worse – but it is on the lower end of the income scale. The houses run in various need of repair; three in a row meticulously kept while the next two look more like crack houses, etc. A house number means nothing until you happen upon it. One never knows what they'll run into.

As I reach the door to the parking lot, Garner's voice booms behind me. "Parnell, my office!"

Well now, there's a balance for my mood. Pissed off for me and sorry for Vic. At least I get out in the fresh air. I should probably send him an invite for a beer after work. If I had any idea when that 'after' might be, I would. But then, Vic has a wife, a family and a home to get to. He'll be good. I'll see him tomorrow.

* * *

It's a small brick ranch house at the end of Perch Street. Yellow crime scene tape already cordoning off the area from the borders of the front yard extending all the way around the side to the alley out back. Two patrol units are in front of the house while another two units take up camp in the alley, and the forensics van sits out front. I park behind the van after flashing my credentials at the stop point and hop out.

"I'm here with Everlee Remington," I tell the approaching officer at the scene. "The forensics investigator."

His brows rise and fall a few times and his eyes widen as he grins and points his thumb toward the house. "You mean that fine piece of as . . ."

"Finish that statement and you'll be eatin' your teeth."

It's a five-second stare down, his in shock, mine in unmistakable anger, before he clears his throat and mumbles, "She's inside."

I step past him toward the front door, noting the band on his finger. He's not that young, probably my age – shouldn't be that stupid. Pausing because, well – I can't help myself, I turn back. "Is that a wedding ring?"

He lifts his left hand as if he's forgotten what's on it. "Yeah."

"Remember why it's there, asshole. Do better."

My urge to punch him is strong. I'm well aware what a fine ass it is. I've seen it naked and I've had flashbacks ever since that morning over and over. *More please*. I enjoy the female form as much or more than any guy I know, but that asshole is married. It's no wonder the divorce rate is what it is. Yes, I've been a hit it, quit it, and never commit to it kind of guy. But for the first time in my life, I don't want to be anymore.

I would commit to forever with Everlee and never look back . . . or anywhere else. She will always be the most beautiful woman I've ever seen, but it's her heart that makes her who she is. But I can't fight for what isn't mine to have. I've had to concede to a man a thousand miles away because she's in love with him. I want her to be happy. So why does her happiness have to make me so fucking miserable?

Chapter 23

Everlee

Slipping on my usual white latex gloves on the way, I cross the lawn to the front door of the small, somewhat rundown, brick home in the lower income neighborhood known as "the sticks". It wasn't always like this. The older folks usually settled here for an easier lifestyle with low maintenance homes. The closest thing to an affordable lock-and-leave you could get with friendly neighbors and still have a stash in the bank. But with time and aging, things changed. Quick buyers snatched up properties and turned them into rentals. The ones who sensed what was coming and could afford to leave, moved out. The ones who couldn't, stayed behind without choice and made the best of a bad situation.

"You must be Ms. Remington," the grimacing, middle-aged detective standing on the small front porch says as he scratches the back of his head.

"That'd be me." I smile and raise my hand, but don't offer it as I've already gloved up. "You can call me Everlee."

"Detective Miller," he says with a nod. "We haven't moved anything. The old lady's body is in the living room. The neighbor called in because she hadn't seen her out in the yard in a few days and wanted us to check on her. Looks like natural causes. No bruising, no signs of a struggle, she's old, but . . ." he hesitates then shrugs. "We'll know more after the coroner takes her in."

"Okay," I say slowly as we enter the house through the rickety screen door and already opened front door behind it. I scout out the surroundings, seeing not much more than a substandard elderly living style – other than the body lying on the floor. Floral furniture from the sixties covered in plastic, ivory drapes on the windows, gold carpeting that has to be more than a few decades old but surprisingly in good condition. The ceilings are peeling but not water stained. The walls could most definitely use a coat – maybe ten – of new paint. Taking the few steps necessary to reach the kitchen, I note the cupboards are painted an avocado green and some of the doors hang loose or crooked as if ready to fall off the hinges with the next opening. Harvest gold appliances. There is linoleum on the floor; a pattern similar to one in my Gram's kitchen when I was a child, shortly before she had it replaced, and it was old at that time. The small dining room houses a yellow Formica table with vinyl covered chairbacks and seats of a slightly faded, but same color. On a few shelves there is a scattered collection of hens made from red and blue Bullicante glass. On the wall hangs a custom made rack to hang spoons collected from individual states. Apparently at one time or another, the lady traveled as there are a total of 37.

"Is there a specific reason you called for forensics, detective?"

"What we need you to see is back here," he informs me as he waves his hand toward the back of the kitchen where a door stands open and uniformed officers are gathered together in a small group.

The floor creaks beneath our feet on our way as if stability may be in question. "Is there a basement?"

He shakes his head as we continue to what obviously is a tiny back porch. "Just a crawlspace. We've already checked it. Just some old paint cans. Probably petrified by now. Haz mat teams will be out to clean those up tomorrow. I think you're goin' to be a lot more interested in what we got back here."

There's a large, mint green, deep freezer against the north wall of the tiny porch, and an electric air purifier in the corner, but otherwise the room is empty and devoid of windows, yet the walls are a bright sunny yellow color. The floor is meticulously clean and looks as if it's been scrubbed regularly. No cobwebs in the corners, none in the upper corners of the ceiling. No musty odor. Unusual for a room like this.

"What are we looking at?" I ask one and all standing in the room.

One of the uniforms grins cockily and looks to the detective. "Do we let her do it or we gonna do it for her?"

Another chuckles and asks in an exaggerated southern drawl that only makes him sound stupid, "Think we should git her a bucket before we introduce her to the package we been keepin' on ice for her?" It's no wonder southerners gain the reputation we do. It's not the accent per se; it's the poor grammar and chosen dialect. AKA: lazy. Even worse? Some think it's charming.

"How about you do your fucking job and get the hell outta the way so she can do hers?" Deacon's low harsh growl comes from the doorway behind me. I don't have to turn to see him to know he's pissed. I know that tone. I know that F-word. Yet, I'm not sure if it's because I left without him, he's had a bad day, or these jackasses are being, well – jackasses.

"Gray," the detective that led me back here greets him and extends his hand. "Surprised to see you here."

Deacon offers a quick explanation though it's forced, "Only here to assist Ms. Remington. Not stepping on your turf, Miller."

"Yeah, I hear you two come as a pair sometimes, especially when it comes to carnival rides." He laughs at his own joke while Deacon glares. "Just yankin' your chain. How you been? Heard about your takedown this afternoon. Shelly doin' okay?"

"She'll be all right," he tells him. "I'll tell her you asked about her."

I turn at the news, concern for not only Deacon but the perky brunette officer who's always been friendly toward me. "Did Shelly get hurt?"

"No." Deacon's response is short and business-like as if it's an everyday thing or . . . none of my business, then pulls a pair of gloves from his pocket and tugs them on. "What have we got?"

One of the uniforms holds up his hands, palm side out. "Think we're gonna let you take it from here. Ain't done nothin' more than open and close the lid. But to tell ya the truth . . ." He smirks and looks to me. "I'd kinda like to stick around and see her reaction when she opens that thing up."

Deacon's throaty growl is not one I would want aimed at me, unless of course we were alone and in the midst of . . .

He glares at the uniformed cop, enunciating each word as he orders, "Get the fuck outta here." All of the others follow in the uniform's footsteps as if in fear, but Detective Miller stays. It's not as if there's a lot of space in this room. It's more like a sunporch, minus the sun; lit by only the incandescent bulb overhead.

As Deacon steps up beside me, I reach for his forearm and squeeze. "Did you get hurt today?"

He studies my face, his gaze flitting from my eyes to my mouth and back again. "Be careful, Ms. Remington," he warns so low only I can hear. "It sounds like you might actually care."

"Ha!" Detective Miller declares from behind me. "Didn't you know? Deac's invincible."

I will not cry. I will not cry. I turn slowly to face the joking, but oblivious cop. "No one is invincible, detective."

Were it not extremely inappropriate, I would kiss the two forensic team members who appear in the doorway after squeezing past the uniforms standing around in the kitchen and break the uncomfortable tension in the room.

"Got your bag, Everlee," Jamie says, holding it up in the air. "Coroner is waiting for the green light to transport the body in the living room. His best preliminary guess is natural causes."

The detective nods at the freezer. "Got a body in there. Didn't want to touch anything until forensics got here. I'll step back and let you two take over."

"Tell him to wait, Jamie. Let's see what we have here first." I turn to Corey, the usual photographer on the team. "You got pics of the rest of the house?"

"All done," he replies with a grin. "Nothing seems out of

the ordinary." He glances at the freezer and grimaces. "Am I to understand it's not the same for back here?"

Pulling a face mask out of my bag, I strap one loop around my left ear and begin to pull it across my face when the compressor on the freezer comes to life. I tilt my head as if to listen intently, furrowing a concentrated brow. This freezer is ancient – a literal dinosaur! My eyes meet Deacon's and our brows lift in unison.

"It's still running," I whisper in fascination.

Detective Miller chuckles behind me. "Still cold as a witch's tit on a winter night in there too. I tried to find the brand name. They don't make 'em like they used to. You can bet your sweet ass you won't find a sticker on there that reads eco-friendly either. Can't even buy a damn toilet I don't have to flush twice these days." He snorts loudly. "Don't even get me started on those damn smart phones. Dumbest damn things I ever seen."

Deacon turns his head slowly and arches a brow. "You done, Miller?"

"Yeah, yeah, yeah," he grumbles. "Bitchin' don't do me any good anyway."

In the midst of it all, I'm biting my tongue, resisting the urge to correct his euphemism of the witch's tit on a winter's night. It seems to be lacking without the brass bra. Maybe that's why bitching doesn't do him any good.

What greets us as Deacon opens the lid is not at all what I expect. We'd been gifted with many bodies found in abandoned refrigerators in junkyards or alleyways in Chicago, but they were generally pretty decomposed . . . or in pieces, and the refrigerators weren't running. This though? Well preserved, on its side, legs bent as if trying to find a comfortable and fitting position, arms folded against the chest, and chin tucked. On top of the body's side, neatly folded and placed under one hand is a piece of paper. The longer the lid is open, the foggier the scene becomes with condensation because the view before us is all neatly wrapped in an enormous clear plastic bag tightly sealed at the top with heavy wire wraps.

"What in the hell?" Deacon murmurs next to me.

"Corey," I call to the photographer and pull the mask from

my face, now noting no one else is wearing one. "Need some quick but thorough pics here. We'll close the lid for a while and you can take some of the room itself while the condensation clears. When we open it up again, hopefully we can obtain clearer pictures."

"Got it, boss." The camera starts clicking and whirring before the words are out of his mouth. I roll my eyes. We work as a team. I'm nobody's boss. I give . . . directions. They may look to me and wait for instructions, but it hardly makes me the boss.

"Everlee," I correct him with a pointed look.

He smiles behind the new, upgraded photography equipment I managed to obtain with the funds awarded forensics through the battle with the city. "Whatever you say." He snickers, then murmurs, "Boss."

I've really taken a liking to this team. They're efficient, friendly, smart. They brought me donuts the day after the storm drain tragedy, containing a variety that spanned anywhere from glazed to blueberry and maple bacon. Ever had a maple bacon donut? I hadn't either. Breakfast and dessert in the same bite. It's like a mini orgasm in your mouth.

Looking to a frowning Deacon, who's still studying the freezer even though we've now closed the lid. "Detective Gray, will you help me move the freezer out from the wall a bit? I want to check a wire that was running to the inside of the back wall of the freezer."

I move to the end of the freezer, ready to nudge it from the wall inch by inch – if he would be accommodating enough to do his part from the other side. Instead, he moves behind me and tries to move me out of the way and play Hercules. I spin around quickly and in the process bump him in the ribs with my elbow. It was totally accidental, but the moment I hear his sharp intake of breath and see him wince, I know it couldn't possibly have been all me.

"You did get hurt today," I let out on a breathy, worried whisper.

His jaw is set and tics furiously as he narrows his eyes. "Move, Ms. Remington."

"No, Detective Gray."

"Move," he says again, a heated flare in his eyes I've only seen once before.

"No." I place my hand on his chest and slide it lower toward his rib cage. "Show me where you got hurt."

The entire room and everyone in it disappear and the bubble around us grows smaller as Deacon's eyes light up and a cocky grin smatters his face. In a slow, sexy, southern drawl I've never heard him use, he inquires, "Why? You wanna fix it?"

Oh God, do I. I'd take top, up against the wall, sink to my knees, lie back on the counter.

My teeth sink into my bottom lip and a small whimper leaves my throat before he gently removes my hand from his chest and holds it by my wrist in his. He bobs his eyebrows once and flashes me a sexy grin. "Let's finish up here first, Everlee." Goosebumps race across my skin with his touch and the way he says my name before he leans in close and whispers, "Then you can go home and call *Theo*." He drops my hand as if it's burned him and steps back.

Two seconds flat. Because a dick is a dick.

He calls out to the uniforms standing in the kitchen, "One of you want to help me move the freezer out from the wall for Ms. Remington?"

Flashlight in hand, as one of the uniforms takes one end and Deacon takes the other and begin to slide it forward, I tell them, "Just a few inches is all I need."

"Aw shit," the uniform sputters a deep groan as he drops his top half over the freezer. "A guy can only take so much."

"A few inches sounds like a job for Murphy," one offers from the kitchen.

The other laughs. "I can give her more than a few."

Deacon glares at Detective Miller. "Get them outta here before I kill 'em myself."

My massive blunder occurs to me as Miller addresses his officers. "Boys, you took it too far. Best go wait in the livin' room before Deacon cuts 'em down to stubs."

As they make their retreat, Corey swings his arm around my shoulder, his camera held securely in his other hand. "Men have a tendency to lose about a hundred IQ points when a beautiful woman is in the room, boss. They just go all . . . stupid."

I narrow one eye and lift a brow. "So, what keeps you well-mannered and behaved?"

"Ha!" he chuckles. "My mama would kill me. Not to mention my beautiful wife and the two little rugrats that worship the ground I walk on. They're my once in a lifetime. I ain't no dummy. I knew the day I saw her she was my one and only. Had to wait for her to find her way back to me. Against all odds, but she was the hill I was willing to die on."

"Sounds like a lucky woman, Corey."

"Nah." He smiles brightly, his blue eyes shining, and winks. "I'm the lucky one."

Deacon studies us from where he stands by the freezer as if intently listening to our conversation, soaking it in. Miller taps the top of the freezer with a flat hand. "Let's do this, Deac. I ain't gettin' any younger."

"Could you move it out a little farther?" I ask as I flash the light behind the prehistoric appliance, spotting the black wire I was searching for. The outlet for the electrical plug is higher on the wall with easy access, but the thin wire I'm searching for came from inside the freezer, up and out the back via the lid. I don't want to disrupt any of the contents inside, so inch by delicate inch of movement is the only way to do this.

"Found it!" I announce. On the back of the freezer cabinet, close to the floor is a magnetic thermometer that monitors the temperature inside. As I said before, this thing is a dinosaur. Good grief! It's an analog thermometer. No digital readouts here. -38 degrees Fahrenheit. Holy Toledo. Some morgues don't even keep bodies that cold. But then, how long has this body been in here?

"Corey." I pop my head up from behind the freezer. "Have you heard back from Paul yet?" Paul Neilsen is the state's head forensic pathologist. In a case like this, I'm a bit more comfortable with his input before we move anything.

"Jamie!" he yells out from the doorway toward the living room. "Any word from Paul yet?"

"He's on his way," she replies. "Are we clear to move the lady out?"

He looks to me with questioning raised brows and sees me blow out a long sigh. "I'll take that as a no?" I raise my own brows and shoot him a wry look. He nods once and shouts back to Jamie, "Tell the coroner he'll eat when we eat."

The doorway is soon filled with one county coroner by the name of Jack Daniels – no, not kidding – who stands with folded arms across his chest and scowls. "What seems to be the hold up, Ms. Remington?"

I step around to the front of the freezer, open the lid, and watch as his eyes go wide, then close it. "Oh, I don't know, Jack," I sneer. "I'm one of those odd people who like to have all the ducks in a row before we let them loose in the pond. If you're that hungry, call Subway and order a sandwich. I'm waiting for Paul before we release anything. Got it?"

"Damn," he murmurs. "That really a body in there?"

"Don't think the old lady ordered a side of beef with clothes on it," Deacon snarks. "Why don't you go wait with the others and we'll let you know when it's time."

Annie Mick

Chapter 24

Deacon

Every minute I spend in this small space with her is agony. Her hand on my chest and lowering to my rib cage felt so good. It was sparks and energy, sending a tingle down my spine. I'd forgotten the pain from her hit once she touched me, concerned that I might be hurt. But she's not mine to have. *Theo.* And how can she look at me the way she does if she's in love with another man? I see it. I feel it. Is it the distance between them? The close proximity with us? I'm just not that guy. And I sure as hell won't be his temporary replacement.

So instead, I teased her, warmed her up, inflated my own ego, then burst that horny little bubble and pissed her off. Hope she has a little toy in her nightstand drawer. So long as I never taste her again. Because if I started, I'm not sure I would have enough restraint to stop.

Jack Daniels is an idiot coroner. Simple license, no medical background and no ambition to get one. He and Hawkins worked together a lot . . . and shouldn't have. Two lazy asses make for one huge shitshow and a lot of unsolved cases. I know the state is short-staffed but that should never mean shortcuts. I would rather wait an extra month to know how a loved one died than never know. It's why I've studied Jonah Remington's case over and over, trying to see what they may have missed.

Everlee is so thorough, it almost edges overkill sometimes. But you can bet your ass, if you need answers, she'll be the one to find them. No stone left unturned, no body left behind, no blank pages. I know she wants to nail Jonah's killer and I want that for her. I want to help her.

Miller studies the back of the freezer as we wait for Paul Neilsen, the forensic pathologist to show. He moves his head in odd angles, scrunching his brow as he shines the flashlight and stretches his neck to get a better look at the far corners not easily visible as we only moved it out inches from the wall.

"What the hell are you looking for?"

He scowls as he stands up straight. "The damn brand name! I swear to God, Deac, I've never seen this color before. It's gotta be as old as my grandpappy and he's been dead for ten years! You can bet your sweet ass it wasn't built in China!"

I scrub my hands over my face as Everlee and Corey snicker. "Miller, any chance we could concentrate on the body inside?"

"What?" He raises his hands as if insulted by my question. "It ain't like it's goin' anywhere. Come on, Gray. This is like the Cadillac of iceboxes."

"Ah, my dear Everlee." The voice in the doorway interrupts our stare down as Paul Neilsen appears. "What delightful surprise have you found for me this evening?"

I hadn't realized how late it's getting until his mention of evening. Glancing at my watch reveals the reason my body is ready for my hot tub, a tall tumbler of bourbon, and a good eight hours sleep. It's been a hella long day and the city better be ready to comp me some PTO for this.

"Hi, Paul," Everlee greets him with a smile. "Before we get started in here, any chance we could check the body in the living room, give a prelim, and let Daniels transport her to the morgue? I think it may warrant an autopsy due to other findings, but I wanted your input before we did anything."

He extends his elbow for her to take and grins. "Let's take a stroll to the living room, shall we?"

If it weren't for his age and fatherly charm, I think I might hate the guy. The easy way Everlee takes his arm and walks with him is enviable. But Paul is actually quite likable and quite competent. A bit eccentric, maybe a bit hoity toity, but with a job like his, he's allowed to be anything he wants to be. Dissecting bodies day in and day out, be they old or be they young, determining the cause of death no matter how excruciating it was, has to take a toll on one's peace of mind. He's been around for thirty-some years and nearing retirement.

"Has anyone moved her?" Paul asks from his crouched position next to the body on the floor, looking up at Daniels after pulling the sheet back.

"W-well," Daniels stammers uneasily. "She was on her side and I had to roll her on her back to check her pulse."

"To check her pulse," Paul repeats slowly as he turns to Everlee and rolls his eyes before turning to one of the uniforms. "How long were you on the scene before calling the coroner?"

The officer shrugs before answering. "Good hour or so. The back porch kinda put a kink in the usual process."

"Hmm," Paul hums. "So, you'd pretty much determined the victim was deceased."

His expression sours. "Uh, yeah."

Paul stands and strips off his gloves as he steps toward Daniels. "The victim has been dead for, oh, I'd like to say . . ." He glares at Daniels. "Wait, I can't say for sure because you moved the body hours ago. It could be several hours, could be more."

"But she's cold!" Daniels hollers.

Paul narrows his eyes. "Yet, you needed to roll her onto her back to check for a pulse. Have you been drinking, Daniels? Again?"

"No!" he denies vehemently, though as he does, Paul steps back with a sour expression.

"Are you willing to submit to a sobriety test?"

"You gotta be kiddin' me!" he shrieks. "I was here, doin' my job. Showed up right after they called me. Reliable as hell, just like always."

"In the van, ready to roll?"

"Yeah, o' course." Daniels nods.

Paul pats him on the shoulders. "Sorry I doubted you. The body is ready for transport. You can load her up."

"'Bout time," Daniels grumbles. "Been here long enough. Dinner's waitin'. You gonna help me load her up?"

"The officers will be happy to help you," Paul tells him before he takes one of the three to the side and speaks quietly.

Upon the end of their conversation, which was inaudible as their heads were bowed and their words hushed, Paul utters the end of their conversation with a low warning as he nods toward the yard. "I'll be watching from the window. Keys in the ignition and he starts the engine first. Remember who you serve, officer Murphy." He flicks the badge on the front of his uniform. "I'll have this if you fuck it up."

Paul stands at the front window, arms folded over his chest, observing the body being loaded into the back of the coroner's van by two officers as Daniels observes them doing his job. He pulls the phone from his pocket and texts a message, then tucks it away.

"What are we waiting for?"

"The arrest of one county coroner for drunk driving," Paul says, glancing toward Everlee and me. "Seems Mr. Daniels made a few trips out to the van while he waited. He smelled like a distillery. They're waiting for him to get in, put the keys in the ignition and start the vehicle so the charges will stick. The woman's been dead for a good two days or more. He paid no attention to the color of her extremities and yet he moved her to check for a pulse. I was testing him. He's an idiot." He jingles the keys in his pocket and grins as we watch the officer reach in and shut off the engine and pull Daniels from the van. Paul's smile grows and his eyes twinkle as he looks to us once again. "And now, he's an idiot without a job. Two of my techs are on their way to pick up the van and deliver the body to the morgue."

"Geez," Everlee whispers in astonishment. "I thought he was just hungry."

Paul chortles as we turn away from the window and he offers her his elbow once again. "Ah, my dear Everlee. Some people have a nasty habit of ruining their taste buds with retched alcohol instead of savoring an aperitif post a delicious meal. You must let my Helena and I treat you to a dinner party at our home soon. I have a devilishly handsome and charming son whose company I think you would find to be quite . . ."

"Ms. Remington has a boyfriend," I offer up freely from the few paces I keep behind them. It's none of my business, but by God if something happens between her and Theo, *I'm* next in line. I'm the guy. I've waited six years!

She glances back over her shoulder and scowls. I smirk and mouth the name I've come to despise without any justifiable reason, "Theo." She scowls harder and mouths, "Dick."

She leans into Paul's elbow and cheerily says, "I would love to meet your son, Paul. He sounds delightful," right before she looks back once more and sticks out her tongue.

Brat.

Chapter 25

Everlee

I don't want to meet Paul's son any more than I want to stick needles in my eyes. A social life is the last thing on my agenda. But I have my pride. Deacon virtually accused me of being a cheater. He's never asked who Theo is; he assumed. And in the process put me on the same low level as my mother.

I didn't wake up wrapped around you like a second skin, Deacon. But you did me. I didn't steal your breath with a kiss that you'll never forget. But you did me. I didn't feed your fish. But you did mine. I don't know your favorite kind of pizza or coffee, but you know mine. For a few shining moments you made me feel like maybe . . . just maybe.

"Pics are done, boss," Corey announces proudly as we reach the sunporch. He holds up the camera in offering. "Do you want to check them? Pretty obvious it's a male."

Shaking my head, I tell him, "I'm good, Corey. You know what you're doing. You've never let me down."

Paul lifts the lid on the freezer and blows a light whistle. "Oh my, interesting. Did you check the temperature?"

"Minus 38. There's a note under his hand."

He lifts a brow, impressed, and hands me a mask as well as putting on his own, then reaches for a small scissors in his bag to begin his first cut into the plastic. "Shall we see what the man had to say?"

"Why aren't we removing the body first?" Deacon asks as he leans over the side of the freezer to observe.

"Because you never know what's going to crumble, detective," Paul explains. "We have no idea how long he's been in here. Judging by the age of the woman in the front room, the apparent age of this appliance and the temperature at which it was set, the possibilities are endless. Baby steps. We want as much intact evidence and information as we can retrieve. The body is not going anywhere. The note may hold a goldmine of information."

As Paul makes the initial snip with the scissors into the plastic, very little air is released and no noxious fumes surround us. The note itself is contained in another plastic bag inside the bag the body is in. As soon as Paul obtains the note from the body bag, he closes the lid of the freezer. He sets the note on top of the freezer. "We'll let that thaw for a few moments."

After waiting what he has deemed the appropriate amount of time he retrieves the note from the baggie. Patting the pockets of his shirt, he frowns and hands the note to me. "I seem to have forgotten my reading glasses in the car. Would you mind doing the honors, dear Everlee? Read it aloud for me, please?"

I take the note from his hand and unfold it carefully. I have no personal stock in this case, but tingles rush from the base of my spine to my neck as I hold the words in my hands.

To Whom it may concern:

*My name is Albert Roman. SS# ***-**-**** Rank: Sergeant. Serial#****** Fought in the Korean War. I died on August 03, 2011 at the age of 74. I know this because I planned it. I had cancer in 2006. Underwent treatment once, cost us our life savings, and put my Bess through hell taking care of me. Then it came back. I wasn't gonna put her through that again. Arranged to have my medical records transferred so the dumbasses at the VA would never know the difference. The only thing I had to leave my Bess was a Social Security check to keep her in the house we had been in for years. By God, I paid Uncle Sam since the first day I went to work. I paid my dues to my country. If I wasn't gonna get* *it, my Bess was. We only had each other after losing two sons and I wasn't gonna let her down. I bet if you look down the hall you'll still find their bunk beds in the second bedroom. I had to keep her here. It's where all the memories were.*

When I couldn't take the pain anymore, I put myself in this freezer, took enough pills to kill myself, told my beloved wife how much I loved her and kissed her goodbye. Then I went to sleep to wait until she joins me. Bess only tied the bag and closed the lid once I was gone. If you find me before Bess dies, you need to know I took the pills myself and the money was my doing.

I sure hope you don't though, because that means we're both up here, enjoying our boys again, looking down on you all and laughing our asses off. Which is the way it's supposed to be.

Be sure to tell Uncle Sam to go fuck himself!

Albert P. Roman

It's not until I reach the end that I sense the hand on my lower back and feel the tears fall softly down my cheeks. I turn my head slowly and look up to see Deacon watching me.

"Pretty amazing the things people will do for love," he whispers so low I'm the only one who hears. I simply nod because my throat is full and I'm halfway to a sob. His eyes crease at the corners and sadness shadows the amazing green that struck me the first time I ever saw them. "It's pretty amazing what they won't do either."

"What do you mean?"

"Make a bad situation worse by staying. Sometimes you have to know when it's time to leave." His hand on my lower back slides upward until it gently grips the back of my neck, his mouth so close to my ear I feel his whispered breath on my skin. "He was lucky though. He got to tell her how he felt before he left her."

He releases his grip around my neck and steps back, pure business in his tone as he addresses Paul. "Doc, how do you want to handle this? Do we thaw him out before moving him or do we move the whole deep freeze to the morgue?"

Paul studies the two of us, an amused grin on his face. "I do believe the gentleman inside the freezer has given us more answers than we could have imagined, Detective Gray. However, I think it best we defrost him before we move him and collect the cabinet tomorrow." He claps his hands together twice. "Chop, chop. Unplug the freezer and lift the lid. Should take about two hours in this heat for the body to be pliant enough to move without damage. In the meantime, shall we congregate in the living room and order a bite to eat? I'm feeling a bit peckish."

"You have to fight, Everlee. Get better so you can help Jonah."

"You're so strong. So beautiful. I'm right here, Everlee. Rest, relax. Don't fight the restraints. They're holding your legs in place until they heal. You want to walk for Jonah."

"Dream good dreams, Everlee. Think of Jasmine in bloom, your favorite song, dancing in the rain."

"I will miss you, sweet Everlee. If only we'd met in another lifetime."

It was his voice. Is it that he can't remember me or am I so crazy that I've created my own fantasies over the years to fit a narrative I needed to give me the courage to return to the scene of the crime?

Stripping my gloves off and tossing them in the haz mat bag, I leave the sunporch. "I'm going to step outside for some fresh air if you don't mind, Paul. You guys go ahead and order. I'm not hungry."

Deacon plops down next to me on the steps of the worn down stoop after a few minutes. "You need to eat, Everlee. It's late. You look pale. I ordered you a sandwich."

I smirk before asking, "Did you remember my wine?"

"I remembered it." He tilts his head and grins wryly. "Doesn't mean you're getting it. Is Roscoe okay going this long without food?"

His concern for my fish is a conundrum. But that's Deacon. *Two seconds flat.* My nose wrinkles. "I'll be sure to let him know you cared. I already called Garvis."

He nods once in approval – not that it's his to give. "Did you really shoot at the reporters this morning?"

I chuckle at this morning's memory. The looks on their faces, the take-no-shit determination on my doorman's face. He is scary, unless you know him. "That was James, another of my doormen."

"They really look out for you, don't they?"

The thought of what James did for me; trusting me with his truck, getting me out the back door to avoid the reporters, arranging for his wife to pick him up and bring him back in the morning melts my heart. "They're like friends."

The cicadas are at a near ear piercing level as they announce their presence in the trees. I'll take cicadas over cockroaches any day, but I still keep my eyes peeled to the ground around me. I had already banded my pantlegs before exiting the van, but bugs will be bugs. Don't care to take new friends home with me. I've half a mind to shower at the station before I go home – just in case. They are sneaky little bastards.

"How long has Daniels been a coroner?" The thought strikes me as I watch a new coroner van pull up to the house in preparation to load another body onto it – the first is long gone after Paul called for techs to come pick it up. If Daniels has a history of drinking on the job, could it explain incompetence regarding Jonah? Was he on duty when my brother was murdered? I know Hawkins was the forensics investigator and that knowledge alone is more than discouraging. The man didn't seem to know the difference between an alcohol swab and a shop rag. As God is my witness, he reused microscope slides, didn't properly steam the tools, and never had the machines inspected. I had to clean food crumbs out of the computer keyboard, for crying out loud! My bet is he and Mayor Peters were drinking buddies as well.

"I know he's been around for a while." Deacon shrugs. "I could find out if you want."

"More than six years?"

He stiffens slightly, rubs the back of his neck, and clears his throat. "Why, uh, why do you ask?"

"Random number, I guess." I stand from the stoop, brush off the seat of my pants, and head back inside. The song of the cicadas is more like an obnoxious never ending screech at this point and I can only hold my finger in my ear for so long. I hadn't checked the records for the name of the coroner who collected Jonah's body the night he was murdered. If it was Daniels and he was drinking, there is every chance he lost evidence, or was negligent in handling what there was.

"Everlee," Deacon calls softly behind me.

Keeping my back to him, I hesitate. "You seem confused, Detective Gray. It's Ms. Remington. *Just* Ms. Remington. Like I'm *just* a forensic scientist."

I can handle Ms. Remington; the formality, the coolness behind it. But the way he says Everlee is almost painful. A simple reminder of what I'm not . . . memorable. People forgetting your name is an everyday common occurrence. We all go through it. No big deal – under normal circumstances.

A little sidenote: Stupidest question in the world is Don't I know you? Because the answer is obvious. Apparently not. If you did, you wouldn't be asking. It's a rhetorical question. It also makes you sound like an idiot and it's a lousy pickup line.

Better approach? I believe we've met before but your name escapes me. Would you be so kind as to remind me?

I can't do Deacon's *two seconds flat* anymore. Hot and cold. Sweet one minute, total jerk the next. I'll force myself to work with him until I can get the hell out of here. Until then, I'm on a mission, and he is not it.

Chapter 26

Deacon

"Like I'm *just* a forensic scientist."

I'd told her to never call herself *'just'* anything, to never diminish her accomplishments.

"More than six years?" Random number, my ass. She wants to know if there's any chance Daniels was the coroner on the job the night Jonah was killed. Yes, Everlee, yes he was. I've studied every avenue possible. I've watched the street cam footage of them loading him up. All evidence seemed to be collected as per protocol before they moved his body.

The pizza delivery truck pulls up to the curb and unloads two warming cases from the front seat. He scans the scene and hesitates before approaching; the yellow tape and official vehicles surrounding the property making him wary.

"Uh, did you call for pizza?"

"We did."

He stays frozen by the open door of his car. "Did somebody die in there?"

"Nothing for you to worry about," I reassure him with a shrug. "As long as it wasn't food poisoning."

The poor guy looks like he's about to piss his pants. "Uh, uh," he stammers. "I've never delivered here before."

Rolling my eyes, I pull a twenty from my wallet to tip him

– I prepaid for the food online. "Get up here. I'm yankin' your chain." I hand him the twenty before he unloads the pizzas from the carriers with shaky hands. His eyes widen in surprise. "Wow, thanks!"

"No problem," I reply as I take the pizzas. I imagine tips in this neighborhood are a rarity. After scaring the shit out of him, I should probably add another ten. "Have a good night."

"Uh . . . yeah, mister." He laughs nervously. "You too."

Damn. She is making me human.

"You need any help with those?" Corey asks as I head for the house.

"I'm good."

"I'll grab some waters," he says as he starts for the van.

"Hey Corey. Got a question for you."

He stops and steps back, curious. "What's up, detective?"

"What did you mean when you said your wife had to find her way back to you?"

He chuckles softly. "I had to let her go when all I wanted to do was keep her. Hardest damn thing I ever had to do. I knew we were meant to be together. Just had to wait for her to finally come home."

"How long did it take?"

He scowls. "Two shitty boyfriends and four years of college."

My eyes narrow with skepticism and a touch of, well – disbelief. "You sat back and waited that whole time?"

He grins impishly. "I kept myself busy enough, detective. Wasn't exactly . . . celibate. I considered it practice for the real deal." He tips his head toward the door. "Get those inside. I'll be back with the waters soon."

Everlee eyes me as I walk in with four boxes of pizza in my hands. "I thought you ordered me a sandwich."

"Fold your slice in half like New Yorkers. It works the same." She glares as I set the boxes on the coffee table. "Bread on the outside, meat and cheese on the inside." I turn to meet her glare and wink. "Or in your case, bread on the outside and shrimp and pineapple on the inside."

As I watch her face soften and her chin tremble slightly, the female from the forensics team shrieks, "Shrimp and pineapple! Oh my God! We are sisters from another mother!"

Little does she know, I'm pretty sure Everlee wishes right now they were sisters from the same mother. *Just not Beverly Remington.*

Popping the top on the box marked with a diagonal line indicating half P&S and half sausage, I remove a slice and fold it in half lengthwise. Holding it up to her mouth. "Trust me."

She chomps down hard, nearly taking my fingertip with it, and speaks around a mouthful. "Do you want me to . . ."

"Don't you dare." My voice is low, my eyes narrowed, as I warn her through a clenched jaw. The last thing I need is to get hard on the job with the memory of her asking if I wanted her to spit or swallow.

She chews slowly, savoring the flavors of seafood and fruit – God knows how – then licks her lips and smacks them loudly. She bats her long lashes and grins innocently. "I was going to ask if you wanted me to get you a slice."

Liar.

I'll match her sass. My stubborn ass never could back down from a challenge and Everlee Remington is just too damn tempting. She's come home and Theo is too far away for me to care. "You gonna feed it to me too?"

Her eyes flare in challenge. "Only if you let me stuff it down your throat until you choke." She snatches the slice of pizza out of my hand. "Get your own, detective. I'm too tired to perform the Heimlich tonight."

"You're riding back with me when we're done here."

She scowls as if she's been told she can't go out after dark. "I came with the forensics team. I'm going back with them."

"Garner's orders."

"He's not my boss," she argues. "I don't answer to him, you do."

I take a step closer so as to keep the rest of the room out of our conversation. "If you had heard Garner go up against Peters today on your behalf, you would see him for the friend that he is. He's looking out for you. His orders for me were to bring you back myself. You will either get in the car with me willingly or I will throw you over my shoulder and haul your ass outta here kicking and screaming. Your call."

"You're hurt." She tips her chin and smirks. "Just how do you plan to carry me?"

I lean in close, the scent of jasmine filling my senses as I feel her shudder against my closeness, and whisper, "Over my shoulder with your ass so close to my mouth I'll bite it if you so much as wiggle."

Chapter 27

Everlee

I tried, I really did. The tiny squeak just slipped out from my throat. But sometimes the body reacts of its own volition. It's like involuntary blinking. Your thighs squeeze at the most inopportune times as well. And, of course, he notices.

Deacon Gray: the very definition of conundrum. You never know whether to slap him or climb him like a tree.

"Your pizza is getting as cold as the body in the freezer, detective," Paul warns playfully. Deacon looks over his shoulder at the warning and Paul raises his brows in a knowing look. "Some things are best left for warming up after hours."

My face flushes in embarrassment when I realize the entire room has been fixed on our closeness and probably a good portion of our exchange – leaning forward in their seats on the couch and chairs, heads tilted as if a better position of their ears might give their auditory canals a vantage point. *Service announcement for those wondering: It doesn't!* But that doesn't mean people won't try it.

Deacon snatches one of the two last pieces from a sausage pizza and folds it in half; taking a large bite and chews. After swallowing, he looks to me and grins. "See? Bread around meat and cheese. Just like a sandwich."

Fine, the man has table manners. He didn't talk with food

in his mouth. I wonder if he talks around a bite of butt cheek, or a nibble of nipple or . . . Damnit, Everlee!

"What if I'm a vegetarian?" I snip back. Not sure why, or where it came from but sometimes you just feel like you have to have the last word, ya know?

He chuckles and nods at the half eaten slice of pizza in my hand. "Shrimp and pineapple? I thought you were."

This time I step closer and stand on my tiptoes, tilting my head up – my mouth barely reaching his chin – and whisper close to his ear, "What I think, detective, is you're a dick."

He grasps my elbow and holds me in place as his eyes bore into mine – not a care in the world who might be watching – but keeps his voice low. "Do you hate me, Everlee?"

I gaze into the eyes that I've never forgotten. Moss green with little gold flecks that seem to dance with his smiles, deepen with his frowns, intensify with his anger, and soften with his compassion. My voice is weak as I admit, "I want to. You make it easy one minute and impossible the next."

"I'll work harder on the impossible." He brushes his knuckle across my jaw in a way that feels strangely familiar. "Okay?"

"Why?" I study his face for a reaction, any indication he's made the connection. "Why is it important to you? Do I remind you of someone?"

His brow creases and his lips pull tight between his teeth before he slowly shakes his head. "No, Everlee. You don't *remind* me of someone. You are an original."

And my bubble bursts. Admittedly, I was bleeding, broken, and crying that night. Probably looked like I'd just crawled through broken glass and . . . Oh wait! I had! What a dreamer I am to think I may have been more than just a job to this man.

"We should probably get back to work." My pizza has gone as cold as my insides. Two bites will hold me over until I get home to my wine. After that? I will sleep with Pinot induced dreams. Possibly Chardonnay if I'm feeling feisty.

"Everlee, my dear," Paul says, gently placing his arm over my shoulder as we walk toward the sunporch. "You and your team have more than put your time in today. We can take over from here. It's only a matter of transport of the body. It's nearing the bewitching hour."

Glancing at my watch, I note a time of eleven p.m.

"But what about you?" I gasp, knowing the man keeps long hours himself. The state is desperately seeking new permanent staff, using locums in their place until that happens. Not to mention, Paul oversees and signs off on any and all autopsies out of the normal spectrum and testifies in court on a regular basis in murder trials.

"I'm fine," he reassures me. "I spent the morning in court doing my best to convince the jury that ten stab wounds inflicted by an ex-husband was much more likely the cause of death than the poor woman's plunge out the window of an 18-story building. From there, I had lunch with my dear Helena and did paperwork in my office for three hours before I was called here." He winks and grins. "All in all, a rather easy day compared to most. I have a fishing trip planned for tomorrow. Can you say the same?"

"No," I reply sheepishly.

"Then off you go." He turns me around by the shoulders before lovingly patting one. "There is rest for the weary after all. Take advantage of it, dear Everlee. I will see you on the next job we have the pleasure of working together."

Turning one last time before making my exit. "Thanks, Paul."

He nods and then looks to Deacon. "Detective, I take it you will see Everlee is delivered safe and sound?" He arches a stern brow. "So that she may *rest*."

Deacon dips his chin in acknowledgement, seemingly a bit irritated. "That is the plan."

"And I'm sure you're a man who sticks to the plan," Paul says, leaving no room for doubt exactly what he means. I've never had a father to look out for me; only my little brother and his friends in the band, followed by Theo and Keith. The man delivers a hug with words. Kinda like a vocal teddy bear.

Corey and Jamie bid us farewell as they climb up into the forensics van after we've loaded the equipment. It wasn't much;

three bags to include gloves, masks, and any supplies needed to collect DNA for evidence. In this particular case, not much was utilized. The case was most definitely unique, but pretty cut and dried.

"Over my shoulder or next to me?" Deacon asks as we watch the van pull away.

"How is the captain even going to know if we don't arrive together? It's late. I'm sure he's gone home by now."

"You've got two choices and ten seconds to decide or I decide for you." Deacon raises one expectant eyebrow as he counts, "One, two, three . . ."

Shivers run down my spine as I storm past him toward his car and he chuckles behind me and murmurs, "Good girl. Although it would have been fun to . . ."

I spin on my heel and glare. "So much for working on the impossible."

"Just stating a fact, Everlee."

"That's Ms. Remington to you, Detective Gray."

He rolls his eyes as he opens the door for me. "As long as you're in the car where you're supposed to be. Buckle up, buttercup." He slams the door after I've climbed in and rounds the front of the car to open his own.

We ride in silence on the way back to the station. My gaze is fixed out the side window as my knee bounces in pent-up frustration. It has been a long day, filled with deep emotions – good and bad. A man willing to arrange his death in such a way so his wife won't be left without. Mayor Peters being the jackass he is and Keith coming through for me the way he did. Hearing that Captain Garner stood up for me. And the cold, cruel reality that not only do I not remind Deacon of someone, he probably walked out of the hospital that night, checked a few boxes on a report, and moved along to the next case. I simply want to get home.

"You've been making the car rock from bouncing that knee, Ms. Remington," he teases as we pull into the parking space at the station and shuts off the car. "Trying to expend a little stored up energy?"

I turn my head slowly and narrow my eyes as I unbuckle my seatbelt. "I'm pretty sure you've made cars rock with expending all sorts of stored up *energy*. I'm bouncing my knee in anticipation of getting out of this one and away from you." I reach for the door handle to let myself out, before snarling, "Thanks once again for pissing me off, *buttercup*." My star performance exit is halted when I find the door locked.

"No cars." He unbuckles his own seatbelt and twists slightly in his seat, smirking. "It was my dad's pickup truck. Prom night, I was 17. No accounting for young and horny." He slides his hand across the back of the seat and takes a tendril of fallen hair, twirling it in his fingers. "Pissing you off isn't my goal, Everlee. But it does seem to be what I do best."

"What is your goal, Deacon?"

His hand wraps in my hair as he pulls me closer and leans in at the same time. "Just for now," he whispers as he brushes the side of his nose against mine, our mouths mere millimeters apart. "Just for this moment, I need a memory." The kiss is gentle, tender, sweet, until . . . it isn't.

But it's not Deacon that turns the tables; it's me. My hands fist his shirt until one crawls its way up to his neck and finds the short waves on the nape. They feel so good between my fingers. The soft hum in my throat runs no competition with the song my body is singing. Our tongues dance in a slow rhythm as if they've tangoed for years. One small break in the kiss only leads to one more as if it's not enough. As if it ends, it will never begin again. His throaty groan and exploring hand that slowly moves up my rib cage causes me to arch into him for more, seeking a touch I've yearned for so long. I'll make him remember me . . . or die trying.

He snaps back so quickly, I nearly fall into him. He runs a fast hand through his hair, breathing hard. "I can't do this. It's all or nothing, not either or." He unlocks the doors, snatches the fob from the ignition, and throws his door open. "Let's go."

I sit stunned, my lips swollen, nipples aching. We won't talk about my panties! *What the hell was that? Oh yes, Deacon Gray's two seconds flat!*

By the time I'm out of the car, my blood has reached far beyond the boiling point. Deacon is not the only one who can slam a door. Unfortunately, since his is already closed, it doesn't quite hold the impact I desired so I kick it with the bottom of my boot for extra satisfaction before I storm toward what I thought I was looking for. *My car!* Confusion furrows my brow until I remember I drove James' Ford F150 this morning. I heave an angry growl of frustration before heading toward the building to retrieve the keys I left in my lab. Asshole waits at the door for me. Apparently he doesn't remember I'm a blackbelt either. And if he doesn't get out of my way, whatever injuries he suffered earlier today will only be increased tenfold.

"Everlee, can we . . ." he says as I'm halfway up the steps.

"Don't!" I sneer, my hand in the air. "Do not say my name, do not touch me, do not talk to me. Got it?"

He closes his eyes and dips his chin. "Everlee, I'm not a cheater."

I open the door opposite of the one he holds open. "What you are is a judgmental ass. Have fun up there behind your pulpit, *Deacon.* Do you wear the robe on Sundays, too?"

Snatching the keys from the locked file cabinet, I go home, leave James' keys and a thank note with Garvis, pour the first of what is sure to be a few glasses of wine, feed Roscoe a second time, and turn on my computer to watch the video from the street cam footage. Two hours, three glasses, and buckets of tears later, I give up, take a shower, and drop face first onto the bed for another restless night.

"I'll find him, Jonah. If it's the last thing I do, I'll find him. Then we can both rest in peace."

Chapter 28

Deacon

"Garvis, Detective Gray here. Did Ms. Remington return home safe?"

"She did, detective," he replies. "About ten minutes ago. I must say she wasn't her usual cheery self, no matter how hard she tried. Quite the late hour too. Was it a bad day?"

"Could have been a whole lot better, Garvis. Can you tell me why she's driving a pickup truck?"

He chuckles. "That would belong to James, another doorman. He was on this morning when the paparazzi showed up. He gave her his to drive so she could get out safely and they wouldn't see her. I take it she didn't explain?"

"I appreciate you gentlemen looking out for her," I tell him with all sincerity, avoiding his question at the same time. Everlee didn't tell me shit, and I doubt she ever will again. "James is the one with a shotgun?"

He laughs heartily. "Crack shot as a matter of fact."

"Yeah, well . . ." I grumble, ". . . tell him not to hesitate if her mother shows up again."

"We're all on the lookout, detective."

"Thank you. Have a good night, Garvis."

"You as well, sir."

I'd watched her as she left the building, noting the vehicle she climbed into. Wondering what the hell was going on. I wanted to ask, but figured I'd done enough damage. I'd told myself to stay away, never touch another man's woman. But after my little chat with Corey, I'd gained hope. Hope is a tricky bitch. Guess I forgot hope still means patience. And my impatience will probably send her running back to Chicago right into the arms of *Theo* and as far away from me as she can get.

So, tempting to create construction worker Damien Greene and visit Harbor county. My dick hasn't touched anything but my hand since she came back. But with the Ferris wheel climb still fresh in everyone's memory, it's too early. Thank you once again, Everlee. Not only do you have my balls in a vise, you've got my dick under recognition restriction.

Making my way to the backyard once I'm home and dropped my keys inside, I turn on the spigot and start watering the bushes. I breathe deeply and appreciate the scent of the jasmines in bloom. I told her I needed the memory. Tonight's was so much better than the ones from the hospital or the one from the fairgrounds. Even better than waking up next to her. Because she reacted tonight. She gave as good as she got. I wasn't alone in my desire. But I'm alone now, just like I've been for the last six years. And probably always will be. Without my sweet Everlee.

* * *

Tapping on his open door the next morning, I see Garner concentrating on an open file on his desk. "Gray," he says, tipping his chin. "How's it going? What can I do for you?" *How's it going?* Something about the way he studies me makes me uncomfortable. Edgy. "Need to take a seat?"

Okay, now I know something's off.

"Uh," I stammer and rub the back of my neck. "No, this won't take long. I'd like a transfer."

He closes the file in front of him, leans back in his chair, and crosses his arms over his chest. "No."

"Why?"

"Because I said no."

I lift my hand, feeling defeated and frustrated. I knew he wouldn't be easy. "Fine. I'll put in for it without you. Thought I'd do the decent thing and come to you first."

"Get in here and sit down."

"No need." I shrug casually, battling the urge to flip him off, and turn to walk away. "I can do it with or without you."

"Shut the door and sit your ass down!"

Ah, there's the captain I know.

The door closes exactly the way I intend . . . hard, and I wait approximately ten seconds to open it again to see Rodriguez leaning into it on the other side.

My glower alone would be sufficient, but I make it clear I know what he was doing. "Apparently you like drinking your dinner through a straw, Handy."

"Uh-uh, I…" he stammers, eyes wide. "I uh, I just had a question for the Cap."

"What is it?!" Garner yells. He knows there is no question. The little prick was trying to be a fly on the wall – rather a mosquito at the door. Irritating little fucker.

"Uh…" Rodriguez scratches his head. "I can come back later."

I narrow my eyes and snarl, "Better think of something good before then." I slam the door once again, in his face this time, and take a seat.

"You're not gettin' a transfer, Gray."

"Why not?" I demand. "It's my option."

"Your option, maybe," he says, nodding. "But you ain't gonna get far without my reference or my John Hancock on it."

I slap my hands on my thighs, feigning indifference, and stand. "Fine, have it your way. I'll go back to the 79th. Been there before. Pretty sure they'll take me back without your signature or references. Thanks for nothing."

"Really, Gray?" he taunts. "The 79th? Tell me, is the *Blue Velvet Lounge* still open?"

The blood drains from my face as I watch his bushy

eyebrows rise and he glances back to the chairs in front of his desk. "Care to take a seat, Deacon?"

As my ass hits the chair, I mutter, "Parnell."

"Didn't leave him much choice," he admits. "I had some of the report already, he filled in the missing bits and pieces. Do you trust me, Gray?"

I sigh, resigned. Do I have a choice? "You've never given me reason not to."

"I hate dirty cops. The only thing I hate more is women-beaters, child molesters, and rapists. Sounds like Spencer was only one short of the whole package. You did the right thing both times. I woulda commended you myself. However, in Everlee's case, getting attached to a victim probably wasn't the wisest thing you coulda done. But Vic explained the circumstances. You didn't have the heart to leave her alone."

"She didn't have anybody else." I stare at the floor between my spread knees and folded hands. "Her own damn mother wouldn't accept faster accommodations to get to her. Her brother was just murdered, she was in surgery, and Spencer was so fucking cruel. She had nobody, Cap."

"Does she know you were there?" he asks. "Does she know it was you?"

"No." I shake my head vehemently. "I only entered her room when she was unconscious to check on her. She fought like hell to get out of that bed to get to her brother, so they had to keep her heavily sedated. I lied to her over and over while she slept. They say you can hear even when you're asleep. Told her she needed to rest and get better so she could see Jonah." I look up to see him staring at me and I shoot him a wry look. "Her dead brother. Worse yet? She pleaded with me in the ambulance to not leave her. I told her I wasn't going anywhere."

"Deacon, you didn't go anywhere," he tries to reassure me. "You stayed."

I rake a hand through my hair. "Not so she'd know it. I kept it professional, Cap. As much as I could. She was young. I wasn't trying to be a hero. She didn't need to get attached through trauma."

"But you did."

"I didn't get attached through trauma, but I can't explain it either." I pinch the bridge of my nose and let out a sad huff. "But I did the right thing in the end and let her go. She's done great things, Cap. Look where she is. She's come so far."

"You're in love with her," he says as if it's some great revelation.

I drop my chin to my chest and blow out a deep resigned breath. "Maybe a little. But she has a boyfriend."

"Little my ass." He chuckles. "Boyfriends are a dime a dozen. Lucky for me, there's only one Deacon Gray. Two of you would drive me to drink more than I do. She ain't married . . . yet. Best get a move on."

"She hates me," I grumble, the memory of last night too fresh to accommodate much hope for anything better.

"She doesn't hate you." He rolls his eyes. "Right now, I think you hate yourself. Your confidence is shit. It's not like you." He shrugs and laughs. "I mean, you've always been an ass, but you might want to stop bein' so good at it. Quit walkin' when you want to dance."

My face squirrels in confusion. "What the hell is that supposed to mean?"

"Be smoooooth, Gray," he nearly hums, sliding a flat hand through the air, then grins. "No rough edges. She's a woman, not a perp."

Staring, because this man in front of me is a total stranger. "Who the hell are you?"

"In that moment? Your counselor." He smirks. "Now, I'm your captain. You're not getting a transfer." My shoulders sag. "Forget it," he says, finger pointed hard. "You and Parnell are two of the best this city has to offer. I own your asses. You're here until I retire."

"Can you keep us separated for a while?" I ask, rising from my chair.

"You and Parnell? Not a chance. He was only . . ."

"No," I stop him. "Me and Everlee."

"Two weeks to pull your head outta your ass," he says begrudgingly. "You gotta see the company doc anyway. He may want you off for a bit."

My protest starts with a groan. "My ribs are just . . ." but soon dies with his glare. "Fine," I relent and turn toward the door.

"Gray," he calls out before I can get the door open. "What happened to the woman in the records room? Is she okay?"

Grasping the knob in my hand, gripping it hard before turning, my knuckles white with fury. The picture of Tess on the floor, broken and sobbing, forever etched in mind. "She didn't come back to work after that."

"Damn," he utters. "Sometimes that kind of trauma is just too much. Good job on Spencer's knees though."

Twisting the knob with a white-knuckle hand – *he has no idea* – I yank the door open. "Not good enough. He's still mobile."

"But he ain't on the force anymore."

I look over my shoulder and lift a brow. "You didn't let me finish, Cap. He's still breathing."

Chapter 29

Everlee

My car now has a temporary place in the employees parking lot at the rear of the building so as not to be spotted by paparazzi as I come and go. James saw to it and left my keys with Garvis just as he'd said he would do. It's not really an inconvenience for me and by the time the news of the frozen body in the sticks had spread, the mass shooting and my Ferris wheel climb have taken a backseat to the sudden interest of how the government might recover nearly a quarter million dollars in backpay – from dead people no less, with no surviving family members. I truly doubt an old house in a less-than-desirable neighborhood and a rack of truck-stop spoons is going to be considered full recompense for all those years of social security checks.

My thoughts on the matter? I picture a happy, reunited couple laughing at the scenario down here while enjoying the two boys they lost in this lifetime. I hope they have a puppy or two to keep them company as well. Good job, Albert P. Roman!

It's Saturday night as I stand outside the *Blue Velvet Lounge* staring up at the flashing neon sign. My legs are wobbly, my heart pounding so hard in my chest I feel it in my ears. I glance down at the very spot I held my little brother in my arms. I know it well. The blood stains are gone; washed away by years of rain and age. The police didn't collect any samples to check for another type;

see if Jonah's killer left any evidence behind. Nope, from all the reports I've read, they only collected Jonah and delivered him to the morgue.

Sheer incompetence.

How many footsteps have passed over this spot without notice? Without knowledge of what happened here? Hmph, would you look at that. There's a couple in the process right now. Can't blame them really. This isn't their pain.

The music from inside flows out onto the street as the door opens and people enter. Ah, it's Caleb's voice I hear as he sings the slow, bluesy "Stormy Monday". How apropos. Starts on Monday and ends on Sunday with a desperate plea to find what he's looking for. But it's one of those songs that let you feel the music even more than the lyrics so your body sways without measure, without limits, and of its own volition. In other words, it soothes the savage breast.

Stepping inside once I've gathered the nerve, I'm met with the same atmosphere and smells as six years ago, minus the one component I'll miss most; the sound of Jonah singing and playing on stage. When I look up to see the band, the breath is literally sucked from my lungs when I note the empty guitar stand topped with a brass letter "J" in front of the drum set.

"And bring that woman home…home to me…"

Caleb's deep, smooth voice rings through the bar as he sings the last words of the song with his eyes closed as the slow crescendo climbs and he runs one last fast riff on the keyboard. He looks up with a sexy grin plastered on his face, then scans the crowd as if searching and his eyes land on mine. It's hard to decipher if it's pain, happiness, or initial shock when he shades his eyes from the lights above and does a double take as if in disbelief.

He hollers into his microphone, "We'll be back in twenty!" Then rushes around his keyboard to hop off stage and down to me. He pulls me off my feet and into his arms, burying his face in my neck and whispers, "Everlee. Oh my God." I was hoping he'd be happy to see me, but I didn't expect this type of greeting. His body rocks gently with laughter as he squeezes tighter. "Oh God, I've missed you." When he sets me on my feet again and pulls back

slightly from the hug to look at me, I realize it's not laughter at all –
he's crying. And so am I. Full blown, all out, no holds barred sobs.

"I see the guitar stand up there," I tell him through my tears.

He smiles sweetly as he wipes his face with the back of his
hand. "He's with us every night, Ev. He goes where we go."

"Tell me my eyes are not deceiving me," Trent says as he
turns me away from Caleb and pulls me into his arms. "Everlee
Remington in the flesh."

Micah pulls me away from Trent and gathers me in a hug.
"You are a sight for sore eyes, lady."

"And my eyes are better'n his," Cody jokes, gently tugging
me into his own arms. "My God, you're beautiful. Good to see you,
Everlee."

"Good to see you guys, too," I say to one and all as more
tears spill.

"You gonna do one with us for old time's sake?" Trent
asks, his hands pressed together in a praying position, puppy dog
eyes fluttering, lips pouting as if he's begging for a second cookie.
"Pretty please?"

"No." I hold up a hand in stark warning. "I can't remember
the last time I sang."

"Aw come on, Evs," Micah pleads. "It's like ridin' a bike."

I wrinkle my nose. "Can't remember the last time I did that
either."

He grins cockily and winks. "If you can climb a Ferris wheel
from the outside, somethin' tells me a bike would be no problem."

He only laughs when I wince. "You saw that, huh?"

Trent snort-laughs. "The whole damn country saw you,
Everlee. I bet your Gram had somethin' to say about it. Come on,
sing a song with us."

"Ask yourself this," Cody pipes in, the same lilt of cocky
and southern mix as always. "WWJD. What would Jonah do."

Scoffing, I roll my eyes. "That's for what would Jesus do!"

"Uh, uh, uh," he says, then looks up, pointing a finger
toward the ceiling. "Jesus is up there right now, elbow leanin'
on Jonah's shoulder, laughin', sayin', 'Let's see what they can

talk your sister into'." *Did I mention Cody is a preacher's son? Not your prime nominee for sainthood, but who of us are? Did I also mention Cody is a prime lyricist as well as a fabulous guitar player? Puts a picture in your head with only a few words.* His face softens and a small sheen glosses his eyes as he dips his chin. "I'll put his guitar stand right next to you so he can keep you company. Just one? A little Sarah for me?"

My eyes shift to Caleb to get a read on his feelings. I virtually abandoned these guys after what happened. They tried to visit, but my refusals got old. I asked for time – pretty sure they hadn't anticipated five years. The last time we saw each other was shortly before my departure for Chicago. The time before that was scattering Jonah's ashes.

He stares out into the bar, his eyes fixed on nothing and no one in particular, deep in thought. Then I note him glance toward the ceiling, a mournful expression he tries to hide as he turns his head and swipes at his cheek before he turns back and nods. "He'd love that, Ev."

"Can I get a drink first, loosen up a little?" I ask, feeling my throat tighten at the thought of doing something I haven't done in forever.

Micah throws his arm over my shoulder. "I'm buyin'. Better make it somethin' flat though. Don't wantcha belchin' into the microphone."

A round of laughter ensues as we all make our way to the bar and they proceed to order drinks for each of us. We make easy and light conversation for approximately ten minutes before I ask Caleb how his little sister, Calista, is doing. She used to tag along with the guys whenever she had a chance and had always had the biggest crush on Jonah. He didn't reciprocate the same sentiment and treated her like the little sister they all did. She and Caleb were very close; much like Jonah and I were. I knew she had to have taken Jonah's death hard, but to be truthful, I hadn't given her much thought until now. Being lost in your own hatred, determination, and thought processes have a tendency to steal you away from some of the little things that deserve attention.

"How is your little sister? She must be about what, 23 by now?" I ask Caleb. "All done with college?"

He takes a long pull of his beer and clears his throat, looking out into the bar. His jaw is clenched and his neck flushes. "Callie left a long time ago. Hasn't been back since . . ." he shrugs. "Hell, I don't know. Been a long time."

"Where did she go?"

"Callie lives in her own world, Ev." His tone is bitter yet pained. He blows out a deep sigh before he shakes his head and stands from the barstool. "Keep thinkin' someday she'll be back, but the longer she stays away the less likely that's gonna happen. Probably for the best." He places a gentle hand on my shoulder and squeezes. "Break's over."

Apparently so is the subject of his little sister.

They take their place back up on stage. Three songs into the set, Cody makes a production of announcing their guest.

"Ladies and gentlemen, you may be familiar with the lovely face of our special guest tonight for reasons outside these doors." He looks to me and winks. "But for those who are longtime customers, you'll remember the voice of an angel that goes with it." He extends his hand to pull me up on stage while Trent moves the guitar stand to slightly left of center. "Everlee Remington, would you do us the honor?"

Caleb holds up two fingers. "Give us a couple, Ev. Start with Bonnie to warm up. We'll end with Sarah. Please?"

Cody immediately starts with the opening bluesy notes of a Bonnie Raitt song while the others follow. I thought I might be nervous, but it feels like old home week, minus my partner in crime. I glance down at the guitar stand with the shiny J on top, an overwhelming sense of nostalgia and a deep sense of gratitude to these men on stage. He'll never be forgotten – by me or by them.

Four songs later – just a couple my eye – I look to Caleb as the audience cheers. "One more, that's all."

He beckons me with a curled finger and I approach him next to his keyboards cautiously. His forehead creases and a sadness envelops his eyes as they glisten. "This is the last time, isn't it?"

He knows I won't be back. This is closure. "Don't make me cry, Caleb."

"You're not gonna be here when we finish this set, are you?" I only shake my head. He extends both arms. "Better give me a hug now then." As we break apart, he releases a deep breath and says, "I miss him, but I miss you too." He turns to the keys and starts the song he knows will give us the closure we all need.

I don't sing the song for the audience – no, I sing it for us. Each of us, as I take a turn at one point or another throughout the song to glance at my brother's guitar stand and make eye contact with Trent, Micah, and Cody; ending with Caleb as I sing the last drawn out phrase, *"weep not for the memories"* of Sarah McLachlan's "I Will Remember You".

I leave the stage in the midst of the audience's cheers and disappear into the crowd, out into the night. I'm stronger than I used to be, more determined than ever. I step around and past the spot I came upon Jonah's body six years ago, and whisper, "I'll find him. I promise you." As I reach the parking lot, the slow purposeful footsteps sound from close by.

"What a pleasant surprise. City didn't pay you enough to keep you away?" The slimy, evil snicker from behind me laced with taunting causes my body to tense and the two drinks I consumed earlier are ready to make a reappearance. "Not only is she flexible enough to climb Ferris wheels, but she can sing too. Wonder if I can still make you scream, you little bitch."

Get a grip, Everlee. You're stronger now. Recall your training. Don't get between the cars. You know where to aim. Roundhouse, throat, upper cut, solar plexus, balls, knees. Remember what he did to yours.

As I turn to see him standing close, the excruciating pain and agonizing loss of that night return as if it were happening right now. My brother in my arms, my knees being ground into the broken glass as punishment for my refusal to let go. The crushing blows to my back and the resultant broken vertebrae.

"Lieutenant Spencer," I sneer, feeling the shackles of fear break free one by one as I face the asshole who cost me a year of my life, a chance to say goodbye to my baby brother, multiple surgeries to repair the damage. I'd only seen pictures of him. I've watched the street cam footage over and over. He's haggard compared to then. His face is deeply creased with signs of stress and heavy drinking, a bulbous, ruddy nose to match. More gray than brown in his thinning, greasy hair. Dark, hollow eyes void of emotion; only hatred for the world and everything in it.

"Good to know you remember me, Everlee Remington," he says snidely; his eyes making a slow, sleezy perusal of my body as he takes another step closer.

Sparring with your enemy head-on has its advantages. A little bit of prep if needed. There's about a six-inch height difference. Too much distance makes contact too soft. Too close and you have to settle on the body part accessible. I want this fucker's head to spin. One more step and he'll be just close enough.

"You ruined my life you little cunt," he sneers. "I'm gonna make sure mine is the last name on your lips while I . . ."

"Don't finish that statement, Spencer," Deacon snarls as he appears out of nowhere and pulls him back in a chokehold that makes his knees buckle. "Wouldn't want you to deprive me the honor of yanking it from your throat along with your tongue."

"Get your h-hands off m-me, rook . . ." Spencer garbles through a sputtered cough as his energy is spent struggling against Deacon's hold around his throat; his face turning beet red as he fights for air. I watch as his eyes bulge – set on me with a flare of hatred like I've never seen. He gasps for a few final breaths, his body goes limp, and Deacon lets him drop to the ground.

"I – I could have taken care of it," I utter, chin tipped in defiance then drop my defiant chin, internally chastising myself, and instead offer, "But thank you."

He stares at the motionless yet still alive – I think – body on the concrete. He pulls his phone from his pocket, hits one button and waits only a moment. "Yeah, need a little clean up, aisle nine in the parking lot of the Blue Velvet Lounge." He pockets the phone and turns to me. There's a look in his eyes I can't quite decipher; a cross between pain and anger maybe, as the edges crease. His brow furrows slightly. He tilts his head as if searching for answers then shakes it slowly and sighs. "Go home, Ms. Remington."

A black SUV pulls up in the lot and two men hop out, making their way to us. I don't recognize either of them. Not that it matters; they don't speak and pay me not one lick of attention as they pick the body up off the ground and haul it to the vehicle. Spencer looks pretty limp, offering no resistance to being carted off.

"ER?" one asks Deacon.

Deacon nods. "You know the one. See you there." He turns back to me and takes my elbow in a gentle grip, turning me in the direction my car is parked and away from the scene. "Go home."

The initial shock of what just happened is wearing off. "Wait a minute." I whip my head up but hesitate while pondering which question I want answered first. "What are you doing here? You know him, don't you? You said his name."

"Doesn't matter why I'm here. And yeah, I know him. He's a dirty cop. We've been watching him." He avoids my gaze and grips my elbow harder, leading me a few steps toward my car. "You need to go home, forget you were here, Ms. Remington. Snuggle up, call Theo."

I yank hard from his grip. "You stubborn ass! If you would ever . . ."

He places a finger over my lips and halts my tirade with a pained whisper, "No, I wouldn't ever. No matter how beautifully you sing. No matter how much I want you, Everlee." He narrows his eyes and arches one brow. "Because I'm a *principled* stubborn ass."

And there you have it: Deacon Gray – two seconds flat.

I study his face, those eyes I've never forgotten, that mouth I've wanted on mine since the last time it was. I need to bank this bitter tone of his and forget the velvety smooth one I've clung to so tightly, because he's forgotten me. And he thinks I'm a cheater.

"I guess I was wrong. You don't make it so impossible.

Good night, Detective Gray."

Chapter 30

Deacon

Staying in the back, in the dark, kept me hidden; so well hidden. Hearing her sing took my breath away but watching her on stage with her brother's friends – the way they welcomed her back into the fold as if they were lifelong friends – was a scene to behold. She fit right in as if she'd been doing it for years.

I'd been waiting for Spencer to show his face, eventually screw up. The incessant newscasts of Everlee's climb up the Ferris Wheel and rescue and delivery of a newborn was bound to bring the cockroach out from under the wood. The records from the lawsuit against the city may have been sealed years ago, but the real danger was Spencer finding out she was accessible. She was hidden before the publicity. She was his prey after. Her building was safe, but anywhere outside that building was a landmine.

Calling in a few favors, I'd had her surveilled over the last week. As I said before, keeping your friends close but your enemies closer has its benefits. Petty thieves and third time offenders looking at hard time if arrested make for better usage than prison fill. I use them, they stay clean. It's a give and take. As it turned out this evening, it was one simple call to let me know of her whereabouts.

It was selfish of me to let it go as far as I did. I should have taken him down before he got within fifty feet of her. But I thought if I gave her enough pieces of the puzzle she would put them together and possibly remember who I was; that it was me who rode with her in the ambulance. Me who held her hand that night. And tonight, me who came to her rescue.

She sure knew who Spencer was. She didn't have a damn clue who I had been.

* * *

Tess's former fiancé, Micah, waits inside the old warehouse on the outskirts of the south side of Hasselback, where Spencer sits in a chair, hands and feet tied so tightly he can barely move; mouth gagged with a filthy rag that probably smells like ass crack and last week's sweatpants after a good workout. I'm just guessing due to the fact he looks like he's ready to retch.

He's joined by three other men who sit leaned back in chairs, arms folded across their chests, eyeing Spencer as if deciding which body part to remove first. I recognize them as Micah's best friends. We had met a few times before, created scenarios to fit individual circumstances; agreed to no rash decisions. Micah deserved the honors.

I nod in approval as I assess the situation then look to Micah. "He looks comfy."

Spencer struggles in the chair and gags behind the rag stuffed in his mouth as he tries to protest. I smirk and release an evil chuckle. "What's the matter, Spencer? Somebody put something in your mouth you didn't want? Are you chokin' on it?" He growls behind the rag and as he breathes back in, begins to retch. "Hmmm," I hum. "Sounds familiar."

"Did you know Tess was my fiancé?" Micah says as he steps in front of him; the bat held in one hand as he slaps it onto the other. Spencer stares up at the man who's endured enough pain for an army, shock and fear enveloping his eyes as his body begins to tremble. It ought to; Micah's been waiting a long time for this.

"Struggled for a really long time to get over what you did to her," Micah continues on a low deep, threatening growl. "Thing is, she never got over it. Did you know she committed suicide?"

Spencer's head wobbles as he shakes it nervously, his lungs only granting him short spurts of breath as he struggles between choking to death and survival. "Yeah," Micah all but grunts. "Four years ago. Where have you been all this time, Spencer? Hiding under a rock? Assaulting women, raping them?"

Spencer rocks the chair so hard it nearly tips backward but one of Micah's buddies holds it upright. Micah taps the bat against his hand once more and narrows his eyes. "I hear your knees are titanium so I'm not gonna waste my time with those. How about a femur or two?" He swings the bat down hard on the top of Spencer's right thigh; the crunch of bone audible over the scream Spencer tries to release from under the gag.

Micah tips his chin to the guy bracing the chair up. "Nah, I want to hear his next scream. Remove the gag. Let him puke. That's what my Tess did, isn't it, Spencer? From you stickin' your filthy dick in her mouth? She told me what you did to her. My Tess was the best thing ever happened to me and you took her away." Micah chokes on his words as his own pain strikes again then raises the bat. On its way to Spencer's femur he screams, "Burn in hell, you sick sonofabitch!"

Spencer shrieks through the vomit spewing from his mouth before he passes out from the pain. I wish I could feel something, but I really can't. Not for Spencer anyway. I knew what had happened to Tess; I simply hadn't disclosed it to Garner when he'd asked. Micah tried so hard to help her, but she was too fragile. Spencer obviously knew how to aim for the vulnerable, an easy target. *Just like Everlee.* I had promised Micah I would help find him. And here we are.

I remove the bat from the hard grip of one still grieving man and place my hand on his shoulder. "You got your job done. Tess can rest in peace. Let your buddies finish up here."

As I turn him in the direction of the door leading us out of the warehouse, I look back at the men readying to dispose of all evidence and nod at the floor. "Crystal clean. Leave his wallet in his pocket with a couple bucks. There's a gator swamp forty miles south, just off 175. Keep him breathing 'til you get there. Gators like they're food fresh. Make sure he's dead right before you drop him in. Make damn sure he's gator food before you leave. Those knee joints they put in are serial numbered. If they don't find his wallet for ID, they can recover those. Got it?"

"Tony's waitin' for us," one offers up with a grin. "Got the airboat ready. Called him as soon as we got here."

My eyebrows lift in wonderment. "Nice work."

"We'd do anything for Micah," another one offers, then adds, "And Tess."

I can only nod before the last one says, "Thanks for what you did for her, Deacon."

My grimace speaks for itself, but I mumble with it, "I wish I'd gotten there sooner."

Micah and I ride back to the city in my truck, windows open, the night air filled with the sound of crickets and cicadas.

"You did get there, Deacon." Micah sighs wistfully as he stares out his side of the truck. "Who knows what he would have done if you hadn't when you did. You gave me a year and a half with Tess that I wouldn't have had otherwise. I'll never forget that."

"I'm sorry, Micah."

He lets out a sad chuckle. "It's not your fault, Deac. You didn't fail her, I did. I treated her like she might be broken. There's nothin' wrong with goin' back to the way things used to be as a couple, put the past where it belongs and remember what's important." He swipes at his cheeks as if his tears are his enemy. "I couldn't let her touch me that way again. I refused blow jobs, for God's sake! I was so afraid if I said the wrong thing or did the wrong thing, got carried away, it would remind her of somethin' he might have said or did. I loved her so damn much, I would have rather let her go than do somethin' that would hurt her." He bends forward in his seat, head in his hands, and breaks down in sobs. "I not only couldn't save her, but in the end it seems I'm the one who hurt her the most. I couldn't be her hero."

I almost lose my grip on the steering wheel as that night flashes through my mind. *I thought I had a hero, too. But I found someone else to rescue me. He keeps his promises.*

I pull the truck over to the side of the road and put it in park. "Need a minute?" It's not for his benefit alone, but for mine as well. However, as the door flies open and he leans over the edge, emptying his stomach onto the gravel road beneath us, can't say I'm not glad I did.

"Damn," he sputters, wiping his mouth with his sleeve. "Sorry. Didn't see that one coming."

Handing him the water bottle from the console. "It hasn't been opened yet. Rinse and spit."

"I wouldn't care if it was fuckin' backwash." He musters a choked laugh as he grabs it from my hand. "Anything's better than the burn in my throat."

Shooting him a side-eye, I shake my head and shudder. "Well, you can keep it. I ain't drinkin' it now."

He takes a long pull from the bottle, swishes and spits it onto the ground. "God, I could sure use a shot or two of whiskey right now."

"I'd say you deserve it."

He tips his chin and proffers, "I'm buyin' if you're drivin'."

"You got it." I put the truck in drive and start back down the road.

"Hey, Deac?"

"Yeah."

"I didn't mean to make your truck my confessional. I ain't ever told anybody what I told you just now."

"Damn good thing I got two ears and one mouth then, huh?" I glance to where he sits and see him grin. "Your secret's safe, Micah. If you ever want to talk again, let me know."

"Appreciate it, Deacon."

"Just don't ask me to meet you in a church," I mumble. "God would strike me dead before I make it in the door. Let's go get that whiskey."

Chapter 31

Everlee

"Good evening, Ms. Remington," Garvis greets me on my way in the building. "Did you have a nice time?"

"I did, Garvis. Thank you." My legs are still shaky and my knees are weak as I make my way to the elevator. I hadn't even noticed it until I got into my car and hit the gas pedal to leave the parking lot. My foot wobbled against the gas pedal and poor Charlotte wasn't sure if I wanted to dance or drive. *Yes, I named my car.* A mix of adrenaline due to anger aimed at Deacon and fear from Spencer. I guess it takes more than physical healing for the anxiety to go away.

"Hey there, sweet cheeks! Miss me?" Theo's laughter rings throughout the room as the speaker phone once again proves its usefulness as I pour a glass of wine.

"You know I do." I close the fridge, pick up my phone, and head for the sofa with phone in one hand and the glass in the other. Taking a seat, I plop my feet up in the coffee table. "How much longer?"

"Aw, honey. Keith got called away for a few days."

"Where did he go?"

"East coast. He's supposed to be back on Wednesday." The sound of a beer bottle being popped open sounds in the background. "What are you drinking?"

"Chardonnay."

He takes a chug of his and lets out a long breath. "Ah, goes good with the local IPA. What are we toasting?"

I growl out loud and spew without forethought, "Deacon Gray's ass if you can get the fire hot enough."

He laughs so hard he snorts then belches. "Whoa! What did dementia dick do now?"

I explain what happened tonight. Everything from start to finish. Where I was, what I did, seeing Jonah's old bandmates, Spencer, Deacon's appearance, his holier-than-thou attitude. I'd never told Theo that Deacon thinks he's my boyfriend before this evening.

"Everlee," he scolds. "Why didn't you just tell him we're best friends?"

"He didn't ask!" I shriek so loud I think Roscoe jumps. "He assumed and in turn accused me of being a cheater by saying he wasn't one. He didn't shut up long enough to give me a chance to tell him who you are! He stormed out the door. Made me break my favorite coffee cup too," I whine.

"The gloves cup I gave you!?" Theo hollers.

"Yes."

"Well, now I hate him," he grunts. "How did he make you break the cup?"

I hesitate before sheepishly admitting, "I threw it at him."

There's a long pause before Theo breaks the silence, "Evs?"

"What?" I sniffle.

"I love you, and I can get you a new cup."

A sob escapes as I long for a hug from my old friend. "Can you get me a new heart?"

"Baby girl." He sighs so deeply I feel it all the way to my bones. "Why would I trade a Rolls Royce for a Prius? If I could curl up next to you and hold you right now, I would. Everlee Remington, you will get through this. I'll have Keith call you as soon as he gets back. Sweetie, I didn't even see him before he left. Some high security shit. But I promise, we got you. You call me anytime. Facetime me tomorrow, okay?"

"Okay."

"I love you, sweet cheeks."

Giggling at his nickname for me, I return the sentiment, "I love you too, big guy."

* * *

My lab is quiet on Monday morning. No calls waiting. No messages left over the weekend regarding the reports I had sent in over the last three weeks after cleaning up files left behind by Hawkins. How that man got anything done is beyond me.

Setting my coffee on the counter and my purse in the usual file drawer, I press the buttons on both computers to fire them up for the day. I enter my passcodes and within thirty seconds the first beep sounds and the red alert light shines on the screen. My fingers fly across the keys and as I watch the picture develop from the top to the bottom of the screen, my heart takes flight. Name, DOB, current residence, and occupation all listed below the image. Most importantly though: DNA match. He's a long haul truckdriver. Deacon was right on the money.

Now, I can either call Marty Striegel and give him the heads-up or I can turn this over to Deacon and let him take the lead and turn in the evidence to the 81st. There is only one way to handle this case – with care. We need driving logs listing times, places, verify drop offs, pick-ups, etc. More than that? We need a dedicated detective who's going to put full effort into catching a murderer.

Don't get your hopes up, Everlee. You've given them what they need. The rest is their job. How many times did they teach you in school there is only so much you can do? Remove yourself from the situation once your job is done. Turn off your emotions. It's like lost and found. You turn in the lost item. You can't always stick around to see if it's returned to its rightful owner.

Do I hate Deacon so much that I can't hand over the information so he can forward it to the investigating officer in the 81st? Is there an investigating officer in the 81st?

Instead of fighting an internal battle any longer, I print off the information and find myself with file in hand hovering over Deacon's desk. He raises his eyes, a look of casual indifference that I'd like to slap off his face. "What can I do for you, Ms. Remington?"

I toss the file on his desk. "I'd like to see him hang, Detective Gray. I've done my part. Please find someone who will do theirs and not have wasted my efforts. Unless of course you still feel a hooker is just a hooker."

His look is one of surprise and awe, maybe a bit offended as well. I don't much care at this point. I'm still mad at him. I can't hate him, no matter how hard I try. I've scrubbed my lips a dozen or more times and can't get the feel of his mouth on mine to go away. Unfortunately, I also can't scrub away the desire to feel it again.

Whatever shoes he's wearing today don't make any sound behind me as I work my way back to my lab. I push the door open and suddenly find it takes no effort as the weight behind it is relinquished from my hands when Deacon pushes on it and moves me forward, pushing the door closed behind him and turning the lock. He grasps my elbow and spins me around, backing me up toward the closed door.

His eyes flare in a heated gaze that matches the one on the fairgrounds. The one in the car in the parking lot. "Because a dick is a dick, right?"

"If the shoe fits." I tip my chin and grin smugly. "Or would that be a condom?"

The door hits my back as I'm pinned against it; my messy bun a lost cause as his fingers find their way under the loosely held hair at the back of my head, his arm around my waist under a lab coat that I'd give anything to have hanging on a hook right now.

"I tried, Everlee. Remember that. But you make it so damn hard," he whispers before his mouth crashes against mine in a bruising, harsh kiss that hurts as much as heals. It's a balm; a temporary salve that washes away the ache from all that ails me. There's no pain. No wishful thinking. No woulda, coulda, shoulda.

No thoughts of yesterday, no tomorrows. Just the here and now.

My hands find the curls on the nape of his neck and I relish the softness between my fingers. He moans with my touch which, in turn, begs for release of the whimper I let loose as I arch my back and seek more heat from his body. More human touch from the man I've fantasized about for years. By God, I'll make him remember me.

He pushes into me and I raise one leg in an attempt to wrap it around his hip as if on instinct. He reaches under my butt to boost me higher, and I wrap both legs around him; a perfect fit. He's hard, solid, every inch meeting mine in all the right places. Friction meeting friction, heat meeting heat. Pant for pant, moan for moan. An irresistible urge to find satisfaction by any means possible. My release is totally unexpected; too swift, a bit embarrassing, but oh so good as I bite the collar of his jacket and hide my moans of ecstasy.

Way to go, Everlee. Dry hump in the lab. Forensic scientists everywhere are giving you a thumbs up, I'm sure. Thank God I darkened the screen on the computer so the murdering creep didn't catch the show.

My body is spent as I rely on his arms to hold me up; my back against the door, my legs around his hips, my face buried in his neck.

He waits until I catch my breath, kisses my forehead gently, then lowers me to my feet. The guilt in his eyes is unmistakable as he moves me to the side and unlocks the door. He pulls on the back of his neck and grimaces. "I'll contact the 81st and let them know you matched the DNA."

"Wait a minute," I start, reaching for his arm.

He steps away from my reach and takes a deep breath, letting it out slowly. "Even principled asses can fuck up when the temptation is too strong, Everlee. If you don't tell, I won't either."

My jaw drops as I stare at him. If he thinks I was hot moments ago, he's got another think coming as my blood begins to boil. "Who the hell would I tell?!"

And here we go. *Two seconds flat.*

He grins cockily. "Made you forget him already, huh?"

"Fuck you, Detective Gray!"

"Not quite, Everlee." He smirks then winks. "We had our clothes on." He pulls the door open and takes his leave without looking back.

"I hope yours shrivels up and dies!" I scream after him before the door closes.

I was wrong. I do hate him.

Chapter 32

Deacon

"Hey," Vic says as he walks in the men's room where I stand splashing cold water on my face. I could use a cold shower right about now, but guilt seems to work as a good boner killer. The cold water on my face serves to help quiet the sound of her moans in my head. That shit is fodder for my dreams for the next year.

"What was the file Everlee dropped on your desk? You didn't seem too pleased." He stops on his way to the urinal up against the wall. "Then again, you don't look too damned happy right now either. What's up, buddy?"

I grab a paper towel from the wall unit and wipe my face. "Remember the first case we went out on weeks ago? The body in the storm drain?" He nods. "She tracked the DNA and got a hit."

His brow furrows in confusion before he turns and opens his zipper, emptying his bladder into the urinal. "Thought she already found her. Wasn't she a missing person from Houma?"

"This was DNA on the very likely perp." I wait for him to finish his business – you know, shake it twice to clean to bore – but my comment catches him off guard and he turns without thinking and sprays onto the edge of the urinal as well as the floor, and unfortunately in the process, leaving maybe a bit of backsplash on his pantleg.

"Sonofabitch!" he growls, shaking his leg as if it might

expel the liquid from the hem of his pants. He flashes me a glare that should make me shrivel. "You couldn't wait 'til I was done takin' a piss to add that little tidbit of information?"

I shrug and grin. "You asked."

"Hand me some paper towels!"

Grabbing half a dozen or so from the dispenser, I hand them over as he steps away from the mess and concentrates on the bottom of his pants and shoes first. "You asshole. I swear to God, you do these things on purpose."

A quick knock on the door captures our attention and the janitor steps in, tugging the bucket and mop behind him. "Gotta clean the can. Anybody takin' a dump or can I get in here?"

"I'd say your timing is perfect." I nod toward the urinal. "Got some real slobs around here."

Vic scowls as he throws his paper towels in the trash and washes his hands at the sink. As soon as he's done, he yanks the door open and looks over his shoulder. "I owe you one."

I follow him out the door and as we head down the hall, I pat him on the shoulder. "Hey, Vic."

"What?" he grunts.

"Your fly's open. We're even and you're welcome."

He glances around quickly and closes the front of his pants. "You're still an ass, Gray."

"So, I've been told," I say with a heaved sigh.

He eyes me curiously, knowing her hopes and wishes are a helluva lot higher than any chance of success. Trying to nail this asshole to the right place and the right time is going to be next to impossible. The log records have probably been doctored. He's most likely worked up good alibis by now. The DNA is faint at best, I'm sure. His truck has probably been cleaned from top to bottom fifty times since then. I'd only glanced inside the folder before chasing after her, but once seeing "long haul truck driver" as his occupation, my hopes sank. It only confirmed my suspicions.

He grimaces and nods in what he assumes is understanding. *Little does he know.* "I take it you explained it to her."

"Nope. Why break her spirit before the system does?"

"So why did she call you an ass?"

I shoot him a wry look. "Which time?"

He stops us before we get too close to the squad room and scouts the area to ensure nobody is close enough to hear us. "Don't you think it's time you tell her who you are? Let her know that you're aware of what she went through?" He shrugs and smirks. "I don't know, maybe that you're the cop who pulled Spencer off of her?"

Narrowing my eyes and dipping my chin, I challenge his question. "Like you did with the Cap?"

"Deacon, his concern was what Peters was threatening her with. Garner ain't stupid. He's taken to her like a father would. I wasn't givin' him a partial truth. I think his respect for you rose about fifty levels by the time I was through. Spencer's shit was covered up until you did what you did for Tess."

My gut roils over the weekend's activities. *I didn't do enough for Tess. Spencer may be dead now, but so is Tess. Micah's life was ruined. If I'd only been ten minutes earlier.*

"Hey." Vic rattles my shoulder. "Where did you go?"

"Just wishing I'd gotten there sooner."

"Can't be everywhere at the same time," he scolds as if it's something I should know; which it is. "You got there in time. Now tell Everlee who you are and quit pissin' around."

I glance down at his shoes and smirk. "Thought pissin' around was your job."

"Not funny, asshole. Let's go."

"She's got a boyfriend," I mutter as we head back for the squad room.

"Everlee's got a boyfriend?" he asks, brows raised in a question louder than the one he vocalized. "How come we ain't ever heard about him?"

"Theo," I enunciate with a disdain I'm not entitled to. "And he lives in Chicago."

Vic studies my face before he quirks a brow and bursts into laughter, then utters low, "Well, unless he's got a 900-mile long dick, he ain't gonna do her much good down here."

My eyes flare with anger at myself over the little act of infidelity I coerced her into in the lab half an hour ago as I tell him, "I am not a cheater and I will not be a replacement."

I expected understanding from my friend – maybe a little compassion – but in typical Victor Parnell form he lifts a brow and speaks as if he knows the secrets that run to the deepest part of my soul. "Then you'd better stop lookin' at her the way you do. Because you got that woman's hopes up so high, she's gonna hit pretty damn hard when you let her fall. And that, my friend, will be on you."

* * *

Halfway to Harbor county this evening, I turn my truck around and head home toward Hasselback. Why bother? Duncan Greene is dead. That fucker died the minute Everlee set foot back in the state of Louisiana. Damien Greene doesn't exist yet, and quite frankly, shouldn't. My dick is going to be laid to rest in the cemetery named "Only the Good Die Young".

Chapter 33

Everlee

I stare at the phone in my hand on Wednesday afternoon, my hopes skyrocketing as I read the message on the screen.

Keith: *Goods should be delivered by approximately 4:30 tomorrow. Being sent to you at work as special delivery and will need to be signed for by you. It's packaged well, looks very convincing as a gift. Should put a smile on your face. Didn't want to trust a doorman in your building. Hope you're not out on a call. Wish I could talk to you before then, but duty calls. Instructions to follow. Love you, Teacup.*

Me: *You have no idea what this means to me. I wish you were here to open it with me. I love you.*

Keith: *I will be with you, because you promised not to install without me. Right?*

Me: *Right. Can't wait.*

Keith: *Then I'll see your lovely face tomorrow. Facetime.*

"Everlee," Cora nearly sings with an exaggerated southern

drawl through the front desk phone. My heart has been racing since noon while I waited for this call. "You've got…uh…a package up here waitin' for you. Gotta sign for it. I'd be happy to put an autograph on this for . . ."

I slam the phone down and head for the lobby before she can finish; my feet flying down the hall as fast as they'll take me to my destination. I dodge a few people on my way, cutting in and out, maybe even under an armpit or two before I reach the grinning group standing behind the front desk.

Winded and anxious, I note a tall, broad-shouldered man standing at the desk chatting with a beaming Cora as well as many admirers behind her. I know the back of that head! As he turns, the rest of the world disappears when his face splits in a beaming smile I know so well and his arms open up at the same time his deep booming voice calls out to me, "Sweet Cheeks!"

"Theo!" I jump into my best friend's arms and he picks me up off my feet as if I weigh nothing, squeezing the air from my lungs.

Keeping one arm wrapped around my waist, he gently holds the back of my head with his beefy hand, tucking my face into the crook of his neck like he's done so many times over the years as I sob, and whispers in my ear, "Breathe, baby girl. I missed you too."

"Hey! You gonna leave enough for me there, Bub?"

I raise my head at the sound of my other bestie from the north. My voice is shaky as I gasp at another jolt of surprise, "Keith?"

He smiles those magnificent pearly whites and spreads his arms wide, waiting for Theo to set me down. He bobs his eyebrows. "In the flesh, Teacup. I told you it would be packaged well, didn't I?"

He plucks me off my feet and holds me in his arms as I cry, "The best packaging and you didn't even have to gift wrap it."

"Hey, hey," Theo chides. "I dressed up for the occasion."

Cora nearly pants as she fans her face then begs, "Can somebody put me in the middle of that bad boy sandwich? I swear to God, the Loozeeana sun don't get this hot."

We all laugh. Theo winks at her as he rubs the scruff on his chin. "Think you could scrub a few tickets for me?"

"Oh honey," Cora proffers with a heavy sigh. "I'll cut you loose from a holdin' cell if ya need." She winks back. "But only if I get to play with you first."

"Oh my God," I groan, glaring at the woman who flirts with the UPS man on a daily basis. UPS, FedEx, postman; she's not picky. "Cora! You're married!"

Theo leans over the desk and flashes her his megawatt smile. "And I'm gay."

She places her hand over her heart and juts her bottom lip in a pout. "And I'm devastated."

"Deacon Gray?!" Keith calls over my head down the short passageway as if stunned. "Is that really you?"

I turn to see Deacon, along with several of the squad room officers, watching the spectacle at the front desk. My eyes flit back and forth from Keith to Deacon and watch as Deacon squints for moment before his face lights in a dazzling smile of recognition and surprise.

"Sommers?" Deacon hastens his pace toward us and the two embrace in a man hug, slapping each other on the back over and over. "Been a long time, Keith. How the hell are ya?"

"Ornery as ever." Keith laughs and slaps his back again. "You look good Deac.

Theo gently pulls me into his hold from behind and wraps his beefy arms around my shoulders, knowing I'm ready to rip Keith a new one.

I whirl my head up against his tight hold and solid chest, glaring. "You knew!" I whisper accusingly. "I told you both his name a long time ago."

Theo's attempt at a soothing whisper and dry humor does little to calm me as his lips nearly touch my ear. "Don't go getting your panties in a twist or I'm gonna have to pinch your ass and pull 'em outta your butt crack." He chuckles at his joke. I don't. "Trust us."

"Come over here and meet my other half," Keith tells

Deacon as he waves his hand toward us. "Deacon, Theo Masters. Theo, you've heard me speak of Deacon Gray. My captain the first two years I was in the Army."

Theo releases his grip around my shoulder from one arm and reaches his hand out to shake Deacon's. "Deacon Gray," Theo says cockily as he squeezes my shoulders with the other arm a little tighter. "Sounds familiar. You're the guy who chased my Sweets Cheeks up the Ferris wheel, right?"

Deacon quirks a brow at me and without missing a beat responds, "By my recollection it was Everlee's sweet cheeks." He eyes Theo and finishes, "And you might know me better as dementia dick."

Theo bends in laughter and in the process, takes me with him. "You told him about that?"

"I didn't have to," I huff. "He overheard you. We were in his truck together. You're like a megaphone when you get upset."

"Only because I was worried about you. I love you, sweet cheeks." He kisses my temple as we're still bent in half, my body swaddled in a beefy cover that gave me more shelter in five years than I'd had my entire life. "I know it's your weekend off. Take tomorrow off and spend three days with us. We're here until Sunday."

I nod against his chest. "I can do that."

As he uprights us, Deacon looks to Keith. "You said Theo is *your* other half?"

"Yup." Keith holds up his left hand, showing his titanium band and grins. "Almost a year now. We refused to let Everlee move out of the condo until they both finished school and she was ready to make the big move here. These two have been best friends for over five years. Love at first sight. Inseparable ever since."

Deacon tilts his head as he studies my face. "I was given the impression Theo was Everlee's boyfriend."

"No, you weren't. You *assumed*," I say, emphasizing his error. Moving toward him and placing my hand on his forearm, I tug downward as I stand on my tiptoes and whisper in his ear, "And you can keep your half of that equation, Deacon, because you only made an ass out of yourself. Even principled *asses* fuck up big time . . . with and without their clothes on. I would never forget Theo and he would never forget me. He was my hero when I needed one. Get over yourself."

I turn back to my two besties. "You guys want to see my lab?"

"Lead the way, Gorgeous," Theo says as he wraps an arm around my shoulder. "I'll follow you anywhere."

"Can I come?" Cora calls after us.

"Faster than anybody we know," someone answers before I can and the lobby fills with laughter, taking with it the tension that occupied it moments ago.

I love the front desk crew. They're a small mix of men and women. Always pleasant, always kind. Seemingly quite competent. I'm beginning to like it here, but not sure I want to stay. I can move my Gram to Chicago, can't I? Maybe Florida.

Annie Mick

Chapter 34

Deacon

"Join us for dinner tonight." Keith's invitation is sincere, but I'm not sure Everlee wouldn't use the silverware as dissecting devices while the staff wasn't watching. That, and if she and Theo were fellow students, she'd have assistance in doing so. She's learned a lot in her time here. My wrinkled penis wouldn't need a dumpster. She'd probably burn it in effigy. Then again, she may roast it and chew slowly. Spit or swallow? Definitely spit. Possibly leave it raw and feed it to the gators.

"I'm good. Thanks." I raise my hand to ward off any protests. "You probably have a lot of catching up to do."

"Are you kidding me?" Keith stares as if I've insulted him. "I haven't seen you in what, ten years?" He waves toward the hall Everlee and Theo have entered toward her lab. "I'll spend the whole weekend with Evs. We're here until Sunday afternoon."

I smirk before asking. "Think we can go somewhere they don't have knives?"

He rubs his scruff before grimacing. "How bad did you piss her off?"

"Scale of one to ten?" I eye the ceiling and scratch my temple. "About a hundred."

He slaps my shoulder and leads us toward the hall to the lab. "I'd say you got some ass kissing to do, Deac. Better find a good steak house with some fine lobster. The lady likes her wine but get enough Southern Comfort in her and she'll forget what she's pissed about. Sound good?"

If the guy only knew what kind of southern comfort I'd rather give that woman. I did assume, and in the process probably made her feel pretty low. Her reactions to me weren't out of loneliness. She wanted me as much as I wanted her. I've got to fix this.

I shrug. "Worth a shot."

He chuckles. "No, it's gonna take about four, maybe five. Theo or I will carry her upstairs to put her to bed. Now show me where the lab is."

As Keith opens the door, Everlee's apparent scolding stops midsentence on a harshly whispered, "and if you had just . . ."

"Hey!" Keith announces our presence to a scowling Everlee. "Deac's going to join us for dinner this evening. Thought I could catch up with him while I can and then the three of us will have the rest of the weekend to ourselves. Okay?"

Everlee's scowl deepens before it slowly turns into a smirk. "Ah, so we're having shrimp and pineapple pizza?"

"What!?" Theo sputters. "Everlee, it's bad enough to watch you down Canadian bacon with that godawful shit on pizza. What in the hell are these people doing to you down here?"

She pins him with narrowed eyes. "It's Cajun."

"It's garbage," he argues.

She tips her chin and counters, "Put enough jalapenos on it and you will never know the difference."

He towers over her so high Everlee has to stretch her neck to meet his eyes. The guy is built like a tank but it's easy to see she doesn't feel threatened in the least. His voice is low as he demands, "I want steak. You know I'm a meat eater."

"Oh, I'm well aware, Theo." She smiles slyly. "But shouldn't you be asking for a big, fat, juicy bratwur…"

Theo's hand covers her mouth in time to capture the rest of her statement, but her giggle can't be contained. He matches her laugh as he lifts her off her feet. "If you weren't so damn cute, I'd paddle your ass. God, I've missed you."

"He rescued her," Keith utters next to me in the doorway where we watch their exchange. "Couple of thugs on the subway. He was on his way to check out a condo, she on hers to check out an apartment. They connected like long lost friends. It was perfect. I was still active duty. They attended the same school. She needed him, he needed her." He glances at me and grins. "Kismet."

"They always like this?"

He snort laughs. "Never a dull moment. Let's plan on dinner about seven. Meet us at Everlee's."

"I'm not sure she really wants . . ."

"Deacon," he stops me short. "Meet us at Everlee's at seven." He grimaces as he eyes me head to foot then shudders. "And don't wear a suit. Loosen up, you tight ass."

On the way back to the squad room, feeling better, and more hopeful, than I have in months, I get distracted by Garner's voice echoing into the hall. *Damn, I was so close.*

"Gray, a minute?" *More like ten, but here goes.*

"What's up?" I ask as I lean on the doorframe. If I step in too far, I fear I'll be stuck for an extended amount of time that I don't have to spare.

"Neil Morris at the 81st called a little while ago." He leans back in his chair, arms folded over his chest. "They bagged him, think they just might have a case. Kinda funny how they were delivered the perp's company records for the last year as to his whereabouts as well as reports of two other murders in two of those same areas that corresponded with his log books, give or take a hundred miles. Fresher bodies. They're crossmatching DNA samples as we speak."

My mouth opens and closes, then opens again. But before my brain catches up to close it again, I erupt without forethought, "There were three companies in total! He bounced around like a fuckin' rubber ball."

His brows lift and he flashes me a knowing look. "So, it was you. How much sleep did you lose doing that search?"

Ignoring his inquiry, I put forth one of my own. "Do they

really think they have a case?"

He nods. "He's hopeful. Wanted me to thank Everlee for her diligence and thoroughness. Once he told me about the info he had received, I knew it didn't add up. That had investigator written all over it. Good job, Gray."

"Don't tell Everlee." I sigh and shake my head. "I've been on desk duty, remember? I had the time. It's not always going to be that way. The sooner she realizes she can't solve them all . . ."

"The sooner she'll be like us?"

"God I hope not, Cap."

He points a hard finger and threatens, "You either give her the kudos without the details or I will give her the kudos with the details. Don't break her spirit, Gray. We need somebody with her drive and ambition around here. She's a bright light in a dark place, not to mention an antidote for your attitude." He smirks and adds, "Got it?"

"Got it," I reluctantly agree.

"Good." His face brightens as he tilts his head in the direction of the lobby. "Was that her boyfriend that came to see her?"

I bite my lip, though it does little to hide my grin. "Not her boyfriend after all."

"Smoooooth, Gray," he reminds me with a grin and a wave of his flat hand through the air. "Don't be an ass."

I chuckle. "Too late for that, but I'm willing to start from scratch if I have to."

"If you need any advice, my door's always open."

"I'll keep that in mind." I snicker and ask, "Would that be before or after shuffleboard at the senior center?"

He plants his forehead on his palm and groans, "Get the hell outta my office."

Garvis is at the entrance before my hand reaches the buzzer and opens the door for me. "Detective Gray," he greets me cheerily before his brow furrows. "Is Miss Remington expecting you?"

"Is there a reason you're asking, Garvis?" I know why he's

asking, but he doesn't know that I know, so I may as well have a little fun at his expense. Rodriguez was out today and I missed being able to piss anyone off. It's my favorite pastime because, well – a dick is a dick.

He looks around nervously as if disclosure may put him six feet under or make him an alligator's appetizer. "She has company already, sir. They looked rather burly."

"Ah," I say with feigned surprise, then worry my brow. "Think I can take 'em?"

He sucks in a breath through his teeth and shakes his head. "Do you want me to call James for backup?"

I give him a reassuring pat on the shoulder. "Let's keep James out of jail, shall we? I know where to bury the bodies, Garvis."

The poor guy looks like he's ready to shit his pants. Maybe I'm not that much of a dick. I pinch the bridge of my nose and chuckle. "Garvis, they're friends of hers from Chicago. Harmless. I promise there will be no bloodshed."

He grins smugly and puffs his chest. "I knew that, Detective. She introduced them. Just watching out for you. I know how protective you are."

He's watching out for her, too. Truly sincere. "Thanks, Garvis. Have a good evening," I tell him as I punch the button for the third floor and watch the elevator doors open.

"Oh, Detective," he singsongs before I can hop on. "All meat pizza with a side order of pecan rolls would be great, thank you."

Two taps on the door before it flies open and I find Theo waiting on the other side. The twinkle in his eyes and sinister grin smattered on his face should be my first clue, but it doesn't prepare me for his cocky greeting. "DD! Glad you could make it."

Dementia dick. So much for promising Garvis no bloodshed.

Unamused, yet knowing I'm desperate to get through this evening without compromising my already shaky status with Everlee, I simply reply, "Didn't find it funny the first time, Theo. Don't give up the day job."

He waves his hand in dismissal. "Pfft. I meant designated driver. But if you're stuck on that dementia dick, at least now we know your memory's good." He arches a brow and narrows his

eyes. "For some things."

Chapter 35

Everlee

"Not one more word!" I grind through a clenched jaw as I grip Theo's forearm in the bathroom before we leave for dinner. I overheard what he said to Deacon at the door. "If you so much as hint one more time, I will personally see to it no one's enjoying your *meat* for the next month. Got it?"

"Somebody's gotta jar his memory," Theo protests with a whisper. "I see the way he looks at you. If he's as sharp and tactical as Keith claims, then he's a total moron in the emotions department and nothing more than a walking dick that only wants to get laid. You're better off without him."

I poke him in the chest so hard, he winces with the pain. "You will not say another word, not one more hint, not one more push to try and make him remember something he obviously doesn't. Leave it alone, Theo. I'm here to solve Jonah's murder and then I'll come home. I'll bring Gram with me or I'll move her to Florida. They're always looking for forensics workers."

He pulls me into his arms and leans his chin on my head. "I don't like it. You were the one who was injured yet remember more than he does? Something just doesn't add up. Are you sure it was him?"

I shrug under the weight of his hold. "Maybe I am wrong. It was a long time ago. He would have said something by now, wouldn't he? Let's look at the footage and see what we can find. Help me do what I came here to do. Then . . ." I move away and crane my neck so I meet his eyes. "I'll come back and drive you crazy."

He taps my nose and laughs. "Never. Let's go eat. Dementia dick is driving."

"Would you stop calling him that!"

He grins impishly. "I take it he hasn't forgotten how to use it?"

"You could ask," I tell him as I turn the doorknob to make my way to the living room, then turn back and wink. "But I don't think you're his type."

Before we make it out the door, Deacon asks, "Did you feed Roscoe?"

"Oh!" I exclaim, embarrassment flushing my cheeks as I turn back to feed my fine finned friend. "I almost forgot."

Deacon takes my shoulders in his hands and gently squeezes. "I got him."

Keith and Theo track his movements toward Roscoe's tank, then look to me with raised eyebrows. I scowl and mutter, "Oh shut up."

In the restaurant, Theo and Keith strategically sit Deacon next to me while taking the other side of the booth for themselves. I'm still ready to strangle him, but as I've stated before, try as I may I don't hate him. I mean, really, he just fed Roscoe! His thigh conveniently rests against mine. It's a subtle move; totally unnecessary as there is more than enough room in this booth. Good grief, Theo and Keith sit on the other side without bumping elbows. I swear he's spreading his thighs under the table so we can connect. Oh wait, maybe that's me.

"So, how often do you two work together?" Keith asks before shoveling another bite of steak in his mouth.

Swallowing the bite of lobster I have in my mouth, I reply, "Whenever I can't get away fast enough in the forensics van for Deacon to catch up with me."

Deacon flashes me a smile and tilts his head, his leg brushing mine a little firmer. "Still manage to catch you when you least expect it, Everlee. Always will."

Does he mean the Ferris wheel? The south side with the body in the freezer? Spencer? Monday in the lab when he held me off my feet while I ground my crotch against his and . . . My thighs squeeze with the memory of that orgasm and Deacon spreads his wider so as not to lose contact. Damn him! He knows what he's doing. I look across the table to see Theo and Keith observing our exchange.

Feeling the need to break the spell he has me under, I turn back to Deacon and shoot him a wry look. "Unless you're following me down storm drains. Hard to catch someone when you're behind them."

"Speaking of which." He holds up a finger. "Garner wanted me to let you know the captain at the 81st called him today to extend his gratitude and let you know how much they appreciate your diligence on that particular case. If not for your fine skills, they may never have been able to find him."

My heart blooms as the possibilities fill me with hope. If I can do this for someone else, maybe I can still find Jonah's killer. "They think they have a case?"

"More than likely," he says with a nod.

I'm not sure what compels me. My sense of decorum is usually a bit more controlled, but at this given moment my excitement can't be contained as I lunge toward him and wrap my arms around his neck. "We did it! We did it, Deacon!"

The fit is tight, being squeezed between the table and the back of the booth, but I feel his arms around my waist and hear his soft whisper in my ear, "You did it, Everlee. And you did a helluva job."

I pull back from the awkward hug and look into the eyes I've known in my sleep, my dreams, and my thoughts for years. I know it's him. "*We* did it, Deacon."

He shakes his head. "I was just along for the ride."

My lips tip in a half-smile as I recall that day. "I thought I was along for the ride that day."

"Half a ride." He quirks a brow. "Because a dick is a dick." A hundred apologies are written in those eyes as he slides his arm from around my waist, giving my hip a gentle squeeze, and utters, "I'll try harder."

A throaty growl lets loose from the other side of the booth before, "Damnit!" My eyes dart to the guys sitting across from us to see Theo glaring at Keith as he rubs his bicep. "My trust-o-meter isn't as high as yours."

Keith waves a hand in our direction. "It didn't take her four shots of Southern Comfort and three glasses of wine. Get over it."

Deacon and Keith exchange a quick nod and knowing grins – amongst themselves. Theo simply rolls his eyes and mumbles, "Military."

I hold up a fist to his and we knock them together. "Yeah," I say smugly. "But we know how to hide the evidence, don't we?"

He laughs. "That's my girl."

* * *

Three hours later, Deacon pulls his truck into my parking lot. Keith reaches over from the backseat and grasps Deacon's shoulder tightly. They had shared their man-hugs and handshakes outside the restaurant before we hopped in.

"Damn good to see you, Deacon. Have Everlee give you my number. Stay in touch. Come see us in Chicago, or we'll see you the next time we're here."

"Good to see you too, Sommers. Been a long time." He glances back at my other best friend. "Good to meet you, Theo."

"That's it!?" Theo hollers. "No 'hey it's been fun, Theo'? No "gee I'm glad you're not her boyfriend'?"

Keith lets out a combination laugh and groan. "Get out of the truck, you moron."

They both hop out and slam the doors, making their way to the door of my building; Theo glancing behind him every few seconds to monitor the situation until Keith shoves his shoulder and moves him forward.

"I can understand now why I heard you tell him you love him." Deacon pinches the bridge of his nose and chuckles as if chastising himself and apologizing to me at the same time.

"What?" I turn in my seat and stare. "When did you hear me . . ."

"It doesn't matter, Everlee." He takes my hand off the console, lifts it to his mouth and kisses my knuckles. His smile is sincere as he says, "Enjoy your weekend. I'll see you on Monday."

As I walk in the lobby, Theo and Keith are entertaining an amused Garvis. "Ah, Ms. Remington. Did you have a good evening?" He glances over my shoulder as if searching for something. "Is Detective Gray not joining you?"

"Does Detective Gray make a habit of joining her often?" Theo asks him, his tone laced with suspicion. As if his size isn't terrifying enough, his narrowed eyes and arched brow only add to it. Poor Garvis turns to me and grimaces, fearing he's disclosed information that will place Deacon in the trunk of a car with custom orders for disposal of his body.

Grabbing Theo's sleeve and shoving him forward, I snap, "Go push the button for the third floor or I will make you sleep in the lobby tonight!"

Garvis watches our exchange, tongue in cheek as Theo marches toward the elevator. "For a big guy, he finds you rather threatening, doesn't he?"

I roll my eyes and shake my head. "He's a teddy bear wrapped in a grizzly's body. Don't let him fool you."

He eyes Theo warily once more. "Still, I'd rather not have him the lobby. I've seen pitbulls that looked less threatening."

Once in my apartment, the guys take a seat while I grab two beers for them and a glass of wine for myself. Setting them on the coffee table, I move down the hall to my bedroom and return with my laptop and set it on the table as well. "Shall we get started?"

Keith calmly moves it to the side. "Not until morning, Teacup. We are not about to watch a scene like that right before you go to bed. We'll start fresh with open eyes and see what we can come up with. I'll install the software first thing, we'll have breakfast, and then we will study the footage. Okay?"

Theo's fists clench tightly and he rolls his neck. His voice is but a low growl as he adds his two cents worth, "The last thing I need to see before I try to sleep is what that asshole did to you. It's going to be hard enough to leave Louisiana without killing him myself."

"It doesn't show much," I murmur next to him.

He tips my chin up with two fingers, his jaw set, his eyes dark and threatening. "*Any* is going to be too much."

"Why did it take you so long to get this software?" I ask Keith.

He squares me a look I don't know well, but in it I see turmoil . . . and conflict. He runs a hand through his gorgeous locks and dips his chin. "It didn't, love. This isn't a bird's eye view, Evs. This is like a telescopic lens. You shouldn't be alone. That's why we're here."

I stand from my seat and plop down between them on the sofa. "Bear hugs?"

Who needs a weighted blanket when you have the real thing? Four arms, the heat of two bodies, and the love of two men that I wouldn't trade for the world.

Chapter 36

Everlee

"Mornin' Everlee," Alva greets us with three coffee cups on a tray and a fresh steaming pot in her hands.

I decided a trip to the diner might be a good thing before we start our journey back to six years ago. A time and a place that is sure to put a damper on the rest of my day. I want to, but I don't. I may be holed up for hours studying that damn footage. Keith suggested a short run after he installed the software; maybe even a walk if I didn't feel up to that. But I wanted to treat them to this place. A southern delight with a selection to fit a king and his court.

"I see you brought your own southern comfort today. Watch out for the female diners. They may scratch your eyes out to get to these boys." She bobs her eyebrows at both Theo and Keith as she pours the coffee like a pro. "I could take 'em back to the kitchen and spoon-feed 'em myself if you want."

Theo leans his head back and opens his mouth before he licks his lips and grins. "Will you hand-feed me grapes and fan my face while I take in all the glory of your loveliness?"

She giggles and slaps his arm with her notepad. "If my son talked to a woman like that, I would paddle his ass."

He winks and grins. "Sounds like fun. You game?"

Keith drops his face in his hands and groans. "I can't take him anywhere."

Alva sighs heavily as she inquires, "Newbies on the force?"

"Oh God, no!" I reassure her. "These are my besties from Chicago. They're just visiting. Theo, Keith, this is Alva. She makes the best pecan rolls you can sink your teeth into. Her pancakes are top notch as well."

"Well, Alva," Theo says, setting his menu on the table. "I'll have one of your best pecan rolls as well as an order of your top notch pancakes. However," he says, holding up a finger. "I need meat. What do you recommend?"

"Just bring him sausage, Alva," I tell her without hesitation and smirk at Theo. "Theo is a big fan of sausage."

Keith sputters a laugh while Theo scowls. Alva snickers as her eyes light with mischief. She looks to me before she asks, "Would that be Deacon's squishy, wrinkled sausage or do ya think he likes his firm?"

Keith shoots coffee from his mouth all the way across the table and Theo's brows lift in curiosity as my cheeks heat with a flush I cannot hide. "I … I'll explain it later," I stammer.

"Oh, sweet cheeks," Theo singsongs. "You can bet your ass you're going to explain it."

Alva pats my shoulder and giggles. "Sorry, sweetie. Couldn't help myself. I ain't never seen Deacon one-upped the way you did him that day." She refills Keith's coffee and turns toward the kitchen. "Orders will be right up."

Keith eyes me as he wipes up the splattered coffee with napkins, then grins. "Dick in the dumpster day?"

"Yes." I scowl and square my shoulders. "He tried to make me look like a prostitute. Served him right."

He drops his chin to his chest as he shakes his head and laughs. "Theo, I think we can quit worrying now."

* * *

"There's something missing here, Evs." Keith rubs his hand over his well-groomed facial hair as he studies the screen of my computer. "They spliced the recording."

I already knew this, but the picture is so much clearer with this new software he's installed. It's like the difference between HD and an old black and white on the TV screen. Much less fuzziness. It's not exactly crystal clear, but it's a damn sight better than anything I was looking at before. I would have never seen Jonah like this if I hadn't stripped the white sheet off his body, but I was in a panic that night. I knew deep down in my soul it was my little brother under that cover and it was my job to get to him.

"Don't focus on Jonah, Evs. Don't focus on the asshole pulling on you," Keith whispers. "Focus on the surroundings. Wait a minute." He freezes the shot right before what has always been known as "when the camera stopped working then started again" and points at the screen. He rewinds the clip and says, "Watch here."

He starts the clip again as I lean closer. The only thing I detect is Spencer being separated from me by someone in the crowd as I fall forward with my baby brother in my arms; limp and bleeding.

"That isn't somebody from the crowd, Evs. That's a cop. Look at the shoe, the pantleg." He zooms the shot in so close the only thing we see is the shoe as well as the bottom half of a navy blue pantleg with the classic darker uniform stipe. The leg is angled in an offensive position at Spencer's side in such a way, it's obvious this person was not an observer. They were moving in to end the chaos.

Theo and Keith exchange glances between themselves over my head but I don't miss it.

My eyes flit back and forth from one to the other. "What?"

"Didn't the records state it was somebody in the crowd moved in to break it up?" Keith asks. I nod.

Theo leans his elbows on his knees and bows his head. "Does anybody here know you're originally from the area?"

"No," I answer quickly. "Other than Jonah's friends. Maybe Mayor Peters. But that's only because he dug deep enough. And Keith took care of him." I look to Keith and smile. "Thank you by the way. The others all think I'm from Chicago. But what do

I know?!" I throw my hands in the air in frustration. "I thought Deacon was the man in the ambulance too! I think we've pretty much established he's just . . ." I roll my eyes and finish, "Horny."

Keith smirks. "You could do worse."

Don't I know it, but I'm not about to tell them that.

"Please tell me you're not going to spend every night going over that footage, Everlee. If you can't, I'll uninstall the software right now," Keith warns. "There's a lot in the background footage that may help you recognize something. A person, familiar clothing, even tattoos. What I'd like to do, if you'll let me, is blur the images of Jonah and you. I think it's too much for you to bear. Will you let me do that?"

Theo wraps his arm around my shoulder and taps my temple. "You have the most important part of Jonah up here." Then he taps gently over my heart. "And here. You don't need to see that shit again."

"You're right." I nod against his against shoulder and look to Keith. "Blur it."

Theo pats my leg and squeezes my thigh. "That's my girl. Then we'll go see Gram."

My mouth pulls tight as if sucking on a lemon and I can't help but giggle. "You realize her sweet tea will make you pucker."

He laughs boisterously. "Baby girl, all that woman has to do is pull out a wooden spoon and my ass cheeks pucker. I doubt the sweet tea can do any worse."

Little does he know.

Chapter 37

Deacon

"Two blocks north of Everlee's apartment near the park. Black sweats and a green T-shirt. Meet me there in thirty minutes. Four seasons."

"You're damn lucky I wasn't in the shower, asshole," I mutter to myself. "Or still in bed." *Four Seasons. Sommers. It's what we called him in the service. Heat was unbearable in Afghanistan; 120 degrees somedays.* I throw back the rest of my coffee – slightly burning my tongue – and head for the bedroom to toss on some clothes. The park near Everlee's is about twenty minutes away. It's also six thirty on Saturday morning. What the hell could Keith want this early?

I find him easily. He's sweaty, looks like he's just finished a run, and quite frankly ready for battle. Alone. He approaches my truck before I'm parked and opens my door once I am.

"Let's talk, Deac."

I kill the engine and unfasten my seatbelt. "You gonna let me get out first?"

He steps back and waits as I climb down and shut the door. "Got something on your mind, Sommers?"

He crosses his arms over his chest, feet shoulder width apart. "How long have you been a detective?"

"Couple years. Why?"

"How long were you a cop before then?"

The hairs on the back of my neck start to rise and an uneasy feeling creeps over me. "Why are you asking?"

"How long?" he asks again slowly.

I shrug casually though it's not at all how I'm feeling. Keith is no dummy. He's special ops. Highly trained, sharp shooter, tech wizard. Mind like a steel trap. Hands of a killer. "About five years."

"How many of those were spent in the 79th division?"

Breaking the eye contact I was so determined to hold, because while I can be evasive, I won't lie to him either, I keep my answer general. "The first couple."

He aims his gaze toward the sky and narrows one eye as if calculating, though I know it's total bullshit. He's got this all figured out. "So, you were there, what, a time span between five to seven years ago?"

"Spit it out, Sommers," I grind through clenched teeth as if I were still his captain.

A cocky grin spreads across his too-handsome-to-be-a-killer face. "You're the one who pulled Spencer off of her, aren't you?" We don't blink, don't waver from our glare; just wait to see who will break. His cockiness grows as he lifts a brow. "I watched the street cam footage."

"It was spliced," I enunciate slowly, our eyes still fixed as if the war ain't over. I know I'm the only one who has the unedited version. It's locked away in a hidden safe in my home, buried under the floorboards. I'll be dead before they ever find it and by then, it won't matter. I haven't even watched it.

"It was also grainy. I have access to enhancement features." He grins like the Cheshire cat. "There's no mistaking a cop's uniform pants, nor his shoes."

Conceding the battle of eye contact as well as the battle of wills, I pinch the bridge of my nose. "Does she know it was me?"

"Nope."

The plea for mercy must be written all over my face because his arms drop to his sides and he lets his guard down. "You gonna tell her?"

"Nope," he says once more. "But you are."

"I can't, Keith." I let out a pitiful sigh. "I never found Jonah's killer."

"Why did they splice the footage, Deac?"

"So, I wouldn't lose my job!" I rake fast hands through my hair in frustration. "I beat the piss out of him. I was a rookie on the force at the time. My supervisor knew I'd be fired immediately without question. He got me out of there as fast as possible and they blamed it on someone in the crowd. Spencer never knew the difference."

"Where did you go after?"

"Home." The word is out of my mouth before I can stop it. I don't make a habit of lying, but until I can someday explain to Everlee why I had to leave her, no one outside the tiny circle of cops who already know the truth needs to. "I had the next three days off and my supervisor told me to lay low. So, I did."

His mouth twists as he ponders my answer but seems satisfied. "Where is Spencer now?"

My eyes are cold and my voice low, my only regret being not watching that sorry sonofabitch feed the gators. "Dealt with."

His lips twitch in amusement. "Permanently?"

"As soon as he came out of hiding." I grit my teeth and shoot him a wry look. "Which was as soon as Everlee's name was spread across every news source after the Ferris wheel incident."

"Any chance Jonah was dealing drugs?" It's a question he would hate a positive answer to, but we all had to ask under the circumstances.

I shake my head. "Not according to all of his friends and the customers I've talked to. Jonah's only interests were his music and obtaining a recording contract. They made good money doing what they were doing. His sights were set. The bartender said it was a rare occasion that Jonah even had a beer and never until the night was over. His friends explained his mother was a drunk and the last thing he ever wanted to be."

"Oh," Keith mutters with disdain. "They got the mother part right. Beverly Remington is a walking, talking nightmare. The woman has been through more one-night stands than two Navy ships full of horny sailors."

I forgo sharing my interaction with the mother from hell.

"How long are you guys going to be here?"

He grins knowingly. "Anxious to get rid of us?"

"No, Sommers," I lie through my teeth and chuckle. "Just wondering."

He grasps my shoulder and squeezes . . . hard. "We leave tomorrow afternoon. You're a good man, Deacon." He pauses and studies my face. "But Everlee is amazing. I've never known anyone like her. Don't hurt her."

"I'd sooner kill myself."

He nods, then squares me straight in the eyes and smiles cockily. "Good to know, because if you didn't, I would. Thank you for pulling Spencer off of her. I owe you one. But sparing you won't be the favor if you hurt her. Take care, Deac. Stay in touch."

He turns to start his jog back to Everlee's. "Hey, Keith."

He stops and looks back, brows hitched as he waits.

"Are you happy?" I ask with all sincerity, remembering the determined young kid I was assigned when he entered the service, proud of the huge steps he'd made by the time I left. Now in awe of the man he's become.

His smile shows damn near every tooth as his face lights up. "Wondered how long it would take you. He's a smartass, but he's loyal as hell. Perfect match. Yeah, I'm happy."

"That's all that matters."

"Mm-hmm," he hums and tips his chin. "I remember somebody telling me that about ten years ago. Have you forgotten to take your own advice? Better not wait too long, old man. That gray hair at your temples is gonna start spreading."

My jaw drops as I reflexively raise a hand to my blonde locks.

"Damn," he breathes a deep sigh of satisfaction. "Always wanted to do that."

"Smartass."

He laughs heartily before he turns to run again. "Good

seeing you, Cap. Don't forget to manscape."
First thing I'm doing when I get home is checking for grays.
After that? Manscaping . . . of course.
Asshole.

Chapter 38

Everlee

"Hey," Theo soothes me as he lifts me off my feet. "No crying or I tuck you in my pocket and take you back with me. What would Roscoe and Gram do without you?"

"I wish you didn't have to go," I cry softly as I bury my chin in the comfort of the crook of his shoulder and neck. "Next time stay longer. Might want to give me a heads-up too."

"Why?" he asks cockily. "You plan on jumping the bones of a hot detective?"

Slapping the shoulder I'm not buried in, I growl, "Go jump your own bone, you idiot. I'll be busy collecting the ones left behind for evidence."

"Don't forget the gloves, baby girl. I left your reminder on the counter," he says as he sets me back on my feet.

"You got me a new mug?"

"Got you two in case he pisses you off again." He taps me on the nose and winks. "Next time make sure you hit him with it. Never waste a good cup of coffee."

We each hug one more time. Three 'I love yous', a few more tears, and then they're out the door. Gone until the next time.

* * *

At six o'clock my doorbell chimes and I look through the peephole to find those 'bones' Theo teased me about standing on the other side. Of course it is. He's the only one that can get past Garvis without permission from me. All 206 of those bones, wrapped in sinewy muscle that I've watched flex on occasion, topped with some pretty interesting tattoos that I've yet had the pleasure of admiring up close for any length of time.

Stand strong, Everlee. You don't want to break a new coffee mug. He hasn't tried hard enough. Make him fight for you.

Taking a deep breath and rolling my shoulders once, I open the door. "Detective Gray," I greet him with feigned surprise. "I thought we were seeing each other tomorrow morning."

He leans a solid forearm on the door frame, the heat in his eyes searing my skin as he arches a brow. "Theo's not your boyfriend."

Rolling my eyes, I laugh. "No shit, Sherlock. A little slow for such a good detective but when the awards competition comes around again, I'll be sure to submit your name. You never know, might get you an honorable mention."

He heaves a sigh. "I assumed."

"You did," I retort with a slow nod.

"I should have asked."

"Which part?" I tilt my head and smirk. "If Theo was my boyfriend or if you could just pop into my lab and make me come?"

A low throaty groan bubbles out of him and his voice is strained as he forces a somewhat sincere, "I'm sorry."

"Be a little more specific." I smile cockily. "For assuming Theo was my boyfriend, questioning my principles, or for making me come?"

His nostrils flare and his eyes narrow. "Never." He takes two steps closer; the door closing behind him. Taking a tendril of hair between his fingers and twirling it between his fingers, he whispers, "For the rest, yes. Giving you pleasure, Everlee? Not one ounce of remorse." His eyes drop to my mouth and he brushes his thumb over the swell of my bottom lip. "For that, I will never apologize."

"What do you want me to say, Deacon?"

His hand wraps in my hair as he bends my head back, the perfect angle for taking and giving; his resolve at the breaking point as he pleads, "Anything but no."

"If you stop in the middle aga . . ."

His mouth crushes mine before I can proceed with my threat; swallowing my words and stealing my breath. I swear if he stops again, I will break both of Theo's coffee mugs over his head. I've never been kissed like this. There is no give and take; this is all Deacon. He's in full control, demanding, all encompassing, harsh but not hurried.

He breaks the kiss with a pop and leans his forehead on mine, his eyes squeezed closed, his breaths broken as his chest heaves. "You're not Theo's."

"No, you idiot," I groan as I fist his shirt.

"You need to want this." His grip around my waist tightens and his hand in my hair tugs my head back. His eyes are ablaze as he stares into mine, a hint of something I cannot decipher. It seems almost desperate, maybe even pain. "Because once we start, I'm not gonna be able to stop, Ever . . . lee."

My nose scrunches the tiniest bit. "Play on words?"

His expression doesn't change, nor does his tone. "Just the truth."

"I want this, Deacon."

As he picks me up by the waist, I wrap my legs around him, and he carries me toward the bedroom. He mutters against my mouth before locking lips with mine, "So fuckin' long I've waited for you."

It's a flurry of clothing being tossed here and there; his boots and socks, my T-shirt and leggings, his T-shirt and jeans. And here we stand, the last stitches of clothing before all is laid bare. The bedroom is dim, but it's not dark. Oh shit! My scars. It hits all at once. This will let me know everything I need to know. If Deacon is the man in the ambulance, he'll ignore them completely like they don't exist. If he's not, he may be turned off by them or heavily inquire. It's not like they're prominent; the shin scars are minimal. But the knee gashes could only be altered to a certain extent. Tendon repairs suck. If we don't go at it doggy style or keep the lights off, he'll never see the scar on my back.

Get out of your head, Everlee! Get laid and enjoy the sex. How long has it been?

"Uh, uh, uh." Deacon stops my hands before they can reach the enclosures on the back of my bra and brings them down to my sides. "Final packaging is mine to unwrap."

"Expecting something spectacular?"

He palms my cheeks and tips my chin up with his thumb. "I've already met her. The rest is simply icing on the cake." His mouth dips to take mine in a kiss that's much gentler than what he delivered in the foyer. Patient, slower, savoring every last dip and corner. He tugs at my bottom lip with his teeth, then soothes the sting with his tongue; the sensation of which sends a flood of desire straight to my core. My nipples stiffen into tight peaks against the thin layer of lace separating us and I press into his chest, causing the slight friction I need to tease them. He reaches behind me, releases the hook enclosures with one flick of his fingers, and waits for me to step back to let it fall.

My arms still wrapped around his neck, my chest to his, I look up. "You want to see what's under here, don't you?"

He grins impishly. "Yeah, baby, I do. But only when you're ready."

I'm not ample-chested, a C-cup at best. Not exactly fried eggs on a platter, but not what you'd call busty either. A perfect balance of no shoulder strain but still in need of support. I take a step back and let the bra fall to the floor.

Deacon bites his lip and takes in the sight before him. "Damn," he breathes in appreciation. "That is some mighty fine icing."

He picks me up and takes me to the bed where he gently lies me down, then follows above me. "You are perfect," he whispers before dropping a lingering kiss to my mouth. That kiss continues on a slow journey from my jaw to the sweet spot behind my ear, onto my neck, my collarbone, and finally settles on a nipple that he nips and tugs with his teeth, then soothes with a flat tongue while twirling the other between his fingers. His mouth moves from my breasts down my belly and onward to the lace covering the most intimate part of my body where he buries his face and breathes deeply. "You smell fucking delicious."

His words alone nearly make me spiral off the bed and out of my own skin. My back arches with need and desire as a moan escapes, followed by a whimper, "Deacon."

He rises to his knees, places his thumbs under my panties on each side, and slowly removes them. Agonizingly slow. As if torture is a sport slow. He takes one ankle in his hand and leisurely places kisses from the inside of my calf to the inside of my thigh, then moves to the other, repeating the process. He's deliberate, nearly methodical, but so gentle. It's like a mix of intimacy and reverence. It's not exactly distracting from the foreplay, but adds an element I've never experienced, nor expected. I don't even care about the scars. For the first time in six years, it's like they don't exist; a sensation like none other I've ever felt in my life. I'm beautiful in my own skin. Nothing to hide and nothing to hide from.

As he reaches the top of my second thigh, my knees bend and I find giving Deacon Gray access and control to every inch of me is easy, comfortable, and oh so magical.

He slides his tongue along each side of the target, teasing and tempting, until I'm nearly growling in frustration. He chuckles, sending vibrations through my center without actual touch, which only makes it worse. I lift a foot and dig my heel into his back while grabbing two fists of his hair, and whine, "Stop teasing me."

He dives in as if he's starving, a throaty groan of satisfaction that adds to my pleasure and increases the sensation. He inserts one thick finger, then two, moving them slowly in and out. I arch into the motions, pleading with my moans and whimpers. He sucks my clit into his mouth and curls his fingers in harmony, hitting that sweet spot only a wise man can find, and I am . . . gone. The sun, moon, and stars flash beneath my eyelids one after another.

"Deacon!" My cry is one for mercy because the man is

relentless. I don't have a chance to come down from the first one before he's coaxing another out of me. I've never . . . but I do. And it's just as good as the first. I'm breathless but fully aware of every touch, every soft kiss he plants on my body as he slowly makes his way back to me.

He hovers above me, burdening his weight on his elbows. His smile is one I've never seen before as he whispers, "I love the sounds you make. The whispers, the moans, the way you say my name. Be careful, Everlee, someone might think you actually like me."

I shrug a shoulder against the mattress beneath me and grin. "You must be growing on me."

He grinds against me and winks. "As we speak."

I take his cheeks in my palms, feeling the delicious scruff in my fingers, and study the face and eyes I want to see for whole different reasons than I thought just days ago. "Thank you, Deacon."

"We're not done, Everlee," he says, brushing his nose against the side of mine. "I warned you once we start, I wouldn't be able to stop."

"I'm well aware, detective." I reach for his jerseys and begin to slide them off his hips, tugging harder when they resist my efforts.

"Whoa, baby," he groans and jolts back, halting my efforts. "There's a package in front we need get past first. I guarantee they weren't this tight when I put them on." He rises up on his knees and slips his jerseys down and off. I take a peek. I shouldn't have. If I have that once, my dildo is going to develop a complex and be lost in the land of wishful thinking. It's going to feel like the wiffle ball on a soccer field.

He reaches for his wallet that he tossed on the nightstand before he removed his jeans and extracts a strip of condoms. XXL. Of course he is. Only 1% of men necessitate an XXL. *Excuse me, I'm a research scientist.* My thighs were squeezing in anticipation before. Now they're quivering in fear. I don't think I have an XXL capacity vagina. I do have to walk tomorrow. If I get called out for an investigation, I may have to bend, squat, or God only knows what.

"Breathe, baby," he whispers above me after taking his position, edging in slowly, back and forth. He brushes the hair away from my face and places soft kisses on my mouth, my cheekbones. "So tight."

I expected Deacon to be so much more dominant, controlling, maybe even demanding. Never in my wildest dreams did I anticipate such gentility and patience. I know he's holding back. I can see it in his tense muscles, the tic in his jaw, the flare in his eyes. Hear it in the strain of his voice.

"Eyes up here, Everlee," he commands through a clenched jaw as he stops moving, demanding my attention before he delivers any more pleasure.

I hitch my legs tighter around his hips and squeeze as I meet his heated gaze and whisper, "More."

He pushes all the way in, the movement stealing my breath and making me gasp. His eyes don't leave mine as he releases a shuddered breath and says, "And now you know who you own."

He doesn't give me time to process what he's said because his mouth takes mine in a hungry, powerful, passionate kiss that helps detract from the few painful movements it takes to adjust to size and drive. And drive he does. This is the dominant and controlling Deacon I was expecting.

And I want more.

So much more.

Annie Mick

Chapter 39

Deacon

She does own me – has for a long time. She will always come first, last, and be my top priority every minute in between. Right now it's in the bedroom as I coax one last orgasm from her just so I can hear more of her moans, feel her clench around me, and bask in the sound of my name as she lets go.

"One more, Everlee." My breaths are fast and hard, my spine feeling that familiar rush before I explode.

"I can't," she whimpers, yet stares at me, her jaw set, as if in challenge to make it happen.

I drop my weight to one elbow and reach between us, pressing a thumb to that screaming bundle of nerves and drive hard one last time, exploding inside the condom, the quantity of which I can only hope it held. Never in my life has anything felt so fucking good.

"Oh God," she pants as she arches into my touch and lets go one last time. I much would have preferred my name, but that's a discussion for another day, and if I had to share the credit, better Him than some rando.

The muscles in the one arm holding me up are on fire so the moment she stops gripping my dick like it's a lifeline, I'm able to give it a reprieve and balance my weight on both. I bury my face in the crook of her neck and chuckle. "I knew you could."

She giggles, but with every motion she squeezes my dick and I swear she's resuscitating him. I've never tried so hard to stave off a release.

"That was . . . that was," she breathes hard.

I raise my head from the crook of her neck, studying her face; those eyes that captured my heart so many years ago. "Just the beginning, Everlee." I plant a soft kiss on her mouth and rise off the bed, heading for the bathroom to dispose of the condom. I've never minded condoms. They've been my best friend for a long time. Wouldn't know what sex without them is like. But I'm suddenly getting the urge to find out.

After finding a washcloth in the cabinet, I run it under warm water and wring it out. I glance in the mirror above the sink. "Forever, Gray," I whisper to myself. "Don't fuck it up."

Returning to the bedroom, I find her under the blanket, all the way up to her chin. I hold the washcloth up. "Lose the blanket."

"Why?" she asks on a shocked whisper.

"Aftercare," I say softly, not that I've ever provided it. "Unless you want to get a warm bath. I can pour the water for you."

"Um." She squirrels her face before sitting up, bringing her knees up to her chest and wrapping her arms around them. "I'll uh, I'll," she stammers before pointing to the chair in the corner. "Could you hand me the robe over there? I can take care of myself. If you'll just, um . . ." She waves her hand up and down. "Put some clothes on, I'll be out in a minute."

Under any other circumstances I would remind her I've seen most of it, tasted a lot of it, but this is Everlee. It's her scars that are making her self-conscious. It's also making me once again regret not watching the gators feast on Spencer.

"The long one," she insists when I snatch the first one off the top. I grab the other, surreptitiously smirking at what I see underneath, and hand it to her. "Thanks."

I pick up my briefs and slide them on before collecting my jeans; forgoing the T-shirt – I'm not planning on leaving unless she insists. As I get dressed, I note she carefully slips her arms into the robe and holds it tightly closed as she slides out of bed on the other side and assures the bottom half falls over her legs as she stands.

When she steps out into the living room five minutes later, dressed in a T-shirt and leggings, I'm at the fish tank with food in hand. "Has Roscoe had dinner yet?"

She laughs and shakes her head. "No, go ahead."

"How about you?" I ask, dropping a few flakes into his tank and capping the jar. "Have you had dinner?"

She tries to scowl but fails miserably. "Kinda got distracted."

I wrap her in my arms and nuzzle into her neck. "The kind of distraction that works up an appetite?"

"I'm starving," she whines then giggles as I rub my scruff against her ear. I've never heard Everlee giggle before tonight. Not for me anyway. I want to bottle it. Best damn antidepressant ever created.

Tugging at the hem of the T-shirt she wears, I tease, "Why didn't you put my shirt on?"

She gasps. "What?"

"I saw it on the chair. Have you been sleeping in my clothes?"

"It's...it's soft," she stammers.

"Everlee . . ."

"An...and comfy. You left it behind and . . ."

"Everlee . . ."

"What?"

I tip her chin up and smile. "I missed you too."

It's nearing midnight before the activities – those which included dinner, three more orgasms for her, two for me – are winding down and we lie in comfortable silence. Spent, sated, and yet I'm not ready to go home.

"We have to work tomorrow," she reminds me as if I didn't already know.

"Yup." I turn and roll her over to her side, tucking one arm under her pillow, the other around her waist, spooning her from behind. "We'd better get some sleep."

"You're going to stay?" she asks, probably half expecting I

would have been out the door and home half an hour ago.

"Unless you're kicking me out." I adjust myself a little closer, holding her tighter to me, and kiss the tip of her shoulder. "I've never done a sleepover before. Never wanted to, 'til now." I take a deep breath and let it out slowly. "Mmm….jasmine."

"Who?"

"Not who," I whisper. "What. It's your scent. My favorite. Has been since the first time I smelled it on you."

"It's my shampoo." She chuckles softly. "I've used it for years."

"Hmm, have you now?" I say playfully. "It's a scent that causes a man to dream."

"Do you snore too?" Her shoulders shake gently as she hides the sound of her laugh.

I nuzzle her neck. "I could sleep with my mouth on your pussy and guarantee you will not care."

She clears her throat loudly and adjusts the blankets around her shoulders. "Goodnight, detective."

"It's Deacon," I clarify before kissing her temple. "And you can use it even when I'm not making you come. Goodnight, baby."

* * *

Six o'clock in the morning, the sun barely cresting the horizon, and my internal alarm is busting my balls from the inside out. No "Whippin' Post going through my head. The only dread I feel is having to leave this bed. She's so peaceful. Her breaths are deep, slow, measured. I want to pull her into my arms and breathe her in for a kickstart to my day. Instead, I slowly and tactically remove myself from my side of the bed and put my clothes on. I need to go home, get a shower, and get ready for work. I also need to water the jasmine bushes out back as I neglected to do it last evening and the evening before. I was so desperate to get to Everlee I forgot to do the one thing that cannot be overlooked. Why I don't install a damn sprinkler system is beyond me. It's the personal touch I've always enjoyed, the effort it takes to keep them alive and thriving.

As my hand reaches for the doorknob, her voice rings behind me. "You're leaving, aren't you? Couldn't even say goodbye?" The hurt in her words hits hard. I wasn't leaving, I was trying to let her sleep in. I was going to leave her a sweet note on the kitchen counter. I planned on seeing her in . . . Aw shit! In her eyes, I was leaving.

Dropping my boots on the floor, I make my way back to her side of the bed and take a seat. She's turned away so I caress her shoulder and tug gently. "Hey, look at me."

She pulls away and sniffles. "It doesn't matter. Just go."

Like hell it doesn't matter. I crawl across her onto the bed and take her in my arms. "I was gonna run home and grab a shower and get ready for work. I need a suit today. You were sleeping so soundly I didn't want to wake you." She sobs lightly against my chest as I cradle her in my arms. "I was going to leave you a note on the kitchen counter. Everlee, please don't cry. Baby, you're breaking my heart."

She pulls back from my hold and swipes at her cheeks. "I'm just being stupid." She sniffles and hiccups.

"Don't ever say that again. I've never met anybody with your dedication and brains." I kiss her forehead. "I think we're dealing with something else here, though. And I don't want you to hold back what you're feeling, okay?" She nods against my bicep while keeping her head low. "Use your words, Everlee."

"Okay," she whispers in agreement.

"Now kiss me." I try to tip her chin up again, but she holds it firm against my against my fingers.

"I have morning breath."

Gripping her chin between my fingers and thumb, I tilt her head back. "You have Everlee's mouth and I want a morning kiss." I couldn't give two shits what her breath smells like. I simply want what I've missed for so long.

"Next weekend," I whisper against her mouth when the kiss ends. "We'll start on Friday and wake up together two mornings in a row. My house. How does that sound?" I grimace. "Provided one of our city's finest doesn't pull us out on an emergency call."

"I'll try not to climb any Ferris wheels."

Arching a brow, I make my stance clear. "You won't be climbing any Ferris wheels again . . . ever."

"But you'll still catch me?"

I plant a soft kiss on her mouth. "I'll still catch you."

She needs to know the truth. I can't keep pretending we have no history. I'll explain it was me in that cop's unform. It's a start. If she's at my house, she can't run away as fast. Can't kick me out the door. Maybe I'll even tell her it was me in the ambulance, explain why I left when I did. Do I dare bring out the uncut version of the street cam footage? Might she see something I missed? It's only foot traffic, my pummeling the shit of out Spencer. Everlee being gently coaxed away from Jonah's lifeless body by the EMTs – the way it should have been done to begin with.

"What about Roscoe?"

I chuckle at her dedication to a fish. Just like Everlee. Everyone is somebody's someone. "We can come back here twice a day and take care of Roscoe. Or we can have Garvis come up. What do you think?"

"He does kinda like you."

"Roscoe or Garvis?"

She scrunches her nose. "Depends on who you're feeding at the time."

"So, they only like me for my food, huh?"

She kisses the underside of my jaw and nips at the skin. "I like you for more than your food."

"You make being late for work very tempting, Everlee," I groan as I bury my face in her neck, her hair, her jasmine scent, in all that is Everlee Remington. I could live inside this woman.

The jasmine bushes? The sun isn't on them until after noon. They'll wait. Work? Yeah, they're not going anywhere. I'll tell them I made a quick stop in the ER. They don't have to know it doesn't stand for emergency room.

I'm on my way out the door half an hour later. ER? Everlee Remington. Morning sex? Who knew? Damn. I gotta do that more often.

The elevator door opens to not only the lobby but to two raised voices. Stepping out, I'm greeted with a visual that wipes out any good mood I was holding onto moments ago.

"I would say since I'm lookin' at a picture o' your ugly mug, you ain't s'posed to be here. And since you just snuck in while there was two people walkin' out, you entered this property illegally," the large intimidating doorman barks at the ever familiar mother from hell. He points a beefy hand toward the door. "Now go on, git. 'Fore I boot your irritatin' ass outta that door myself."

"You must be James," I greet him as I walk to the front desk. "I've heard about you. Thanks for staying on your toes. I'll be happy to escort her *irritatin' ass* out the door for you." I scowl at the leering she devil who is donning a red wig today. "Apparently you've decided to violate those no-contact orders, Beverly. Need a few nights in a jail cell to remind you what happens when you break the law?"

"You again," she sneers.

"Always will be," I retort with a cold, hard stare. "This is your first mark against you. Last chance. Leave now, don't come back, or go to jail. What'll it be?"

She extends her hands and paints on a salacious smile that makes me want to retch. "You gonna cuff me, officer?"

"Nope. I'll save that for the two female officers coming to get you." I smirk. "We know your type. Did you make the call, James?" I ask the doorman without looking his way. My hope is that he's as fast at taking a hint as Garvis is.

He holds the receiver to the desk phone up. "Got 'em on the line. They're waitin' for your orders, detective." *Good man.* Apparently he knows who I am too.

She bares her teeth and as God is my witness, foams at the mouth. "Fuck you, detective."

Hard as it is, I simply arch a brow. "Door. Now."

As soon as the door closes behind her, James blows a low whistle. "That is one nasty woman. How many personalities you s'pose she got?"

I shoot him a wry grin. "I s'pose as many as it takes until she gets what she wants."

Chapter 40

Everlee

My heart races as I sit in my car in the parking lot. How do we do this? We didn't discuss it. Do we pass each other in the hallways like always? Do we sneak peeks while no one is looking, as if sharing a secret, and picture each other naked? Do we hide it? There's no policy against it. Not us anyway. We're not inter-department.

"Mornin' Everlee," Cora singsongs loudly as I enter the building. "My Roger says to thank you for all the sex this weekend."

My eyes nearly bug out of my head. "For what?!" My voice is nearly an octave higher and four decibels above normal. "I don't even know your husband!"

"Oh honey." She flags a hand in the air. "I didn't mean *from* you. Your Chicago muscle gave me enough fuel to start the embers. Roger put out the flames. I told him you shared some new ideas. He doesn't need the details."

My face fills with mortification. Don't people usually watch porn for that? I stare at her, scrunch my nose, do a double take, scrunch once more, and blow an exasperated breath, then shake my head of the visual she's just planted in there. "You are weird!" I whisper shout across the lobby.

She waggles her eyebrows. "He's puttin' in a trapeze bar next weekend."

"You worry me, Cora." I shudder before turning for the hall, leaving a front desk full of laughing people behind. That's the thing about me: I'm never sure if people are joking or not. I'm sure not going to hang around and find out.

An hour later, Deacon steps into the lab. "Thought I'd stop and see you before I take off for court." He looks pensive as he studies my face. "Did you get to work okay?"

I spread my arms wide and grin. "One piece."

While my arms are spread, he takes the opportunity to slide his around my waist and lift me off my feet. "Don't forget the weekend." He kisses me as if he hadn't just been inside me two hours ago and sets me back on my feet. "I have court this morning and Parnell and I have a stakeout tonight. If it's a success, we'll be lucky. If not, it could last a bit longer. More nights, less days so I won't be around. I'll try to catch you before I go."

"Be careful."

He grins cockily. "Why, Everlee Remington, I do believe you just may like me after all."

"Jury's still out," I sass. "Don't push your luck."

"I'm trying." He chuckles and kisses me once more then heads for the door.

"Deacon?" I call after him before the door closes. "I'd rather have the real you. Don't change."

He turns, his body half in and half out the doorway. He smiles so sweetly it lights up his eyes. "Everything changed the day you showed up here, Everlee." The door closes behind him and I'm left with the sound of his heels echoing in the hall.

Staring at the closed door, I mutter to myself, "No shit, Deacon Gray. You were not in my plans and I cannot let you get in the way of them. Dammit, Everlee, focus!"

I spend the rest of the week in the lab cleaning up the last of Hawkins' messes – yes, it's taken this long – and analyzing evidence as well as interpreting blood smears for state examiners. I love my job. It's challenging and demands precision. It also convicts the criminals and exonerates the innocent.

I spend my evenings glued to my computer screen zooming

in and out on every last inch, every last nook and cranny of the street cam footage, searching for a lost clue. Keith said to concentrate on clothing, faces, tattoos I might recognize. There is nothing. By Thursday I'm ready to throw my computer through the wall. I don't know where to turn. I was counting on this footage giving me something to go on.

My phone pings with a text.

Deacon: *Pick you up at seven tomorrow. Pack a bag, you won't be going home. We'll feed Roscoe before we leave. Same restaurant we took your besties to.*

"Assuming again, detective?" I speak to my phone as if he can hear me, though I do it with a smile. I have missed him. He has sent a good morning text every day before he goes to bed, and a goodnight text while he's on the stakeout. He's stopped in the lab once this week, virtually attacked my mouth, and left like a thief in the night, stealing my breath and leaving me, well – horny.

Me: *What if Roscoe gets lonely?.*

Deacon: *We'll call Garvis and have him take the phone up and you can sing him a lullaby. Seven o'clock. Be ready.*

Me: *You're driving?*

Deacon: *All. night. long.*

If my hands weren't shaking, I might respond. But what would I say? Instead, I pack a bag with enough clothes for two days, two nights of PJs consisting of tank tops and leggings, set out a sleeveless sweater dress that falls just below my knees, and ankle boots for the restaurant tomorrow night. My phone pings once again.

Deacon: *Did I scare you?*

Annie Mick

Me: *I get a break from midnight to two.*

Deacon: *No worries, baby. I'll break you.*

Pretty sure he will. Just don't make it my heart, Deacon. It's been under wraps for so long, it wouldn't just crack. I'm afraid it might explode. And I'm afraid you're just the man to do it.

Chapter 41

Deacon

"What are you grinning at over there?" Parnell glances at me from his side of the car, then slides another fry in his mouth. He finishes chewing and swallows – one of the many reasons we get along so well. "You don't text. Ever."

"Lee." I pocket my phone and shoot him a cocky grin. "Everlee. And yes I do."

He chuckles, having caught the play on words. "I take it you've lost your *ass* title."

"Wouldn't go that far, Vic. Still working on it."

We both throw our wrappers on the floor of the car when our target leaves the building with bags in their hands, and in unison say, "They're moving. Let's go."

Two hours later, we're on our way back to the station, mission accomplished . . . somewhat. It's three o'clock in the morning, we still have paperwork up the ass to complete, one cop in the hospital, two dead perps, and four more in holding cells. Let's not forget a shitload of cocaine and fentanyl in a warehouse as well as an extremely large amount of cash being collected by state and federal authorities at the current time. Yeah, we've earned our keep and our sleep.

By six o'clock we've finished booking them, the paperwork is complete, and I'd love to stick around and wait for Everlee to arrive, but I've got a cop to check on at the hospital, some adrenaline to work off, and a bed that's calling my name. I'll see her tonight. Whether or not she'll ever want to see me again after this weekend is a crapshoot.

* * *

Garvis has the door open and is waiting for me when I'm within ten feet of reaching it. "Ms. Remington has already asked if I might be available to feed Roscoe tomorrow evening. I informed her I would be happy to be of service if necessary," he tells me as I enter.

I roll my eyes. "All meat with pecan rolls?"

"Oh no," he breathes in disappointment. "Wife caught on to that. I spilled sauce on my uniform the last time. Better make it a steak and baked potato with all the toppings and a salad with French dressing on the side from that fancy restaurant you're going to this evening. They do deliver."

Now I know Garvis is not that ballsy. The fact he mentioned the fancy restaurant leaves only one option. "Everlee told you to say that, didn't she?"

He nods, his mouth twitching at the corners. "She may have recommended it."

I pinch the bridge of my nose, debating whether to laugh or growl. "How do you want your steak?"

"Medium rare is good," he says. "About 8:30 would be perfect. Have a wonderful time, detective."

Well, there goes sixty bucks..

She is breathtaking. Her hair is down, something I seldom see. The soft, nearly black waves frame her face, the stormy gray eyes the perfect juxtaposition; the light to the darkness. My darkness. She always was. That inner smile I could never find, no matter how hard I tried. Until she came home.

"Deacon?" Her voice breaks my thoughts as I stand frozen in the doorway.

"You look beautiful." I can only hope my sentiments are

audible because I'm rendered nearly speechless by the truth.

"You okay?" she whispers, her question sincere as her brow furrows.

I step inside the door and lift her off her feet before the door closes. She lets out a tiny squeal of surprise and braces her hands on my shoulders. "Better than okay. Miss me?"

Her mouth twists to one side as if in contemplation. "Depends. Are you still taking me to dinner?"

"I'll feed you breakfast, too."

She narrows her eyes. "Are you going to feed Garvis?"

"Shut up and kiss me, Everlee," I threaten with a squeeze of one delectable ass cheek. "Before I bend you over that sofa, make you forget all about food, and we won't be needing Garvis because we won't be leaving your apartment."

"Sweet talker." She giggles before delivering a kiss that makes it damn tempting, but I won't. I want her in my house, my bed, where no woman has ever been.

* * *

We barely make it in the door before I have her pinned against the wall, hands above her head, commanding the kisses as if I owned her mouth. Keeping her hands pinned with one of mine, I roam with the other, gently lifting the fabric of her sweater dress higher on her legs, gaining access to the silky skin underneath. She lifts one leg against my hip as the skirt rises, moaning with the motion, pressing into me, struggling against my hold on her hands. I release them, cup both bare ass cheeks as she's in a thong and lift her up. She wraps her legs around my waist and squeezes. So reminiscent of the lab.

The lights are dim; one lamp in the living room lit at its lowest setting, a light in the kitchen that casts an offset glow through the walkway, one small light in the hallway upstairs. All done intentionally for her comfort. I want to see all of her, appreciate every last dip and curve by sight as much as by feel. But for now, I'll settle on Braille if it's all I've got. I'll work with the shadows she's willing to offer.

She slides the jacket off my shoulders and immediately works the buttons on my shirt, nearly ripping them from the holes. I don't shave my chest, nor do I wax it. I'm not a hairy beast, but I do have chest hair. The perfect amount, if I'm to take the word of the women who've admired it. Apparently, Everlee is a fan. Because as soon as she has that shirt open, pulled the hem out of my pants, and stripped it off my shoulders, she's palming my chest like a long-lost teddy bear.

She whimpers as she runs her fingers ever so lightly over my chest. "I love the way this teases my nipples."

If I didn't see the want in her eyes and if my dick weren't bursting through the zipper of my pants right now, I would laugh. She is so honest, so sincere, so open, so damn Everlee. "Then we'd better get you out of this," I whisper, reaching for the hem of her dress that's bunched at her waist, and slide it up and over head. She wears a sheer black bra that does nothing to hide the anxious hard peaks underneath. "And this," I add, reaching behind her, undoing the two clasp binder that releases with one quick flick. Her thighs squeeze a little harder around my waist as she reaches for the straps and rips them away, throwing the bra somewhere behind me.

"Wait!" She struggles to reach between us to unfasten my belt buckle. "You need to lose the pants. I want both things at once."

"Let me grab a condom out of the pocket first."

"Just unzip them," she pants impatiently as she squirms.. "I'm on birth control."

My eyes nearly bug out of my head. "You want me bare?"

"Are you not clean?" she snaps indignantly.

"Of course I am!" I growl. "I wouldn't risk that with you! But I've never . . ."

"Neither have I!" she retorts with a sneer. "But no one's ever made me this horny!"

Me either, sweetheart.

With anyone else, I wouldn't even consider it. This isn't exactly the way I'd planned on losing my rubber virginity, but I sure as hell ain't going to turn it down. I reach under her legs, undo my belt and button on my pants, lower the zipper and let my pants and jerseys fall to my ankles. Grabbing the side straps of her thong, I tear it off.

"Well then, Everlee," I say with a smirk as I line myself up with her warm and wet heat. "Shall we break each other's condom cherry?" I enter her with one deep thrust.

She gasps then groans a quiet, "Oh, God."

"It's Deacon," I mutter in her ear before I start to move. "Get it right or I'm not going to let you come."

"Deacon," she whimpers.

"Everlee," I whisper with all the reverence she deserves and start to move within her. I'm slow at first, savoring every sensation of this delicate wonder. She does enjoy the chest hair; brushing her nipples against it as if it's a new toy. I want those nipples in my mouth, but I can share – this time. I'll take 'up against the wall' sex if it makes her happy. We've got the whole weekend. We're just getting started. And from now on, I get Everlee . . . bare.

Annie Mick

Chapter 42

Everlee

"Where do we go from here?" I whisper to myself as I believe he's drifted off to sleep behind me; his chest to my back, arm wrapped about my ribs as if in the same bed isn't quite close enough. We've had enough sex to last us for who knows how long. It's more than I've had in probably ten years. And he's so good at it, it makes me wonder if there's a room in this house filled with trophies. And why pursue me? Am I one of those trophies? I told myself not to fall for him, to remain on track, never lose sight of my goal. When I thought he was the man in the ambulance, it hurt to think I was so forgettable. But now, even knowing he's not, I still find myself getting attached, and distracted. My whole reason for returning was to find Jonah's killer.

"Forward," he reassures me, tightening his hold around my waist and pulling me closer to him. "I'm right here, Everlee. I'm not going anywhere."

If someone were to hold a pillow over my face right now, it would be easier to breathe. I feel like a bucket of ice water has been poured over me. Those words. That voice. I'm back there all over again.

"Do you say that to all women in distress or just the ones you think you'll never have to face again?"

"Oh fuck," he breathes heavily into my neck before he

buries his forehead against my shoulder. "How long have you known?"

I whip the blanket back and try to get up, but he doesn't release his hold. "I need to go."

"You need to stay," he demands, pulling me tighter to him. He's never used this tone with me, and quite frankly it's a little scary. I've never felt threatened by Deacon, but in this position I feel vulnerable. Something I swore I'd never be again.

"Let go of me right now, detective," I demand, enunciating each word, giving him one chance to lose his grip or take an elbow to his face and a heel to his shin, before I twist and plant a forearm on his throat with a knee to his balls. I may be small, but I'm agile, quite flexible as well – two things I should have never given him the pleasure of experiencing.

He immediately removes his arm from around my waist and I'm off the mattress, snatching my overnight bag from the floor, and headed for the bathroom.

He's off the bed and right behind me but doesn't stop me from slamming the door. "Everlee, we need to talk."

I order a Lyft and tuck my phone in the bag before I get dressed in leggings and a T-shirt and slide into a pair of flip-flops; my hopes high the Lyft will be waiting by the time I reach the bottom of the stairs. If not, I can wait at the curb. I throw open the bathroom door as soon as my clothes are on and find Deacon standing in front of the bedroom entrance, shirtless, jeans hung low on his hips. The light is on, the room much brighter than it was minutes ago.

He heaves a deep sigh. "We need to talk."

"You," I sneer, "need to get the hell out of my way." When he doesn't budge from his position, I warn him once more, "Do not make me hurt you." Not that I'm sure I could do a lot of damage, but I can leave a lasting impression.

His shakes his head as he steps to the side and lets me pass. On my way down the hall, another light goes on, then another on my way down the stairs.

"I can find my way around in the dark!" I yell. "I don't want to see you!"

"Everlee, wait. Please," he calls out as he follows me down the stairs.

Another light is flicked on in the foyer that virtually lights up the entire entrance to the living room – a room I hadn't been in yet – drawing my attention. And that's when I see it. On the coffee table; a black three-ring binder notebook with a white label on the spine that reads:

J. P. Remington

Deacon must note what I'm staring as he mutters, "Oh shit."

I drop my bag on the floor and rush to pick up the binder, opening it to examine the contents. Inside I find copies of the same witness statements, initial reports and findings, and the sloppy coroner report that I already have, i.e. the items I stole two months ago from the records room.

I slam the binder closed and stare at a watchful Deacon. "What the hell are you doing with my brother's file?"

"I can explain," he says softly.

"Who are you covering for, Deacon? Spencer?" It's not a question. No, I've had too many of those over the years. I narrow my eyes as a new thought occurs. He was there, then rode with me in the ambulance. What better alibi is there than to be absent from the scene? "Or are you covering your own ass?"

A car horn blows out front.

"What!?" he hollers as he charges toward me.

"Don't come near me!" I throw the binder at him as a distraction and rush past him, snatching my bag off the floor, unlatching the deadbolt, and run out the door. I don't check if he chases after me. All I know is I make it to the car, pull open the door, slide inside, and order the driver, "83rd precinct as fast as you can."

* * *

Dashing down the hall to my lab as inconspicuously as I can once inside the station, I pull up the list of contacts stored in the computer.

"Yeah, what is it now?" he answers in a gruff, groggy tone that one might hesitate responding to. It's two o'clock in the morning; he's entitled to it.

"C-captain G-Garner," I stammer. "It-it's Ev-Everlee Remington."

"Everlee?" He sounds suddenly alert and I detect rustling in the background. "What is it? Where are you?"

"I- I'm at the station," I whisper so as not to sob openly. "In my lab."

"Stay there," he says calmly. "Are you in any danger?"

I look toward the door, then rush to lock it. Hadn't even thought to lock it behind me when I came in. "I d-don't think so."

"I'm going to have a couple officers posted in the hall until I get there. Stay put. I'll be there as fast as I can. Okay?" I nod as if he can see me. "Everlee?"

"Yeah," I agree, aloud this time.

* * *

The knock on the door is followed by the booming voice I've come to trust over the past few months. "Everlee, it's Captain Garner. Unlock the door."

He can obviously see the mess that is me in front of him because as soon as he enters, he pulls me into a bear hug. "Whatever it is, we'll sort it out," he soothes with a calming voice. "What do you say we go up to my office?"

I sob in his arms before spilling words that should never leave an investigator's mouth before the investigation is complete, "I-I think Deacon killed my b-brother. I found his file in Deacon's house tonight."

He holds my shoulders while pinning my gaze. His brows furrow so deeply the hair meets in the middle as he blows a deep sigh from his nostrils. So many emotions fill his eyes; sadness, pity, sympathy, maybe even a little bit of understanding. "I think I'd better put a pot of coffee on." He shudders. "Not what's in the squad room. That stuff would fuel a fire before puttin' it out. Got a special pot in my office. Come on."

He sends a text while we're on our way to his office, then pockets his phone.

"Did you send somebody to arrest him?" I ask as he double pats his pocket.

"Nah," he says then chuckles and winks. "Gonna make him sweat a while. Wait to see who kicks his ass first."

* * *

"I'm not from Chicago," I explain as the captain sets down two cups of coffee on his desk, one in front of the chair in which I'm seated. "I only went to school there. My little brother and I grew up in Hasselback. He was murdered a little over six years ago outside the Blue Velvet Lounge. You guys never solved it." Tears gather along the rims of my eyes once more and I blink fast to hold them back, but it only makes them spill. The captain offers a tissue and I take it. "There's so much more. I don't know where to start." I pause to wipe away tears and sob.

The captain rounds his desk and sits in the chair next to mine, placing his arm over my shoulder. "I know, kiddo. You don't have to do this."

My head whirls toward him. "You know about all of this?" He nods, a slight wince joining his confession. "Does everyone?"

"No," he denies adamantly, looking me straight in the eyes. "Only a couple, and they would never."

A few sharp raps on the door is followed by it opening. A rather angry looking, sleep deprived Victor Parnell steps in and closes it behind him. "Thought about stoppin' at his house and kickin' his ass first, but I'll save that for later. Mornin' Everlee, or should I say top o' the mornin'? It is rather early."

"What is he doing here?" I shriek, staring at the captain and shooting a hand out toward Victor. "They're best friends! He's only going to cover for him!"

Victor's eyebrows rise to an extraordinary height as he eyes the captain. "Got himself in pretty deep, huh? Why that dumbass can't just tell a woman how he feels, I'll never know."

The captain slaps the tops of his thighs and stands, walks to his desk and takes a seat behind it. "She found her brother's file in Deac's house. Take over, Vic."

"Pour me a coffee," Victor tells Captain Garner then yawns. "Better be caffeine in there." He takes a seat on the edge of the desk, one leg propped on it, his hands clasped together.

"Everlee, I'm just gonna get straight to the point here. Six years ago we were called out to a scene at the Blue Velvet Lounge. You broke through every barrier to get to your little brother. Pushed through a crowd, yellow tape, line up of cops. Dylan Spencer was an asshole. He was cruel, abusive, and handled the situation in the worst way possible. Deacon saw what was happening before anyone else did. He was on top of Spencer faster than I've ever seen a man move. Beat the livin' hell out of him. We watched for a bit before pullin' him off." He shrugs. "We all hated Spencer. Figured somebody oughta enjoy it. Deac was a rookie at the time. Hadn't even been on the force for a full year yet. I needed to get him outta there before Spencer figured out who it was, make sure the other cops kept their mouths shut, and splice the cam footage so his face was never visible." He stops to take a sip of his coffee and sets the cup back on the desk.

"I sent Deacon in the ambulance with you to get him outta the way and to make sure you had an escort." He lifts his brows and grimaces. "You were an emotional and physical mess. I didn't know your circumstances beyond what had happened outside that bar and that your little brother had just been murdered, nor did I know Deacon would become so enamored with you in the little amount of time it took to get you to the ER.

"He hunted down your emergency contact, stayed until he got a hold of your mother, offered her a plane ticket to get her to you faster . . ." He dips his chin and narrows his eyes, ". . . which she refused by the way. And decided to stay with you until you had someone by your side."

"But my mother," I try to interrupt and he holds up his hand to halt my words and shakes his head.

"Let me finish. Deacon had the next three days off after that night, two of which he refused to leave the hospital and spent either sitting outside your room or by your side while you were unconscious. He never left until your mother finally showed up." He dips his chin and raises his brows, emphasizing, " Two days later."

"My mother said she was there the whole time," I mutter, shocked at more of her lies. She probably hadn't had Jonah cremated yet either. I could have seen him one last time. Where was my Gram?

"No, she wasn't," Victor says with a disgusted shake of his head. "Deacon was. He couldn't stand the thought of you being alone. He wanted you to have someone."

"Somebody's someone," I whisper as I stare at the floor. Words that I build my work ethic on, but Deacon actually lived up to them.

Victor stands and lays a gentle reassuring hand on my shoulder. "Guess he was yours." He heads for the door and tosses back over his shoulder to the captain. "I'm goin' back to bed. Remind the dumbass I warned him."

"You gonna tell her why the file's in his house?" Captain Garner asks.

He sighs and turns back. "Deacon's never given up lookin' for your brother's killer. He spends his off time viewing that damn footage and goin' over statements, believing something was missed. Thought maybe someday he'd be able to call you with an answer. He is nothin' if not stubborn but there is not a man on this earth I'd rather have coverin' my back. Go home and get some sleep, Everlee."

The door closes behind him, leaving me to study the white knuckles of my clenched fists. "What have I done?"

"Reacted the same way anyone would without an explanation," Captain Garner says.

"But I didn't give him a chance to."

"He would have never given you the whole story, Everlee."

He shakes his head. "Even Vic didn't share it all."

For half past three in the morning, my eyes hardly struggle to widen, and it has nothing to do with caffeine. I haven't swallowed but three sips from the cup he's poured. "There's more?"

"You sure you want to hear this?" I nod. "Deacon found Spencer in the middle of assaulting a woman in the records room about six months after the incident with you. He literally blew out his kneecaps by stomping on them. Crippled him for life. Made damn sure he never came back on the force." He furrows his brow as he takes another sip of coffee then aims an intentional glance at my knees. "I can't help but see the irony in it. Your knees, Spencer's knees. I think it was Deacon's roundabout way of finally releasing the anger he had in him for the damage Spencer did to you."

My hand flies to my mouth in horror. "Spencer assaulted a woman."

He winces. "In the worst way. He had a history of beating his wife, did what he did to you, assaulted a woman. Who knows what else he did and got away with." He snorts. "I give Deacon credit for not killin' him."

I suddenly recall Spencer in the parking lot a few weeks ago, but I don't mention it to the captain. Two men stuffed him a van and drove away. *"Clean up in aisle 9 at the Blue Velvet Lounge."* Was that code?

"Everlee?" The captain's voice jolts me out of my thoughts.

I clear my throat and blink fast. "Th-that's a lot to take in."

"Just givin' you a little food for thought," he says pointedly. "If I know Deacon, he woulda let you go on thinkin' he's an ass." He holds his hand up and tilts it back and forth. "He's really more of a smartass. But he's a good man."

"I know."

"Go home, get a nap." He dips his chin, sparing me a look of compassion and understanding. "You two will get it figured out."

Chapter 43

Everlee

Trying to get a nap was futile. I tossed and turned for a couple hours on the sofa until I decided there was no point in putting it off any longer. How many ways can you apologize, beg for forgiveness? Roscoe's only advice was a gentle bubble he released which contained a tiny piece of food, probably took too big of a bite. No help at all.

There's a car in his driveway when I pull up in front of his house at ten o'clock in the morning. Never seen it before, and it makes me pause before I find the nerve to walk the distance to the door to ring the bell. I could have sent him a text and given him a heads-up, I suppose. But what if he never wants to see me again? I even put on a dress, left my hair down the way he likes, and wore some heels for the occasion.

I hesitate over and over again, my finger inches from the button that looks like a hot pot I'm afraid might burn if I touch it, before finally pushing the doorbell. He's not quick to answer, but footsteps eventually sound from the other side of the door and the knob turns.

"Everlee." His voice is monotone, as cold as the look in his eyes. He's not greeting me, hardly an acknowledgement. More of a *what the hell do you want* demand.

"I'm sorry," I whisper, the dryness in my throat causing a

rasp I didn't expect. "I should have let you explain."

The casual indifferent eyebrow lift mixed with the same tone nearly breaks my heart when he asks, "That all?"

"I-I wanted to . . ."

"Eww, Deacon, there's a dirty thong in your waste basket!" A female shriek comes from deep inside the house. "My God! You tore it off of her, you horny cretin. Get out here and empty your own trash."

Mortification fills my face as I fight to breathe. The car in the drive must belong to his next conquest. What was I thinking? I was in his bed hours ago and he has another woman in his house already. I take a few steps back and hold up my hands. "I-I shouldn't have come. Just forget I was here."

I spin on a wobbly heel and head for my car. How could I be so stupid? The door slams behind me, sounding like a bullet ricocheting off the walls of a building. Worse yet? It feels like one through the walls of my heart.

As I reach my car, a large hand grabs my bicep and spins me around, pinning me to the driver's door. "Forget you were here!?" he yells. "I've spent six fucking years trying to forget you! I walked away because it was the best thing for you, but it was the hardest thing I've ever had to do. I've spent six fucking years trying to solve your brother's case so you could find some peace! You came back here, Everlee. You walked into my squad room! You walked back into my life! I tried to stay away, I tried to do what I thought was best, but you made it impossible!"

"I didn't know . . ."

"Shut up, Everlee," he grinds through a clenched jaw, pressing harder against me as if he can't help himself. "I'm nowhere near done. I know you didn't know, but I'm not sure what I'm more pissed about right now. You thinking I murdered your brother or that I could be with another woman after being with you." His eyes flash with pain before he tilts his head toward the house. "That's my little sister in there. Big mouth, no filter. I threw your thong away because I ruined it last night and it was still in the hallway when she showed up. I didn't want her to see it."

He drops to one knee, lifts my foot and strips my shoe off, throwing it over his shoulder, then strips the other off and does the same. "Stupid fucking heels." He grabs my hand and pulls me back toward the house. "Come with me."

Opening the gate on the side of the house, he leads me through the grass and the gate slams behind us. No wonder he removed my heels. They would have sunk in the wet grass.

"Where are we going?" I question weakly, fumbling on bare feet in the wet grass. He is rather angry. The ground is soft. Perfect burial spot to hide a body if you know what you're doing. Oh God! He's had enough time to dig the hole.

He ignores my question and continues to pull me toward the backyard. Once beyond the back of the house and in the yard, he stops and waits while I take in the splendor that surrounds the edges. Jasmine bushes in full bloom along the entire border. The scent fills my nostrils and I breathe deeper to capture the intoxicating aroma. My eyes follow the path from one end of the yard to the other, admiring the tiny white clusters that cover the shrubs from top to bottom.

"What is this?" I ask, the stunned whisper barely audible as I recall him sharing his favorite scent.

"I couldn't have you," he explains. "But I could save the memory. It's where I sit in the evenings to find some sanity and peace after a long day of dealing with the shit this city hands out. I hear some people choose lavender. I chose the memory of the most beautiful girl I'd ever seen. The scent of her hair, her soulful eyes."

"I thought you didn't remember me." Tears flood my eyes, making the view of the bushes blurry.

He runs a gentle finger down the side of my face, brushing a tear away with his thumb. "I could never forget you, Everlee. I just didn't want to be the connection you made with the worst day of your life."

"You were the only comfort I had that night," I confess before releasing the sob I've been holding back. "Everything else was so cold and calculated. Doctors and nurses shouting orders. Victor told me what you did; that you stayed with me to keep watch. You were my someone for two days, and I never knew it."

He takes my cheeks in his palms and tilts my head up to meet his gaze. "You've been my someone for six years. About time you came home, Everlee Remington. Because now I get to love you for the rest of my life."

"You're not still mad at me?"

He narrows his eyes. "Not sure. You haven't kissed me yet."

I melt into his touch, the kiss, all that is Deacon Gray. Everything I never knew I wanted. Never knew I needed. *The man in the ambulance.*

"I love you, too," I tell him when the kiss ends.

"Nope, definitely not mad anymore." He chuckles and kisses me once again then places an arm over my shoulder and leads me toward the house. "Come on, let's go meet my sister. She's been glued to the kitchen window and I want to make sure she's the one who wipes the nose prints off."

"I don't want you to feel bad, Deacon. I don't think I'll ever find Jonah's killer either." I sigh in resignation. "I've studied that footage so many times it makes my head spin. Keith even installed enhancement software on my laptop. It hasn't helped. I need to face the fact that I can't solve them all."

His brow furrows as his mouth twists and he seems to ponder unspoken thoughts. "I don't want to get your hopes up," he says, seemingly more to himself than me. "But I think we may have one more shot at it. We'll talk once we get rid of Dory."

"She saw my underwear!" I whisper in embarrassment.

"It was a thong," he says with a grin and a wink. "I'll buy you a dozen more and tear off only eleven of them. You won't even miss it."

Chapter 44

Deacon

Getting Dory to leave without insulting her is a pain in my ass, but eventually with promises of dinner out with both of us, a girls' day at the spa with Everlee, and a gossip phone call with me – 't ain't never gonna happen – she's on her way out the door by two. Gotta admit, the girl makes a helluva pancake.

"She's fun!" Everlee giggles.

I shoot her a wry look, hating the admission now that I've seen it. "Kind of a female version of Theo."

She gasps, her face lighting up brighter than a Christmas tree. "Oh my God, she is!"

"Think you've found a new friend?"

She closes one eye, narrows the other and studies the ceiling as if weighing the options. "Do I have to keep you to keep her?"

"Yup."

She grabs my face and plants a hard kiss on my mouth that I'd love to take full advantage of, but first things first. "Another new best friend," she says sweetly.

"Good to know." I arch a brow. "No sharing secrets at the spa." She giggles before I tap her butt. "Now let's go."

"Where are we going?"

"Your place. We have a laptop to pick up."

Annie Mick

* * *

One hour, a change into comfy clothes *for* her, twenty questions *from* her, avoidance of direct answers from me, and a nervous stomach later, we're sitting on my sofa in front of a big screen TV with her laptop on the coffee table. I collect the uncut version of the street cam footage from the safe and set the thumb drive on the coffee table next to the laptop.

"What's this?" she asks, picking it up and turning it in her fingers.

I run a fast hand through my hair, send up an even faster request that this is the right thing – known to most as a prayer – hoping He's listening on her behalf. Been a long time. "It's the uncut version of the street cam footage. Might be something on there you haven't seen and if we hook it up to the big TV, it'll give you a better view. Don't concentrate on you and Jonah or Spencer. Watch the crowd. See if you see anything you couldn't before. Okay?"

"That's what Keith said."

I take her hand in mine. "You don't have to do this, Everlee. It's a longshot at best. May lead to nothing."

"I've got to try," she whispers as she stares at the thumb drive in her fingers. "It's all we've got."

She fires up the computer while I run the cable to connect it to the TV. She inserts the thumb drive once we're seated. Having already programmed the computer to accept the file type she'd stolen from the records room, it plays immediately.

I watch her watching it; my fear that it will stir every horrible memory from that night like it happened yesterday. The picture is much clearer than anything I've studied before. The big screen only adds to its clarity. Jonah leaves the bar and waves to someone in the distance, disappearing from the camera's view, then returns, stumbling onto the wide sidewalk from the street and collapses on the ground. I wait for Everlee to crumple in tears but she doesn't. She's looking beyond him, as if she needs to stay zoned in on the commotion around him. She is focused; her fingertips on

310

the mousepad ready to click right or left – dependent on what she needs to do. There is no audio, no sound to adjust; simply film to watch. Her eyes are fixed on the screen in such a way, I'm tempted to remind her she can blink, that we can play the recording again. The flashing lights of the patrol cars appear against the windows of the buildings in the background and cops are soon performing the requisite duties of crowd control as they break up the groups of gawkers and some of those trying to help. This scenario is all in the cut version but she seems set on watching this again, as if starting from the beginning. I understand. I've done it a thousand times over the years. Just never with this type of clarity.

So much movement, so many observers. Two cops bent over Jonah checking for a pulse and shaking their heads, yellow tape being posted to cordon off the area, people being held back, but one girl shoving her way through to get to her brother. I try to focus on the crowd, but my eyes always find their way to her. Her knees drop into the broken glass surrounding her brother and she pulls him into her arms, rocking back and forth before she screams at the sky. The footage may be silent but the echo of those screams rings in my mind as if the volume is turned to its loudest setting. I glance at Everlee, but she pays no attention to the main attraction on the screen. Her eyes are scrupulously studying the background, the view between the main attraction and the building. The small details. Spencer moves into the camera's view and begins his cruel treatment of Everlee, yanking her upward, then throwing her back down, his knee on her back grinding her into the broken glass. All hell breaks loose which in the spliced version, is all anyone else has ever seen. Today, however, the scene continues in its original state; unedited, nothing hidden. The crowd moves closer toward the scene in a fit of anger while the cops are trying to hold them back, oblivious to what Spencer is doing; the moment I moved in on him.

She leans forward, eyes fixed on the crowd in the background until a horrified expression fills her face. She freezes the picture and zooms in on two figures. It's a dark-haired young man with what looks to be a teenager, wearing what appears to be a cheerleader uniform, arms flailing as they argue, before he grabs her arm and rushes her around the corner and into the alley at the side of the building. Slowly rewinding the footage, Everlee stops at a point where she's satisfied and starts it again. The tension in her jaw only worsens as she watches once more, freezing the recording and zooming in on the faces and the tattoo of a hula dancer decorating the arm of the young man, then zooming in on the blood stains on the cheerleader's uniform. On the grainy film, it could easily be mistaken for dirt. The picture is black and white, but the splatter pattern and depth of contrast makes all the difference in perception.

I've seen that tattoo; recently, in fact. I've seen her hug the man who wears it. The girl? Not a clue. But from the look on Everlee's face, she knows exactly who she is.

The scene resumes to the spliced video that was presented as evidence in the civil lawsuit, to the city officials in order to hold Spencer accountable to his actions.

She pulls the thumb drive from the computer and shuts it down. "I need to go see somebody," she says softly, closing the lid on the laptop.

"Not alone." I take her hand in mine and kiss the knuckles. "You will never be alone again, Everlee Remington."

* * *

"Everlee?" The shock in Caleb's eyes is only matched by the choked rasp when he opens the door. When he notes me standing behind her, it's hard to tell if it's an enormous amount of guilt or actual relief that consumes him as his shoulders sag and he sighs. "You're the detective. I've seen you around a few times."

"Where's Callie?" Everlee forgoes any pleasantries, seeking only the answers she's spent years yearning for.

Caleb opens the door wider and waves to the room behind him. "I think you'd better come in."

It's a modest apartment, but comfortable. An electric keyboard sits in the corner of the living room, acoustic guitar on a stand next to it. Sofa, two chairs, TV on the wall. Typical bachelor pad. Neat and clean. On an end table sits a picture of the band when there were five of them. Everlee's brother with a navy beanie on his head. I know it's him because their smiles are identical. His eyes the perfect storm, just like hers. We take a seat on the sofa and Caleb sits on the edge of one the chairs.

"Can I get you guys something?" Caleb asks sheepishly.

"Answers," Everlee says without waver. "Where is Callie, Caleb? I asked you the night I came to the club. You never did tell me."

He presses the heels of his palms into his eyes then runs his hands through his hair, leaving it standing on end. "She didn't mean to do it, Ev. She went off the deep end." He crosses one arm over his chest and tucks the hand under his bicep as if hugging himself, and rocks back and forth. "She was so obsessed with Jonah. He tried to be nice about it but she got pretty bold. I told her not to come around anymore. To go date some guys her own age and leave my friends alone.

"I came running out of the building when I saw all the lights. I'd been in the basement helping the bartender carry up some kegs. I didn't know what had happened to Jonah, what was going on. Callie ran up to me out of nowhere. She was too damn young to be at a bar. She had blood on her cheerleading outfit. She was freaking out, said she did something terrible. I panicked. I didn't give her a chance to tell me what it was. I led her down to the alley and told her to go home. That we would take care of it when I got there."

He bends so far his head is nearly between his knees as he sobs. I place my arm around a crying Everlee's shoulder as we wait for him to gather his bearings.

He lifts his head, his eyes on Everlee. "I had no idea what that cop did to you. You were in the ambulance and gone. All I knew was Jonah was dead. I put two and two together and rushed home to Callie. When I got there I found her sitting on her damn bed, still in that cheerleading outfit, staring at the wall. All she would say is, 'He didn't want me'. I screamed at her, told her to go change and that I was taking her to the police station." He sobs harder, his body rocking with convulsions, and buries his face in his hands. "Oh God."

My voice is calm as I gently urge him to continue. "What happened, Caleb?"

"She cut her wrists instead!" he wails, the sound of which reminds me a wounded animal. I suppose in some ways he really is.

Everlee falls into me, grasping my shirt and quietly weeping. I hold her because there are no words for what she must be feeling. These were her friends. Her circle. Maybe it would have been best had she never known.

"Where is Callie now?" I ask him once things have calmed . . . a bit.

He sniffles, clears his throat, swallows hard. "A convalescent home." He snorts sarcastically. "Though I don't know why they call it convalescent. Doesn't that mean there's hope for recovery? She suffered anoxic brain injury from lack of oxygen to the brain for too long. Too much blood loss. They spoon-feed her. She can't walk, talk, bathe herself. Has no idea who we are. I didn't find her in time."

"It wasn't your fault," I tell him.

His eyes are nearly black as he glares at me. "Do you have any idea how many times I've heard that? Your words are as empty as all the others, detective. She was my little sister. I should have seen it." He looks to the woman in my arms. "I'm sorry I wasn't there for you, Everlee. Maybe now you understand. That trip to the Gulf to let Jonah's ashes go damn near killed me. I couldn't say goodbye to him. I could only say I'm sorry."

He stands from his chair, stoic and determined. "I think we're done here."

"Caleb." Everlee stands and reaches for him but he steps away.

He shakes his head and gifts her with a sad smile. "Don't waste your energy hating me, Ev. I do enough of that myself."

She hurls herself at him, wrapping her arms around his neck; not giving him the option of getting away. "I don't hate you, Caleb. Jonah and Callie don't either. We've both lost so much already. Let's not lose each other, too."

Is it any wonder I love this woman?

Epilogue

Everlee

Ten months later

Deacon wondered if I'd regretted the path I followed to get where I am today. If forensics was my true calling. If investigating murder scenes, collecting evidence, feeding computers information; waiting for days, weeks, sometimes even months before getting a hit proved satisfactory for me.

My answer? Absolutely. If I only solve or assist in solving a dozen murders a year, it's that many families that don't have to suffer any longer as well as that many murderers who will pay for their crimes. It's a dirty job, but somebody has to do it.

I'll never forget my first job in Louisiana. The woman in the storm drain. I wasn't foolish enough to think that my evidence alone was sufficient to find and convict her killer. Deacon had his hands in it all along. We make a good team.

And that would explain today . . .

"I already had my little talk with him." Theo's stern voice comes from about my knee level as he straightens the hem on my gown. The gown he chose, the gown he demanded be paid for by him, the gown he recommended have a chastity belt sewn into just to piss Deacon off.

"You did what?" I demand, pulling his hair to lift his eyes

to meet mine.

"Hey, hey, hey!" He reaches for his scalp to straighten his locks. "Don't mess with perfection. I'm giving you away. I gotta look as pretty as you do."

Gram laughs as she sits in the chair just feet away. Theo looks over and tips his chin. "Tell her how pretty you think I am, Gram."

She waves her hand as she stares at her phone. "You'll do in a pinch, you big lug. I'm checkin' the video camera on the crowd. This Rodriguez guy is tryin' to flirt with one o' the guests. He just pinched her titty and she threw a drink at him and slapped his cheek."

I gasp. "He didn't!"

She nods and smirks. "He did."

It's not a big crowd. We kept it small; limiting the number to only 75 or so. Deacon's backyard is the perfect setting and he wanted the scent of jasmine in bloom while we said our vows.

"What does she look like?" I ask, dread filling my every sense.

"Little spitfire if you ask me," she says. "Blonde hair, purple dress."

"Oh God, no," I whimper, knowing Dory is the only one in purple today. She's my maid of 'royalty and loyalty' as she put it. A stand-in just in case my man of honor, Keith faints. Theo is giving me away.

"Whoop, no worries," she reassures me as if a pot of flowers has been stood back up, intact. "Deacon just punched him." She shakes her head and studies the tiny screen. "Nope, wait a minute. That's Keith who punched him."

"Are you serious?" I shriek.

She holds up her phone to show a game of solitaire on the screen and winks at Theo. "Told you we could get her 'drenaline goin'."

Theo stands and helps Gram off the chair, then extends an arm to me. "You ready, Sweet Cheeks?"

Keith meets us downstairs and sees to Gram to ensure she

gets to her seat in the front row, kisses her cheek and leaves her to take his place.

Deacon stands waiting by the arch decorated with a mix of white orchids, pink lilies, and babies' breaths. The preacher behind him, Vic by his side while Keith waits for us on the other.

Theo whispers on our way down the makeshift aisle, "Your man in the ambulance looks pretty damn happy."

When we reach the waiting groom, Theo takes my shoulders and holds my gaze as his eyes water. "Five of the brightest years of my life were spent with you. Day in and day out. You make people matter, living or dead. But the one thing you said that I will never forget is *'everyone is somebody's someone'*. I'm gonna hand you over to yours now. Call me if he ever fucks up."

Deacon scowls. "You done?"

Theo grins cockily. "Should I stick around and kiss the bride for you?" Then leans into Deacon and whispers, "You might forget, *dementia dick.*"

The End

Annie Mick

Thank you for taking the time to spend with me and the characters I love. Please feel free to leave a review. They mean a lot to your author and give you, the reader, a voice in the pages.

Other Books By This Author

<u>The Crew Series:</u>

<u>Run To Me</u>

<u>Wicked Lemonade</u>

<u>Find Another Hero: Just Make Sure He Can Dance</u>

<u>Tell Me Why, Jannie</u>

<u>The Fresh French Connection</u>

<u>Old Farts and Pop Tarts</u>

<u>Saari, Not Sorry</u>

<u>The Chauffeur: Phoenix Rising</u>

<u>Manipulation 101: Code of Ethics</u>

About the Author

A diehard laughaholic who has learned to take everything with a grain of salt, Annie Mick loves to dish it out with a good dose of sarcasm.

If you can giggle while you wiggle, it's added exercise and spares you ten minutes on the treadmill.

It is true that if you can laugh while you cry, the tears are saltier and it makes the margaritas taste better.

If you can find your hero in one of her books, therein lies her success. If you can find a bit of yourself in one her characters, therein lies her joy.

Life is too short to not get lost in a fantasy; if only for a day, if only in a book, one page at a time.

Sweet dreams.

324